Chamber Music

THE GROWTH & PRACTICE
OF AN INTIMATE ART

HOMER ULRICH

NEW YORK · COLUMBIA UNIVERSITY PRESS

To My Wife

PREFACE

This book lays no claim to being a history, nor does it pretend to be an essay in music appreciation. A history presents all the pertinent facts about the subject, uncovers principles and trends, and accounts for the phenomena it brings to light. An "appreciation," on the other hand, concentrates on a few significant works, tells its readers what to look and listen for in them, and in so doing becomes a guide to musical understanding. But while this book is neither one nor the other exclusively, it does contain elements of both. What, then, is its purpose?

No major field of musical literature is as little known as chamber music. True, certain works in the repertoire are widely performed, and many persons have heard that Haydn fathered the string quartet. In general, however, its history has remained obscure, its importance to the whole literature of music has been misunderstood, and many laymen whose contact with the field has been limited consider it highbrow. To introduce chamber music to the wider public which admires it from afar and to remove misconceptions about its quality and appeal, two things are necessary: an orderly account of its evolution to the point where the contemporary concert repertoire begins and a survey of the works which form the bulk of that repertoire. Those things this book hopes to supply.

Its first seven chapters, having to do with music that is seldom heard today, are designed to introduce the principal musical events, works, and tendencies of the two centuries before 1750. Subsequent chapters, beginning with the account of Haydn, are concerned with orienting the reader in the extensive and important chamber-music literature by major composers since 1750.

Chamber music is one of the oldest of instrumental literatures.

While the book has been planned to illustrate, at times merely by implication, the continuity of that literature, it has been impossible to include all composers. For example, Luigi Boccherini, Ludwig Spohr, Ernest Chausson, Alexander Glazounow, and many other composers of similar stature are scarcely mentioned. One may with justification omit accounts of such men and their works, largely because they have been of little influence upon their successors. The essential composers and the essential works, however, have been discussed in detail.

With sincere gratitude I record the part Mr. Ferdinand Volk played in my student days, in stimulating my first interest in chamber music and in helping to provide the solid musical background out of which this book has emerged. Likewise, the efforts and sacrifices of my mother to enrich that background went far beyond parental responsibilities. Such debts, while they may be publicly acknowledged, are not easily repaid.

The book itself owes its existence to my erstwhile colleague Dr. Donald Grout. His many helpful suggestions, his constant stimulation, and his patient reading of preliminary chapters are gratefully remembered. Without his encouragement the book might not have been written; nevertheless, he is not to be held responsible for its defects. Dr. Paul Henry Láng's interest in the work began when it was still in its early stages. His great help at crucial steps in its path from desk to press is deeply appreciated. To Dr. Warren D. Allen, Dr. J. M. Coopersmith, Dr. Karl Geiringer, Dr. Wiley Housewright, Mr. Kent Kennan, Mr. William Kroll, and Dr. Paul Pisk, all of whom read portions of the manuscript, I am indebted for factual corrections and stylistic improvements. In all matters of bibliography I acknowledge with thanks the technical assistance of Miss Jean Cassel, whose patience and good will seem inexhaustible. Finally, my sincere thanks go to Mr. John Scabia, for his help in preparing the musical examples; and to the individuals who are the Columbia University Press, particularly to Miss Ida M. Lynn, for their help at all stages of the book's progress. The professional skill and great interest Miss Lynn exhibited in the final preparation of the manuscript are especially appreciated.

My thanks are extended to Music Press, Inc., New York, and to the editor of the Alessandro Scarlatti *Sonata a quattro*, Dr. Hans Theodore David, for permission to quote a phrase from that work. An extended quotation in the text is reprinted from *Music in Western Civilization*, by Paul Láng, by permission of W. W. Norton & Company, Inc., New York, copyright, 1941, by the publishers. The passage from the Arnold Schönberg Suite, Opus 29, appears by kind permission of Universal Edition, Vienna. The example drawn from the string quartet of Anton von Webern is reprinted by permission of the copyright owners, Boosey & Hawkes, London and New York.

The list of chamber-music publications and recordings found as an appendix to the book has been compiled from a purely practical standpoint. I venture to hope that the reader, stimulated by the textual account, will wish to become better acquainted with chamber music itself. He will then turn to that list for information about the availability of a particular composition, and will go further along the path of musical enjoyment with the score or the records in his possession. If that should be the case and the music should thus become a vital part of his musical life, the book will have served its purpose.

HOMER ULRICH

Austin, Texas
March 27, 1948

CONTENTS

1. BACKGROUNDS   3

2. FROM CHANSON TO CANZONE   20

3. CHAMBER MUSIC BEGINS   45

4. THE DANCE SUITE   69

5. SONATA DA CHIESA AND SONATA DA CAMERA   90

6. THE TRIO SONATA   115

7. THE EMERGENCE OF CLASSICAL STYLE   145

8. FRANZ JOSEPII HAYDN   178

9. WOLFGANG AMADEUS MOZART   210

10. LUDWIG VAN BEETHOVEN   239

11. SCHUBERT AND THE ROMANTIC PERIOD   281

12. BRAHMS AND THE DECLINE OF ROMANTICISM   317

13. THE CONTEMPORARY WORLD   354

BIBLIOGRAPHY   387

CHAMBER MUSIC PUBLICATIONS AND RECORDINGS   395

INDEX   417

TABLES AND CHARTS

THE USUAL COMBINATIONS IN CHAMBER MUSIC   11

LIFE SPANS OF PRINCIPAL SEVENTEENTH-CENTURY COMPOSERS   49

THE SECTIONS OF A GRILLO *canzone*   54

THE EVOLUTION OF SONATA TYPES   91

THE SECTIONS OF A ROSENMÜLLER *sonata da camera*   106

LIFE SPANS OF EIGHTEENTH-CENTURY COMPOSERS BEFORE HAYDN   119

THE FORMAL PLAN OF BUXTEHUDE, SONATA, OPUS 1, NO. 1   123

THE FORMAL PLAN OF BACH, *Das musikalische Opfer*   136

THE FORMAL PLAN OF BACH, *Die Kunst der Fuge*   141

SONATA-FORM MOVEMENTS IN GLUCK   154

EVOLUTION OF CHAMBER-MUSIC COMBINATIONS   165

TABULAR VIEW OF HAYDN'S STRING QUARTETS   199

MOZART'S TRAVELS   211

SONATA FORM IN SCHUBERT'S PIANO TRIO, OPUS 100   296

SONATA FORM IN SCHUMANN'S PIANO QUINTET, OPUS 44   310

SONATA FORM IN FRANCK'S STRING QUARTET   338

MUSICAL EXAMPLES

MODAL HARMONY AND *musica ficta*   24

VIADANA, *Canzone francese*   50

ROSSI, *Ruggiero*   62

MARINI, *La Orlandina*   64

BYRD, PAVANE   74

FRESCOBALDI, *Canzone da sonar*   93

PURCELL, SONATA VIII (1697)   103

ROSENMÜLLER, *Sonata da camera*, NO. 11   107

CORELLI, *Sonata da camera*, OPUS 4, NO. 1   113

DALL'ABACO, *Sonata da camera*, OPUS 3, NO. 9   118

DALL'ABACO, *Sonate da camera*, OPUS 3, NOS. 5 AND 9   120

CALDARA, *Sonata da chiesa*   121

BUXTEHUDE, TRIO SONATAS, OPERA 1 AND 2, FUGUE THEMES   124

HANDEL, TRIO SONATAS, OPUS 5, NOS. 1 AND 3   132

J. S. BACH, TRIO SONATA, C MAJOR   135

J. S. BACH, *Das musikalische Opfer*, "THE ROYAL THEME"   137

J. S. BACH, *Die Kunst der Fuge*, CYCLICAL THEME   139

PERGOLESI, TRIO SONATA, NO. 1   149

SCARLATTI, *Sonata a quattro*   163

STAMITZ, ORCHESTRAL TRIO, OPUS 1, NO. 4   169

STAMITZ, ORCHESTRAL TRIO, OPUS 1, NO. 2   171

RICHTER, STRING QUARTET, OPUS 5, NO. 3   174

HAYDN, STRING QUARTETS, OPUS 17, NO. 2, AND OPUS 33, NO. 2   195

HAYDN, STRING QUARTET, OPUS 17, NO. 2   196

MOZART, STRING QUARTET, K.465   224

MOZART, STRING QUINTET, K.515   230

MOZART, STRING QUINTET, K.516   231

BEETHOVEN, PIANO TRIO, OPUS 1, NO. 3   250

BEETHOVEN, PIANO TRIO, OPUS 97   253

BEETHOVEN, STRING TRIO, OPUS 8   257

BEETHOVEN, STRING QUINTET, OPUS 29   263

BEETHOVEN, STRING QUARTET, OPUS 18, NO. 1, MOTIVE   265

BEETHOVEN, STRING QUARTET, OPUS 18, NO. 1, SCHERZO   266

BEETHOVEN, STRING QUARTET, OPUS 59, NO. 1   268

BEETHOVEN, STRING QUARTET, OPUS 59, NO. 2   269

BEETHOVEN, STRING QUARTET, OPUS 59, NO. 3   270

BEETHOVEN, STRING QUARTETS, OPERA 130–133, BASIC MOTIVE   275

BEETHOVEN, STRING QUARTETS, OPERA 130–133, TRANSFORMED

  MOTIVES   276

BEETHOVEN, STRING QUARTET, OPUS 133, FUGUE THEME   277

BEETHOVEN, STRING QUARTET, OPUS 131, VARIATION THEME   278

BEETHOVEN, STRING QUARTET, OPUS 131, TONAL RELATIONSHIPS   279

SCHUBERT, STRING QUINTET, OPUS 163   298

BRAHMS, PIANO QUINTET, OPUS 34   325

BRAHMS, STRING SEXTET, OPUS 36, "AGATHE" MOTIVE   326

BRAHMS, HORN TRIO, OPUS 40   327

BRAHMS, RHYTHMIC PATTERNS   333

BRAHMS, STRING QUARTET, OPUS 51, NO. 1   333

BRAHMS, PIANO TRIO, OPUS 101   333

FRANCK, PIANO TRIO, OPUS 1, NO. 1   337

FRANCK, PIANO QUINTET, CYCLICAL THEME   337

DVOŘÁK, RHYTHMIC PATTERNS   351

SCHÖNBERG, SUITE, OPUS 29   367

WEBERN, VON, STRING QUARTET, OPUS 28   369

CHAMBER MUSIC

I

BACKGROUNDS

THE MUSICAL repertoires of artists and performing groups the world over have at least one characteristic in common: they are drawn to a great extent from music written after 1750. Orchestras, for example, seldom perform works earlier than the symphonies of Haydn, except for an occasional Bach or Handel masterpiece. For violinists, music seems to begin with Mozart, even though Bach, Handel, and their Italian contemporaries are represented to some extent. Singers know of a dozen arias by early—that is, seventeenth-century—composers, but confine themselves largely to post-1750 works. When do opera companies reach any further into the past than a Mozart performance requires? Organists in general are faithful to the pre-Bach masters; but even their interest lessens as they approach the early years of the eighteenth century.

Chamber-music groups are perhaps more restricted in their choice of works than are any other musicians. Almost never do they choose works older than the Haydn quartets of 1755. Not even Bach or Handel or any of these giants' contemporaries is performed with any degree of frequency. It is as though the year 1750 (round numbers are convenient) marks a gateway labeled "Ancient music; proceed at your own risk." And scarcely anyone today dares enter that enclosure farther than is necessary to exhume a few of the innumerable pieces which lie buried there, notably Bach and Handel.

One might infer that music beyond the gateway is not worthy to be performed. One might assume that it is the work merely of forerunners; that it has no significance of its own. Or worse, one might remain entirely ignorant of its existence. In the field of chamber music, then, one would be forced to conclude that the string quartet, which is without doubt among the greatest musical achievements of western civilization, has no ancestors; that it emerged from the pen of Haydn as a new invention.

To give an account of the one hundred and fifty years of chamber music which preceded the quartets of Haydn, to describe the many forms which flourished during those years, to trace the many threads which lead from the earliest instrumental forms to the latest, to indicate how greatly every age is indebted to that which went before—these purposes are among the motivations for the first portion of this book. Later sections will attempt to guide the reader to the rich and extensive literature which constitutes present-day chamber-music repertoire, namely, that from Haydn to the present. One of the most satisfying and stimulating fields of music lies before us.

Chamber music is a bountiful source of pleasure to those who know the field. It is at once one of the most enjoyable and the most dignified of literatures. The musical amateur often makes it his hobby and considers it the mainspring of his musical existence. The experienced layman finds himself richly rewarded for his intelligent listening. The professional musician turns to it for relaxation and for a kind of pleasure that no other field offers.

Furthermore, it has challenged the greatest composers to their best efforts. Make a list of the chamber-music works of the masters from Haydn to Debussy; you have at once a catalogue of their finest works. The string quartets of Beethoven, for example, and the quartets and quintets of Brahms, are among the most profound and moving works in the entire literature of music—even though only a few instruments are required for their performance. "E'en little things can yield a perfect pleasure, e'en little things may be supremely dear"—so run the lines of a Tuscan love song beautifully set to music by Hugo Wolf. And of nothing is that so true as of the "little things" of chamber music. One finds in that field no necessary correlation between size and quality.

Again, chamber music provides a medium for the expression of particularly intimate musical ideas. There are people who grow tired of bombast and pretension and appreciate some degree of subtlety and refinement in their musical fare. Chamber music is for them, for it does not depend for its effects upon great splashes of sound, great variety of tone color, or great virtuoso display. In chamber music there is room only for essentials; all mere padding is avoided. One is aware of the musical essence, of the composer's inmost intentions, and is not distracted by extraneous glamor.

Until well into the nineteenth century chamber music was amateur music, confined to small rooms and private homes. In a day when every cultured person played an instrument [1] and professional musicians played several, chamber music provided the natural outlet for their activities. Every home of any size or pretension to culture harbored a chamber-music group; the sounds of trio sonatas, quartets, and even flute duets were heard throughout Europe.[2] In the time of Beethoven, however, professional chamber-music players became active,[3] and the two classes of musicians—namely, performers and listeners—took a long step away from each other. It became more fashionable to listen than to play, and the amateur status of the field deteriorated somewhat. As the music became more difficult to play

[1] Baldassare Castiglione (1478–1529) wrote a treatise on manners, social problems, and general behavior for the sixteenth-century courtier, *Libro del cortegiano*. Here one can learn how important musical accomplishments were to the well-being of educated persons of that age. Similar accomplishments at the Elizabethan court are too well known to require comment.

[2] Among the first public concerts of chamber music were those presented by John Banister, from 1672 to 1678, at his home in London.

[3] Ignaz Schuppanzigh (1776–1830), friend of Beethoven and Schubert, founded the Rasoumowsky Quartet in 1808. The Koella Quartet, composed of four brothers of Swiss parentage, played during the 1820's. The four Mueller brothers (born between 1797–1808, died between 1855–1875) began their quartet playing in 1830. Confining themselves to Haydn, Mozart, and Beethoven and traveling in all parts of western Europe (and Russia in 1845), they did much to create interest in and to set standards for chamber-music playing. The quartet founded by Joseph Helmesberger, Jr. (1829–1893), played from 1849 to 1887 and was influential in making the last quartets of Beethoven widely known. In 1869 Joseph Joachim founded his quartet, perhaps the most famous of all nineteenth-century ensembles. To these must be added the name of the Kneisel Quartet as the first well-known American chamber-music group, active from 1885 to 1917. The Flonzaley Quartet (1903–c. 1930), the London Quartet (1910–c. 1935), and the Kroll, Gordon, and Budapest Quartets of the present decade have maintained the high standards set by the earlier groups.

(there can be no question but that each new composer made greater demands upon the player), it became more and more a specialized field; consequently, fewer amateurs played it and knew it as a living literature.

But it is true that the finest musicians, the most enthusiastic amateurs, and the most cultivated listeners had not lost sight of chamber music. Concerts were well attended, the most competent amateur groups throve, and the field not only remained alive but also continued to draw new admirers in the decades just preceding and following 1900. The general awakening of a larger music audience since the turn of the century, plus the advent of phonograph recordings in the past three decades and of radio broadcasts in the past two, have done much to make chamber music better known to the public at large. Nothing more has been needed. To know chamber music is to revere it; to hear chamber music is to enjoy it. It is fast returning to the favored position it held throughout the seventeenth and the eighteenth centuries. The prejudices and misconceptions that surrounded it in the past are rapidly disappearing; they are being replaced by honest appreciation and real understanding. Chamber music, long known to musicians and listeners as the repository for the finest music in western civilization, is again being recognized as one of the most satisfying manifestations of the human spirit.

Why was chamber music once clouded by prejudices and misconceptions? Why do some laymen, even today, mistrust the field? It is largely because chamber music, like every other branch of music, has certain limitations along with its positive characteristics. One thing is true of all branches of music: each has a particular function to perform, and each has peculiar possibilities and particular disadvantages. Sacred music, for example, is well adapted to contribute to church services, to help establish an attitude of reverence, to testify to the presence of the divine in the human; sacred music is unsuitable as a source of dance tunes. An orchestral piece gives the composer ample opportunity to develop a musical idea with great variety of tone color and to create effects which depend upon tonal mass for their success; an orchestral piece cannot successfully meet the requirements of intimacy and economy in music. So with the other branches: each does one thing well, other things less well or badly. A single composition or literature cannot be all things to all men; to this the field of chamber music is no exception.

The character of chamber music makes its limitations follow as a matter of course. Since it is a medium for expressing subtle musical ideas, it cannot serve more general or obvious musical purposes. It is not a medium for elaborate display or extensive verbosity. It does not lend itself to vivid color effects or to dazzling passages which impress one sheerly by a large number of players or mass of tone. It is not a medium for storytelling—for delineation of this or that extramusical effect. It is not often suited to the purposes of the virtuoso, whose appeal is by means of technical facility rather than musical worth. Since there is only one player for each part, certain types of writing which can afford to ignore human frailty and the limitations of physical endurance are not successful in it. All these things chamber music is not.

The person who looks for the color of an orchestra, the pomp and display of an opera, the rhythmic vitality of a military band, looks vainly for these things in chamber music. Disappointed or disillusioned, he calls it dull or austere or colorless. He is bored by it and considers it a subject fit only for the music historian. But why should one listen negatively and look for characteristics which properly belong to other branches of music?

Where else can he find such clarity of texture? The listener to an orchestra is often so lost in a maze of sound, in variety of tone color, and in the great number of tonal lines that he is aware of only a formless mass; in a musical sense, he cannot see the trees for the forest. His enjoyment of the finer points is greatly hampered, and his overall appreciation of the work is made difficult. He who listens to a string quartet, on the other hand, seldom has to follow more than three tonal lines, the mass of tone is never so great as to overwhelm him, and he is able to look within the music—to hear between the notes, much as one learns to read between the lines.

Where else than in chamber music is there to be found the economy of resources that eschews all padding and flamboyance? [4] Where else can there be accomplished so much with so little (and by so many, the author is tempted to add)? The extramusical effects which impress the naïve listener through sheer novelty or sheer weight, the kaleidoscopic colors whose appeal is mainly sensuous—these are seldom found in chamber music. And their absence allows the music to stand on its own feet with all its beauties and strengths revealed. The result is that its shams and weaknesses are uncovered also. Chamber music is honest music, if it is successful. No insincerity is possible in good chamber music, for the characteristics of musical insincerity go hand-in-hand with noise, bluster, and confusion; and these are, of course, lacking.

Where else than in chamber music can he find the flawless balance and ensemble, the selfless teamwork, the achievement of which is one of the finest manifestations of the human spirit? Loyalty to the composer's intentions requires the perfection of ensemble which the chamber musician strives for and only the chamber musician can hope to achieve. And where else than in chamber music can he find the feeling of intimate contact with the music itself? Undistracted by sensuous appeals, undisturbed by flamboyant delivery, unencumbered by overstuffed detail, he can give himself up to the pure enjoyment of the tonal lines themselves, can follow their paths and their encounters, and can come close to realizing the composer's ultimate intention. Let the person who mistakenly looks for the color and pomp of an orchestra in a string quartet address himself to the positive values that chamber music has to offer. He will not be bored or disappointed.

The dictionaries define chamber music as instrumental music written in the larger forms for combinations ranging from two to ten players, having one player on a part, and designed to be heard in a small room or chamber. The limit as to the number of players is not made arbitrarily. For one thing, chamber music implies ensemble

[4] The well-informed listener will say, "Why, in any of the choral music of Palestrina and other sixteenth-century composers." But here the author's rhetorical question is meant to confine itself to instrumental works in the present-day repertoire.

music; since one player can hardly be said to engage in ensemble activity (except in the case of a pianist whose left hand knows not what his right does), two is the minimum number to qualify under the dictionary definition. Then again, it is rarely feasible for more than ten players to remain in good ensemble without a conductor. Players must sit some distance apart, even ten players can produce so large a tonal volume that the end men cannot clearly hear each other, and more than ten different musical natures make compromise rather difficult and accurate ensemble almost impossible. Thus the upper limit of size is arrived at. So it happens that musical reference books list all combinations from sonata for piano and one other instrument to and including ensembles for ten instruments as chamber music.

For the purposes of this book, however, the dictionary definition will be amended somewhat. There is a general understanding of the term "chamber music" among musicians and concert-goers, a restricted use of the term, that deserves recognition. It is based in part upon present-day traditions in the concert field, in part on economic factors, and in part upon the fact that very little music for nine or ten instruments exists. For all practical purposes, chamber music consists of trios, quartets, quintets, and sextets in which string instruments play the leading roles. When an informed music lover attends a chamber-music concert, he does not expect to hear a sonata for violin and piano; that form he looks for on a violin recital program. When a number of enthusiastic musicians assemble for an evening of chamber music, they look forward to playing quartets or quintets, with perhaps a trio or a sextet thrown in if the music is available; they do not expect to have the evening ruined (for them) by being forced to listen while two of their number play through the violin or cello sonata repertoire. Finally, chamber music for wind instruments is, for reasons of tradition and limited literature, largely a field for the specialist; it does not often appear on concert programs and is of interest mainly to the wind players themselves.

This does not mean to imply that violin or cello sonatas and wind instrument ensemble music deserve no place in chamber-music lit-

erature.[5] It merely calls attention to the fact that the technical definition of the field and the general description (among those who live
and work and thrive in it) do not agree. Since this book is not meant
to be an exhaustive history of all instrumental music, it seems justified, even appropriate, to introduce the subject within its more
usual limits. A restricted definition is called for, a definition that will
determine what works shall be discussed in the pages to follow. And
so we arrive at the following.

Chamber music is, for our purposes in this book, instrumental
music written in the largest forms available to the composer for
groups of three to eight players, having one player to a part, in which
string instruments supply the principal interest.

Thus we are arbitrarily disregarding hundreds of sonatas for violin
or cello and piano, we are ignoring scores of divertimentos for string
and wind instruments written by the early masters of the Classical
period, we are paying no attention to many eighteenth-century
works, pieces which are popularly referred to as being for "chamber
orchestra," and we shall not mention the many excellent works for
woodwind and brass ensembles.

What remains of the field if so many categories and compositions
are not to be included? The following table gives the combinations
of instruments engaged in chamber music in the sense of the above
definition. In addition to these most common combinations, there are
a few works in which a wind instrument is substituted for a string,
as in the Mozart and Brahms clarinet quintets and the Brahms horn
trio (violin, horn, and piano). There are also a few combinations of
winds and strings, notably the Beethoven septet and the Schubert
octet. All but the *Sonata a tre* are among the post-1750 combinations
to which contemporary chamber music groups customarily address
themselves. The latter, on the other hand, is the predominant instrumentation for the great majority of pre-1750 forms; these include
the trio sonata, the *sonata da chiesa*, and the *sonata da camera*, and

---

[5] The interested reader is referred to von Wasielewski, *Die Violine und ihre
Meister;* Beckmann, *Das Violinspiel in Deutschland vor 1700;* van der Straeten, *The
History of the Violin.*

to a large extent the *canzone*, the form in which the first true chamber music was written.

THE USUAL COMBINATIONS IN CHAMBER MUSIC

Sonata a tre (Trio Sonata)

Violin I and II
Cello and/or bass
Harpsichord

String Trio

Violin
Viola (or Violin II)
Cello

String Quartet

Violin I
Violin II
Viola
Cello

Piano Trio

Violin
Cello
Piano

String Quintet

Violin I and II
Viola I
Viola II
Cello

or Violin I and II
Viola
Cello I
Cello II

Piano Quartet

Violin
Viola
Cello
Piano

Piano Quintet

Violin I and II
Viola
Cello
Piano

For the purposes of this book we have chosen to identify our field as a branch of instrumental music; therefore we ignore vocal ensembles, which a less rigid definition might include among chamber-music media. By doing so we are spared a long excursion into the history of vocal music. Nevertheless, we must begin this survey with two subjects related to that field: the emergence of instrumental music out of the dominant mass of vocal music and the transformation of the vocal chanson into the instrumental *canzone*.

On the strength of what little evidence has as yet been presented, one may assume that music written after approximately 1750 differs from that written earlier. Let us postpone real evidence for the moment, but refer to 1750 as marking a change in musical style. While a particular date may be taken for convenience in establishing style boundaries, actually no such exact limit exists. Styles in music do not change as rapidly as styles in clothes, let us say. There is nothing in music comparable to the devastating effect of a New York or Paris style show which overnight relegates yesterday's modish garments to today's stock of old-fashioned ones. Rather, the process is a gradual shift on the part of many composers from one kind of writing to another, a shift which may persist throughout several decades. At some point during those decades one composer, usually a reactionary or a conservative, sums up in a blaze of creative genius all that has gone before; at the same time another composer is the first successfully to codify the new practices. At that moment the differences between the old style and the new come clearly to light; as a matter of convenience one may refer to the date and call attention to the style change. Such a date was 1750, and such composers were the conservative Bach and the successful codifier Haydn.

Another such convenient date marking a major shift in musical trends was the year 1600. Again several decades were involved in the shift. The three centuries before that date had been concerned largely with vocal contrapuntal music. The expressive possibilities of that music, the purity and consistency of its style, and the economy of means employed are to be observed in the great composers of the late sixteenth century. Palestrina, whose work ended in 1594, is usually singled out as the great representative of that century, although there is no reason why Lasso, Byrd, or Victoria should not have been so honored. And the new style, coming after 1600, is characterized in part by the appearance of instrumental music with a lessened use of vocal counterpoint.

Among the many generalizations current in the textbooks, none is so firmly implanted as that which refers to the sixteenth century as the "golden age of *a cappella*." In his state of having a little learning, which is a dangerous thing, the unsuspecting person may think of that century as one great splurge of vocal music, with everyone singing sixteen-part counterpoint at sight, unaccompanied. Then on the stroke of midnight, December 31, 1599 (to the chronologically-minded this is obviously wrong, for the century ends in 1600, but 1599 makes a better picture), all unaccompanied vocal counterpoint ceases, and everyone miraculously begins to compose and to perform instrumental music.

Herein lies a great misconception, and withal a pair of half-truths. For while it is true that the sixteenth century witnessed the glories of Lasso and Palestrina and Byrd, all of whom wrote unaccompanied vocal music, it is equally true that music of that kind was not always performed without accompaniment and that it continued to be written until well into the eighteenth century. While it is true that the decades after 1600 saw the emergence of instrumental music as a separate branch of the art, it is equally true that instrumental music was performed as early as the thirteenth century. Here is another case in which a style change developed throughout several decades, gradually shifting the emphasis from vocal to instrumental music. It is only for convenience that one attaches a date to the moment (figuratively speaking) when the two styles were most sharply differentiated. In this case the date is 1600.

Instrumental music did not suddenly come to life in the seventeenth century, but was well established and assiduously cultivated in the 1200's. While there are few manuscripts giving direct evidence, numerous paintings testify to the number and variety of instruments in common use.[6] Lute, zither, vielle, guitar, and harp are among the string instruments played in those years; the recorder, flute, oboe, and horn are the wind instrument contemporaries. Chaucer and Boccaccio give added evidence that instrumental music was a part of everyday life among certain classes of people. Especially in the *Decameron* do the characters make use of instruments, both in solo playing and to accompany singing. Professionally, too, instrumental music was on a firm basis; guilds of trumpeters, pipers, and fiddlers were established late in the thirteenth century.

[6] Leichtentritt, "Was lehren uns die Bildwerke des 14ten–17ten Jarhunderts," *Sammelbände der Internationalen Musikgesellschaft* (April–June, 1906), VII[8], 315–364.

From the fourteenth century through the sixteenth, instruments gradually encroached upon vocal music.[7] One of the early great French composers, Guillaume de Machaut, who died in 1377, set the pattern for secular music in France until well into the fifteenth century. Machaut seized upon the old Gothic motet, a sacred choral piece in contrapuntal style with a Latin text, and by substituting French love lyrics and performing it with one part played [8] (probably on viol or lute) and the others sung began the process of transforming vocal into instrumental music. This method of performance underwent certain changes in the course of many decades: at times an improvised instrumental part was added; in the absence of a singer an instrument played the missing part; occasionally a drone bass was added. The end result was that vocal music, which is to say choral music, was often performed by instruments alone. In such performances viols predominated; but other instruments were there in abundance, not in families of similar tone color, but in as great a variety of color and sonority as possible.[9] The organ and lute also took part in these transformed vocal pieces to a great extent; the large number of collections containing lute transcriptions of instrumental music which itself was derived from vocal music testify to the popularity of this form of activity. This type of arrangement, the lute transcription of a vocal piece, remained in favor for more than two centuries. We shall see it again in Italy about 1550.

Toward the middle of the fifteenth century a similar step was taken in Germany; there, too, instrumental music was freed from the position of merely supporting the voices. The German folk song had been popular since the twelfth century; it was sung on many occasions and often provided the music for dancing. About 1450 it became the basis for a new type of composition.[10] Certain

[7] Cf. Nef, *An Outline of the History of Music*, tr. by Pfatteicher, pp. 62–65.
[8] Láng, *Music in Western Civilization*, pp. 153–154. Cf. Haas, *Aufführungspraxis der Musik*, pp. 103–105.
[9] Adler, *Handbuch*, I, 383.
[10] New, that is, to Germany. A discussion of the similar French motets of the thirteenth century, as found in the Montpellier *Codex* (modern edition published as *Polyphonies du XIIIe siècle*, ed. by Yvonne Rokseth; Paris, 1935–1939) would lead too far afield.

folk-song melodies (called "tenors") were supplied with two or three accompanying countermelodies, and were otherwise expanded and ornamented. These three- or four-part contrapuntal arrangements of folk songs were then given over to groups of instruments for performance. In addition to these popular arrangements, designed for home (i.e., chamber) music use, a number of leading composers of the time applied the same devices to original tunes. Conrad Paumann, a famous blind Bavarian organist, who died in 1473, was among the best known of these men. Three sources for music of this kind are the *Lochamer, Berliner*, and *Münchener Liederbücher*,[11] all from the period about 1450–1460. The arrangements contained in these books are perhaps the earliest recorded music for amateurs: *Hausmusik*, which large numbers of Europeans have held in esteem up to the present day. The *Münchener Liederbuch* contains trios by Paumann, along with many arrangements of "tenors" similar to those described.

Again following these models is a set of arrangements by Hans Gerle (1532) for *Grosz- und Kleingeigen Quartet*. These are still folk-song transcriptions, but arranged with more regard for instrumental style and with less slavish adherence to the vocal originals. Still later, in 1561, Martin Agricola's (c. 1486–1556) work *Duo libri musices* was published by Rhau in Wittenberg; this work contains sixty-seven textless trios and quartets for groups of viols.[12] Meanwhile, Heinrich Finck had written, in 1520, "songs . . . lustily to be sung, and suitable for instruments."

From the fourteenth century to the seventeenth there existed, principally in Germany, a branch of music which owed nothing to vocal models: tower music. Brass ensembles employing *Zinken* (a type of conical wood or ivory instrument with a cup mouthpiece, provided with holes to produce notes lying between the natural overtones, also called cornett), natural horns, and trombones had many functions in the German medieval and Renaissance towns.

[11] *Das Locheimer* [Lochamer] *Liederbuch*, prepared in facsimile edition by Ameln. Cf. Moser, *Geschichte der deutschen Musik*, I, 349–354.
[12] Moser, *Geschichte der deutschen Musik*, I, 429.

Their activities were varied: playing short concerts from the town hall tower at stated hours, taking part in religious and municipal ceremonies, playing for town dances, alarming the town at the approach of the enemy, and giving fire warnings. Regulations concerning instrumentation of the group, behavior, terms of service, and the like are common in the Acts of the burgomasters of the several towns as late as 1650.[13]

The dance had, of course, been accompanied by music since ancient times. During the Middle Ages the duty of playing for dancers was assigned to the *jongleur;* the medieval chanson provided the music, the *estampie,* the step.[14] Throughout the fourteenth and fifteenth centuries dance music remained in the humble hands of the itinerant *Musikant* or the performing musician of the courts. It did not enter into the purview of the "composer" or into the realm of art music (as opposed to folk music) until the beginning of the sixteenth century. From that point its influence on chamber-music forms of the seventeenth century can be traced. An account of dance music thus belongs more properly in a later chapter of this book, hence need not be elaborated here.

On the basis of considerable evidence, of which the foregoing paragraphs are only a fragment, it is no longer permissible to think of the years from 1400 to 1600 as a purely vocal, *a cappella,* period. The view borne out by the results of modern research is that instrumental music was at first a substitute for vocal music, that it grew in importance during the fifteenth and sixteenth centuries, and that it finally emerged as a separate branch of music in the seventeenth.

It is true that it came into the light of day about 1600 without a true style of its own. Instrumental melodies remained within the easy range of the human voice, contained no intervals that the voice could not sing easily, and had no awkward or rapidly shifting rhythmic patterns. Above all, the characteristic melodic shapes which today identify a melody as being suitable for the violin or the trumpet or the piano were completely missing from early instrumental music. Organ music, as well as that for strings, employed the

---

[13] *Ibid.*, pp. 304-307.   [14] Láng, *Music in Western Civilization*, p. 107.

same general texture found in vocal contrapuntal music; indeed, many of the early instrumental forms (the *ricercari* and the *canzoni*) have the appearance of textless motets and chansons—which is, after all, what they were. It was one of the great accomplishments of the seventeenth century to create separate musical styles for the organ, the harpsichord, and the violin and to make each of these styles an eminently satisfactory medium for carrying its wealth of musical ideas.

The reader will have noticed that the instrumental music discussed thus far has appeared only in connection with secular pursuits: folk song, love song, tower music, and the dance. It must not be forgotten that however much emphasis may be put upon the secular uses of music during the fourteenth, fifteenth, and sixteenth centuries, the backbone of the art was polyphonic vocal music placed at the service of the Church. The great number of masses, motets, and magnificats outweigh in importance and probably in quantity the rudimentary instrumental music of that period. The vocal contrapuntal writing of those centuries reached its highest peak of development in the music designed for church use.

But not all polyphonic vocal pieces were sacred music. The madrigal in Italy and in England and the chanson in France were both secular forms, making use of the same type of love and lovesick poetry we associate with the Elizabethan period in literature. A host of composers were active in those countries, and in Germany as well, in the field of secular music—even though their chief concern was with sacred music. Palestrina in Rome, Lasso in Munich, Byrd, Morley, and Gibbons in England, Hassler in Augsburg, Jannequin and Le Jeune in France—all of whom were active in the late sixteenth century—are typical of the group. Many of them, regardless of location, made use of the French chanson. The latter was by far the most popular secular vocal form in France. Important in its own right, it was destined to have a strong influence on the early chamber-music forms of the seventeenth century.

What of the circumstances under which the various sacred and secular forms were performed? One can distinguish rather clearly three main lines of musical activity in the years just before 1600.

(1) *Music in and of the Church and of the private chapels of the aristocracy.*—Motet and mass formed the core of the choral portion of the service, along with Gregorian plainsong. The organ and other instruments at times supported, at times substituted for, the choir.

(2) *Music at the courts and in the homes of the aristocracy.*— There, in addition to its private chapel, every establishment was supplied to some degree with secular choral and instrumental groups. Madrigals and chansons for the one, dance tunes and dinner music for the other—there was sufficient material to keep the hard-working servant-musicians busy. In most cases the secular and religious musical duties were combined; one man was responsible for all the music. Orlando di Lasso in the sixteenth century at the court of Munich, Heinrich Schütz at that of Dresden in the seventeenth, and Joseph Haydn at Eszterháza in the eighteenth—these are outstanding examples of the quality of the men placed in such positions.

(3) *Amateur music of all types.*—In this line are included all such activities as communal music purely for self-entertainment, village dances, accompanied songs, and, perhaps most important for the future, the *Collegium musicum.*[15] Organizations bearing that name had been established in the middle of the sixteenth century, simultaneously with the decline of the chairs of music in the Renaissance universities. They were, in a sense, the lower and middle class counterparts of court groups and professional ensembles, to which the common man had access neither as performer nor as listener. Originally devoted to choral music, both sacred and secular, they opened their ranks to instrumentalists late in the century and were the arenas in which many of the newly emerging dance suites received performance. One cannot speak of the instrumentation of the *Collegium musicum,* or for that matter of any sixteenth- or seventeenth-century group, as one can of the standardized symphony orchestra after the 1740's. A uniform instrumentation did not occur to Renaissance musicians; only considerations of range determined

---

[15] Riemann, Preface to No. 44 of *Collegium musicum.* This is a series of seventeenth- and eighteenth-century chamber-music works.

the disposition of instruments. Tone color and blending of diverse tone colors were not to become factors of musical expression until the middle of the eighteenth century. About that time, which is about the time public orchestral performances came into being, the *Collegium musicum* declined in popularity, and it soon died out.

In summary, the years just before the end of the sixteenth century are noteworthy in several respects. Culturally, they mark the transition from the late Renaissance to the early Baroque periods. From the point of view of musical texture, they usher in the decline of vocal counterpoint and the beginnings of the age of accompanied melody. Technically, they mark the deterioration of the system of ecclesiastical modes which had persisted, with many alterations, for more than a thousand years, and the establishment of our system of major and minor tonalities. For our purposes they bring forth independent instrumental music as opposed to instrumental music derived from or in direct imitation of vocal music. Let us now look at the years from about 1550 to 1600 in greater detail, in order to have a firm grasp on the musical forms, styles, and ideas of the seventeenth century, the century in which chamber music began.

2

FROM CHANSON TO CANZONE

It is one of the more pleasant moments in life when one can identify an important event with an easily remembered date. Historians will always be grateful to Charlemagne for having assumed the imperial crown in the year 800; students, while they greatly lament Chaucer's death, are happy that he died in such a convenient year as 1400. Likewise, it is a boon to the music historian that an obscure canon named Giovanni Artusi (c. 1550–1613) chose the year 1600 to publish a diatribe, *L'Artusi overo della imperfettioni della moderna musica*,[1] thereby being the first to call attention to revolutionary changes, to the new music that was sweeping over Europe. This *nuove musiche* (we shall hear this phrase again, later in the chapter) was to give birth to the opera, was to give instrumental music, and thereby chamber music, its first long trousers, and was to make possible the homophonic style of the Classical symphony. The new musical practices which Artusi inveighed against were a part of the great changes in all the arts, in the Church, and in all European life that took place in the last years of the sixteenth century and were to give rise to a new style period. So extensive were these changes, so wide their influence, and so lasting their results that historians have found it necessary to give that period a name: the Baroque. The name hardly gives a clue to the nature of the changes, for "baroque" means grotesque, bizarre, irregular. It is a rather neat coincidence that another derogatory name was given to an earlier period closely allied to the Baroque: the Gothic. It will be remembered that "Gothic" was meant to be rude, barbarian; historians have been

[1] Published by Vincenti at Venice.

equally uncomplimentary to the Gothic period's relative, the Baroque.

The period that intervened between the two just mentioned, namely, the Renaissance, extended roughly from the middle of the fourteenth century to the middle of the sixteenth. The Renaissance was a time of romance; man had found himself, and the world was his to conquer. It was a time for reforms, for recasting civilization according to the models of Greece and Rome. It was, in the arts, a time of symmetry, proportion, and balance. And inevitably it became in time a period of excesses and exaggerations in all directions (the Baroque begins to rear its ugly head). The Church had lost its hold on the common man and had found it necessary to revive the Inquisition to combat the cancer of heresy. Its whole position had deteriorated mightily. Split half apart by the Reformation in the early sixteenth century, it suffered under the neglect of political popes and worldly prelates.

With the Catholic Counter Reformation, in which the Council of Trent, meeting interruptedly from 1545 to 1563, took a prominent part, a change took place. The Jesuits took the lead in reestablishing the Church as a spiritual and moral power, and rescued large parts of central Europe from the Protestants. They realized the advantages of stimulating art of all kinds, provided that it remained within the orbit of the Church. A new architecture arose, based on the old Gothic. Classic symmetry and proportion gave way to exaggeration of detail, flamboyant ornamentation, and distorted forms. Ritual and ceremonial events within the Church rose to new heights of display. Colorful processions captured the public imagination. Mysticism, the cult of saints, and a belief in miracles again became aspects of the Catholic mind. Fervor, energy, and display characterized the Catholic life of the times.[2] And so the Baroque period was born.

In the Protestant countries, where by now the erstwhile heretics were politically well established, the exuberance and initiative of the south turned toward other fields. Tradition had lost its hold; in-

[2] Láng, *Music in Western Civilization*, pp. 314 ff.

dependent inquiry became more and more of a force as the seventeenth century flowed on. A list of names of the century's leaders in thought and action gives a truer picture of the stimulating life of the times than a long account of its accomplishments: in the sciences, such men as Descartes, Galileo (although an Italian), Kepler, and finally Newton; in philosophy, Descartes again, Spinoza, and Locke; in literature, Milton, Molière, and Bunyan; in art, Rubens, Rembrandt, and Velásquez; in politics, Cardinal Richelieu, Cromwell, and Gustavus Adolphus.

The mention of the last group calls attention to the turbulence of the century. The devastating effects of the Thirty Years' War (1618–1648), from which Germany did not recover for a century, point to the zeal and the endurance of the religious antagonists. The period of the Commonwealth in England and the absolute monarchy of Louis XIV in France give evidence of the contradictory nature of some of the Baroque period's elements. In short, the period, especially its middle portion, the seventeenth century, was a time in which the rational spirit and calm perspective of the late Renaissance had given way to action, to emotional impulse. Drama was felt everywhere. Color contrasts were dramatic; the rich ceremonial processions and the elaborate Church art were dramatic; the new architecture provided an excitement akin to drama. And it is out of the emotional state kindled by the century's color contrasts and dramatic excitement that the new music of the Baroque period arose. Color was present everywhere: in the vivid frescoes and paintings with which the new churches were adorned; in the brilliant civic and religious pageants; in the ceremonial robes of church dignitaries. Dramatic color in the poetry and stage plays of the time found its natural counterpart in the music. And along with their mirroring of color, composers became able to create particular moods. Among the first of the Baroque composers to sense music's ability to reflect particular moods was Luca Marenzio (c. 1553–1599), an Italian composer of madrigals.

Josquin des Prés (c. 1450–1521), several decades before Marenzio,

had laid the groundwork for a more intimate kind of expression.[3]
It remained for Marenzio to achieve a really close connection between text and music. In his madrigals, the music followed the implications of the words so closely that not only the intellectual
content of the text but also the dramatic idea behind it appeared.
In his efforts to paint true pictures, to give a faithful account of
the poem in music, to read between the lines, Marenzio found that
the ecclesiastical modes in use at the time hampered him. He turned
away from the modes to a great extent, in favor of major and minor
tonality and a degree of chromatic harmony; and here is his great
importance from a historical point of view. Only the system of
tonality could give him the necessary harmonic freedom to express
in his madrigals the poetic and dramatic content of his texts. We
must look for a moment at the essential differences between the
modal and the tonal systems properly to evaluate Marenzio's contributions.

The modal system in the sixteenth century made use of six pairs
of scales or modes, each less than two octaves in range, and each with
a different arrangement of half and whole steps. Thus, the Dorian
mode consisted of the notes D-E-F-G-A-B-C-D, with its half steps
between the second and the third and again between the sixth and
the seventh scale steps; the Phrygian had E-F-G-A-B-C-D-E, with
its half steps between the first and the second, and between the fifth
and the sixth. Likewise, the other modes differed in this regard.
Each mode was rigidly adhered to, except in a few instances where
melodic considerations warranted the change of an F in the Dorian
mode, for example, to an F sharp when the melody was ascending,
or a B to a B flat when the melody descended; such changes, coming
under the head of *musica ficta* (fictitious music), were banned by
the Church, but were in general use among all singers without being
written down (hence the term "fictitious music"). Interval leaps in

[3] A discussion of *musica reservata* would lead too far afield. The interested reader
is referred to van Crevel, *Adrianus Petit Coclico,* for a complete account of this
subject.

the melodic lines were traditionally prescribed, could not be exceeded, and in effect limited the choice of melodic shapes to a few
general patterns. Certain intervals were to be avoided at all costs,
for example from F to B in either direction. Chords which resulted—
and since the modal system was melodic there were no chords as
such to choose from—in three- or four-part contrapuntal writing
were always consonant triads, except insofar as a short passing
tone might create a very brief dissonance. Chords were connected
on the basis of the melodic line, the chord progression being conditioned by whatever notes succeeded each other in the upper line.
Thus, a melodic line, let us say, of A-B-C-B-A might have below it
three other melodic lines which result in the triads of A, G, F, C, G
minor, and A (see example).

(Example of musica ficta)

It is this feature of modal music which gives it its characteristic
color, and this feature in which it differs so widely from tonal music.
   The tonal system has, as we know, two scales, major and minor,
each of which can appear in twelve different keys. The root, or first
note of the scale, is the tonal center around which the melody and
its harmony revolve. Chords of varying degrees of complexity and
consonance are built on each note of the scale, or on chromatic
alterations of scale notes. In the tonal system the strong tendency
of the seventh scale step to progress to the octave, and of the fourth
to the third, is satisfied or deliberately (for expressive purposes)
avoided. The satisfaction of such tone tendencies gives the feeling
of repose which is so evident in a typical tonal cadence. Chords are
used to strengthen these tendencies: a dominant seventh chord, for
example, contains both the ascending seventh and the descending
fourth of the tonic scale, and gives the fullest feeling of finality and
repose when it appears before the tonic chord in a cadence. Further-

more, through the ability to employ chromatic alterations of scale steps (really, notes borrowed from other scales) it is easy to pass from one key to another.

The expressiveness of a melody, any modal or tonal melody, lies in its contour, in its satisfaction or avoidance of tone tendencies, in the choice of chord to strengthen the latter, and in the relation of the melody to other tonalities (keys). The modal system, in its pure form, ignored tone tendencies; its chords were in a sense the accidental result of three or more parts meeting at certain intervals from each other. Modal melodies were so organized that certain leaps and certain general contours were not permissible. True, the device of *musica ficta* overcame the ignoring of tone tendencies, but that device was a late development in modal music, and was in itself an approach to the tonal system. Thus, in modal music certain types of expression were possible, and in the hands of the great composers were achieved with marvelous subtlety; but not all types of expression were possible. Whereas in tonal music, with no restrictions on melodic contour, harmonic color, or change of tonality, and with freedom to use the expressive possibilities of all intervals and all scales, the field was wide open. Marenzio was among the first composers to seize upon the possibilities of tonal music, and he succeeded in writing madrigals which depicted human emotions in a way that was completely foreign to modal music. His influence on his followers, particularly Carlo Gesualdo (c. 1560–1613) and Claudio Monteverdi (1567–1643), was tremendous. The latter, carrying the torch to harmonic and tonal distances undreamed of by Marenzio himself, established the tonal system firmly enough to call down upon himself the wrath of Canon Artusi, the mention of whose diatribe against "modern music" opened this chapter.

But obviously a system as well established as the modal one did not give up without a struggle. Throughout the seventeenth century the modal and the tonal systems existed side by side. The former remained more in the province of church music, the latter in the secular forms. Even with the best of revolutionary intentions no composer could quite throw off the shackles of the older system of expression. Modal feeling, the feeling engendered by connection of chords on a melodic rather than a harmonic basis, persisted in all of Monteverdi's works, even though they were built on a tonal foundation. In Heinrich Schütz (1585–1672), in Henry Purcell (c. 1659–1695), and well into the eighteenth century modally flavored music is found. Until the time of Rameau's codification of harmonic laws (1722) modality was a potent means of expression no composer could do without.

The outstanding musical phenomenon of the Baroque period was the emergence of independent instrumental music. An outline of the steps in practice and performance that led to such music has been given in Chapter 1; it is desirable to give a similar outline for the musical form in which it first appeared. That form is the instrumental *canzone* as we find it at the very end of the sixteenth century. The *canzone*, in turn, was at first an instrumental (lute or organ) arrangement of a French vocal form, the chanson. So we must briefly examine the latter properly to evaluate the *canzone*.

From the Gothic period until well into the Baroque, which is to say from about the fourteenth century to the seventeenth, Frenchmen, and Frenchwomen too, sang chansons. Composers had taken the short lyric poems of their day, poems of a secular nature, poems full of love and springtime and pining away and rosebuds and the like, and set them to music: the resultant musical form was the chanson. Much of the time the chanson was set for four voices, in contrapuntal style; in phrase structure and general form it always mirrored the form and the rhyme scheme of the poem. And since repetition and recapitulation of verses were characteristic of the poetry, the musical forms ABBA and ABA became characteristic of the chanson.

During its three hundred years of popularity the chanson underwent many changes in length, style, and general content. By the time it began to serve as a model for the Italian *canzone* it had resolved itself into a composition from twenty to sixty measures in length, well separated into sections marked by a change from contrapuntal to note-against-note style. A parenthetical word about these two characteristics (measures and style) may not be amiss.

1. Almost all the music composed up to 1600 was notated without being divided into measures. A rhythmic unit did exist: the half-note, roughly equivalent to our modern quarter-note in moderate tempo. And a succession of multiples and divisions of the rhythmic unit was employed, ranging from the breve (⌐◻⌐) to the eighth-note; but such notes were employed without reference to regularly recurring accents. In general, since most music of the time was vocal, the accented syllables of the text provided the rhythmic accents of the music, and the music was unmetrical in the way that prose may be unmetrical. Thus, bar lines, which are needed only in metrical music, were unnecessary. However, as the sixteenth century ran its course, such accents came more and more to be four units apart, and a metrical rhythm of 4/2 became usual.

In the nineteenth century, with its great preoccupation with editing and reprinting the music of the sixteenth, it became customary for editors to insert bar lines at regular intervals in the music in order to facilitate reading. Thus, when we speak of measures in a sixteenth-century piece of music, we do so with the knowledge that the composer himself made no use of this convenient metrical symbol. In this sense a measure becomes a group of four half-notes (or three in the case of a triple meter) which correspond in modern notation to quarter-notes. In the case of the chansons of the period under discussion (1520–1540) this grouping is especially justified, since the overwhelming majority of chansons of this period were in duple meter, with their phrases built in multiples of four half-notes.

2. It was pointed out also that sections in contrapuntal and note-against-note style alternated. It is interesting to observe the lack of contrast between these two opposing terms. The word counterpoint is merely the English equivalent of the Latin *contrapunctum*, which is in turn an abbreviation of the phrase *punctus contra punctum*; this means "note against note." Yet the direct translation and its shortened form are set up as contrasting terms. It is well to keep this contradiction in mind. In this book "note-against-note" will be used to characterize the style in which no rhythmic diversity occurs between the voices, regardless of whether the voices have independent

melodic integrity or not.[4] "Counterpoint" will be used when, in addition to melodic integrity, the voices also show rhythmic diversity.[5] This procedure will conform to existing practice, even though it does bring in the possibility of inaccuracy.

Let us now return to the chansons. We have mentioned their length and a characteristic of their sectional form. In addition to the change in style of succeeding sections, there was often a change in meter: a duple-meter section would be succeeded by one in triple meter, where the change in textual rhythm made such a metrical change necessary. The chansons were distinguished by a considerable use of quarter-notes (eighth-notes in modern notation), which provided a certain amount of bustling rhythmic vitality. Finally, they so frequently began with a dactylic motive (♩ ♪ ♪) that the motive almost became a trademark for the form.

The extreme popularity of the chanson is made evident by the hundreds of publications and dozens of collections appearing in Paris, Antwerp, and Venice before 1550.[6] But equal in popularity to the chanson as a four-voice contrapuntal piece of vocal music was the instrumental arrangement of the chanson. It will be remembered that one of the practices of the sixteenth century was, in the absence of the required singers, to substitute instruments for the lower voices of a vocal work and to perform it with one part sung and the others played. Viols were so used, and to some extent other instruments. But whereas string and wind instruments could play the missing voices directly from the part books (which were like present-day orchestra parts in that they contained only the part for one voice),

---

[4] The example on p. 24 is in note-against-note style.
[5] The example on p. 74 is contrapuntal.
[6] Attaingnant, at Paris, published several hundred chansons in half-a-dozen collections between 1527 and 1549. Other Parisian publishers, imitating his example, were similarly active: Jacques Moderne published between 1538 and 1543; Le Roy et Ballard, 1552–1599; in Antwerp, Tilman Susato, c. 1540; in Venice, Andrea Antico, 1520–1536, and Antonio Gardano, 1531–1548. The latter was joined later in the century by Vincenti, who was still publishing chansons in 1588. Cf. Crocker, "An Introductory Study of the Italian Canzona for Instrumental Ensembles," an unpublished dissertation (Radcliffe College, 1943), I, 80–83. I am much indebted to Miss Crocker's excellent work.

a "harmony" instrument, such as the lute, required that the parts to be used be combined and if necessary arranged for it. Thus, one finds arrangements of chansons for solo voice and lute, with the original lower voices written in the lute tablature of that period. Publishers, with an eye to increasing their sales through "plugging" their best sellers, often undertook to make these lute and voice arrangements themselves, or had them made.[7] Another type of arrangement, which is perhaps more important than the voice and lute version for the subsequent history of chamber music, is that for lute or keyboard instrument alone. Chansons were arranged for lute by many mid-century Italian lutenists. The form appears arranged for the virginal in the *Fitzwilliam Virginal Book*,[8] one of the important sources of Elizabethan music in England.

The transcriptions for organ, however, had the greatest influence on the later history of the instrumental version of the chanson. We must notice the use of the word "transcription" in place of "arrangement" here. The practice of ornamenting a melody, improvising embellishments, runs, and the like, was an established part of the organist's trade. When this practice was applied to a work previously existing in a vocal form, the piece was so greatly altered by the florid ornamentation that it ceased to be an arrangement, made merely to facilitate its performance in some other medium, and became in effect a piece recomposed by the ornamentor. We must henceforth speak of transcriptions, for many sixteenth-century examples of the chanson adapted to the organ show to a great degree the results of this practice.

The first transcriptions of chansons for organ appeared in Italy in 1523, in a collection of organ tablatures by Marcantonio (Cavazzoni) de Bologna. Girolamo Cavazzoni followed his father in including two "canzoni alla francese" in his *Intavolatura, cioè recercari*,

---

[7] One such work was published by Attaingnant, in 1529, and contains chansons by Crequillon, Clement non Papa, Gombert, and others, many of which he had published in the original form a few years earlier. This work was republished in modern notation by the Societe française de Musicologie (Paris, 1934), and includes also publications of Phalese (1553) and Le Roy et Ballard (1571).

[8] In modern editon by Fuller-Maitland and Squire.

canzoni, himni, magnificat,[9] published in 1542.[10] The younger Cavazzoni's teacher, Andrea Gabrieli (c. 1510–1586), continued in
the same tradition with many similar transcriptions, most of which
were published posthumously in two books, in 1605.[11] Many of the
canzone transcriptions by these three composers bear as subtitles the
names of the chansons on which they were based. Those of Marcantonio and Gabrieli do nothing more than "color" (i.e., ornament
with runs and flourishes) the original chansons. Those of Girolamo,
on the other hand, are much freer; contrapuntal parts are changed,
some are omitted, and some new material is added.[12] Even as early
as this, youth was bound to have its fling.

One of Gabrieli's *canzoni* may be singled out for closer attention; [13] it is based on a chanson by Crequillon. The latter is typical,
in that it begins with a section in imitative counterpoint and is followed by other sections in note-against-note style; remaining true
to form, a short section in the middle of the chanson is set in triple
meter, as opposed to the duple meter of the remainder. Gabrieli
remains faithful to the model, retains the triple-meter fragment in
the midst of the contrasting duple, and does nothing more than em-
bellish that section with running scale figures.

If the author may be permitted another digression at this point,
he would like to point out that an apparently unimportant detail
such as the one given in the paragraph above may be of vital significance in the future evolution of musical forms. He asks the reader
to remember that a *canzone* usually contained a short section of
triple meter in the midst of prevailing duple. He will show in Chapter 5 that this triple-meter fragment is the germ out of which the
entire second movement of the Classical sonata form grew. It is not
too much to say that had the fragment not existed, the four-
movement form we know as the symphony might not have arisen.
"Mighty oaks," and so forth, is as true in music as in botany.

[9] Reprinted in Torchi, *L'arte musicale in Italia*, Vol. III.
[10] In 1543, according to Eitner, *Quellen-Lexikon.*
[11] *Canzoni alla francese—per sonar sopra istromenti da tasta; Lib. V e VI.*
[12] Crocker, "An Introductory Study of the Italian Canzona for Instrumental Ensembles," I, 90.   [13] In Torchi, *L'arte musicale in Italia*, Vol. III.

To return to Gabrieli: he did not, however, confine himself to mere elaborations or "colorings" of pre-existing chansons. He wrote other transcriptions as free as some of the young Cavazzoni's, and he wrote original *canzoni* for the organ, perhaps the first original works in this form.[14] In these works the same formal scheme of sections in contrasting meter was adhered to; the same imitative beginning, and the same dactylic motive. The subsequent history of these keyboard works cannot occupy us here; it is sufficient to mention that the original organ *canzoni* (i.e., not the transcribed ones) of Gabrieli provided the models for the next development in instrumental music.

As the sixteenth century ran its course, transcribed and original *canzoni* became well established in all parts of Italy. We can imagine that string and wind players became envious of this growing literature in the unfolding of which they had no part. As a matter of fact, string and wind instruments began to amplify the organ, and even to substitute for it, just as they had long accompanied and substituted for voices. In line with the Baroque feeling for tone color, and with such diversity of color as viols, cornetts, trombones, and woodwind instruments supplied, what was more natural than that the whole group of available instruments should be called to take part. Thus arose the development which followed hard on the heels of the original organ *canzoni* mentioned above: the *canzone* form written for string or wind groups appeared, modeled on the organ *canzoni* of Gabrieli. And it is with these ensemble works that instrumental music attained the status of a separate branch.

The first instrumental *canzone* of which there is any bibliographical record did not see the light of day until 1572, when Nicolò Vicentino published *La Bella* (*canzone da sonar*) at Milan.[15] A host of other works followed in short order.[16] Among the innovations

[14] Crocker, "An Introductory Study of the Italian Canzona for Instrumental Ensembles," I, 91.

[15] Most histories credit Maschera's publication of 1584 as being the first in this category. The latest authority, Miss Eunice Crocker (*ibid.*, p. 109), has uncovered much valuable information about the early history of the *canzone*.

[16] Vincenti at Venice, in 1596, published a collection containing *canzoni* by Merulo, Guami, and others. Amadino, also at Venice, published a work of Banchieri's which

this new development brought in its wake was a new version of the name: the *canzone da sonar* mentioned above. We have seen in the younger Cavazzoni's publication of 1542, for organ alone, the name *canzone alla francese*, which is obviously the Italian form of chanson plus the modifying phrase "in French style." Now, with Vicentino we meet the new version, *canzone da sonar*, or *canzone* to be played: that is, played instead of sung. The distinction is an important one; it points first to the fact that music up to this time could have been performed by either a vocal or an instrumental group, or by both, that the composer henceforth found it necessary to specify which group he had in mind, and that the possibility of distinguishing between vocal and instrumental style was at hand.

Many other works of this period included the phrase *da sonare o cantare* or *da sonare e cantare;* in other words, they could be sung and/or played. Works so designated were obviously not independently instrumental, but were hybrids, partly in vocal style and yet not sufficiently removed from vocal to be in instrumental style. The chief difference between these hybrids and the purely *da sonar* works was that the latter were tending toward a type of workmanship which took into account the mechanics, characteristics, and sonorities of the viols, cornetts, or woodwinds for which they were meant. Hence the former, the "and/or" variety, are on a side path, so to speak, and do not lead to the independent instrumental style the development of which is one of the great achievements of the Baroque period.

The original *canzoni* for organ written in the period from 1523 to about 1597 were of three different types, the characteristics of which were quickly taken over by the composers of instrumental *canzoni* of the type just mentioned. The three were: (*a*) those whose chief appeal lay in florid, elaborate ornamentation or coloring, a type which lost ground when the form was transferred to instrumental

---

contains several *canzoni alla francesa a quattro voci per sonar*. Floriano Canale composed nineteen *canzoni da sonar a quattro*, published by Vincenti in 1600. These are only a few items drawn from Miss Crocker's extensive bibliography of *canzoni* ("An Introductory Study of the Italian Canzona for Instrumental Ensembles," Vol. II, Appendix).

ensembles, had little influence on the evolution of subsequent forms; (*b*) those which were in imitative style throughout and were closely related to another form which turned out to be the ancestor of the fugue, the *ricercare;* (*c*) those characterized by many short sections in contrasting duple and triple meter, in a diversity of styles very much akin to the French chanson discussed above. The two latter types, one largely contrapuntal and in one meter throughout, the other homophonic to some extent and characterized by many short sections in contrasting meter, existed side by side throughout the late sixteenth and the early seventeenth centuries. The first of these, the formally unified type, is less significant here; its later history, however, leads to Henry Purcell, and will be taken up again when that composer is reached. The other, the type with many short and diversified sections, was of immediate and great importance in the further evolution of chamber-music forms and will be discussed as a characteristic of the later Venetian school of composers, of which Giovanni Gabrieli is an outstanding exponent.

This younger Gabrieli (1557–c. 1612), a nephew of the Andrea Gabrieli mentioned earlier, was, like his uncle, an organist at St. Mark's in Venice. He was another of the long line of famous Venetian organists and composers which had begun with Adrian Willaert early in the sixteenth century, which included such men as Cypriano de Rore, Claudio Merulo, Andrea Gabrieli, and which was later to number Claudio Monteverdi among its members. To the Venetian school is ascribed the first use of the antiphonal principle in western Europe, a principle which makes use of two organs or two choirs heard alternately. Giovanni Gabrieli, as one of the most distinguished composers of this school, inherited the traditional use of the double organ and the choir. And he inherited the instrumental *canzone da sonare*, to whose literature he contributed a number of works. His collection, *Sacrae symphoniae*, published by Gardano, at Venice, in 1597, contains forty-five motets, fourteen *canzoni da sonar* and two sonatas. This collection was one of the most important works of the early period of *canzone* composition (1572–1600). The *canzoni* included in it are typically Baroque in their brilliant writing and display; in them Gabrieli carried the antiphonal principle at least as far as any of his predecessors. They are full of great masses of sound; and they show the first extensive use of the sectional principle characteristic of the third type of *canzoni* mentioned above, a principle which was to be of great importance in the early years of the seventeenth century.

Another innovation of Gabrieli's was the use of more than four voices (voice is here used in the contrapuntal sense, meaning a separate musical line or part, and does not refer to the singing voice). Some of his later *canzoni*, in a posthumous publication of 1615,[17] are for as many as twenty-two voices. The dramatic impact of this music, when heard for the first time, must have been tremendous. It is small wonder that the music of Gabrieli contributed to the speedy decay of the pure, reserved style we associate with the works of Palestrina.[18]

Let us examine one of the Gabrieli *canzoni da sonar* from the *Sacrae symphoniae* of 1597; one is reprinted in Hugo Riemann's *Old Chamber Music*, Vol. I.[19] It is an eight-voice piece, with the voices arranged in two groups; two high voices, one middle voice, and one low voice in each group. In keeping with the practice of the times, the instrumentation is not specified.[20] Riemann, in his modernized edition (with bar lines), suggests an instrumentation of two violins, one viola, and one bass and/or cello for each group. There are in

[17] *Canzoni et sonate—per sonar con ogni sorte di instrumenti.*
[18] So quickly was that style outmoded and misunderstood that Giovanni Francesco Anerio (c. 1567–c. 1620) edited some of Palestrina's masses with instrumental accompaniment; a similar fate befell some of Lasso's motets. And the famous Palestrina *Missa Papae Marcelli* was enlarged, provided with a *basso continuo*, and transcribed for a gigantic polyphonic chorus; quoted by Láng, *Music in Western Civilization*, p. 324. See Arnold, *The Art of Accompaniment from a Thorough-bass*, p. 90n.
[19] This work, containing four volumes of instrumental music from c. 1600 to c. 1700, will often be referred to in the following pages.
[20] Particular instruments were rarely specified in sixteenth-century compositions. Crocker, "An Introductory Study of the Italian Canzona for Instrumental Ensembles," I, 233, mentions the fact that two or three of these *canzoni* of Gabrieli's have a specified instrumentation, but points out that that was unique in the early *canzone* literature.

the piece seven sections, ranging in length from three to twenty-four measures, and in all of them the antiphonal device is much in evidence. The odd-number sections are in broad duple meter, have the dactylic motive ($\downarrow$ $\downarrow\downarrow$) characteristic of *canzoni*, and are contrapuntal. The even-number sections are in fast dance-like triple meter, are in note-against-note style, and are even more antiphonally arranged than the duple-meter sections. At the end of each section the antiphonal device is abandoned in favor of an eight-voice texture. There is in this *canzone* a fourfold alternation of tempo (slow—fast); of meter (duple—triple); of instrumentation (first group—second group); of texture (four-voice—eight-voice).

The main element of expressiveness in this and similar works is to be found in some manifestation of this principle of alternation. In addition to the four just mentioned are dynamic alternations (loud—soft),[21] stylistic alternations (counterpoint—note-against-note), plus certain sub-manifestations implied in the above, such as that caused by alternating a strongly rhythmic content with a more introspective contrapuntal one. Certain applications of this principle persisted in music for another century and a half, namely, the dynamic and tempo alternations. Additional manifestations appeared in the early 1600's to do their part in changing the look and sound of music: thematic alternation (as in the rondo forms) and mass alternations of concertino-ripieno groups (as in the later *concerto grosso* form). And it is not too much to say that even the eighteenth-century principle of thematic dualism, the basis of the Classical sonata form, is related to this Baroque principle, for it had its inception in harmonic alternations (of tonic and dominant groups).

What has been said about Giovanni Gabrieli above applies largely to him alone. His was the first considerable use of the sectional principle in the *canzone*, and his was the first extensive use of more than

[21] As illustrated by Giovanni Gabrieli himself in his sonata *Pian e forte*, one of the two contained in the *Sacrae symphoniae* collection of 1597; by Marini in *La Bemba*, 1617; by Riccio in *Sonata a 4*, 1620; the last two quoted by Crocker, "An Introductory Study of the Italian Canzona for Instrumental Ensembles," Supplement, II, viii and xiii.

four instrumental parts.[22] Until his works became generally known, other composers in other localities, notably Brescia, Milan, Bologna, and Rome, wrote *canzoni* in the old way, with four voices and a rather unified formal scheme (that is, in one meter and one tempo throughout). But so great were the innovations of Gabrieli, and so successful the music in which they appeared, that imitators in the years immediately following 1597 adopted the principles of this founder of the new Venetian school.

In northern Italy several other schools of composers flourished toward the end of the sixteenth century.[23] In Brescia, Floriano Canale was active. He published *Canzoni da sonare a quattro et otto voci, libro primo*, in 1600. Like Maschera's before him (1584), Canale's *canzoni* are unified in form, thus they belong to the style type which Gabrieli does *not* represent. But the Venetian influence may be seen in that some of Canale's nineteen *canzoni* are for eight-voice ensemble. In Milan, Gaspar Costa, who has one *canzone* in Giovanni Rognioni's *Canzoni a 4 et 8 voci*, 1605, and Agostino Soderino, with fourteen *canzoni a 4* and one *canzone a 8*, 1608, were the principal composers of this form. Here the Venetian influence is felt still less. In Bologna, too, the absence of the sectional *canzone* is noticed, for both Aurelio Bonelli, with *Il primo libro de ricercari et canzoni a quattro voci*, 1602, containing eight *canzoni*, and Adriano Banchieri, with a number of publications between 1596 and 1612, wrote in the old form.

But even in the old form, that is, in the *canzoni* written in one meter throughout, there were sections well marked by cadences and by a shift from contrapuntal to a more homophonic style. In the truly sectional type the consecutive sections were, of course, marked by the most obvious of contrasts, a contrast brought about by a change from duple to triple meter, or vice versa. Thus, in both types

---

[22] In both these innovations, members of the earlier Venetian school had led the way. Francesco Spongia (*detto* Usper) and Claudio Merulo, Gabrieli's predecessors, had occasionally written sectional *canzoni;* occasionally a texture for more than four voices had appeared. But what were tendencies in the older Venetians became characteristics in Gabrieli; and it was the latter's works which influenced later composers. See Crocker, *ibid.*, I, 181, 244, 246 ff.   [23] *Ibid.*, pp. 161 ff.

composers adhered to a structure that originally had been necessary (in the French chanson) because of the strophic text, but now was merely a matter of traditional usage. Consequently in none of the *canzoni* from 1572 to those appearing in the first decades of the seventeenth century was real unity of form possible. That development had to wait until composers attacked the problem from the other side. Instead of attempting to achieve unity within the many sections of the *canzone*, they expanded each individual section to greater length. Finally, through sheer size the *canzone* fell apart into a number of separate movements of contrasting style, tempo, and meter. We shall see the course of that development in the chapters which follow.

With Gabrieli [24] and the other pre-1600 *canzone* composers disposed of, it will be necessary to make one more excursion into the late sixteenth century before examining in detail the works that are the first true chamber music.[25] This excursion takes us to Florence in the period between 1580 and 1600, and has to do with the work of the Camerata.

The Renaissance had been peculiarly successful in rediscovering the art, architecture, and to some extent the literature of classic Greece. From the fourteenth century through the sixteenth the forms, aesthetic purposes, and styles of those fields became known to large groups of educated Europeans, were widely imitated, and became the bases upon which the new forms of the Renaissance were constructed. A rebirth of Greek music had not fared so well. It was

[24] Not only for his innovations in the *canzone* are we indebted to Gabrieli, however. He, with others of his school, did much to bring instrumental style to the polyphonic *ricercare*, casting off the last traces of vocal writing. When that point had been reached, the way was clear to fugal style. In this development Frescobaldi (cf. Moser, *Geschichte der deutschen Musik*, I, 505), with his solidification of monothematic structure, was of outstanding importance. The subsequent history of the fugue, however, lies outside the field of chamber music.

[25] It will be made clear in Chapter 3 why the pre-1600 *canzoni* are not considered the first chamber music. It is sufficient here to point out that these works were largely imitations of vocal pieces, did not include a specified instrumentation, and were still inclined toward vocal style. Later works, post-1600, were specifically designed for instruments and evolved their own forms—even though they were still called *canzoni*.

suspected that music had been combined with speech to form the Greek drama, but detailed knowledge was lacking.

In the 1580's, at Florence, steps were taken to effect this rebirth of Greek music. A group of noblemen, poets, and musicians met at the home of Count Bardi to engage in aesthetic discussions about the classic arts. The members of this group, called the Camerata, felt keenly that however successful artists in other fields had been in reviving classic forms and practices, musicians had not realized anew the supposed union of speech and music. The Camerata, among whose members were Ottavio Rinuccini, a poet, and Vincenzo Galilei, Emilio del Cavalieri, Jacopo Peri, and Giulio Caccini, musicians, experimented to restore the supposed connection. But instead of realizing their aim of rediscovering the past, they stumbled upon an entirely new mode of expression and gave birth to a new style: accompanied recitative. The particular portion of their accomplishments which concerns us here centers in their development, out of this new style, of the principle of monody: the use of a solo vocal line accompanied by a bass instrument. The new principle is of basic importance in the great bulk of seventeenth-century music, and of great influence on the future course of all music.

Vincenzo Galilei, the father of the astronomer, was one of the Camerata's leading figures. He felt that the union of speech and music must be achieved by subordinating the music—in other words, by letting a sort of singing speech carry the textual idea. The singing was to mirror the actual speech rhythm and be supported at appropriate places by chords which had the dual function of enhancing the punctuation of the text and relating the melody to a particular mode or tonality. To illustrate his principles, Galilei set to music portions of pastoral poems written by fellow Camerata members and parts of the Lamentations of Jeremiah. Others of the group, notably Peri and Caccini, followed the same principles and emerged with the style which was to make opera possible: the recitative style. Unfortunately, the works of Galilei have been lost.

Now, hurling several new terms at the reader, as the author has done in the paragraphs above, is bound to cause distrust or confusion, depending upon how kindly the reader is disposed toward the author at this point. In the interests of allaying both the distrust and confusion with one stroke of the pen (a figure of speech; it will take several paragraphs) it becomes desirable to examine the parts of the new principles in as much detail as seems necessary. Most seventeenth-century music makes use of them in one way or another, and clear understanding of the principles and terms is essential if the chaos that is Baroque music is to be understood at all.

The new terms are (1) principle of monody, (2) recitative style, (3) accompanied recitative. Actually, all three terms are related; the second and third are practically synonymous, and both are contained within the first. The difficulty arises from the fact that the monodic principle consists of several factors. First there is the essential idea that the function of the music is to carry the text, and nothing more. There should be no preoccupation with making the music expressive in its own right, no concern with lyric melody, no formal ideas of balance or symmetry in the musical form which results. The words of the text are recited to music, and out of that idea grows the second factor.

The second factor is concerned with the melodic shape implied in the word "recitative": a melodic shape whose contour follows to some extent the natural inflections of the speaking voice; whose rhythm reflects the natural rhythm established by the text itself. Now when the inflections of the dramatic speaking voice, with its natural cadences and rhythms, its rise and fall in intensity, its very punctuation, are all mirrored in the music, it becomes possible for the music to transmit the emotions implicit in the text. And finally, the second factor is concerned with the proper proportion between melody and accompaniment, insuring that the melody will always be more important than the lowly accompaniment—this in keeping with Galilei's idea that the music (i.e., the accompaniment) must always be subordinated to the text. This brings us to the third factor, the accompaniment itself.

The accompaniment includes the bass line, the choice of chords implied by the interaction of melody and bass, and the manner of performing the chords; this aggregate is brought together in the term *basso continuo*,[26] or continuous bass. In its simplest form, the bass was a continuous line of long notes corresponding to whole and half-notes in modern notation. The function of the bass line was, not to provide a pleasing countermelody below the superior reciting melody, but simply to act as a foundation upon which chords could be erected. Actually, the idea of using a bass line to accompany a melody was not an innovation of the Camerata. As early as 1553 Diego Ortiz had published at Rome a treatise dealing with this problem.[27] During the course of time (we are dealing with the years between 1580 and about 1600) several other kinds of bass line had come into use; these are distinguished by the terms *basso generale, basso seguente,* and *basso ostinato*.[28] While the new bass types all played their part in seventeenth-century music, and while they differ to some extent from the *basso continuo*, we shall ignore their special characteristics and treat them all together under the term *basso continuo*—which is exactly what seventeenth-century musicians did with them. But one related new term must be introduced at this point: figured bass, a device for indicating chords in these two-voice (melody and bass) compositions.

One of the musicians of the Camerata, namely, Jacopo Peri, set to music a pastoral poem written by his friend and colleague Ottavio Rinuccini. This work, *Dafne*, was first performed about 1597,[29] but has since been lost. *Dafne* was the first drama that had been set to music throughout its entire length; hence it deserves the distinction of being called the first opera. A later collaboration of Peri and

[26] The interested reader is again referred to Arnold, *The Art of Accompaniment from a Thorough-bass.*

[27] *Trattado de glosas sopra clausulas y otro generos de puntos en la musica de violones* [Treatise on ornaments over cadences and other kinds of notes in music for bass viols].

[28] The reader interested in more exact details about these types of basses is referred to Kinkeldey, *Orgel und Klavier in der Musik des 16ten Jahrhunderts*, p. 198; to Arnold, *The Art of Accompaniment from a Thorough-bass*, and to the general reference books.

[29] The exact date of this first performance seems uncertain. Many historians agree on 1594; Riemann holds for 1595, while Donald Grout, the latest authority, in his *A Short History of Opera*, gives 1597.

Rinuccini produced another opera, *Eurydice*, performed in 1600. Giulio Caccini, another of the Camerata musicians, composed an *Eurydice* to the same text and published it the same year; this opera, however, was not performed until 1602 or 1603. Both of these operas on the story of *Eurydice* made use of the *basso continuo* in the simple form described above, with the addition of figures placed above certain notes to indicate the nature of the chord above those notes. Thus, the new device, figured bass, emerges to play its part in the evolution of music.

The origin of the figures to indicate chord intervals is not very clear. In the earliest preserved works that first show the *basso generale* type (1594) sharps and flats had appeared above certain bass notes to indicate that the corresponding chords were to have major or minor thirds.[30] At any rate, the figured bass did appear in the two versions of *Eurydice* (1600), and in the course of the next decades was widely copied. Many divergent practices existed side by side in those early years, some composers indicating every chord, some figuring more sparsely, and some not at all. For more than one hundred and fifty years (as late as 1765) theoretical works appeared which gave instructions for using unfigured basses, but recommended that composers use the figured type.[31]

There were, then, these four main forms of bass, the device of figuring being common to all. Many of these main forms were loosely grouped together under the common term *basso continuo*. Later, when tradition had settled upon a keyboard instrument to carry the bass line and fill in the indicated or implied chords (with doublings of the bass line by a cello and/or bass viol, trombone, or bassoon), this whole factor of the accompaniment was called *continuo*, and it was incorrectly spoken of (and still is) as playing the *continuo*, as if it were an instrument.

The three operas mentioned above, the lost *Dafne* and the Peri and

[30] Arnold, *The Art of Accompaniment from a Thorough-bass*, pp. 7-9. Cf. his p. 8n.
[31] *Ibid.*, pp. 66-67. Arnold mentions Werckmeister's *Harmonologia musica*, Gasparini's *L'armonico practico al cimbalo*, Heinichen's *Der General-Bass in der Composition*, and K. P. E. Bach's *Versuch über die wahre Art das Klavier zu spielen.*

Caccini versions of *Eurydice*, were among the first works composed in the new monodic recitative style; inevitably they had departed from modality and were strongly flavored with elements of the tonal system. It is this new style, with all its implications, that Artusi had in mind when he attacked Monteverdi in his polemic of 1600. But the new style was not confined to the stage. Between *Dafne* and *Eurydice*, that is, roughly between 1595 and 1600, Caccini and his colleagues kept at work in their newly discovered style and even applied it to other musical media. One of the results of this work is Caccini's collection of madrigals and canzonettas published in 1601, which he proudly entitled *Le nuove musiche*. These are solo songs with a figured *basso continuo*, true enough; but they are not all in the recitative style. It is apparent that even the innovators themselves realized that the new monodic principle need not be confined to recitation, but could become the vehicle for lyric melody as well.

It is argued by some historians that the Camerata achieved little that was really new. They point to the close union of text and music in the French chanson; they remind us that long before the 1590's madrigals, motets, and chansons had emerged as solo song accompanied by a bass line; they point to the appearance of an independent accompanied solo in the musical illustrations given by Diego Ortiz in his treatise of 1553; they find that figured bass was known in a rudimentary form to many late sixteenth-century organists. All that remains of the Camerata's efforts, according to this view, is the particular outline of the melody. We might even demolish this remaining achievement by pointing out that plainsong, too, is a kind of recitation, and *its* origin is ancient indeed. If one grants that this view has some truth, what remains of the Camerata's work? There are two essential features.

(1) While the union of text and music had been achieved in the chanson, it was essentially the intellectual aspect of the text that was satisfied. It remained for the Camerata's compositions to satisfy the emotional aspect; not necessarily the emotion expressed by the words, but the emotion implicit in the situation out of which a singer (or speaker) was acting. There is a vast difference between

the two. Because of the latter feature it became possible to portray dramatic situations in music even when the text was absent, that is, in instrumental music. The Camerata, in establishing the monodic principle to bring about a union of dramatic text and music, provided the means for dispensing with the text entirely and establishing the possibility of dramatic instrumental music. (2) The other feature grows out of the fact that while the Italian theater of the time was full of music, it made no use of music in a connected way. A dramatic action on the stage was halted while the orchestra or ballet performed something that was designed to act as a commentary to the drama. The Camerata's contribution was to make it possible for music to accompany dramatic action throughout the course of a play, thus to achieve the long-sought connection between text and music. This feature makes the opera medium possible; as we have seen, the first operas were the direct result of the Camerata's work. Further concern with the history of opera can serve no purpose here; while certain formal developments within that field had some influence on chamber music, their larger aspects lie outside our immediate province. Let us return to the nonrecitative factors of monody.

The practical results of the new principle of monody were far-reaching. (1) The contrapuntal style, with its short motives and imitative developments, was virtually abandoned by those composers who championed monody. A new style resulted, a style in which only melody and bass were indicated, in which inner voices were created only to complete the harmonics and in which a note-against-note accompaniment predominated. (2) A new type of melody appeared, a type not dependent upon contrapuntal associates to complete its significance. The melody was self-contained (that is, it had a beginning and an end), was cast in phrase or period form of four or eight measures; and, not being bound by modal restrictions of range and intervals, it contained the possibility of all kinds of emotional expression. This the contrapuntal melody had had only rarely, for it was always one part merely of a polyphonic texture which depended upon the interaction of several melodic fragments for its emotional appeal. (3) The corpus of harmony became more vigorous as the figured-bass notation made convenient and practical the use of a greater variety of chords. At first largely restricted to triads and the few passing dissonances typical of modal harmony, it gradually acquired unprepared dissonances, employed chromatically altered chords, and the like, until the modal aspects of the music were so much weakened that we can speak of the breakdown of modality and the emergence of the tonal system.

3

CHAMBER MUSIC BEGINS

SIXTEENTH-CENTURY organists were often faced with a situation that is all too familiar to the modern choirmaster with a volunteer choir. What, for example, is the latter to do on a Sunday morning if only his soprano soloist (who may be a paid singer or only the minister's wife) and his organist appear for the church service? He can substitute a soprano solo in place of the four-part anthem his choir had rehearsed the previous Thursday, or he can perform the anthem with the soprano part sung, and with alto, tenor, and bass parts "filled in" by the organist. The sixteenth-century organist adopted the latter course, largely, of course, because there was no literature for solo voice and organ in the prevailing contrapuntal style. As a consequence, four- or five-voice motets and other sacred forms were often performed in this way: the organist played a condensed contrapuntal version of the lower voices and allowed only the upper part to be sung.

With the appearance in 1601 of Giulio Caccini's *Le nuove musiche*, which was mentioned in the chapter above, a solo literature (albeit a secular one) in the new monodic style, with figured *basso continuo*, begins to emerge. In the following year Lodovico Grossi da Viadana published a similar work entitled *Cento concerti ecclesiastici a 1, 2, 3, 4 voci*. But Viadana's collection differs from Caccini's in two important respects: (1) it includes not only solo songs, like those of Caccini's, but also duets, trios, and quartets; (2) it contains sacred pieces, hence would serve the organist in his dilemma in the paragraph above. In other respects the works are similar, for both are in the monodic style, both are supplied with a *basso continuo* designed to be realized at the organ.

Lodovico Grossi da Viadana was born at Viadana, on the Po River, in northern Italy, about 1564. From 1594 to 1609 he served as chapel master in the cathedral at Mantua, during which time he joined the Franciscan Order (1596) and published the *Cento concerti ecclesiastici* (1602). He held posts as chapel master in other cathedral towns in northern Italy (Concordia, 1609, Fano, 1612, Piacenza, 1615, etc.) and died in a Franciscan convent at Gualtieri in 1645.[1] Viadana wrote many psalms, canticles, and other religious music, but he is remembered primarily for the *Cento concerti*. To him is ascribed the invention of the term *basso continuo*, although the device itself and its related forms (for example, *basso generale* and *basso principale*) were in use in the sixteenth century.

The reader who has followed our account of the monodic style thus far may ask two questions, for Viadana's are multi-voiced works, and monody has been described as a solo-voice style: (1) Is not this use of several voices a contradiction of the essential idea of monody? (2) How do these works of Viadana's differ from the accompanied motet and madrigal of the late sixteenth century? Both questions may be answered together by pointing out that the function of the topmost voice was not impaired (it was still the carrier of the textual idea); that the inner voices are no longer independent melodies running with a degree of integrity equal to the upper voice (together with the bass they create the chords which harmonize the latter); that the bass line is consciously designed to supply a chordal foundation for the upper voices, sometimes consisting of one long sustained note over which the upper voice is free to run its course. This is obviously different from the melodic bass of the earlier polyphonic piece.

The chief purpose of bringing the *Cento concerti ecclesiastici* into these pages is not, however, what has been discussed thus far. The origins of solo song have little connection with the history of chamber music, and the above paragraphs might well have been omitted—

[1] Láng, *Music in Western Civilization*, p. 358, gives 1627 as Viadana's death date.

except that an orderly account of the growth of monodic style seemed appropriate. But in an appendix to Viadana's work is a small piece that does deserve to be mentioned, that justifies a discussion of the rest of the work, and that actually marks the beginning of our historical survey. This small piece, tucked away at the end of Viadana's more pretentious vocal works, may be singled out as the first which conforms to our definition of chamber music. And as such, it is the direct ancestor of all orchestral and chamber music from Haydn to the present.

The careful reader will have observed that the concept of monodic style, as defined by its inventors, had by 1602 been broadened considerably. The earliest works in this style had been, of course, solo songs or group songs, with *basso continuo*. We should have expected the first step beyond this to be the transfer of monodic style to solo instrumental pieces; then, as a second step, the appearance of instrumental groups as carriers of the style. Unfortunately, that first step, while it must have been taken, has left no evidence of its existence: solo instrumental works that correspond to the solo songs of the period from about 1585 (Galilei's setting of the Lamentations) to 1601 (Caccini's *Le nuove musiche*) have not been found. The second step can be traced, however, and the Viadana work, in the appendix to his *Cento concerti* of 1602, supplies the evidence. This work is designed for instruments alone, not for instruments and/or voices, and its title is "Canzona francese a quattro, a riposta."

The title may be translated as "French chanson for quartet, in responsive style," the quartet in this case being a violin, a cornett, and two trombones, with an unfigured *basso continuo*. It is interesting to observe, and important to remember, that the *continuo* was never included in the numbering of the voices. According to the practice of the times, which practice soon became traditional, this work was performed by the four instruments just mentioned plus a keyboard instrument. Similarly, duo sonatas for violin and bass, let us say, turn out to be trios in performance (we shall meet such works later in the century) when the keyboard instrument is added. It should not be surprising, then, on examining the Viadana *Canzona francese* to find that we have to do with a quintet. Nor is the combination of instruments as strange as would appear at first sight, for a "cornett" is not a "cornet." The former, known as *Zink* in Germany, was an instrument made of wood or ivory equipped with holes like a flute or recorder, but with a cup mouthpiece like a trumpet or horn. Its tone was closer to a woodwind than to a brass instrument, and it provided a quality somewhere between the violin and the trombone.

The Viadana *Canzona* is reprinted in modern notation in *Old Chamber Music*, Vol. I. We are immediately brought face to face with three important innovations. First is the presence of an instrumental work written in the monodic style. All the other *canzoni* we have referred to earlier, including the transcriptions of vocal chansons, were in the polyphonic style. Second is the use of the *basso continuo* in an instrumental work, with its implication of a dominant melody and a subordinate nonmelodic bass line. Heretofore the *canzone* had been written in a style which allowed all four or more voices equal participation in the ebb and flow of the music; in the Viadana work the texture is divided between melodic instruments and those that accompany, and the function of the two groups is quite different. Third, although the piece is written for four instruments, it is in effect for two, for as we shall see below, one melody and one accompanying instrument are grouped together, announce the themes, and are then echoed by the other similar group. The piece turns out to be a series of accompanied phrases for two instruments. This is the first appearance of a line of *canzoni* with less than four voices, a line that will be further discussed and seen to be of great importance. In these respects Viadana's work is of great historical interest.

As indicated in its title, the piece is antiphonal (that is, in responsive style) throughout. The melodic material consists of a large number of motives ranging in length from two to eleven beats; each motive is accompanied by a differently styled bass motive. We speak of beats (single half-notes) rather than measures for metrical measurement here, because the diversity of 2/2, 3/2, 3/4 measures in this music would not accurately show the comparative lengths of the

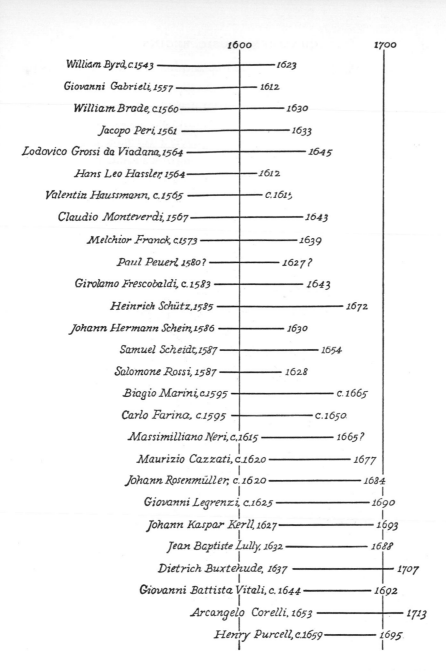

	1600	1700
William Byrd, c.1543	———————— 1623	
Giovanni Gabrieli, 1557	———— 1612	
William Brade, c.1560	———————— 1630	
Jacopo Peri, 1561	———————— 1633	
Lodovico Grossi da Viadana, 1564	——————————— 1645	
Hans Leo Hassler, 1564	——— 1612	
Valentin Haussmann, c.1565	——— c.1614	
Claudio Monteverdi, 1567	——————————— 1643	
Melchior Franck, c.1573	——————— 1639	
Paul Peuerl, 1580?	——— 1627 ?	
Girolamo Frescobaldi, c.1583	——————— 1643	
Heinrich Schütz, 1585	——————————————— 1672	
Johann Hermann Schein, 1586	——————— 1630	
Samuel Scheidt, 1587	—————————— 1654	
Salomone Rossi, 1587	——— 1628	
Biagio Marini, c.1595	———————————— c. 1665	
Carlo Farina, c.1595	——————————— c.1650.	
Massimilliano Neri, c.1615	——————————— 1665?	
Maurizio Cazzati, c.1620	———————————— 1677	
Johann Rosenmüller, c.1620	———————————— 1684	
Giovanni Legrenzi, c.1625	——————————— 1690	
Johann Kaspar Kerll, 1627	———————————— 1693	
Jean Baptiste Lully, 1632	————————— 1688	
Dietrich Buxtehude, 1637	———————————— 1707	
Giovanni Battista Vitali, c. 1644	—————————— 1692	
Arcangelo Corelli, 1653	———————— 1713	
Henry Purcell, c.1659	——————— 1695	

LIFE SPANS OF PRINCIPAL SEVENTEENTH-CENTURY COMPOSERS

melodies. No bass motive is quite like another. Sometimes it consists of a few whole-notes; sometimes it is in the same rhythm, but in contrary motion to the melody; often it is purely contrapuntal and provides a brief bit of countermelody. On two occasions it provides merely a harmonic bass, and in one place it forms a canon at the octave for three measures. This example of canonic imitation between bass and melody is strong evidence that very soon after its inception the monodic style began to take up again elements of the not-so-dead polyphony of the sixteenth century.

There is thus a strange mixture of old and new in this work, a mixture of melodic and harmonic association between the two voices of each pair which points to both the sixteenth and the seventeenth centuries at once. The shape of the melodies, too, is worthy of attention, and is again a mixture of the two periods.

Melodic fragments from CANZONE FRANCESE

Viadana

The first melody, for example, is a typical *canzone* type, with the familiar dactyl (♩ ♩ ♩) *canzone* trademark. The second and ninth are self-contained melodic units which would not, except for their typically modal cadence patterns, sound out of place in an eighteenth-century work. Others are scale fragments; still others are merely rhythmic figures with no melodic contour to speak of.

There are three well-defined parts in this *canzone*, the first part roughly as long as the other two (53–27–22 measures, respectively, in the three parts). But there is also, in the third part, an exact recapitulation of the first ten measures of the first part. There is thus a distinct and recognizable three-part form, in spite of the unequal lengths of the first and third sections. In all three parts one characteristic is very prominent: the difference in distance apart of the responsive entrances, of the entrance of the second pair of voices carrying the same melody as the first. For example, in the first section: one pair of voices is heard in the first melody, the second pair "answers" with the same melody after eleven beats; the same melody is heard again in the first pair, but this time the answer in the second pair comes after seven beats; then five melodies, each one shorter than the previous one (ten, eight, five, three, and two beats, respectively) are heard, first in one pair of voices, then in the other. That characteristic appears throughout the entire *canzone*. Why is this difference in distance important?

One of the ways in which the listener to music is moved, one of the ways in which an emotional effect is achieved, is by altering the degree of the listener's attention to the music. Let any particular texture, or style, or melodic device be continued for a considerable length of time; the listener will be attentive at first, less attentive as the music goes on, and finally become inattentive. But let the texture, style, or melodic device be changed, and his attention is restored; he again listens. In this alternation between attention and the relaxation of attention, between different states of emotional tension, lies one of music's powers to affect the emotional interest of the listener. Now, if it be realized that in any pair of antiphonal entrances the second one of the pair momentarily reattracts the listener's attention and provides an emotional accent through the mere fact of entering the tonal structure, it will be seen how a closer series of entrances increases the attention and thereby the emotional interest of the listener. Further, if the texture is changed from a two-voice to a four-voice section, with the temporary abandonment of the antiphonal device, the emotional interest is increased.

Both these devices are present in the Viadana *Canzona,* and give evidence of intelligent planning of musical effects. The antiphonal entrances come closer together as the end of each of the three sections is approached, and at each section's end the four instruments are heard together in the cadence which terminates the section. Thus, the interest of the listener is increased, and he experiences the three-part form; for after each cadence a pair of more distant entrances is heard, and he may momentarily relax again. The degrees of emotional tension and relaxation may be diagramed in somewhat the following way. A greater degree of shading represents a thicken-

A: *53 measures*   B: *27 measures*   C: *22 measures*

ing of texture, or closeness of entrance, or both. It is not to the point here to discuss whether Viadana was the first to achieve this expressive device. But the device is of considerable importance here and later in the century as one means of making a rather amorphous texture able to convey musical interest and emotional excitement to the listener.

In the Viadana *Canzona,* as we have seen, is perhaps the first example of the application of monodic style with *basso continuo* to a group of instruments. A very few years later, in 1608, a collection of *canzoni* was published by Raverii in Venice. This collection was for instrumental groups ranging from four to sixteen; Giovanni Gabrieli, Claudio Merulo, Florentino Maschera, Girolamo Frescobaldi, and Giovanni Battista Grillo are among the better-known composers represented in the collection. Let us look at one *canzone* by Grillo and at portions of another by Merulo, both reprinted by the indefatigable Riemann.[2]

The Grillo work is a *Capriccio a 4, Canzona da sonar.* The sectional nature of this type of *canzone,* found first in the chanson, carried further by Giovanni Gabrieli (see Chapter 3), is seen here

[2] Riemann, *Handbuch der Musikgeschichte,* II[2], 126–138.

in its extreme manifestation. This *canzone* has ten sections, varying in length from five to twenty-one measures; but the sections are not completely unrelated. The first, third, eighth, and tenth sections are in imitative style and are thematically related; in fact, the eighth section is a recapitulation of the first, and as we shall see below, the ninth recapitulates the second. The third section is a modified recapitulation of the first, and the tenth has melodic similarity to the first, third, and eighth. Thus, in the three sections at opposite ends of the piece there is a strongly modified but easily recognizable aba—aba form.

The relationship among the four middle sections is curious: sections four and six are in duple time, sections five and seven in triple. In point of style, the parts bear a resemblance to pavane and galliard dance types,[3] respectively. In section four there is a kind of introduction of four measures to the six measures of pavane type; in section seven there is a four-measure extension of the galliard-type material. Let us recapitulate the foregoing two paragraphs in tabular form, as we have done on page 54.

This is not the place to speculate whether this beautiful formal relationship in small and large details ($\frac{A}{aba}-\frac{B}{cdce}-\frac{A}{aba}$) was a conscious construction of Grillo's, whether it was influenced by some other work not yet generally known, or whether it arose by coincidence. The important thing is that it shows the instrumental *canzone*, in this example at least, to have its small sections—one might almost call them fragments—justified by a larger form principle at least as valid, led us say, as the eighteenth-century rondeau. This form was also afflicted by numbers of sections tied together in a sort of ABACADAEA relationship. Unfortunately, the collection of Raverii's is not available at the present writing. Examination of other works by Grillo and of other *canzoni* generally would show whether this was an isolated case, doomed to die unrecognized, or whether it was a fairly common formal pattern that has until now gone unnoticed.

[3] See pp. 69–70.

SECTIONS	TYPE	NUMBER OF MEASURES	FIRST CHORD AND CADENCE	FORM	
1	Imitative	7	G-G	a	
2	Galliard	11	G-D	b	A
3	Imitative	21	G-G	a	
4	Pavane	4 & 6	C-C	Introduction and c	
5	Galliard	8	C-C	d	B
6	Pavane	6	F-G	c	
7	Galliard	8 & 4	G-D	e and extension	
8	Imitative	7	G-G	a	
9	Galliard	11	G-D	b	A
10	Imitative	5	G-G	a	

In the works we have examined thus far, most of the melodic development has been achieved by simple repetition of motives or by sequence (repetition on other scale steps). In a few cases the melody has dissolved into figuration of various kinds, for example, in the first phrase of the Viadana *Canzona francese*. We must turn to another work contained in the Raverii collection for an example of another kind of development: the last *canzone* [4] in that set of thirty-six is by Claudio Merulo (1533–1604), the predecessor of Giovanni Gabrieli at Venice. This work is not characterized by the small sections which were so evident in the Grillo work just discussed. Here the prevailing duple meter is only once broken off by a short section in triple time, a dance-like phrase ten measures long. The type of development characteristic here is one in which a short four-note motive is spread out among all the voices and is manipulated in such

[4] Reprinted in Riemann, *Handbuch*, II², 132–138.

a way that several other phrases and longer melodies grow out of the original motive. Many of the contrapuntal devices typical of the six-teenth century are found here: imitation at several different intervals, small countermelodies, and the like. In fact, the piece is much more in the style of the *ricercare*, the ancestor of the fugue, than it is in *canzone* style. In this composition is to be observed the beginning of a technique that was to culminate in the work of Beethoven two hundred years later: the use of a motive rather than a theme and the participation of several voices in the creation of the theme, with the eventual theme the result of the motive's development. The first movement of his ninth symphony and the second theme of the Eroica symphony's first movement are cases in point.

As we enter the second decade of the seventeenth century,[5] we must digress from the *canzone* form and turn our attention to new style elements which were becoming more and more prominent in that form, were finally to overwhelm their parent and crystallize into a new form: the sonata. With the period beginning about 1613, sonata-style elements are defined clearly enough to justify speaking both of a sonata and of sonata style. This is true, however, only in some works of some composers. The *canzone* proper, with its style elements intact, continued to flourish for years. But chamber-music history must now concern itself with the sonata, leaving the *canzone* behind.

The first half of the seventeenth century is, perhaps, the most confused and complicated of all periods in music history. The con-tinued presence of the old polyphonic style, the emergence of the new monodic, the appearance of instrumental music with vocal style in some cases, with well-developed instrumental style in others, with mixtures of the two in a third group, the lack of uniformity in labeling the forms, the stylistic differences in the same form when written for a larger or smaller group of instruments, the presence of two diverse formal styles (sonata and *canzone*), the corresponding musical forms partaking of the one style sometimes, of the other at

[5] I must again acknowledge my indebtedness to Miss Crocker's dissertation (*op. cit.*) for guiding lines in this difficult period.

other times—these are a few of the factors which make the period from about 1600 to 1650 so chaotic, that make it the repository for so many generalities. Order can come out of this chaos only if one outlines several distinct trends, differentiates between the two main styles as much as possible, and separates the period into two sub-periods. In the discussion which follows, each of these elements will be treated separately; obviously such a separation is contrary to the actual course of events during this time, for none of the elements was present in a vacuum, apart from the others.

First, the careful reader will have noticed in the paragraph above three pairs of adjectives modifying the word style. (1) We have spoken there and elsewhere of polyphonic or contrapuntal style as opposed to monodic style; (2) we have discussed *canzone* style and are about to engage sonata style; (3) we have called attention to the fact that in much of the music since the thirteenth century there is a difference between vocal style and instrumental style. Six different styles? Scarcely that, for the three pairs are not mutually exclusive. The first pair has to do with the general texture of music; it differentiates between a contrapuntal piece made up of a number of equal, independent melodies and a piece made up of one or more accompanied melodies provided with a bass line and a chordal accompaniment—but it says nothing about the form or structure of either piece. The second pair has to do with the structure of music; it differentiates between a piece of music which has the general characteristics we discussed in Chapter 2 and a piece of different form known as the sonata, the characteristics of which we shall disclose in the pages that follow—but it says nothing specific about the texture of either piece. The third pair has to do with the melodic shapes and contours of music; it differentiates between a piece of music whose melodies are most suitable for the human voice and a piece whose melodies or melodic figures are most suitable for and designed for an instrument —but it says nothing about texture or form. The context will—or should—make clear in each case which aspect of style is being discussed.

Second is the fact that shortly after 1600 the *canzone da sonar* split into three main lines: (1) *canzoni* written for more than four voices, (2) those for the traditional four voices, (3) those for less than four. The first line, especially the *canzone a 8* based on the large works of Giovanni Gabrieli (1597), traveled far afield and emerged in Germany in the works of Hans Leo Hassler; his *Sacri concentus,* of 1601,[6] includes three *canzoni a 8* modeled on those of Gabrieli. And Giovanni Priuli, in his *Sacrorum concentum* (Venice, 1608) included ten *canzoni* for six, seven, and eight voices. Samuel Scheidt and Hermann Schein wrote several *canzoni a 8* in the years between 1609 and 1621. Paul Peuerl included a few *canzoni a 8* in his dance publications of 1613 and 1621. The second line, being the traditional size, enjoyed a healthy life for a few decades, but it too went into a decline in the 1620's. A collection entitled *Seconda aggiunta alli concerti raccolti dal . . . Francesco Lucino a 2, 3, e 4 voci*, Milan, 1617, was among the last to be devoted mainly to the *canzone* for four voices, although a few scattered works exist, notably those by Salomone Rossi (Mantua, 1608), Stefano Bernardi (Venice, 1613), and Tarquinio Merula (Venice, 1615). The third line was, in point of influence on subsequent developments, the most important. *Canzoni* of this line (for two or three instruments) provided the greatest amount of innovation and progressive change. Giulio Belli (publication of 1613), Giovanni Battista Riccio (1614 and 1620), Biagio Marini (1617), and Giulio Mussi (1620) were among the early contributors to the literature of the *canzone a 2* and *canzone a 3*.

The three lines differed widely as to style and form, also. (1) The larger *canzoni* (usually for eight voices) were more inclined toward chord masses and toward homophonic style in general. The *basso continuo* was of small importance in these massive works and tended toward the *basso seguente* type, with figuring sparsely employed. (2) The traditional size of ensemble (four-voiced), because it was more traditional, attracted the more conservative composers and retained conservative characteristics longer than did either the larger or the smaller *canzoni*. The style tended to remain more contrapuntal, and often appeared without the *basso continuo* (for example,

[6] Reprinted in D.D.T., Vols. XXIV and XXV.

throughout the Lucino collection of 1617 and Rossi's *canzoni da sonar* of 1608.[7] (3) The smaller groups (*canzoni a 2* or *canzoni a 3*) contained a greater proportion of new style elements and innovations in general. In these groups more interest was shown in the possibilities of instruments; independent instrumental style advanced a step, and some specific instrumentation was often called for by the composer. Three types of instrumentation are specified: the more conservative among composers for this size of *canzone* (for example, Mussi) were content with a mixed ensemble of strings and winds; progressive composers, of the type of Marini and Riccio (1620) allowed an option of strings or winds, but no mixing of instrumental families; only Riccio (1620) specified a particular family—winds in some cases, two violins in others.[8] In the use of the *basso continuo*, too, these smaller *canzoni* differed from their larger relatives. In them the *continuo* approached a melodic contour, took a greater part in thematic imitations, and tended to be more completely figured. The last-mentioned was made necessary, of course, by the incomplete triads in the two parts above the bass. Finally, in general content the *canzone a 2* or *canzone a 3* found it expedient to provide for particular instrumental effects, because the thinness of the instrumentation brought simple chord progressions or routine imitations close to the point of monotony. Further details of the style of the *canzone a 2* will be seen below, when it is compared to the similarly instrumented *sonata a 2*.

Third is the fact that throughout the period under discussion, namely, 1600–1650, composers with conservative traits were as much in evidence as progressive ones.[9] The conservatives tended to favor a contrapuntal style, use forms closely allied to the old *ricercare*, write *canzoni* for four voices, and use the *basso continuo* in a restrained manner. The progressives favored the monodic style, *canzoni* for two or three instruments, advanced use of the *basso continuo*, and they composed in the newly emerging sonata style.[10] They experi-

---

[7] Crocker, "An Introductory Study of the Italian Canzona for Instrumental Ensembles," I, 314.   [8] *Ibid.*, pp. 329-331.
[9] *Ibid.*, pp. 334-339.   [10] Elements of this style will be discussed below: see p. 60.

mented with the innovations of Gabrieli, with self-contained melody, technical innovations of tremolo, passage work, and echo effects. Of the last group of composers mentioned above, Belli (1613) and Mussi (1620) were the conservatives, while Marini (1617) and Riccio (1614) were in the progressive camp.

Fourth is the lack of uniformity in labeling forms in this period. A number of terms were in use, were used almost interchangeably by different composers, and often meant different things to different composers. "Sinfonia," "concerto," "fantasia," along with "canzone" and "sonata," were used indiscriminately at the beginning of the century. In time they took on their specialized meanings, and by 1650 the confusion had disappeared to a great degree.

Fifth is the fact that a new style, which we may call the sonata style, was emerging quite separate from the *canzone* style, whose course we have followed so far. Elements of the sonata style can be traced back well into the sixteenth century, in the organ *canzoni* of Andrea Gabrieli (c. 1575) and in the instrumental ones as well as in the sonata *Pian e forte* (published 1597) of Giovanni Gabrieli. A great deal of the confusion in the minds of music historians writing on the early decades of the seventeenth century comes from the mixture of these two styles. Sonata-style elements are found in the *canzone* long after the sonata had achieved a separate form; and conversely, at that time many sonatas still contained elements of *canzone* style. Furthermore, some composers issued conservative *canzoni* and progressive sonatas in the same collection (for example, Riccio, 1620). Finally, the sonata style between 1597 and 1608 was quite different (in general, more conservative) than the style from 1610 to 1621. Let us look at the *canzone* and sonata styles side by side, taking them at a period when they were most clearly differentiated—about 1610.

Canzone style, as we have seen it during the course of the last chapter and a half, and in the *canzoni* since the middle of the sixteenth century, was derived from a contrapuntal and imitative texture. The melodic material consisted of short motive-like phrases, with repeated notes much in evidence. The dactylic motive was characteristic, rhythmic diversity was not great, and the melodies ran largely in scalewise fashion. The quarter-note was the prevailing metrical unit, thus giving the effect of a moderately fast tempo. A definite rhythmic beat was typical of the *canzone*, and duple meter was most usual. The triple-meter sections we have seen in Gabrieli (1597) are themselves elements of sonata style obtruding themselves into the older form; when later, in Grillo (1608), they appear again they are evidence of the further mixture of the two styles. Equality of voices is typical of the *canzone*, as it was typical of contrapuntal vocal works of the time. Finally, the *canzone* was not greatly concerned with the instrumental medium. We saw above that the traditional line (those for four voices) did not specify instrumentation; works in that line were more concerned with presenting music for music's sake.

The sonata was largely of homophonic texture. Note-against-note style, with tentative use of passage work and instrumental figurations, predominated. There was a distinct effort to lengthen the melodic phrases, to achieve melodic expression within a period structure four or eight measures long. This required the use of a greater amount of rhythmic diversity, a greater range in the melody, and the use of note values ranging in length from a half-note to a sixteenth. The half-note was the prevailing rhythmic unit; thus, the sonata was characterized by a slower tempo than the *canzone*. Being primarily expressive, the sonata lacked the regular pulse typical of the older form. In line with the tendency to achieve melodic expressiveness, the upper and lower voices took on added importance, with a consequent lessening in importance of the inner ones. Greater care was shown in details; tendencies to introduce phrasing marks and to write so that the nature of the instrument was taken into account were typical.[11]

The sonata literature [12] of the period under discussion (1597–1621) is not extensive. The dozen or so collections include works by

---

[11] This summary of elements of the two opposing styles is based on Crocker, "An Introductory Study of the Italian Canzona for Instrumental Ensembles," I, 375–383, where numerous musical examples are given.   [12] *Ibid.*, pp. 384–387.

Giovanni Gabrieli, Salomone Rossi, and Biagio Marini, to mention only the more important composers. And it is noteworthy that the year 1608 seemed to mark a stylistic change in the sonata. The works written before that date are all for four or more voices; there is very little contrast between sections; they are largely homogeneous in form and tend toward a slower tempo with less rhythmic diversity; they are more vocal in character, and they have no *basso continuo*. Thus, they belong in most respects to the conservative line, and are not far removed from the progressive *canzone*. The sonatas from 1610 to 1621, on the other hand, are in general *sonate a 2* or *sonate a 3;* they are at times fragmentary in their many-sectioned form, and there is a greater contrast between sections; the tempo is faster, and there is more rhythmic diversity; instrumental style and instrumental effects are much more in evidence, and they are written with a *basso continuo*. One new feature introduced into the sonatas of this second group is the set of variations found first in the sonatas of Salomone Rossi (1587–1628).

The two sonatas by Rossi which contain sets of variations are found in the third book of his set of *Varie sonate*, 1613.[13] One is "on the Romanesca Air," the other, "on the Air of Ruggiero." The two tunes which supply the themes for these sets of variations were extremely popular in their day and inspired many composers, both vocal and instrumental, to treat them as Rossi did; we may mention Marini and Frescobaldi among this number. Rossi, however, was the first to set them for instrumental groups.[14] Each sonata contains eight variations over a *basso continuo;* each variation, as has been common practice ever since, is confined to one type of figuration. The figurations found here grow naturally out of the instrumentation Rossi employed: two violins and *basso continuo*. This instrumentation, des-

[13] Riemann, *Handbuch*, II², 87–94. Eitner, in *Quellen-Lexikon*, VIII, 325, indicates that Rossi must have been born before 1587, for in that year he was employed at the Mantuan court. The full title of the work here referred to is as follows: *Il 3 lib. de varie sonate, sinfonie, gagliarde, brandi e corrente per sonar 2 viol da braccia, & un chittarrone, o altro stromento simile* (Venice, Vincenti, 1613). Eitner mentions only the 3d ed. of 1623.
[14] Crocker, "An Introductory Study of the Italian Canzona for Instrumental Ensembles," I, 395.

tined to be the most popular chamber-music combination throughout the seventeenth century, must next be examined.

Rossi's first experiments with string-instrument trios date back to
1607, to a collection of *Sinfonie et gagliarde a 3, 4, et 5 uoci . . . per
sonar 2 viole, ouero 2 cornetti, et un chittarone.* The first *sinfonia*
of the second book has been reprinted by Robert Haas in *Die Musik
des Barock.*[15] The piece is entirely homophonic, with the viols playing in parallel thirds above an angular bass line. By 1613, the date of
the *Varie sonate,* Rossi has substituted violins for viols and indicated
the bass instrument simply as *basso continuo.* This is, perhaps, the first
appearance of this instrumental combination in the century; it is the
instrumentation of the later trio sonata, one of the most widely used
forms of the Baroque period. In the "Romanesca" and "Ruggiero"
variation-sonatas the parallel thirds are again in evidence. But with
them appears a new device which contributed much to the future of
instrumental style: the figuration is distributed between the two
violins. The following example will show the device (taken from
the "Ruggiero" sonata).

The antiphonal or responsive style, the principle of alternating
two opposing groups, is again at work here, even if in a miniature
way. We saw the principle at work in the massive *canzoni* of
Gabrieli, in the alternation of two large tonal masses; we saw it again
in the *Canzona francese* of Viadana, where it became a factor of the
monodic style and was concerned with the alternation of two pairs of
instruments and several pairs of long melodies. Here we see it again,
this time in the monodic sonata, and we see it used to divide a single
melodic figuration among two instruments, producing the effect of
a single instrument. The type of figuration, the rapid repetition of
broken-chord patterns, marks a decided step forward in the evolution of violin style. A comparison of this passage with one, let us

[15] Page 90.

say, of Corelli's later in the century will show how the latter was derived from such humble beginnings. Salomone Rossi stands at the very beginning of the line of composers who gradually developed violinistic music. Because of his consistent use of parallel thirds in his trio sonatas as well as in his *sinfonie* and in the variations discussed above, his use of dialogue-like passages between the violins, and his use of note-against-note style in his instrumental music generally, we must consider Rossi to be one of the foremost champions of instrumental monody. And we must give him credit for having established the instrumentation of the trio sonata.[16]

We turn now to Biagio Marini (c. 1595–c. 1665), a composer whose excellent writing and fertile imagination did much to influence the music of the later seventeenth century. Marini was a composer of progressive *canzoni,* as well as the founder of the solo violin literature, and he was active after the middle of the century in writing in the new forms of that time. His importance for us here lies in his contributions to bi-thematic composition, to the development of two- and three-note chord writing for the violin, and to the evolution of violin technique generally. Marini published his first work, *Affetti musicali,* at Venice in 1617 while a violinist in the orchestra of St. Mark's in that city. This work contains two pieces which Marini calls *sinfonie;* both are for solo violin or cornett, with *basso continuo,* and the first includes also an optional part for bass viol. Both have subtitles: "La Orlandina" [17] and "La Gardana" [18] respectively.

"La Orlandina" consists of five sections, ranging in length from seven to sixteen measures, containing duple meter in two sections, triple in three, and having a variety of tempos from slow to very fast. It would almost serve as a model for the summary of sonata style given above. The piece begins in homophonic style, with a lyric melody; the metric unit is a half-note. Succeeding sections employ more rhythmic diversity. The most obvious difference between this

---

[16] Riemann, *Handbuch,* II², 139.
[17] Reprinted by Riemann, *ibid.,* pp. 96–99.
[18] Reprinted by Schering, *Geschichte der Musik in Beispielen,* No. 182.

work and a sectional *canzone* is that in the former the imitative section based on the manipulation of the *canzone* dactyl motive is missing. On closer inspection, the piece is not nearly as broken up as the formal description would imply. The second, third, and fifth sections all contain figures found in the first section, and the second actually grows out of the first.

The effect of these works of Marini's (published 1617) is quite different from that of the *canzoni* of Gabrieli (1597), Viadana (1602), and Grillo (1608), to mention only those we have examined in detail. In Marini one feels the attempt to establish a longer melodic line—rudimentary, it is true, and characterized by extreme changes of tempo and meter. But the dead stop between sections is not present here, and melodic material used in one section appears in another.

"La Orlandina" and "La Gardana" are important for other reasons also. The reader will recall that no instrumental works representative of solo monody are known in the years immediately following the Camerata's first achievements. In the years since Galilei's experiments took definite shape (c. 1581), there are operas (the two versions of *Eurydice*, 1600), solo monodic songs (Caccini's *Nuove musiche*, 1601), group songs utilizing the monodic principle (Viadana's *Cento concerti*, 1602), and instrumental ensembles (Viadana's *Canzona francese*, 1602). These works of Marini's are the first representatives of solo instrumental monody that have yet been discovered. In them is definite evidence of the growth of the instrumental style. Types of figuration and passage-work found in them are eminently playable on the violin and are entirely unsuited to the voice; broken-chord figures and scale passages that have been stock-in-trade among string composers ever since the seventeenth century emerge in Marini's work. We saw similar devices above, when we examined the trios of Salomone Rossi; those works antedate Marini's by a few years, so we cannot speak of the latter as having established the instrumental style. But Marini's importance in helping at its birth cannot be denied, especially if other works of his are considered.

Among such other works are "La Foscarina," another of the *Affetti musicali* of 1617. Here is found probably the first use of the tremolo in violin music, seven years before Monteverdi's more famous use of that device in *Il combattimento di Tancredi e Clorinda*.[19] Later, in his *Sonate, sinfonie, canzoni*, 1629, Marini wrote a "caprice in which two violins play in four parts" and a "caprice for solo violin with three strings in the manner of a lyre." [20] Thus, Marini, as probably the first known composer of solo instrumental monodic pieces, is also the first to use the tremolo as well as double and triple stops through long passages. We shall return to Marini below, when his place in the evolution of the trio sonata is discussed. His further importance in the development of the solo violin sonata must remain outside the confines of this book.

Let us review briefly the ways in which musical length had been achieved up to this moment (1617), the ways in which a composer had extended his musical ideas. (1) In the *ricercare* type of composition the composer was constrained to present his first motive or theme or melody briefly, let it be imitated contrapuntally in other voices,

---

[19] Riemann, *Handbuch*, II², 100.
[20] Fragments reprinted in *ibid.*, pp. 101–102.

go on to another theme, let the same process be repeated, and so forth. He ended finally with a group of themes more or less unrelated, imitated after a fashion but not developed or extended. This type of treatment, satisfactory enough in the *ricercare's* vocal counterpart, the motet, where the text kept the various elements in proportion, was not capable of achieving unity of form nor great interest in content. Not until the *ricercare* had abandoned all but one theme and centered its attention on imitations of that theme was its future assured; it led the way to the monothematic fugue. (2) In the sectional *canzone* type the composer began with a section in imitative style which soon gave way to another section in contrasting (often dance-like) style, tempo, and usually meter; this section, in turn, made way for another contrasting bit, and so forth. Here again the unity of form was threatened by the number of unrelated fragments (an exception was noticed in the case of the Grillo *canzone* discussed above), although the interest in the content may have been sustained through the quick introduction of new bits. (3) In those portions of Marini's *Affetti musicali* that have been discussed, the attempt at lengthening the line and achieving unity of form is seen in the effort to let one section grow out of the previous one, to repeat in a later section a melodic figure heard in an earlier one, and to relate the types of figure generally. Here the unity of form is closer at hand, although unity of style has not been achieved. (4) In those works of Salomone Rossi which consist of variations built over a *basso ostinato*, the repetition of the bass phrase in each variation provides a unity of form, and the number of different versions of the melody contributes to the lengthening of the composition.

Let us now look at one more achievement of Marini's which stands side by side with his attempts to create greater melodic integrity. We refer to his use of an independent countermelody not derived from the imitation of a previous phrase. Marini's trio sonata "La Foscarina" was mentioned above in another connection; also, in this work we find the tentative use of a countermelodic device. At the beginning of this sonata the first violin announces a theme which the second later imitates; but while the second violin is so occupied, the first announces another theme to accompany the original one. Later in the work the same pattern occurs. The device appears nowhere else in the trio sonatas of Marini.

Another example of the use of a countermelody is in the works of Girolamo Frescobaldi, the last of the great Italian organists and one of the great masters of polyphonic writing. We turn to the second of his *Canzoni a due canti*, that is, *trio canzoni*. Here there is one section, twenty-one measures long,[21] in which a melody and its countermelody appear twice; this situation we also found in the Marini, above. Several other times one or the other of the melodies appears, but each time it is counterpointed differently; hence, these cases cannot be considered as examples of this latest step forward. Here, again, the step was taken in isolation; in two other *canzoni* of this set [22] no trace of countermelody appears at all. These two examples by Marini and Frescobaldi, eleven years apart, may have been the first appearance of true countermelody in music.

We have followed the course of the *canzone* from Gabrieli (1597) to Frescobaldi (1628), and have taken note of the principal changes that have occurred in it during those years. We have seen two distinct types of *canzone:* the old, with much counterpoint and a homogeneous form, and the new, with emphasis put upon contrasting sections and written in the monodic style. We have seen the birth of a new form, the sonata, with style elements drawn from the old *canzone*, from the new, and from the imaginations of composers active in that form. We have seen the emergence of two or three types of sonata, and the appearance of sets of variations scored for two violins and bass. Finally, we have seen the rudimentary beginnings of countermelody.

In the years after 1628 the innovations made by Viadana, Grillo, Rossi, Marini, and Frescobaldi were seized upon and improved by Tarquinio Merula,[23] (c. 1590–c. 1655), Maurizio Cazzati (c. 1620–1677), and Massimilliano Neri (c. 1615–1665?). A distinct and independent countermelody became the rule in the works of these men,

---

[21] *Ibid.*, p. 142.   [22] Reprinted by Riemann in *Old Chamber Music*, Vol. I.
[23] Not Claudio Merulo of Venice.

and a tendency arose to reduce the number of sections in the *can-zone* to four. When that point had been reached, about 1644, the way had been prepared for the forms which were to succeed the instrumental *canzone* as the popular form for chamber-music groups: the *sonata da chiesa* and the *sonata da camera*, or church sonata and chamber sonata, respectively. Both of these new forms made considerable use of dance tunes; in fact the last-named was at times merely a collection of such tunes. Before examining the new forms, then, it is necessary to leave Italy, where we have been since the middle of the sixteenth century, and move to Germany, in order to trace the evolution of the dance suite.

4

THE DANCE SUITE

WILHELM FISCHER, writing in Adler's *Handbuch der Musikge-schichte*,[1] calls attention to the stylistic differences between the dance music of Renaissance "society" and that of people more humbly placed. The dances of the latter included a small number of types, with relatively few musical examples of each type. The dance steps employed were rather simple, implying a straightforward rhythmic scheme in the music, and the tunes were repeated more or less without change as long as the desire to dance was present. The dance music of "society," on the other hand, was characterized by a greater number of types, more numerous musical examples of each type, and a greater degree of elaboration and complexity, both in the steps and in the music. And in place of the constant repetition of one tune, a number of tunes of the same type were played one after the other.

But both kinds, "society" and folk dances alike, had one characteristic in common. each tune was composed of two contrasting parts, both of which almost always appeared together. The first part of the pair was a relatively slow, stately dance, usually in duple meter; the second one a lively dance in triple meter, with a strong melodic similarity to the first. This pair of melodically related dances was common to all countries of western Europe in the early sixteenth century, and was the germ out of which the seventeenth-century dance suite grew.

The most common of the duple-meter dances was called, with great variety of spelling, *paduana, padovana, pavane, paven,* and *pavin* in Italy, France, England, and Germany. Its triple-meter asso-

[1] I, 394.

ciate, that is, the second of the pair, was most usually a *galliard*, *saltarello*, or *courante*. In Germany the distinctive names of the pair often disappeared, and the pair was called *Dantz und Nachdantz* or *Hofdantz und Nachdantz*. In Italy the *passamezzo*, closely related to the *paduan* in steps and music and often substituted for it, was popular. In France the pair of dances named *basse danse* and *tourdion* was often used; here, however, both dances were in triple meter.

Dance music broke into print early in the sixteenth century; and, as was also the case with the French chanson, dance music was arranged for the lute. The lute at that time, and for many decades afterward, enjoyed a favored position much like that of the piano in the early twentieth century (and like that of the radio-phonograph combination in the present day). Dance music arranged for the lute was among the first printed music of which there is any record. As early as 1508 Ottaviano dei Petrucci, the inventor of the process of printing music with movable metal type, published at Venice several sets of dances for that instrument. These dances appeared in sets of three: the pavane and the saltarello are joined by another lively dance in triple meter, called *piva*.

Dance music was not confined to the lute, however. It was written, arranged for, and played by organists and clavichordists as well; and it appeared, not in the familiar notation which employs notes and the staff, but in the various tablature notations current in the early sixteenth century. Tablature notation differs from staff notation in that figures or letters are used to show pitch levels, various other symbols to show length and rhythm, and hooks and crosses attached to letters to show chromatic alterations. Among the many examples of dance music of the time, a few may be characterized briefly.

In a clavichord tablature made by Hans Kotter, an organist at Freiburg about 1530, is a pair of dances by Hans Weck,[2] a contemporary and fellow-townsman. The first of the pair is a *Spanyöler Tancz*, that is, a Spanish dance; [3] the second, a *Hopper Tancz*, de-

---

[2] Reprinted in *Klaviertänze des 16ten Jahrhunderts*, ed. by Halbig.
[3] Because of its title, its broad triple meter, and the placing of the secondary accent on the third beat of the rhythmic group, this dance gives evidence of being a sara-

rived from the German *hoppsen*, to hop. Both are in triple meter; the first is slow and sustained, the second, fast and sprightly. Melodic relationship between the two is slight, being in fact confined to the first phrase. Both dances are essentially harmonizations of elaborately decorated melodies; as such, they are among the earliest examples of homophonic style (some seventy years before the Camerata began the experiments which led to monody).

In France, too, lute and clavichord tablatures appeared in great numbers during the early sixteenth century. One such lute tablature was published by Pierre Attaingnant, one of the foremost of Parisian publishers at that time; its title is *Quatuorze gaillardes, neuf pavanes, sept branles et deux basse danses*.[4] On examining a modern reprint of several of these dances,[5] one finds that they are short (24–32 measures, with repeats), that they have well-established periodic structure, and that they appear in either homophonic or contrapuntal style.

Forty years later, in Germany in 1571, we find in a tablature for clavichord by Elias Ammerbach several sets of dances, five of which have been issued in modern notation.[6] The first four of these five sets consist of the usual pairs having the duple-triple relationship common to most sixteenth-century dances. The first, third, and fourth pair bear titles which call attention to the humble origin of the dance tunes; the titles may be translated: "He Who Wants the Little Daughter," "Must I Die, Then," and "The Maidens Are from Flanders." The second pair is called simply "Pastorum Dantz." In each case the second dance of the pair is a triple-meter variant of the first, and is called "Proportio." [7]

The fifth set of these dances is no longer merely a pair, but a miniature suite of three movements. The first movement, in place of a bucolic title, is called "Passamezzo d'Angleterre"; the second, called "La Reprise," is essentially a transposed repetition of sections of the

---

bande, appearing in Germany many years in advance of its reported debut in France, about 1585.
[4] A facsimile reproduction in *Chansons und Tänze*, ed. by Bernouilli.
[5] *Klaviertänze des 16ten Jahrhunderts*, ed. by Halbig.   [6] *Ibid.*
[7] Referring to *proportio tripla*. Cf. Adler, *Handbuch*, I, 396.

first dance. The third dance is the expected triple-meter variant of the first, and is called "Proportio, oder Galliard." In all the dances discussed in this section we have to do primarily with note-against-note style, and with a very evident regular phrase structure. The phrases are, with a few eight-measure exceptions, four measures long; since each dance consists of no more than two or three phrases, no great length of composition is attained.

The dances and dance pairs mentioned in the paragraphs above are typical of the large bulk of sixteenth-century music in this form. Large collections such as the Attaingnant set, with its thirty-two single dances, and small ones such as the Ammerbach, with its few pairs, were published throughout the century. But a tendency to arrange dances in groups of three to eight or more movements, in a word, to create a suite of dances, also was present. The subsequent history of dance music, until well into the seventeenth century, must take account of that tendency. Several different methods of combining single dances into suites are to be observed; in general, one method was confined to one country. We shall next examine the developments in England, France, Italy, and Germany from about 1550 to 1650, taking each country separately.

We turn first to England where the composers for the virginal, in the last half of the sixteenth century, contributed an important step in the evolution of the dance suite. The virginal, a keyboard instrument almost identical with the clavicembalo, had been popular in England since the beginning of the century. Most of the well-known English madrigal composers—among them William Byrd, Thomas Morley, John Bull, Thomas Weelkes, and Orlando Gibbons—wrote virginal music too. And in their hands the music for the virginal acquired two characteristics: one is the characteristic of writing music really adapted to the instrument for which it is intended; the other is the extensive use of the variation principle.

The first characteristic appears most clearly in the fancy (fantasy), derived from the Italian *ricercare*. The fancy, while not a dance form, may be mentioned briefly here for the part it played in the development of instrumental style. Some of the fancies were among the first instrumental pieces which took into account the sonorities, difficulties, and technical characteristics of the chosen instrument, thus among the first to have an individual style. But the fancy remained relatively untouched by the inventions and innovations characteristic of the Italian *nuove musiche* of the late 1590's, and continued in its contrapuntal style with fugue-like imitations until well into the middle of the seventeenth century. John Jenkins (1592–1678) and Henry Lawes (1595–1662) wrote fancies until about 1650, resisting strongly the Baroque influences present elsewhere in Europe. From that date the fancy lost popularity and was abandoned in favor of newer forms; but it appeared later, remodeled by the continental influences that had gone unnoticed for almost a century, in the works of Henry Purcell about 1680. Those works we shall discuss in a later chapter,[8] where we shall also see how English composers benefited by having for so long cultivated instrumental polyphony.

In the dance forms, on the other hand, English composers for a decade or two before and after 1600 apparently felt that the variation principle offered the best means of disclosing the musical possibilities of the virginal. English keyboard music of that period is largely based on the variation forms. And it is the application of the variation principle to dance forms that enabled composers such as John Bull (c. 1562–1628), William Byrd (c. 1543–1623), and Orlando Gibbons (1583–1625) to make the next step in the evolution of the suite, a step which was to be imitated widely in Germany in the following decades. Among the most important sources of virginal music of the period from about 1585 to 1625 are three collections known respectively as the *Fitzwilliam Virginal Book, My Ladye Nevelles Book*, and *Parthenia*.[9] We may look at a few typical dance tunes from these collections in order to see the results of that step.

[8] See pp. 101 ff.
[9] *Fitzwilliam Virginal Book* reprinted and edited by Fuller-Maitland and Squire; *My Ladye Nevelles Book*, from 1591, in modern edition by H. A. Andrews; *Parthenia*, from 1611, reprinted by The Musical Antiquarian Society; new edition by M. Glyn.

The "Spanish Paven," by John Bull,[10] is one such dance tune; it consists of a theme and seven variations, each of which is sixteen measures long. All but two of the variations conform to the theme in being in duple meter. The two exceptions, the fifth and sixth variations, are in triple meter; in modern notation they appear as 6/8 meter, thus are actually a compound of triple and duple (3/8 and 3/8). The theme is in a kind of half-contrapuntal, half-homophonic style. In some measures a chordal accompaniment is present; in others, a degree of inner-voice motion that takes on the appearance of four-voice counterpoint. The first of these variations is concerned with imitations of a ♫♫ ♫♫ motive; the texture is in general contrapuntal. The following five variations are concerned entirely with running figures, first in the bass, then in the treble, and then in bass and treble together. In the seventh and eighth variations a return is made to four-voice imitative writing. Nowhere during the variations is the form or the harmonic structure of the theme altered. The variations are purely ornamental figurations of the theme, and as such are characteristic of the great bulk of virginal music in the variation forms.

A pavane by William Byrd [11] is another of the pieces in the Fitz-william collection. In this work there are three distinct, melodically unrelated sections. Each section is sixteen measures long, and each is followed by one variation. Thus a form of AA′ BB′ CC′ results. This piece, quite different from the "Spanish Paven" discussed above, is largely in four-voice counterpoint, even though there are a few running figures in the variations. A fragment of the A′ section will show the type of treatment.

[10] Republished by Schering, *Geschichte der Musik in Beispielen,* No. 147.
[11] Reprinted and ed. by Bantock in *Three Dances of William Byrd.*

The third section, both in its C and C' versions, abounds in cross accents and other types of rhythmic complexity. There is throughout this piece no trace of technical display such as characterized the "Spanish Paven"; this is a dignified piece, with the impressiveness of the themes retained in the variation sections.

In the Fitzwilliam collection is another piece by Byrd: a set of five variations on a galliard.[12] Even here, where finger activity dominates the texture, where running scale passages and passages in thirds are characteristic, contrapuntal writing is not long absent. Melodious inner voices, imitations of small motives, and the like indicate that even in his virtuoso moments Byrd could not forget his interest in solid writing and good voice-leading.

Judging by the numerous dance pieces and other bits found in the three principal collections of virginal music, one gathers that the polyphonic and homophonic styles existed side by side in England through the first quarter of the seventeenth century. Along with strongly contrapuntal pieces, such as the examples by Byrd mentioned above, are others by the same composer (for example, "A Gigg," "Rowland," and "Wolsey's Wilde") and by his contemporary John Bull ("Pavana" and "Duke of Brunswick") which are equally homophonic. Nor is there great uniformity of style and tempo within dance pieces of the same type. Byrd's "Sir John Gray's Galliard," for example, is moderately slow and rather somber; his galliard with the five variations mentioned above is animated and filled with lively figurations.

It must not be supposed that English dance music and dance variations were confined to the virginal. As early as 1599 suites of dance tunes written for groups of viols—the suites were called "consorts" —had appeared in England: Thomas Morley's *Consort Lessons, for six instruments to play together* (1599); John Dowland's *Lachrymae; or, Seven Teares, figured in seaven passionate pavans, in five parts* (1605); Phillip Rosseter's *Lessons for Consorts* (1609), for five voices. A number of manuscripts from this time exist also, among

12 *Ibid.*

them John Cooper (Giovanni Coperario), "Fancies for Viols," William Lawes' "Royal Consort of Viols" and his "Great Consort." It is in this form, as music for groups of viols, that English music so greatly influenced the German in the years after 1600.

William Brade was a forerunner of the many English musicians who fled to Germany after the ascension of James I (1603) and continued to compose in the style they had brought from England. Brade, beginning in 1594, lived in several north German cities, enjoyed considerable reputation as a violinist and composer, and published several dance suites, mostly for five and six voices, in the years between 1607 and 1621. John Dowland and Thomas Simpson were two of the better-known expatriates to follow Brade. These composers had great influence on their German contemporaries and opened a new epoch in German music, the epoch of the suite for orchestra and chamber ensemble. While the south German and Austrian centers were more influenced by the Italians, north German composers adopted the style and instrumentation of the English, seized enthusiastically upon the consort, and transferred their attention to that vehicle.[13] Thus in the instrumental field the school of Elizabethan composers split into two lines: the emigrants to Germany carried with them instrumental dance music, to the great advantage of continental musicians; the composers who remained in England stayed largely within the framework of the suite for virginal and the fancy for sets of viols. Not until 1656, with Matthew Locke's (c. 1630–1677) *Little Consort of Three Parts*, did the English ensemble suite appear, to lead the way to the suites of Henry Purcell in the 1680's.

The process of enlarging the suite in France transpired quite differently. Dances for the lute retained the melodically related pair pavane-galliard or pavane-courante until well into the seventeenth century. But instrumental composers, writing both for the "society" dance and the staged *ballet de cour*, added a second pair, melodically unrelated to each other and in the sequence of triple and duple meter. *Branle* was the collective name for the set. The individual dances of

[13] Láng, *Music in Western Civilization*, p. 402.

the suite about 1600 were usually *branle double, branle simple, branle gay,* and *branle de Bourgogne.* They were in duple, triple, triple, and duple meter, respectively, with slow, fast, fast, and slow tempos alternating. The second was melodically related to the first, but the third and fourth were completely independent.

During the early part of the seventeenth century the dance suite was again taken over by the lutenists, particularly Denis Gaultier (c. 1597–1672). The content of the suite had changed by that time. About 1650 a typical suite was made up of allemande, courante, sarabande, and gigue; the metrical scheme was still as indicated above, but the tempo relations had changed to moderate, fast, slow, and fast. Melodic relationship was still confined to the first pair. In this form the suite was taken over by the clavecinists, notably by Louis Couperin (c. 1626–1661) and Jacques de Chambonnières (c. 1600–c. 1670). A sarabande and *double* by the last-named composer, reprinted by Schering,[14] show the degree of embellishment found in clavecin works of this period. The dance suite in this form was destined, later in the century, to remove all other forms of the suite from the field.

In 1906 Jules Ecorcheville published a collection entitled *Vingt suites d'orchestre du XVII siècle française.*[15] The collection contains a great number of dance movements found in the *Landesbibliothek* of Cassel in central Germany and composed by obscure Frenchmen and Germans between 1650 and 1668. There seems to be considerable doubt in Ecorcheville's mind as to whether the movements found here were originally composed in sets and can thus be called suites, or whether they were written separately. While there is no positive evidence that they really are suites, he has so arranged them in his publication. The twenty "suites" range from two to twenty movements; the majority contain from six to twelve. Occasionally a bit of melodic relationship is found between duple- and triple-meter movements of the same set, but not enough to prove that the relationship is intentional. According to Fischer,[16] these sets which

---

[14] Schering, *Geschichte der Musik in Beispielen,* No. 218.
[15] Published by Fortin at Paris.   [16] In Adler, *Handbuch,* I, 571.

Ecorcheville has edited are, perhaps, the only examples, except for the lute and the clavecin dances and the dance suites appearing in the French opera, particularly in the works of Lully and his pupils, of the emerging suite by French composers.

Steps leading toward the development of a unified suite were also being taken in Italy. The popularity of the lute in that country during the sixteenth century has been mentioned, along with the appearance of pairs and occasional sets of dances for that instrument. In 1607 Monteverdi published a *Balletto* for instrumental ensemble, including it at the end of a set of several small vocal movements called *scherzi*. This ballet is composed of an instrumental *entrata a 3*, followed by six dances with text: *pavana, galliarda, corrento, volta, allemanda,* and *tripla*.[17] A similar set of dances is found in the works of Antonio Brunelli, dated 1616. Here the sequence is as follows: *balletto, altro ballo per sonar solo* (another *ballo* to be played only), *corrento, ballo grave, gagliarda, corrente.* Here again the indications are that the dances were to be both sung and played.[18]

One of the early adherents of instrumental monody was Giovanni Battista Buonamente. In his seventh book of sonatas, published in 1637, are included eight sonatas consisting of *sinfonia, brando, gagliarda, corrente.* The *sinfonie* of these sonatas follow in general a three-part form: slow first section, fast section in triple meter, slow section often recapitulating the first part.[19] We shall return to these movements in Chapter 5, where their contributions to the later development of the dance suite are examined. Nor was the tendency to arrange dances in sets confined to ensemble groups. For example, in Tagliapetra's *Antologia di musica antica e moderna*,[20] Volume V, are a number of Frescobaldi's keyboard works from 1637. Here one finds a set of dances consisting of four melodically related courantes, a *balletto* I with its triple-meter variant, a passacaglia, and a *balletto* II with related courante II—nine movements in all. This is obviously not a dance suite in the sense of the French and German versions

[17] Alfred Einstein, in a note to Riemann's *Handbuch*, II², 526.
[18] *Ibid.*, pp. 530–531.   [19] *Ibid.*   [20] Published by Ricordi at Milan.

of the suite; but it does serve to show that Italy, too, was concerned in the effort to combine dance movements into sets having some inner thread tending toward unity of form.

We now turn back to Germany at the beginning of the seventeenth century, where still another method of suite expansion and development occurs. Hans Leo Hassler (1564–1612), perhaps the greatest German composer of the late Renaissance, published his *Lustgarten* in 1601. This collection contains thirty-nine vocal and eleven instrumental pieces. The instrumental pieces are six-voice *entradas* (related to "introduction"), stately and pompous, designed for civic banquets and patrician dances.[21] Of the vocal pieces, many are themselves dance tunes; they contain the expected triple-meter variant of a foregoing duple-meter piece, sung to the same text. And still more significantly, successive verses have their own music; thus miniature suites or dance-song cycles are created.

Renaissance and early Baroque instrumentation was not standardized. The same piece could be, and was, played on brass instruments by the tower musicians, on wind and string instruments for dances, and on strings and lute for intimate chamber-music purposes. The composers following Hassler were greatly influenced by him, and followed the prevailing practices in regard to flexible instrumentation. Among the more important composers after Hassler were Melchior Franck (1573–1639) and Valentin Haussmann (c. 1565–c. 1615). These men retained the old practice of writing pairs of dances in which the duple-triple and melodic relationships were present. Hugo Riemann, in his *Old Chamber Music*, Volume II, reprints two of Franck's dances, taken from the *Neue musikalische Intraden* (1608), and *Deutsche weltliche Gesang und Täntze* (1604), respectively.

The "Intrada" is in compound time; Riemann notates it in 6/8. There are three short sections, all of which are repeated; the texture is all note-against-note, the melody is almost entirely in scalewise motion and rarely exceeds a sixth in range. The "Tantz," in duple time, likewise has three short sections, and is also in note-against-

[21] Moser, *Geschichte der deutschen Musik*, I, 502.

note style. The outstanding characteristics of both these six-voice dances are the regular periodic structure, the lack of counterpoint, and the complete absence of any tendency toward monodic style devices. Franck remained true to the old practices and issued his dances in sets of similar type out of which the players made their own suites.[22] Haussmann, on the other hand, experimented with his own sequences of dances: the usual pair of *Tanz-Nachtanz*, most often a pavane and a galliard, served as a nucleus to which other pairs were attached. One finds [23] a *passamezzo* and reprise, or a Polish dance and fugue, or an occasional set of variations.

But the distinction of adding a second pair of dances melodically related to the first pair, thus creating a unified whole based on the use of the variation principle, falls to Paul Peuerl (Bäurl) (1580?-1627?) with his *Newe Paduan, Intrada, Däntz und Galliarda*, published in 1611. From the beginning of German activity in this field and including the works of Hassler and Franck, the dance forms had been given to an ensemble of strings: five or six voices in the case of the older composers, four in the case of Peuerl. One of Peuerl's suites from the publication of 1611 is included in *Old Chamber Music*, Volume II.

In this suite Peuerl follows the sequence indicated in his title. The four dances are respectively in duple, triple, duple, and triple meter. There is no longer evidence of mere melodic relationship; these dances are actually variations of the motive on which the pavane is based. Each of the four movements is in three parts, and each part is repeated. But the movements are not all the same length: the "paduan" contains thirty-two measures; the others range from sixteen to twenty. This is caused by the unique way in which phrases are elided, omitted, or expanded during the course of the respective dances. There is a respectable amount of "development" of the basic motive throughout the suite; yet the harmonic relationship of one movement to the others is never lost sight of. Contrapuntal writing, too, is more evident here than in Hassler's and Franck's *intrade*, and the demands made on the lowest instrument, bass viol in this case,

---

[22] *Ibid.*, p. 509.   [23] In D.D.T., Vol. XVI.

are greater than in the works discussed previously. In the "paduan," for example, the bass takes part in the contrapuntal imitations of the basic motive and engages in rapid parallel-third motion with the alto viol.

The variation suite thus originated by Peuerl was carried further a few years later with the publication by Johann Hermann Schein (1586–1630) of his *Banchetto musicale*, Leipzig, 1617. The tenth of the twenty suites contained in this publication has been reprinted in *Old Chamber Music*, Volume II. This suite is for five instruments, and Schein specifically mentions that these are meant to be violins, not viols.[24] In this he follows the innovation of Haussmann, who had introduced the violin into Germany in 1604. There are five movements in this suite instead of the usual four: *padouana, galliarde, courente, allemande,* and *tripla*. The variation principle is employed somewhat more freely here than in Peuerl's works. The "galliarde" is almost independent of the "padouana"; in only one or two passages is there a sign of melodic similarity between the two dances. The other movements do show, however, a considerable amount of relationship to the first. The lengths of the five movements are forty, twenty-four, twenty-eight, twelve, and twenty-four measures, respectively. It will be noticed that with regard to length in both the Schein suite and the Peuerl the "paduan" is the most important movement. Even at the beginning of the seventeenth century the first movement was taking on some of the characteristics that were to lead to its domination of the sonata structure in the middle of the eighteenth century.

Not all composers adopted Peuerl's innovation in the direction of a unified suite, however. Single dances and dances arranged in pairs still appeared until the century was well on its way. One such pair was a *Paduana e galliarda a 5* by George Engelmann,[25] a Leipzig musician in the early years of the seventeenth century, taken from his *Fasciculus quinque vocum concentum* (1617). There is a greater amount of contrapuntal writing in these dances than in any of the

[24] Moser, *Geschichte der deutschen Musik*, I, 509.
[25] In Riemann, *Old Chamber Music*, Vol. II.

other German works so far examined. There are short sections in canonic style, two or three passages full of cross accents reminiscent of Orlando di Lasso, and a general air of contrapuntal competence; in the galliard the two violins at times engage in antiphonal imitations. These dances have gone far on the road toward true instrumental style; bustling rhythmic figures based on chord intervals as found in them are clearly written for the violin and would be impractical for the voice.

Nor was the Italian influence passed by in Germany during these years. A *Pasameza con variazioni* is found in Thomas Simpson's *Opus newer Paduanen*, also published in 1617.[26] The *passamezzo*, it will be remembered, was an Italian dance similar to the pavane, but a bit more sprightly. Simpson, one of the Englishmen transplanted to north Germany in the early seventeenth century, here combines English and Italian influences by writing a set of variations on an Italian dance tune. Italian works and style were coming into Germany about that time. The "pasameza," in duple meter and thirty-two measures long, is followed by three variations. The harmony remains unchanged throughout the variations; the bass part is confined to playing chord notes, takes no part in thematic imitations, and has quite the look of a *basso continuo*. We shall see later that Samuel Scheidt is given credit for introducing the figured bass to Germany in 1621. This work of Simpson's may well have prepared the way for that innovation by introducing the simpler *basso continuo* form four years earlier.

One other composition must be mentioned to indicate the spread of Italian musical ideas to Germany. Erasmus Widman (c. 1572–1634), a south German musician, published a set of *Gantz neue Cantzon, Intraden, Balletten, und Couranten* at Nuremberg in 1618. From this set a "Canzone auf den Schäfferstantz" (*Canzone* on the Shepherd's Dance) is included in the *Old Chamber Music*, Volume II. Widman's work consists of two parts, both repeated, thirty and thirty-five measures long, respectively, with a five-measure coda after the second part. Here is no trace of the familiar dactylic

[26] *Ibid.*

motives so typical of *canzoni*. The piece begins with a contrapuntal, fugue-like section, after which it settles down to a more homophonic texture, the bass taking on the sustained nature of the *basso continuo*. The second part introduces a new theme and returns to the fugal texture of the first part. Riemann points out [27] that Widman was among the first German composers to write *canzoni*, but that many of them are really pavanes.

The next important step in the development of the dance suite was taken by Samuel Scheidt, one of the three great "S's" of the seventeenth century: Heinrich Schütz (1585–1672), whose work lies outside the scope of this book; Johann Hermann Schein (1586–1630), the composer of the *Banchetto musicale* mentioned above; and Samuel Scheidt (1587–1654), who is now under discussion. That step was the addition of the figured bass to the dance suite. Let us look at a "Paduan und Courante dolorosa," from Scheidt's set of *Paduana, Galliarda, Couranta,* 1621; again we look into *Old Chamber Music*, Volume II. These dances are for two violins, viola, and figured *basso continuo*. Scheidt has here returned to the custom of melodically relating the pair of dances, for the "Courante" is a triple-meter variant of the "Paduan." Each of the dances has three sections, totaling forty measures in the one and fifty-five in the other. The "Paduan" shows several unique features; each of the three sections is in a completely different style. In the first section the first and second violins run in parallel thirds and sixths, but they are in counterpoint with the viola, while the bass is in the conservative *continuo* style. In the second section all the instruments, including the bass, break out into rapid figurations, syncopations and considerable rhythmic diversity. In the third section the figuration ceases, the middle voices harmonize a descending scale melody, and the bass resumes a *continuo* role. The "Courante" is largely in mixed homophonic and note-against-note style, with the first and third sections following rather closely the corresponding sections of the "Paduan"; the middle section deviates, both in melody and harmonization, from the second section of the previous movement.

[27] *Handbuch*, II², 184.

Scheidt's step of having included the *basso continuo* in his instrumental works seems to have met with approval in Germany. In 1626 Carlo Farina (c. 1595–c. 1650) published at Dresden two books of *Pavane, gagliarde, brandi, mascherata, arie francese, volti, balleti, sonate, canzone.* This collection, as the title indicates, included an array of German, French, and Italian works. Dances in four-voice counterpoint appear next to trio sonatas for two violins and figured bass.[28] These are, perhaps, the first trio sonatas printed in Germany. A "Pavana" and "Gagliarda" from the first book of this set are found in *Old Chamber Music*, Volume II. Both dances are for two violins, viola, and bass; the bass is figured in the "Pavana" only. The first dance is in a mixture of homophonic and contrapuntal styles; the second, like most of the triple-meter dances, is largely homophonic. The noteworthy feature of this pair of dances is that the bass is much freer than in the Scheidt "Paduan" and plays a minor part in establishing the contrapuntal style by imitating the principal melodies.

While this work of assembling the dances into suites was going on, the single dances themselves were undergoing considerable internal transformation. In the early years of the seventeenth century the pavanes, *intrade*, and galliards had been solidly rhythmical. Based largely on note-against-note texture, the regular pulse of the dance tune was clearly perceived. During the course of the century's first half, several factors caused the dance to lose its pristine rhythm and take on a stylized character. Among such factors were (1) the use of contrapuntal devices, imitations, and the like, which tended to obscure the rhythm; (2) the adoption of the *basso continuo*, which allowed a greater degree of rhythmic diversity and figuration to develop in the upper parts; (3) the development of self-contained melody to such a degree that lyric expression became a part of instrumental style, and appeared in dances to the detriment of the prevailing rhythm. The end result of this was that the pavane to a great extent became a piece of pure music in two- or three-part form and lost its connection with dance music. Further, a variety of

[28] *Ibid.*, p. 185.

tempos served the same dance; there were slow, fast, and moderate pavanes; courantes could be sprightly, *dolorosa*, moving, and so forth. With the dance characteristics of unpretentious melody and straightforward rhythm obscured and the erstwhile dance tune now simply a piece of concert music, the way was clear for the step which was to complete the formal evolution of the dance suite: the inclusion of nondance forms.

A move in this direction is seen in a suite by Johann Neubauer, a musician in Cassel; his manuscript, dated 1649, is entitled "Neue Pavanen, Galliarden, Balleten, Couranten, Allemanden, und Sarabanden," and contains eight suites. The fifth suite of this set, reprinted in *Old Chamber Music*, Volume II, is for two violins, two violas, and *basso continuo*, and it contains six movements. The bass is figured copiously in the first three movements, sparsely in the fourth, and not at all in the fifth and the sixth. The third movement is the one we shall examine here. It consists of three parts: the first is in fast duple time, is eight measures long, and is called "ballet"; the second is a piece of slow, nondance music in duple time, called simply "adagio," and is eight measures long; the third is a fragment of lively dance music eight measures long, in compound meter, and is marked "presto." Thus we have a combination of fast-slow-fast within a single movement, and the slow section is a lyric melody not connected with dance forms. While such a combination of tempos and styles is justified from the point of view that this movement is a piece of music for a miniature staged ballet (at least it is derived from such a ballet and perhaps is seen here in an idealized form), it gives evidence that the dance movement of the concert suite—that is, the suite not functionally connected either with the theater or with the ballroom—was breaking down and being transformed into pure concert music. Even earlier than Neubauer, however, nondance forms had appeared in the suite: the suites of Andreas Hammerschmidt (1639) contain lyric movements called "airs." [29]

Let us go back for a moment and look at the suite as a whole once

[29] Moser, *Geschichte der deutschen Musik*, II[1], 110.

more. Neubauer's inclusion of an allemande and a sarabande in this and two other suites of his 1649 manuscript gives evidence of the gradual intrusion of the French suite on German soil. The sequence of allemande, courante, and sarabande had appeared in Copenhagen in 1626, whence it had migrated to France.[30] We saw above (page 77), that the typical French suite of the time just before 1650 contained the three movements just mentioned, plus a gigue. In the latter four-movement form it was taken over by the lutenists (Denis Gaultier), clavecinists (Louis Couperin and Jacques Champion de Chambonnières in France and Johann Jacob Froberger in Germany), and we see its partial adoption in the Neubauer suites of 1649. From 1650 on, the French suite became increasingly popular. Johann Kaspar Kerll (1627–1693) in Germany, Matthew Locke (c. 1630–1677) and Benjamin Rogers (1614–1698) in England, and Johann Rosenmüller (a transplanted German whom we shall meet again) in Italy were among the first composers outside France to write ensemble suites in the new form.[31]

The tendency toward stylization of individual movements became almost a characteristic in these new French suites. The allemande, for example, took on the nature of a prelude, with fast passages in eighth and sixteenth notes. The courante and the sarabande acquired a degree of rhythmic diversity and motive manipulation, all within the framework of the homophonic style. The gigue alone retained a bit of contrapuntal imitation; its fast, two-part form usually included a fugal type of exposition complete with episodes and the motive-overlapping structure known as "stretto." Each of the four movements exhibited the combination of a harmonically three-part form within a formally two-part form; in general the diagram

$$\underbrace{\text{tonic-dominant}}_{A} : \lVert : \underbrace{\text{dominant}}_{B}\text{-}\underbrace{\text{tonic}}_{A}$$

[30] Norlind, "Zur Geschichte der Suite," in *Sammelbände der Internationalen Musikgesellschaft* (March, 1906), VII[2], 186.
[31] Adler, *Handbuch*, I, 566.

was characteristic. Wilhelm Fischer [32] calls attention to the fact that just in those countries where the suite was dominant, namely, France and Germany, no collective name for the set of dances was available. In Italy the term *partita* had been in use as early as 1603; Tarquinio Merula had introduced the term *sonata da camera* in 1637. In France and Germany, on the other hand, the suite appeared either with a fanciful title—Schein's *Banchetto musicale* is an example—or as a collection, such as Neubauer's "Newe Pavanen, Galliarden," or with a general term, as *pièces de luth*. In Germany the term *partita*, or *partie*, became general; not until just before 1700 was the term "suite" adopted in France. In the eighteenth century such terms as *ordre*, as in François Couperin, 1713, or "overture," referring to the predominant position of the suite's first movement, came into general use as collective names for the dance suite. But we are getting ahead of the story, and must return to an account of the inclusion of nondance types in the suite.

As noted above, the suites of Andreas Hammerschmidt (1639) contained "airs." Neubauer's tentative introduction of a lyric phrase within a dance movement (1649) has been mentioned. In the period after 1650 new dances and nondance movements were inserted into the suite in ever-growing numbers. Two types may be distinguished: [33] one, usually placed between the sarabande and the gigue, often called *intermezzo;* another, placed at the head of the suite as a prelude or introduction.

Among the *intermezzi* various movements were in common use. (1) Dances of other nations, or native dance tunes that had found no place in the suite heretofore, or revivals of obsolete dances. Polonaise, hornpipe, rigaudon, siciliano, minuet, gavotte, bourrée, and passepied were among the more popular newcomers. One of the last four usually appeared paired with another of the same type (for example Minuet I and II, or Bourrée I and II), with the second in a different key, after which the first was repeated. It became customary in the orchestra suite to set the second dance (Minuet II, for example) with a smaller instrumentation than the first (three voices

[32] *Ibid.*, p. 567.   [33] The following is based on Fischer, in *ibid.*, I, 568–570.

in many instances); thus arose the *trio*, which in the form of minuet-trio-minuet *da capo* persisted in sonata, quartet, and symphony until well into the nineteenth century. And the appearance of the trio in a related key was the first breakdown in unity of tonality that the suite had suffered; heretofore, of course, all movements had been in the same key.

Others among the *intermezzi* were (2) airs, or arias, which were sometimes dances whose names had been lost or simply pieces in two-part form without particular dance characteristics. (3) Rondeaus were, in the French suites, movements whose principal characteristic was an alternation of solo and chorus episodes (of course, in an instrumental sense), each consisting of an eight- or sixteen-measure period. The melody of the rondeau was usually cast in a particular dance rhythm; hence hybrid movements such as *minuet en rondeau* and *gavotte en rondeau* are sometimes found in French suites. (4) Variations of previously heard movements: *double*, which might be a contrapuntal variant of the preceding dance, and *agrément*, which was an ornamented version of the dance heard just before it. (5) *Basso ostinato* forms, the best known of which were the chaconne (*ciaconna*) and passacaglia (*passacaile*). These dances were characterized by a constantly reiterated short phrase in triple meter heard in the bass, over which a series of contrapuntal variations of that phrase was played.

The other group of nondance forms was attached to the beginning of the suite; it is with this group that we shall shortly find our way back to Italy, to the *sonata da chiesa* and *sonata da camera*. The tendency to begin the dance suite with a nondance form can be seen before 1650. It reveals itself in three ways: the nondance form (1) replaces the first movement, (2) is attached before the first movement, and (3) influences the alteration of the first movement itself. We have called attention to the degree of stylization found in the pavane in the 1620's and 1630's. A similar change took place in the allemande about 1650; it, too, lost a great deal of its dance-like character and took on the character of an introduction. As early as 1650 Johann Rudolf Ahle (1625–1673) and Johann Martin Rubert

(c. 1614–1680) had written what they called "trio sonatas," in which the first movement bore the title *sinfonia;* Johann Jakob Löwe (1628–1703) had followed suit in 1658.[34] Movements of the *toccata* type, but variously called *toccata, praeludium,* or *praeambulum,* appeared in the works of Esajas Reusner (1667) for lute and Johann Kaspar Kerll for harpsichord. In the orchestra suites of Johann Rosenmüller, published in 1667, we find an Italian *canzone* [35] used as the first movement. Although the movements are called *sonata, sonatine* or *sinfonia,* the combination of the Italian *canzone* and the French-German dance suite resulted, and the way was clear for the subsequent split of the sonata literature into the separate lines of *sonata da chiesa* and *sonata da camera.*[36] We shall, in the next chapter, return to Italy to trace the events which were to give rise to those two sonata types (*da chiesa* and *da camera*) and were to prepare the way for the direct ancestor of eighteenth-century chamber music: the trio sonata.

[34] One sinfonia reprinted by Riemann in *Sammelbände der Internationalen Musikgesellschaft,* VI, 505 ff.   [35] See p. 108 for an elaboration of this point.
[36] Moser, *Geschichte der deutschen Musik,* II¹, 110.

5

SONATA DA CHIESA AND SONATA DA CAMERA

LET US begin by making an assumption. Assume that the *canzone* and the sonata in Italy about 1650 are still sufficiently related in structure and style to justify a common name; and let that name be The Form (capitalized). We do this in the paragraph which follows, so that we make a generalization about the last half of the seventeenth century, one that will aid materially in clarifying a puzzling situation. We are about to see a number of interesting developments in The Form, which make its influence felt until half a century after its demise in another style period and in another country.

At the end of Chapter 3, in Italy about 1628, The Form was beginning to show four contrasting sections in place of the larger number of sections or fragments it had had earlier. In the present chapter we shall first bring The Form up to 1667. Then we shall watch it disintegrate into a series of four separate movements called church sonata (*sonata da chiesa*). But we shall also see its four sections compressed into a single movement, see it attached at the head of the dance suite we examined in Chapter 4, which by this time is being cultivated in Italy, and see this series of movements called chamber sonata (*sonata da camera*). Thus, The Form has become a whole series of movements in the *sonata da chiesa*, and a single movement in the *sonata da camera*. Later in the chapter we shall see these two types of sonata combine to give rise to the "trio sonata." There we shall have the strange phenomenon of a series of movements derived from the four sections of The Form, with The Form itself shrunk into one movement and serving as the headpiece of the series. From here on the explanation becomes a problem for the

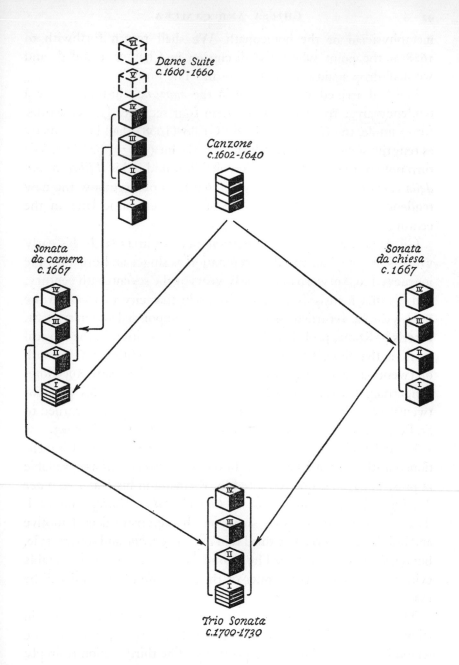

Dance Suite
c.1600-1660

Canzone
c.1602-1640

Sonata
da camera
c.1667

Sonata
da chiesa
c.1667

Trio Sonata
c.1700-1730

THE EVOLUTION OF SONATA TYPES

metaphysician or the homeopath. We shall return forthwith to 1628 at the point where the discussion in Chapter 3 ended; and we shall drop again the common term "The Form."

We had arrived at that place in the *canzone's* history where a tendency arose to have no more than four sections. Earlier works, for example, the *Capriccio a 4*, by Grillo (1608), had had as many as ten; the sonata "La Orlandina," by Marini (1617), had five. We turn now to two *canzoni* by Frescobaldi, found in his *Il libro primo della canzoni ad 1, 2, 3, 4* (Rome, 1628), to observe how the new tendency became a characteristic of chamber music later in the century.

Girolamo Frescobaldi was born at Ferrara in 1583. In his early years he enjoyed an excellent reputation as singer and organist. He journeyed to Antwerp in the early years of the seventeenth century, and his first madrigals were published in that city in 1608. In the same year he returned to Italy and was appointed organist at St. Peter's in Rome, probably the most honored position in the musical world at that time. The popularity and great reputation of this youth of twenty-five were enormous, to judge by the many anecdotes concerning his early successes. Frescobaldi retained this post for twenty years, and after a five-year absence in Tuscany, returned to St. Peter's for ten more years, from 1633 until his death in 1643.

Frescobaldi's collection of five *canzoni da sonar* of 1628 was mentioned at the end of Chapter 3. Three of these *canzoni* are available at present writing: one reprinted by Riemann in his *Handbuch der Musikgeschichte*,[1] and two in his *Old Chamber Music*, Volume I. The first is a true *canzone*, with its characteristic dactyl motive and imitative texture. The third is in mixed *canzone* and sonata style, but is not yet a true sonata. The second, however, shows considerable evidence of being a forerunner of the *sonata da chiesa*, and will be examined in detail.

The piece is for *due canti e basso*, and is in five sections: slow in triple meter, fast in duple, slow in duple, fast in triple, and moderate tempo in compound meter, respectively. The third section is simply

[1] *Handbuch*, II², 142.

a phrase five measures long, heard in the bass and imitated once by each of the upper voices. It is reproduced here as an excellent example of how great beauty is achieved with economy of means.[2]

The features which attract our attention here are found in the first four sections: (1) the use of homophonic style in the first, third, and fourth sections, and the retention of polyphonic style in the second; (2) the slow tempo of the first section, with a consequent lack of *canzone* characteristics; (3) and most important for the future, whereas contrasts between the other sections are introduced abruptly (either through a change from triple to duple meter, or from slow to fast tempo, or both), no such contrast exists between the fourth and the fifth sections. The fifth grows out of the fourth, as the example below shows, and the piece as a whole gives the effect

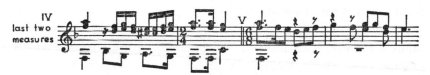

of being virtually in four sections. And this Frescobaldi work is not alone in thus relating sections to one another. Many other pieces of the time exhibit the same device, and a work with more than four sections is seldom found after the 1630's.

The sections themselves become longer and increasingly independent. For an example of this development we turn to the *Symphoniae 1, 2, 3 violinarum*, by Nicolas à Kempis (c. 1610–c. 1660), published in 1644. In these works the tendency is seen to separate the

[2] In this place, as in many others, Riemann's overelaborate realization of the *continuo* destroys the charm of Frescobaldi's inspiration.

sections entirely and to let each stand alone. Riemann reprints the thirteenth *Symphonie* in his *Old Chamber Music*, Volume IV; we may take it as being typical of the set. And although it is for one violin and bass, the form and style characteristics of the *sonata a 3* are present. The work is in four sections; the first is in broad duple meter and consists merely of a broad lyric melody with its repetition. The second section, in fast duple meter, is concerned largely with the development of a short rhythmic motive: ♪♫♫ ♫ ♫♫│♩ The third section, in slow triple, has a similar motive which is similarly developed; a five-measure extended cadence intervenes between the third and the fourth sections. The fourth section, again in fast duple has yet another version of the rhythmic motive. Each of the four sections of this work gives the impression of being longer than it really is, because of the skillful avoidance of cadences, the spun-out nature of the phrases, and the sequential treatment of the various motives. Obviously, when cadences appear only two or three times in an extended section (the four sections range from nine to twenty-one measures in length), when they lead to new sections in greatly contrasting tempo and meter, and when a feeling of unity within sections is achieved, the four-movement form is close at hand.

The next decided step forward in the direction of a four-movement form can be seen in a work by Marco Uccellini (c. 1605–c. 1667), *Delle sonate over canzoni da farsi a violino solo e basso continuo*, Opus 5 (1649). Riemann prints the second of these sonatas in his *Old Chamber Music*, Volume IV. It is now time to speak of separate movements rather than sections: the four parts of this work are extended considerably beyond any we have examined previously. And Uccellini is consistent in his use of one device for achieving this greater length in these monothematic structures: he depends upon sequence repetition of a fairly long phrase, then allows the phrase to dissolve into running scale figures. In this manner he is able to write a piece three of whose parts (first, second, and fourth) are forty-four, sixty-five, and forty-one measures long, respectively. Only in the third part does he revert to the older practice, for here the part breaks off after six measures. Thus, each of the longer parts is more than twice as long as corresponding parts or sections of earlier works in this form. And the feeling of length is enhanced here, as it was in the Nicolas à Kempis work above, by skillful use of cadences, mainly at the end of each part. Further, the use of a well-marked cadence only at the end of a part does more than strengthen a feeling of the part's length; it also serves to separate that part from that which follows. Of all the works examined in these pages, this is the first which can be said to have separate movements. And what was achieved in this work, and in other contemporary works in which the same tendency is to be observed, became common property in the years following 1649. From that date forward we are no longer justified in speaking of sections in this type of sonata; we shall refer entirely to movements.

We turn now to the works of Giovanni Legrenzi (c. 1625–1690). This eminent composer of operas, cantatas, and chamber music was active at Venice as the director of the Conservatory of the Mendicants and during the last five years of his life as chapel master of St. Mark's. His Opus 2, published in 1655, contains eighteen *sonate a due e tre*. We shall examine the thirteenth of the set, entitled "La Valvasona," for two violins and violoncello. This sonata contains four movements, in the expected fast and slow tempos and in the expected duple and triple meters. The first movement, thirty-three measures long, contains elements reminiscent of the old *ricercare*, yet is in an open, transparent style in which nothing more involved than imitations of previously heard phrases is attempted. The second movement, consisting of sixteen measures in slow tempo, contains a broad lyric melody accompanied in part in homophonic style, in part by bits of countermelody. The third movement is forty-seven measures long, and is almost entirely in note-against-note style. The last movement, twenty measures in length, is again fugal; the contrapuntal lines accompanying the principal motives are derived from the motives themselves.

The noteworthy features of this sonata are: (1) the four-movement form, with the greatest emphasis put on the first movement (even though the third is a few measures longer); (2) the intrusion of so many contrapuntal elements in a style that is essentially homophonic. These features are found also in other chamber-music works of Legrenzi's, notably in another work from Opus 2, "La Savorgnana." [3] But in that work the third movement is extremely short, as in the Nicolas à Kempis sonata discussed above, and serves merely as an introduction to the fourth. Thus, hardly a decade after the sonata had been enlarged and quartered, so to say, it began to lose its third quarter. We shall see in the following paragraphs that the next step in the evolution of chamber-music forms is in the direction of a three-movement form—for a few years, at least.

Toward the middle of the seventeenth century the long and noble line of great organists in Italy showed signs of dying out. Two of the greatest masters of that instrument, Frescobaldi and Monteverdi, organists at Rome and Venice, respectively, died in 1643. No worthy successors of these giants being immediately available, many of the duties of church organists devolved upon instrumental groups. Portions of the musical part of the Roman Catholic service were given to string ensembles for performance with appropriate music drawn from the sonata literature existing at the time. A name for the appropriate selections from this literature had appeared in 1637, with Tarquinio Merula's *Canzoni, overo sonate concertate per chiesa e camera*, to be followed in 1655 by Marini's *Sonata da chiesa e da camera*. These works, according to Hugo Riemann,[4] are essentially *canzoni* (presumably of several movements) with some added dance movements. For church use, he implies, the dance movements were omitted, and a church sonata (*sonata da chiesa*) resulted.

A distinct separation of the sonata literature into two functionally different types, however, was not immediately forthcoming. Not until 1667, with the publication of Giovanni Battista Vitali's (c. 1644–1692) Opus 2, did the *sonata da chiesa* as such appear with name and content pointing to its sacred function. The essential fea-

---

[3] A fragment reprinted in Riemann, *Handbuch*, II², 156–164.
[4] *Ibid.*, p. 419. But whereas he calls them *canzoni*, we, in the light of modern research, know them to be sonatas.

tures of its opposite type, the *sonata da camera*, had existed since early in the century (Brunelli in 1616, Buonamente in 1637, both mentioned on page 78); but the naming of the type and the determination of its content were delayed until about 1667, when Rosenmüller became active in Venice. Let us examine Vitali's work and defer a discussion of Rosenmüller until later in this chapter.

The tendencies shown in the works of Frescobaldi, à Kempis, Uccellini, and Legrenzi become characteristics in Vitali's *sonate da chiesa*. The characteristics which this type developed until it began to fuse with its relative, the *sonata da camera*, are in general as follows: (1) three separate movements, often with a short slow movement before the second or third; (2) the first and last movements in fast duple meter and contrapuntal style, with a degree of thematic relationship between them; (3) the second movement a slow lyric piece in triple meter, rather homophonic in style. Vitali's *Sonate a 2 violini col suo basso continuo per l'organo*, *Opus 2*, published in 1667, show these characteristics in general.

Let us look at the first sonata of this set, reprinted in *Old Chamber Music*, Volume IV. There is a first movement in fast duple meter, with a fugue subject which would do credit to any eighteenth-century composer, so far has Vitali traveled along the path of instrumental style; the texture is contrapuntal throughout. There is a second movement in slow, broad duple meter, largely note-against-note, with the violins in parallel thirds most of the time. There is a third movement in fast triple meter, largely in homophonic style, but with a contrapuntal section in which the initial portion of the first movement's fugue theme is employed. So far this sonata conforms. But then there follows another slow section in duple meter and homophonic style, leading directly into a fourth movement, again in fast duple meter and contrapuntal in style. Here the second half of the first movement's fugue theme is much in evidence. It is as though the two halves of one large movement were separated by an interpolated slow section; the halves are unified by giving to each half a portion of a single theme employed in an earlier movement.

The form of the entire sonata might be diagramed: A—B—aca', and the general characteristics mentioned in the preceding paragraph are seen to hold true for this sonata also.

There comes a time in the history of every musical medium when one composer, more gifted than his fellows, arrives on the scene to summarize, clarify, and in a sense give a new impulse or a new direction to the evolution of that medium. In the early history of chamber music that composer was Arcangelo Corelli (1653–1713). At the age of seventeen Corelli was an accomplished violinist and a member of a famous orchestra in Bologna. Moving to Rome in his early twenties, he soon established a reputation as an outstanding virtuoso and an excellent conductor. He was employed by popes, honored by royalty, and died universally admired and respected. His system of violin teaching was copied in all parts of Europe and forms the basis for modern methods. Corelli has rightly been called the "father of violin playing," both for his solid accomplishments in the field of teaching and for his achievements in clarifying and perfecting a true violin style in his compositions. His work in the latter field brought to an end a century of experimenting with the problems of violin style.

Corelli's complete works total no more than six sets of sonatas and concertos, with twelve compositions in each set. On these seventy-two works Corelli spent almost thirty years. Gone was experimenting with form and structural details; instead he was preoccupied with new expressive devices, new ways of making the violin to sound, and new concepts of melodic beauty. The complete works are as follows: [5] Opus 1, published in 1681, containing twelve *sonate da chiesa;* Opus 2, 1685, with twelve *sonate da camera;* Opus 3, 1689, again with twelve *da chiesa,* and Opus 4, 1694, with twelve *da camera;* these forty-eight works are all for two violins and bass with *basso continuo.* Opus 5, from 1700, contains six *sonate da chiesa* and six *da camera* and is for one violin and bass with *basso continuo;* [6] finally,

[5] Published in Chrysander, *Denkmäler der Tonkunst,* Vol. III. Arnold, in *The Art of Accompaniment from a Thorough-bass,* p. 189, attributes the sonatas of Opus 1 to 1681 rather than to the customary 1683.
[6] The twelfth sonata of Opus 5 is the famous variation set "La Follia."

Opus 6, from 1712, contains twelve *concerti grossi*, of which eight are *sonate da chiesa*.[7] Let us look at the works of Opus 3, to see in what important respects Corelli differs from his predecessors.

All but one of the twelve *sonate da chiesa* of Opus 3 have four movements; the exception, the last of the set, has six. All twelve of the first movements are in mixed homophonic and imitative style: some with broad chordal passages, others with lyric melodies above a moving bass line, and ten of the twelve are in slow tempo. Here is the first major deviation from the norm as established in the *sonata da chiesa* of Vitali. Now to Corelli's second movements: nine of the twelve begin with fugal expositions, and eleven are fast. And it is noteworthy that in the one sonata (No. 6) in which the second movement is slow, the movement is very short—fourteen measures—and leads directly into the third movement, which is in turn fast and in fugal style, is the only fast third movement of the set, and has in all details the characteristics of Corelli's second movements. The fourth movements are the least alike: while they are all fast, four are contrapuntal, and eight are homophonic. In content, five are dance movements, three consist largely of broken-chord figurations, three have quasi-fugal beginnings, and one consists largely of short phrases played in parallel thirds.

It is at once obvious that Corelli has added a movement at the head of the sonata as established by Vitali. The other movements conform to the model: the second movements (Vitali's first) are fast, in duple meter, and largely contrapuntal; the third movements (Vitali's second) are slow, generally in triple meter, and almost always homophonic. In the fourth movements (Vitali's third) a new element appears: while they are all fast, and either in duple or compound meter, they are not in the main contrapuntal. Instead of fugal movements Corelli writes dance-like tunes, idealized and stripped of objectionable dance characteristics (be it remembered that these are church sonatas). Through clever and charming employment of dotted rhythms, occasional syncopations, and considerable use of the bass in antiphonal passages (where the bass answers the two violins

[7] Opus 3 was published at Modena; Opus 4 at Bologna; the others at Rome.

which are playing in parallel thirds), Corelli succeeds in introducing an air of lightness and charm in place of the sometimes stodgy contrapuntal movements of his predecessors.

Another important difference between Corelli and Vitali comes to light when one considers the former's addition of a first slow movement. Vitali had established a sequence of forms which ran to a fast-slow-fast pattern. Corelli, by adding a new first movement, set up a slow-fast-slow-fast arrangement. The dualism which had existed earlier in the century returns again: the *canzone*-sonata conflict is again apparent. For where the *canzone* had begun fast and contrapuntally, the sonata had begun in slow tempo and in homophonic style. Vitali's *sonate da chiesa* represent a late flowering of *canzone* elements, concealed and considerably altered, it is true, but still conforming in general to the *canzone* pattern. Corelli, on the other hand, with his slow homophonic beginning movements, held to sonata elements; yet his *sonate da chiesa* contain within them (in their last three movements) what is left of the *canzone*. We shall see in later chapters that Corelli's scheme, or rather shall one say the scheme of the sonata, had longer life. One has only to look at the French opera overture, or even at the slow, homophonic introductions of eighteenth-century symphonies, to see how long-lasting was this particular aspect of sonata style.

There is some danger of thinking that all the eventful development of seventeenth-century music took place on Italian soil. Such is far from true. While we must look for originators or innovators in that geographic region in many cases, we cannot afford to overlook the consequences of such innovators' work in other parts of Europe. Corelli, for example, was not the only great composer to follow in the path marked out by Giovanni Battista Vitali. England had one bright moment in the musical history of the late seventeenth century, centered around the work of one of her greatest composers; that moment was the direct consequence of the work done by other great composers in other countries.

In 1683, two years after Corelli published his Opus 1, Henry Purcell published at London a set of *Twelve Sonnatas of Three Parts.*

Purcell, the son of a violinist in the Royal Band (of violins) of Charles II, was born about 1659. At an early age he came under the influence of French music, for his teacher, Pelham Humphrey, had been sent to Paris to study with Lully and remained an avid and successful imitator of that master's style. Purcell became organist at Westminster Abbey in 1680, at the age of twenty-one, and remained in that position until his death in 1695. He wrote vast quantities of church music, more than fifty works for the theater, including the well-known opera *Dido and Aeneas,* many secular songs, pieces for keyboard instruments, fantasies for strings (three to eight parts) and two sets of chamber-music sonatas: the set of twelve mentioned above (1683) and a set of ten, published by his widow in 1697. All this, and he died when he was thirty-six! Although much of his work is uneven in quality, he remains one of England's greatest composers and one of the great masters of all time.

But not only the French style was influential in England in Purcell's day. Italian works circulated widely, Italian musicians held honored positions in London's musical life, and Italian influences were felt in church and chamber music. It is not surprising, then, to discover that Purcell acknowledges the Italian influence in the preface to his first set of sonatas. He says "he has faithfully endeavor'd a just imitation of the most fam'd Italian Masters" and "he is not mistaken in the power of the Italian Notes, or elegancy of their Compositions, which he would recommend to the English Artists." There is no direct evidence as to which Italian models Purcell had before him; the editor of the composer's complete works, J. A. Fuller-Maitland, surmises that Giovanni Battista Vitali's Opus 5, *Sonate a 2, 3, 4, e 5 stromenti* (Bologna, 2d ed., 1677), may have served, for that work contains sonatas strongly resembling Purcell's.

The two sets of sonatas,[8] the twelve of 1683 and the ten of 1697, may be considered together, for they are much alike. Most of them have five movements; the others either four or six, except number 6 of the second set. The latter is a one-movement chaconne, consisting of forty-four variations of a five-measure phrase. Of the twenty-

[8] In Purcell's *Complete Works,* ed. by Fuller-Maitland, Vols. V and VII.

one sonatas having from four to six movements, all but two of the first movements are slow and in duple time, and all but three are contrapuntal in style. Sixteen of them contain movements marked "canzona," most usually (eleven out of the sixteen) appearing as the second movement. The rest of the movements do not lend themselves to generalizations; there is no system apparent in placing them in the sonatas. While about half of them are arranged in accordance with tempo alternations of slow-fast-slow-fast, the other half seem to overlook this principle of contrasting tempos. In two cases three, and in one case four, slow movements follow one another, with no fast tempo intervening. True, there are differences between an adagio, a largo, and a grave; Purcell was aware of these differences, for in the preface to the 1683 set he defines "—*Adagio* and *Grave*, which import nothing but a very slow movement: *Presto Largo*, *Poco Largo*, or *Largo* by It Self, a middle movement." In the order of meters, too, there is a similar lack of regularity. Two or three movements in duple time are followed by one or two in triple, in most cases. Only in one sonata, number 7 of the 1697 set, is there a regular alternation of duple, triple, duple, triple, and duple. Purcell does make this concession to the god of contrast, however: he does not allow two movements to follow each other without changing either tempo or meter, again with one exception: the fifth sonata of the 1683 set has four consecutive slow movements, of which the first two are both in duple time. This lengthy paragraph forces one to the conclusion that one cannot generalize successfully about the sequence of movements in these two sets. Let us try again, this time examining the contrasts of style.

The sonatas indicate that Purcell was at home in both the lyric French and the dramatic monodic Italian styles. But he was also of the race that had produced William Byrd a few generations earlier, of the race that had been so successful in developing the contrapuntal arts of the thirteenth and fourteenth centuries. Purcell's style, in these two sets of sonatas and in much of his church music, is essentially contrapuntal. And to indicate the quality of his contrapuntal writing, Láng [9] mentions the well-known fact that a *toccata* and fugue of Purcell's, copied out in admiration by Bach himself, were included in the great edition of the Bachgesellschaft as being that master's own work.

We should expect to find, then, and we do find, that the great majority of the movements in these sonatas are in contrapuntal style. Of the more than one hundred separate movements, more than three-quarters are contrapuntal. The nature of the counter-point ranges from a "canon in twofold augmentation in the 5th and 8ve above" (first movement of the sixth sonata of 1683), through the magnificent chaconne which is the sixth sonata of the 1697 set, through movements which contain true fugal expositions, through movements which are full of skillful imitations of one phrase, to movements made up of chains of countermelodies. Purcell is equally competent in fast, moderate, and slow movements, and his skill and

[9] *Music in Western Civilization*, p. 418.

imagination in the chaconne are masterful. He succeeded to a great degree, as Bach did to a greater, in casting his contrapuntal ideas into regular phrases of four or eight measures, thus avoiding the feeling of formlessness one so often experiences in less successful contrapuntal music.

The noncontrapuntal movements (twenty-six of them) are about equally divided between slow in triple meter and slow in duple, with two others in fast triple meter. Nine additional movements, scattered throughout the two sets of sonatas, are in mixtures of note-against-note and contrapuntal styles; these include three in slow triple, two in slow duple, and four in fast triple meter. It is the twenty-nine slow movements which give these sonatas their strongest link with the Italian *sonate da chiesa*. The triple-meter largo and adagio movements especially are close to the corresponding movements of Corelli, in the lyric beauty of their melodies, the freshness of their cadences, and at times their resemblance to sarabandes.

The last-mentioned characteristic, insignificant as it may seem in an overall view of Purcell's sonatas, is of great importance to the future of this sonata type. We saw the tendency in Corelli to depart from contrapuntal last movements (as they were in the case of Vivaldi) and write dance-like tunes in a light and airy manner. This tendency appears again in Purcell, for the last movement of the ninth sonata in the 1683 set is practically a siciliano. Purcell wrote it in 6/4 meter; it is better notated in 12/8. The rhythmic figure typical of that dance form (♪·♫ ♪·♫) is never long absent; the movement flows along in a lively manner, and must have pleased Purcell's patron, Charles II, who is said to have found much church music entirely too dull. Another movement, the fourth movement of the seventh sonata of 1697, one can easily mistake for an eighteenth-century minuet, so dainty, lilting, and charming are the melodic and rhythmic aspects of the piece.

In neither of these two sets of 1683 and 1697 did Purcell indicate the type of sonata he was writing. But the evidence is overwhelmingly in favor of calling them *sonate da chiesa*. The differences between these and other sonatas of that type are largely in sequence of movements and the quantity of contrapuntal writing. And, as we have seen from a comparison of Vitali and Corelli, a hard and fast formula for sequence of movements was not characteristic in the great Italian masters either. The similarities between these three composers lie closer at hand, for there is in all of them an outward adherence to formal models, coupled with a desire to make melodies expressive and suited to the character of the violins for which they were written. Each in his own way was successful; if Purcell's way is more contrapuntal, nothing is lost and the literature of chamber music has gained much.

We have progressed to a point about thirty years past the establishment of the *sonata da chiesa*. With the tendency to introduce dance-like tunes into that sonata type, as we have seen Corelli and Purcell inclined to do, we are approaching the next large event in the history of chamber-music forms: the merger of the *sonata da chiesa* with the *sonata da camera*. But before we allow the former to merge, it will be well to examine the form it is about to merge with. Let us retrace our steps and progress beyond the dance suite as we left it at the end of Chapter 4 in Germany and follow it to Italy.

We had arrived at the stage, in the history of the dance suite in Germany, at which nondance movements were being admitted into the suite. In the decades after 1650 a variety of intermezzos, arias, rondeaus, and the like were found within the suite, and various kinds of *toccate, sinfonie,* and other forms were attached to its head. One composer may be singled out for having been most consistent in the type of introductory movement he employed, for having introduced the German form of the dance suite to Italy, and for attaching to the transplanted suite a functional term, the *sonata da camera*.

Johann Rosenmüller (c. 1620–1684) was born near Leipzig, and received his education and early employment there. Imprisoned for moral lapses, he escaped in 1655, and shortly afterward arrived in Italy. He remained there until 1674, when he was pardoned, recalled to Germany, and given the post of chapel master at Wolfenbüttel. He had written much church music and a number of dance suites before his imprisonment. But the portion of his work that is significant here was written in Italy. We turn to Rosenmüller's publication, at Venice, about 1667,[10] of eleven *Sonate da camera cioè sinfonie* for five instruments. This set is reprinted in Volume XVIII of *Denkmäler deutscher Tonkunst.*

The sequence of movements in eight of the eleven sonatas is identical: *sinfonia, alemanda, correnta, ballo,* and *sarabanda.* In two more cases an *intrata* is inserted after the *correnta,* and in one case an *intrata* plus an extra *alemanda* and *correnta.* We have met all the above dance movements before, except the *ballo.* That is a lively dance in duple meter in which a dotted rhythmic figure (♩♪ ♩♪ ♩♪) is heard throughout the movement. The *sinfonia,* as Rosenmüller writes it, however, is a new form in the dance suite and deserves to be examined. Let us look at one of these introductory movements in detail: the *sinfonia* of the second sonata is typical.

The movement is characterized by a number of short sections, all note-against-note, and contrasting in tempo and meter. The form may be diagramed as follows:

$\frac{4}{4}$Adagio	$\frac{4}{4}$Allegro	$\frac{4}{4}$Adagio	$\frac{4}{4}$Allegro	$\frac{4}{4}$Adagio
3 meas.	*5 meas.*	*3 meas.*	*9 meas.*	*4 meas.*

$\frac{3}{2}$Adagio	$\frac{4}{4}$Adagio	$\frac{4}{4}$Allegro	$\frac{4}{4}$Adagio	$\frac{3}{2}$Adagio
19 meas.	*11 meas.*	*11 meas.*	*7 meas.*	*19 meas.*

At first sight this example of Rosenmüller's style of writing, in which the movement is divided into ten sections, seems to be more extreme than any we have yet seen. But on closer inspection one sees that all sections are in duple meter except the sixth and the tenth, and the two latter are the same length. Examination of the music

[10] These sonatas have been attributed to 1667 ever since J. G. Walther (*Musikalisches Lexikon,* p. 533) gave the dates of their two editions as 1667 and 1671. Karl Nef, in the foreword to D.D.T., Vol. XVIII, refers to the only known printed copy of these sonatas (in the library at Zurich), and finds it dated 1670. He concludes that if 1671 is the date of the 2d ed., then the date of 1670 on the copy here referred to may be that of the 1st ed. But evidence on this point is not conclusive.

shows further that these two sections are identical in all respects. Let us now arrange the ten sections into four groups (labeled A, B, C, and B, respectively), as follows:

(A)

$\frac{4}{4}$Adagio—Allegro—Adagio—Allegro—Adagio

(B)　　　(C)　　　　　　　　　　　　　　(B)

| $\frac{3}{2}$Adagio | $\frac{4}{4}$Adagio—Allegro—Adagio | $\frac{3}{2}$Adagio

This arrangement into four groups of sections or parts is seen to be justified if the other sonatas of the set are examined. In every one of the eleven *sinfonie* in this set, (1) the second and fourth parts are always in triple meter, and the fourth is an exact repetition of the second, (2) the third part always contains an adagio-allegro-adagio group, (3) all parts and sections except the second and the fourth are in duple meter. In every case an ABCB form results.

The adagio sections of parts A and C have several points in common. The style is always note-against-note, and the content is always a chord progression; nothing more. A few measures taken from the eleventh sonata's beginning will show the style that is typical of all the A and C slow sections. Rarely does a phrase consist of more than five or six chords.

Each phrase comes to a cadence, either perfect or Phrygian, a hold is placed over the last chord, and after an empty half-measure a new phrase is begun. And this is not an isolated construction; it is found in practically all the adagio sections of the A and C parts in all eleven sonatas. What expressive purposes may we attribute to Rosenmüller in these movements, written several decades after comparatively long movements, and nonsectional ones at that, were well established?

First is the obvious fact that these *sinfonie* of Rosenmüller's are modeled on the overture of the Venetian opera. Be it remembered that the sonatas were written at Venice, to which city the composer had fled. Rosenmüller had every opportunity to hear the new operas, notably those of Pietro Francesco Cavalli, written in the new, intensely dramatic style that was to make Venetian opera famous for half a century. He absorbed the operatic overture style that was at once pompous and dramatic, sensational and lyric, and adapted it to the dance suite, with one important modification: he always repeats the second part of the *sinfonia*, the section in triple meter. Are these first movements really *canzoni?* It must be pointed out that many histories give Rosenmüller credit for attaching the *canzone* at the head of the suite; this assertion originated in the period when the distinction between the *canzone* and the early seventeenth-century sonata was not well understood. Thanks to Miss Crocker's dissertation in that field,[11] that distinction can now be made. One may indicate that these *sinfonie* of Rosenmüller's are not *canzoni*, but sonatas, as a comparison of their style elements with those of the sonata type described on page 60 will show.

Second is the hypothesis that these slow chordal sections may have provided the violinist with a harmonic background upon which to improvise. It is at this time well established that slow movements of most seventeenth- and early eighteenth-century instrumental works contained only the harmonic and melodic outlines of the composer's ultimate musical intentions. A melodic line of a few long notes, unrelieved by any rhythmic vitality or great melodic charm, was written with the understanding that the performer would improvise an appropriate ornamental variant of the phrase. A judicious selection of mordents, trills, scale runs, figurations, and the like were inserted as the good taste and creative imagination of the performer dictated. We see the results of that practice in the florid, highly ornamented adagios of the Haydn string quartets a century later,

[11] See p. 28*n* for bibliographical data.

except that there the ornaments and embellishments are all specifically indicated by the composer. It seems likely that musicians and public alike would have been dissatisfied with these austere chord progressions separated from the pomp and display of the operatic stage, and would have demanded the same type of improvised embellishment they were hearing in the solo sonatas of no less a composer than Vitali.

The innovations of Rosenmüller were immediately accepted. Diedrich Becker, in 1668, at far-off Hamburg, published a set of *Musikalische Frühlingsfrüchte* (Musical Fruits of Spring) which contained, among other works, four suites having Italian sonatas as first movements.[12] These are expanded beyond Rosenmüller's dimensions and are more contrapuntal and somewhat tighter in form.[13] Johann Pezel's (16?–16?) *Leipzigischen Abendmusiken*, 1669, contains twelve suites, eight of which make use of sonata first movements. The fifth part of Johann Kaspar Horn's *Parergon musicum*, published at Leipzig in 1676, contains five suites on the same model as those just mentioned.[14] And a number of other works published between 1670 and the end of the century are similarly built.

But the innovations of Rosenmüller were in general not long lasting. By 1682, with the publication of Johann Sigismund Kusser's (Cousser) *Composition de musique selon la methode française*, a new type of first movement had found its way into the chamber-music suite, and the suite itself was designed for a larger ensemble; orchestra music emerges, and takes a path of development away from chamber music and toward the symphony. Suites of dances after 1682 are in general for orchestra or for keyboard instruments. For these media they were written until the middle of the eighteenth century, culminating their development in the great orchestra suites of Bach, the suites for solo violin and solo cello by the same composer, and the innumerable French and English keyboard suites by many late Baroque composers.

---

[12] Nef, *Geschichte der Sinfonie und Suite*, p. 64.
[13] Riemann, *Handbuch*, II², 419.
[14] Nef, *Geschichte der Sinfonie und Suite*, pp. 68–70.

The new first movements found in Kusser's suites are modeled on the French overture introduced into the opera by Jean-Baptiste Lully (1632–1688). This was a two-part form: a slow section of large dimensions built on a dotted rhythmic figure (♪.♪ ♪.♪ ♩) was followed by a fugal allegro which often ended with a few measures in slow tempo. The whole was characterized by the high degree of pathos expected of a piece which was to introduce and set a mood for the opera. The French overture form was not only used successfully by Lully's successors in Paris, but found wide application in Germany, in orchestra suites, oratorios, and operas. The style derived from that form is an important part of the familiar Handel style. As late as 1750 its rhythms and its sequence of tempos were influential in shaping the new Classical symphony.

Let us review briefly the various versions of the dance suite as they appeared about 1682. (1) The version we have just examined, represented by Kusser's suites of 1682, very quickly took on an orchestral dress, appeared for combinations of string and wind instruments, and became a suite for orchestra. We lose interest in this version, then, for its further history has little in common with chamber-music forms. (2) The version introduced by Rosenmüller, about 1667, with a sonata as a first movement, was quickly hailed and as quickly forgotten. Rosenmüller, as we know, borrowed his innovations from the Venetian opera overture; separated from the lights, glamor and dramatic atmosphere of the opera house, his fragmentary sonatas seem not to have been adapted to introducing a series of dances. At any rate, there is little evidence that Rosenmüller's sonata movements introduced any permanent changes into chamber-music forms. (3) The version of the dance suite mentioned in passing in the discussion of the suite in Italy [15] (in Brunelli and Buonamente), a version that is relatively little known, seems to have been more influential in the future of chamber-music forms than either of the others. It is this version upon which Corelli based his *sonate da camera*, and from the latter to eighteenth-century chamber music is but a short step.

[15] See pp. 78 ff.

We turn again to Arcangelo Corelli, for his thirty-four works of the above type are, like his *sonate da chiesa*, among the most successful compositions of the late seventeenth century in Italy. The *sonate da camera*, including those for violin and bass and those for *concerto grosso* as well as those in which we are most interested, namely, those for two violins and bass, are found in the following: twelve in Opus 2, 1685; twelve [16] in Opus 4, 1694; numbers 7 to 11 of Opus 5, 1700 (Opus 5 is for violin and bass); the last four of Opus 6, 1712 (these are *concerti grossi*). We are justified in including the portions of Opera 5 and 6 listed above, for the difference in instrumentation does not carry with it a difference in form or style. We shall first look at the twelve sonatas of Opus 4, for they are typical of all of Corelli's *sonate da camera*.

The sonatas in general are short; one has two movements, eight have three, and three have four. There are in each of the sonatas a prelude and one, two, or three of the following dances: allemande, courante, sarabande, gavotte, and gigue, placed in no special order. Six of the dances (one each in sonatas 1, 2, 4, 7, 9, and 10) are preceded by short introductory movements varying in length from five to seventeen measures. The introductions are slow, in duple time, and without dance characteristics. Each of them is attached to the dance which follows by means of a Phrygian cadence. Throughout the seventeenth and the eighteenth centuries this old modal device was used to indicate a half close and to indicate that the movement in which it was found was to proceed directly into the next. Furthermore, the introductions are of two kinds: three are in note-against-note style; three are contrapuntal. But all are similar to the internal slow movements of Corelli's *sonate da chiesa* and would not be out of place in those works, except that they are all in duple meter, whereas two thirds of the slow movements in the church sonatas of Opus 3 and Opus 5 are in triple meter.

An interesting relationship to past centuries comes to light here. In the twelfth and thirteenth centuries, at the time when metrical notation was being established, the only possible meter was a triple

[16] Not six, as Riemann asserts in *Handbuch*, II², 421.

one. Based on its analogy to the Trinity, it seemed the obvious meter for the sacred music of that time. When, in the fourteenth century, the rise of secular music is to be observed, one finds that a duple meter became possible. To distinguish between the two meters, the terms of perfect (referring to the Trinity) for the triple meter, and imperfect (symbolizing the worldly aspects of the music) for the duple, came into use. It seems quite likely that in Corelli's choice of triple meter for the sacred slow movements (in the church sonata) and duple meter for the secular slow movements (in the chamber sonata) we see a faint, idealized reminiscence of this ancient practice. That this practice was not consistently carried out goes without saying; there is probably as much duple-meter church music in the period from 1400 to 1700 as there is music in triple meter. One can, however, account for the appearance of the old *tempus perfectum* in the *sonata da chiesa* and *tempus imperfectum* in the *sonata da camera* by pointing out these metrical characteristics of medieval sacred and secular music.

The dance movements themselves, which make up the body of these sonatas, do not differ essentially from their German and French counterparts. They are almost entirely in homophonic style, are based largely on broken-chord figurations, as the example on page 113 demonstrates. The tempo indications are not invariably in the expected relationship to the dances, however; we find, out of three sarabandes, one in the usual slow tempo, one in 3/4 meter and marked vivace, and one in 6/8 marked allegro. Several of the courantes are marked vivace instead of the more sedate allegro, and two of the seven allemandes are marked presto. Of these last dances, only one of the seven begins with the up-beat characteristic of older and more northern allemandes. Finally, throughout all the dances the bass part has become much more animated, takes part in imitations of violin figures, and requires a degree of technical proficiency comparable to the violin parts.

In *sonate da camera*, as in *sonate da chiesa*, the first movements are always the most important, for they exhibit the greatest changes from one period to another; they best show the prevailing trend of forthcoming changes, and they carry the style elements of the seventeenth century most directly to eighteenth-century sonata form. The first movements of Corelli's Opus 4 are similar to the twelve *sonate da camera* of Opus 2 and the five of Opus 5. They are in a mixed homophonic and imitative style, averaging about twenty-four measures in length; and the majority are slow and in duple meter. Several are based on broad chordal figurations, a few have lyric melodies; but almost all have beautifully moving and expressively melodious bass lines. These characteristics they share with the Opus 3 *sonate da chiesa* we have looked at.

One feels that everywhere in these first movements there is a successful attempt to write dignified, melodious pieces of music, free of formal restrictions and free of pomp and empty display. This is also true of the other slow movements, in *chiesa* and *camera* alike. Lyric charm and expressive melody are found everywhere that the tempo of the music permits. While the fast movements seldom can have lyric moments, because of their speed and dance characteristics, they are like the slow movements in that in both classes every trace of the domination of vocal style elements is removed. The figurations, scale passages, and in general all the melodic contours are those that grow out of the nature of the string instrument, and are those that we have associated with instrumental style ever since Corelli's day. The long road from the *da sonare o cantare* works of the early 1600's, through the attempts of Rossi and Marini, reaches its terminus in these sonatas of Corelli. The patterns for violin style were laid down for all to see, for all to admire, and for all to imitate. Corelli, almost unique among seventeenth-century composers, is as much respected today as he was in his own time.

In the decades following the publication of Corelli's work, the two sonata types branched out into new instrumental fields. We have seen that a large number of erstwhile *sonate da camera* became orchestra suites with French overtures at their head. Similarly, a line of *sonate da chiesa* for keyboard instruments arose, as composers for the harpsichord and organ adopted the forms and style of the church sonata. Johann Kuhnau (1660–1722) was perhaps the first in this field with his publication of sonatas for harpsichord in 1692 and 1696, sonatas which are in all essentials *sonate da chiesa*.[17]

Composers who remained with the chamber-music ensemble instrumentation of two violins, bass, and *basso continuo* continued to flourish in the years following 1685 or so. The types of *da chiesa* and *da camera* mutually began to influence each other, to take on characteristics one from the other. Soon the formal distinctions between the types disappeared, and we can speak of one combined form: the trio sonata. That discussion will form the content of the next chapter.

[17] The keyboard works of Kuhnau, reprinted in Vol. IV of D.D.T., consist of four sets: *Klavierübung*, Part I, 1689, contains seven suites of dances similar to the instrumental *sonata da camera*. Part II (four editions from 1692 to 1726) contains seven suites similar to those in Part I; but also, in an appendix, contains one sonata in B flat, which is probably the first work in *chiesa* form for a keyboard instrument. This sonata, along with seven similar works found in the *Frische Klavierfrüchte* (five editions from 1696 to 1724), transfers the form of the *sonata da chiesa* to the keyboard. It is on these works that K. P. E. Bach built when he founded the three-movement sonata in Classical sonata form. The *Musikalische Vorstellung einiger Biblischen Historien*, 1700, completes the list.

6

THE TRIO SONATA

LET US review briefly the chief characteristics of the two sonata types existing at the end of the seventeenth century. The *sonata da chiesa*, whose four movements were derived from the four sections of the *canzone*, was essentially a serious work, contrapuntal in style, and well adapted to its function of contributing to the church service. Even though the second and the fourth movements of the sonata were in fast tempo, they were still felt to be suitable for sacred use. As much as seventy-five years later Charles Burney reports his visits to churches in Paris in these words: "When the Magnificat was sung he (the organist) played likewise between each verse several minutes, fugues, imitations, and every species of music, even to hunting pieces and jigs, without surprising or offending the congregation, as far as I was able to discover." And about a visit to St. Roque's church to hear M. Balbastre, "great latitude is allowed the performer in these interludes; nothing is too light or too grave, all styles are admitted." [1] Thus, we can account for gay and dance-like movements in some of Corelli's *sonate da chiesa*, and we must realize that they were suited to the needs of the church of his day.

The *sonata da camera*, regardless of whether its first movement was derived from a French overture, from a Venetian opera overture, or from an early *sinfonia*, was still largely a set of dances, usually homophonic in style. The separate dances had, during the course of several decades, become stylized, their dance rhythms had become obscured through the addition of bits of imitation and bits of lyric melody; and, finally, many nondance movements had been inserted

[1] Burney, *The Present State of Music in France and Italy*, pp. 37, 41.

into the sonata. The most obvious of such added movements was, of course, the overture or *sinfonia* or prelude found at its head. Notably in the *sonata da camera* of Corelli, the first movement was in the nature of an introduction; typical violin figures were exploited, or broad passages in homophonic style were presented. Movements within the sonata were often slow in tempo, again in homophonic style and lyric in character.

We have, then, in the *sonata da chiesa* a type of movement which is light and dance-like, and in the *sonata da camera* a type of movement which is slow and serious, and consequently nondance-like. The differences between the two sonata types were minimized still further in the early decades of the eighteenth century, and the similarities became more pronounced. But the terms distinguishing the opposing types continued in use long after the essential differences in the types themselves had disappeared, much as the terms had existed long before the two types had achieved separate status (for example, in Merula's *Canzoni, overo sonate concertate per chiesa e camera* of 1637). Although a number of composers, both German and Italian, continued to use the old terms, an equal number adopted the more inclusive new term, "trio sonata." And the history of chamber music in the first half of the eighteenth century is essentially the history of the latter form.

Among the Italian instrumental composers in the generation immediately following Corelli's we may mention Francesco Geminiani (1680?–1762), Giuseppe Torelli (c. 1658–1709), Antonio Caldara (1670–c. 1736), and Niccolò Porpora (1686–1767). But the most significant of chamber-music composers of that generation was Evaristo Dall'Abaco. This eminent violinist was born at Verona in 1675. In his twenty-sixth year he moved to Munich, and shortly thereafter entered the employ of the Elector of Bavaria, in whose service he remained active until 1740. His works [2] include: Opus 1, twelve *sonate da camera*, c. 1705; Opus 2, twelve *concerti a 4 da*

[2] The works of Dall'Abaco were published without date; consequently, they can be related to particular years only approximately. Sandberger, in the Preface to D.T.B., Vol. I, gives the dates as shown here; he bases his surmises on hints in the prefaces of the sonatas, Dall'Abaco's nearness (in Belgium or France) to places of publication, and similar evidence.

chiesa, c. 1712–1714; Opus 3, twelve *sonate da chiesa e camera,* c. 1712–1715; Opus 4, twelve *sonate da camera,* c. 1714–1716; Opus 5 (c. 1717) and Opus 6 (c. 1730) are concerti for various instruments. Dall'Abaco died in 1742 at Munich.

Three works of Dall'Abaco are contained in the *Collegium musicum* series; thirty-six others are found in Volumes I and IX of the *Denkmäler der Tonkunst in Bayern;* [3] a few other works are scattered in other editions. These works give evidence that Dall'Abaco was a composer second only to the great Corelli in melodic invention, purity of style, and nobility of expression; and in contrapuntal skill he at times overshadowed his predecessor. We shall present examples of his style below, after having examined the form of his trio sonatas. To this end we will select the three sonatas Opus 3, numbers 4, 5, and 9, found in the *Collegium musicum* series.

One is immediately struck by the fact that these works (here we include the thirty-six sonatas in the *D.T.B.* in our generalization) exhibit a regularity of form not found in any of their predecessors; and we shall find later that trio sonatas by Caldara, Locatelli, Telemann, and Handel share this characteristic. Almost invariably the sonatas contain four movements in slow-fast-slow-fast sequence; almost invariably the third movement is in triple meter. This is true in trio sonatas of both the *chiesa* and the *camera* types. Gone are the interpolated introductions to fast movements in the *chiesa* sonatas; gone are the added fifth and sixth movements in the *camera* sonatas. Rather than an arbitrary inclusion of any number from two to six movements, one finds the regularity of number which proceeds in an almost unbroken line down to the middle of the nineteenth century.[4]

[3] Vol. I contains Opus 1, Nos. 2, 4, 5, 6, 7, 11; Opus 2, Nos. 4, 5, 8, 9; Opus 3, Nos. 2, 3, 6, 12; Opus 4, Nos. 3, 4, 5, 6, 8, 11. Vol. IX contains Opus 1, Nos. 1, 3, 8, 9, 10, 12; Opus 3, Nos. 1, 8, 10, 11; Opus 4, Nos. 1, 2, 7, 9, 10, 12. Riemann's *Collegium musicum* contains, in Nos. 41–43, the following: Opus 3, Nos. 4, 5, 9.

[4] The following exceptions to these general statements must be noted: of the thirty-nine available works of Dall'Abaco (see note 3), twenty-seven contain four movements, and all but two of them are in slow-fast-slow-fast tempo sequence; nine of the remainder have either two, three, or five movements; one has a five-measure interpolated introduction to the fourth movement; two have similar short introductions to the third movements.

The first two of the Dall'Abaco works here being examined (Opus 3, numbers 4 and 5) are *sonate da chiesa;* number 9 is a *sonata da camera;* and the sonatas are so labeled by the composer. One sees, however, a continuation of the trend first noticed in the sonatas of Corelli and Purcell: the inclusion of dance-like movements in the *chiesa,* and a considerable use of counterpoint and rhythmic diversity in the *camera* type. The D major *sonata da chiesa,* number 5, contains, for example, a third movement which is in all respects a sarabande; and on the other hand, the allemande and the gigue of number 9 are almost entirely imitative, with a consequent lessening of dance characteristics. One expects *sonate da chiesa* to be written in a contrapuntal style; but when a *sonata da camera* contains passages like the following, the essential differences between the two types have practically disappeared.

In the slow movements of these sonatas Dall'Abaco succeeds in establishing an atmosphere of beauty and reverence, which for purity and charm is not exceeded even by the great Corelli. There is no longer any experimenting with violinistic effects. Corelli had for all time laid the foundations of violin style, and Dall'Abaco is

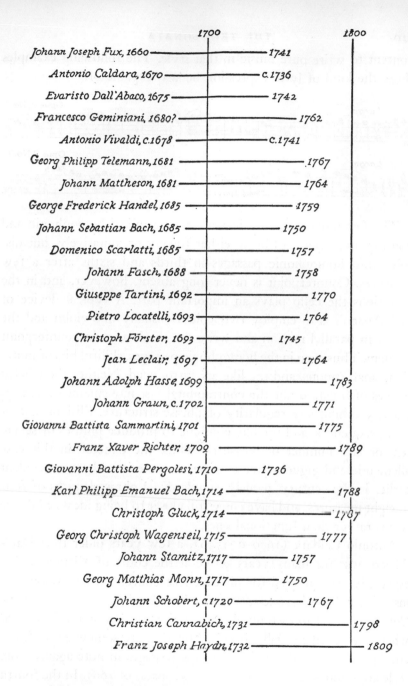

1700   1800

Johann Joseph Fux, 1660 ———————— 1741

Antonio Caldara, 1670 ———————— c.1736

Evaristo Dall'Abaco, 1675 ———————— 1742

Francesco Geminiani, 1680? ———————— 1762

Antonio Vivaldi, c.1678 ———————— c.1741

Georg Philipp Telemann, 1681 ———————— 1767

Johann Mattheson, 1681 ———————— 1764

George Frederick Handel, 1685 ———————— 1759

Johann Sebastian Bach, 1685 ———————— 1750

Domenico Scarlatti, 1685 ———————— 1757

Johann Fasch, 1688 ———————— 1758

Giuseppe Tartini, 1692 ———————— 1770

Pietro Locatelli, 1693 ———————— 1764

Christoph Förster, 1693 ———————— 1745

Jean Leclair, 1697 ———————— 1764

Johann Adolph Hasse, 1699 ———————— 1783

Johann Graun, c.1702 ———————— 1771

Giovanni Battista Sammartini, 1701 ———————— 1775

Franz Xaver Richter, 1709 ———————— 1789

Giovanni Battista Pergolesi, 1710 ———————— 1736

Karl Philipp Emanuel Bach, 1714 ———————— 1788

Christoph Gluck, 1714 ———————— 1787

Georg Christoph Wagenseil, 1715 ———————— 1777

Johann Stamitz, 1717 ———————— 1757

Georg Matthias Monn, 1717 ———————— 1750

Johann Schobert, c.1720 ———————— 1767

Christian Cannabich, 1731 ———————— 1798

Franz Joseph Haydn, 1732 ———————— 1809

LIFE SPANS OF EIGHTEENTH-CENTURY COMPOSERS BEFORE HAYDN

content to write pure music in that style. The following examples show the kind of lyric expression he was capable of.

The fast movements are in general in a mixed homophonic and contrapuntal style. All begin either fugally or imitatively, but dissolve into homophonic passages in thirds and sixths after a few measures. Counterpoint is never long absent, however, and in the imitations the cello plays an important part. A typical device of Dall'Abaco's is to employ two voices (usually one violin and the cello) in parallel motion and write the third voice in counterpoint to them. Thus even in the homophonic passages, skillful bits of imitation, small canons, and the like are introduced. Neither the labeled dances of sonata 9 nor the contrapuntal fast movements of sonatas 4 and 5 exhibit any regularity of phrase structure. Elisions, extensions, sequences, and the like combine to produce phrases of seven, ten, or any number of measures. Thus, the dances—in this case allemande and gigue—have lost the characteristic that was evident earlier in the century, namely, standardized phrase lengths of four or eight measures, and have come still closer to being idealized dance forms rather than functional ones.

Antonio Caldara (1670–c. 1736), a few years older than Dall'-Abaco, was for many years active at the court of Vienna, and is especially remembered for his excellent church music. Among his instrumental works, one *sonata da chiesa* has been preserved in the *Collegium musicum* set, number 44. This work is a bit old-fashioned when compared to Dall'Abaco's. Melodies are somewhat stiff, the counterpoint is traditional, and a few passages in note-against-note style are reminiscent of Rosenmüller's sonatas of 1667. In the fourth movement of this sonata, Caldara makes use of the old broken-chord device found in Vitali, Buonamente, and as far back as Rossi's *Varie sonate* of 1613.

These instrumental works of Dall'Abaco and Caldara were written near the beginning of the eighteenth century. Contemporary with them were the many other trio sonatas and concertos by the great and small Italian masters composing at all the courts of Europe; the Italian gift for melody, the traditions of Vitali, Torelli, and Corelli, were alive in these composers and established the style of the first half of the eighteenth century. But northerners were not idle during this period; in 1696 Dietrich Buxtehude (1637–1707) published his fourteen trio sonatas for violin, viol da gamba, and *basso continuo.*

Buxtehude was born at Helsingborg, near the southern tip of Sweden, in 1637. In 1668 he succeeded Franz Tunder at the organ of St. Mary's Church at Lübeck. There, in 1673, he instituted the *Abendmusiken:* church concerts for the several Sundays before Christmas. These elaborate concerts, replete with soloists, chorus, and orchestra, and for which Buxtehude composed many cantatas became famous throughout Europe. Bach journeyed on foot from Arnstadt to Lübeck in 1705, drawn thence by the great reputation of the concerts and their founder. Buxtehude died at Lübeck in 1707.—In these few lines is condensed the essential biography of one of the great composers of the generation before Bach. Famous as an organist and master of improvisation at that instrument throughout his lifetime, Buxtehude was an important figure in the line from Heinrich Schütz (1585–1672) to Bach. In his music, Italian dramatic and lyric elements and north German seriousness and technical skill are brought together in the light of his own vivid imagination and typically Baroque enthusiasm and humor. Here is no mere predecessor of Bach, but a great composer in his own right, without whom a Bach might not have been possible.

Among Buxtehude's chamber-music works are two sets, with seven sonatas in each, labeled *Suonate à doi, violino e viola da gamba, con cembalo*, Opus 1 and 2, respectively, both published in 1696. Both are contained in the *Denkmäler deutscher Tonkunst*, Volume XI; included with them are a suite for the same combination, a sonata for two violins, viol da gamba, and harpsichord, and a sonata for viol da gamba, violone (bass viol), and *continuo*.

In the fourteen sonatas which comprise Opera 1 and 2, we are immediately faced with a form which contains elements of the German suite of the 1650's, of the Italian *canzone* of the same period, and of the *sonata da camera* of the 1670's. As to the first, there are a few dance movements scattered here and there in the sonatas; as a notable example, Opus 2, number 4, originally contained four melodically related dance movements, which suite was discarded when Buxtehude prepared the sonatas for publication.[5] As to the second, there is no organizing principle apparent in either the type, the order, or the length of the movements; the sonatas range from three to twelve movements or sections, the length of which varies from a four-measure adagio to a hundred-and-thirty-four-measure allegro—these features remind us of the *canzone*. As to the third, there is a short phrase structure broken by pauses, a mixture of homophonic and contrapuntal style, and a use of virtuoso elements —all similar to the early *sonata da camera*. Let us examine the first sonata of Opus 1 in detail; the choice is justified, for all fourteen are of the same amorphous type.

The formal and stylistic elements of the sonata may be tabulated as shown in the chart on page 123.

Thus, it is seen that there is no regular alternation of fast-slow, or of duple-triple, nor is there regularity of any other sort. Key relationships of various movements are likewise impossible to classify. In one case (Opus 2, No. 1) keys of B flat, D major, F major, G minor, and D minor are found; in another (Opus 1, No. 6, with twelve movements) one meets the keys of D minor, B flat, C minor,

---

[5] According to Stiehl, writing in the foreword to Vol. XI of D.D.T. The suite is found in the appendix to that volume.

F major, and A minor. On the other hand, in other sonatas of five to seven movements, one finds only one or two movements in different keys. Harmonically, Buxtehude is much closer to modal writing than are many of his predecessors, Corelli and Rosenmüller, for example. Many cadences and many chord sequences sound harsh to an ear accustomed to the tonal progressions of eighteenth-century Vienna. And in the mixture of styles, Buxtehude is unique. One has come to expect an alternation between counterpoint and homophony in successive movements. But Buxtehude changes style radically within movements. The last movement of Opus 1, No. 1, for example, begins with four measures in homophonic style, followed by a fugal exposition; this gives way to a section in imitative counterpoint, with material unrelated to the fugue; this in turn, to a homophonic section which employs repeated note figures; finally there is a return to fugal construction, with a few homophonic measures added to close the movement. All this occurs within forty-seven measures.

TEMPO	METER & LENGTH	TONALITY	STYLE
Vivace	$\frac{4}{4}$ 27 meas.	F, cadence in C	Contrapuntal
Lento	$\frac{4}{4}$ 6 meas.	F major	Homophonic
Allegro	$\frac{4}{4}$ 40 meas.	F, cadence on the dominant of D	3-part fugal with counter-themes
Adagio	$\frac{4}{4}$ 12 meas.	D minor, cadence in F	Mixed contrapuntal and homophonic
Andante	$\frac{6}{8}$ 40 meas.	F major	Homophonic 3ds & 6ths
Grave	$\frac{4}{4}$ 11 meas.	B flat, cadence in F	Homophonic
Presto	$\frac{4}{4}$ 47 meas.	F major	Fugal-homophonic

The forms encountered in the various movements are of great interest. There is a large proportion of fugal movements, but as has been indicated above, not consistently in fugal style. There are many improvisatory, cadenza-like movements, for violin alone, or for viol da gamba alone. There are several sets of variations over a *basso ostinato* motive. There are a few quasi-sarabandes and gigues. In practically all these various forms the element of brilliance is present, along with dramatic surprises, unexpected turns of phrase, and sudden style changes. This music is exciting, to a degree not encountered previously in any of the earlier Italian or German chamber-music works.

The elements of excitement and enthusiasm are especially evident in the fugal movements. The fugue, derived from the Italian *ricercare*, had up to this time been a rather staid and reserved movement, even when in fast tempo. In Buxtehude we encounter a new type of fugue theme and a new type of fugal treatment. Short rhythmic motives, characterized by many repeated notes, separated by short pauses, full of effervescent humor, are typical of Buxtehude's fugues. A selection of his themes is given, to illustrate the characteristic humor and sparkle of these movements.

These themes are treated in a great variety of ways, used in homophonic as well as contrapuntal contexts, always with energy and liveliness. The slow movements which surround these fast fugal ones (and all the fugues in these fourteen sonatas are fast) serve as interludes or transitions; rarely are they extensive enough to develop lyric melodies in the style of the Italian sonatas. The overall impression one receives from the sonatas is one of speed, virtuosity, and humor, so large is the proportion of fast movements. The rhythmic treatment Buxtehude affords all his musical material is especially noteworthy. There are no dull moments, no feeling of something about to happen; things happen all the time, and there lies the particular charm of these sonatas. /

In summary, one must conclude that while these two sets of sonatas, published in 1696, are in themselves valuable as music and delightful as repertoire material, they are somewhat off the line that leads from Corelli through Dall'Abaco to Haydn. Buxtehude has more in common with his predecessors than with those who come after him. His use of viol da gamba in place of a second violin is a case in point; while his contemporaries were writing trios for two violins and bass, Buxtehude retains a member of the viol family, a family that was well on the way to obsolescence in his day. Earlier north German works, notably the dance suites, had employed five string instruments: violins and viols of various sizes. Buxtehude is among those writing for the trio, but he prefers the darker tone color that only the viol can provide. He stands at the crossroads, musically, harmonically, formally, and instrumentally.

Returning to the path which leads more directly from Corelli to Haydn, we next encounter the chamber-music works of Buxtehude's near neighbor and consistent admirer, George Frederick Handel. Handel was born at Halle an der Saale in 1685, the birth year of Bach and of Domenico Scarlatti as well. Destined (by his father) to be a lawyer, he entered the University at Halle in 1702; but the following year he went to Hamburg and immediately became interested in opera. Within two years (by 1705) he had his first two operas performed, and a year later journeyed to Italy. During the years of his stay there (1706–1710) he wrote several operas and oratorios, was honored by distinguished personages in Venice, Florence, and Rome, and became acquainted with eminent musicians, notably the two Scarlattis and Corelli. The latter was of great influence on the young German master, for the nobility of Corelli's ideals and the purity of his style struck answering chords in Handel's heart. Returning from Italy in 1710, Handel remained in Germany for a short while before moving permanently to London. Dozens of operas, 1712–1736, and many oratorios, 1732–1751, were his main contributions to the musical literature. Organ works, orchestral suites, and instrumental concertos, along with the chamber music about to be discussed, complete the list. Handel died in 1759, and was buried in Westminster Abbey.

The amount of his chamber music is not large, in comparison to his enormous output of operatic and choral works. There is first a set of six trio sonatas for two oboes and *basso continuo*, written, according to Chrysander in Volume XXVII of Handel's *Complete Works*,[6] when Handel was eleven years old.[7] Next, published as Opus 1, in 1724, is a set of fifteen solo sonatas (one instrument and *basso continuo*), some for violin, others for recorder, flute, or oboe.[8] Opus 2, published in 1733, consists of nine trio sonatas for two violins (or flutes or oboes) and *basso continuo*.[9] Opus 5, published in 1739 or 1740, contains seven more for the same combination.[10] All these thirty-seven works are reprinted in Volume XXVII of the *Complete Works*. Volume XLVIII contains a few scattered works, including

[6] Published by the Deutsche Händelgesellschaft.
[7] The complete comment reads: "Handel's earliest composition, from his eleventh year (1696)." It may be stated in passing that Moser (*op. cit.*, II[1], 279) and Leichtentritt (*Händel* [Stuttgart, 1924], p. 820) believe the sonatas to have been written much later.
[8] The first edition, published by Witvogel, at Amsterdam, in 1724, contains twelve sonatas. Several later editions, by Walsh, at London, between 1732 and 1740, contain fifteen. This may explain Eric Blom's assertion (in Williams, *Handel* [London, rev. ed., 1935], pp. 106, 226) that Handel began composing these sonatas (the last three?) in 1732.
[9] The first and second editions, published by Walsh at London, contained six sonatas. When later Chrysander found three isolated sonatas at Dresden, he added them to the original six and introduced them, in Vol. XXVII of the *Werke*, as Nos. 3, 8, and 9 of Opus 2.
[10] It may be well to point out that in Handel's music only the instrumental works bear opus numbers, of which Opus 7 (organ concertos published posthumously in 1760) is the last.

an excellent sonata for viol da gamba and *basso continuo* and a transposed version of one of the sonatas of Opus 1. In line with our arbitrary policy not to consider solo sonatas in this book, we shall omit
any discussion of Opus 1 in the paragraphs that follow, and confine
our observations to the three sets of 1696, 1733 (Opus 2), and 1739
(Opus 5).

Like the trio sonatas of Dall'Abaco, Handel's six sonatas of 1696
are in a four-movement form, in the order slow-fast-slow-fast. The
first movements, all marked adagio, are in contrapuntal style, imitative but not fugal. The difference between these two is, of course,
that in the latter the imitations regularly occur on tonic and dominant, while in the former the interval chosen for the imitation is
most often the unison, and the imitation is in general neither complete nor exact. Occasionally, as in sonatas IV and VI, the counterpoint in the two upper parts gives way to passages in thirds and sixths;
in these cases, the imitations are carried out by the bass—a device
we found in Dall'Abaco also. The style in general is majestic, with
considerable use of dotted rhythms reminiscent of the French overture of Lully and characteristic of Handel throughout his lifetime.
Obviously, there can be no lyric melodies in a style compounded of
short motives heard contrapuntally and many dotted rhythmic
figures; hence the appeal of these movements must be found in their
consistency of style, neat turns of phrase, and inexorable progression
toward the cadences.

The second movements are, on the other hand, fugues of quite
definite construction; they are complete with expositions in related
keys, stretto (a stretto in a fugue is a condensed, overlapping section leading to the climax of the movement), and coda. So large
do the dramatic and melodious aspects of Handel's style loom when
one considers his operatic and choral works, that one sometimes
loses sight of the fact that his contrapuntal skill was second to none.
These movements should do much to remind one that contrapuntally,
too, Handel was one of the great masters. The melodic invention of
the majority of these fugues is not outstanding. Some themes are
angular; some remain tied to one spot. But the effectiveness of the

development of the themes cannot be denied; good proportion, musical excitement, and well-defined climax are all there to a great degree. In all except sonata V the bass is equal in importance to the two oboes; three-voice fugues result. The fifth sonata's second movement is two-voiced, the bass providing a homophonic accompaniment.

In the third movements also, sonata V provides an exception, which it shares with sonata I. In these two cases the third movement is merely a short duple-meter interpolation between second and fourth, has as its first chord the resolution of the dominant chord with which the second movement closed, and proceeds directly to the fourth by means of a Phrygian cadence. The third movements of the other sonatas, however (numbers II, III, IV, and VI), are fairly long (averaging thirty measures), are complete in themselves, and have the further distinction of being in a key different from the tonality of the other movements. When the sonata is in major, the third piece is in the relative minor (III, E flat—C minor; IV, F major—D minor; VI, D major—B minor); in the minor sonata the relationship is reversed (II, D minor—F major).[11] Furthermore, these slow movements are all in triple meter, as opposed to the duple-meter slow first movements. While contrapuntal style prevails, there is a noticeable absence of the dotted rhythmic figure characteristic of the first movements; in its place are melodic fragments which occasionally combine into lyric phrases of no remarkable beauty.

The fourth movements are all fast, all in imitative contrapuntal style, and full of bustling scale figures which require a certain vir-

[11] This reference provides a good place briefly to recapitulate the breakdown in the sonata's unity of tonality. Originally all the movements of the early seventeenth-century dance suite had been in the same key. After 1650, when it became customary to add to the suite two related movements in the same form (in the sequence Minuet I, Minuet II, Minuet I repeated), the second of the two was placed in a different key, usually the dominant (see p. 87, above). In the latter half of the century this practice was extended, in the sonata types, to other movements as well. In Corelli, for example, we find that thirty of his seventy-two sonatas and concertos have one movement in a related key; it is usually the slow movement of the major sonatas which is placed in the relative minor key. By the turn of the century (c. 1705) the practice was general, and any sonata containing all movements in the same key must be looked upon as archaic.

tuosity to play successfully. It is interesting to observe that in these works (for oboes) there is a complete absence of the broken chords and string alternations so typical of violin style. These devices one does find in many of the solo sonatas of Opus 1 and the trio sonatas of Opus 2 and Opus 5, which, be it remembered, are for violins *or* flutes *or* oboes. One can be sure that Handel actually had the oboe in mind when writing this first set of trio sonatas; the "or flute or oboe" phrase must have been added to the three sets of violin works either as an afterthought or at the publisher's suggestion. When one remembers how freely Handel's publishers, particularly Walsh at London, approached the works, one may assume that the alternate instruments were included on the title-page merely to increase the sale of the Opera 1, 2, and 5 sonatas.

With a few exceptions, what has been said about the six trio sonatas of 1696 applies to the nine trio sonatas of Opus 2, for two violins and *basso continuo*.[12] Here again is the four-movement alternation of slow-fast-slow-fast, except in sonata V, which contains a fifth movement in fast tempo, and in sonata IX. In about half of the first movements the dotted rhythmic figure is not found; the style remains contrapuntal, however, and the prevalence of figures with repeated notes may be mentioned. In several of the second movements the regular fugue writing characteristic of the 1696 sonatas is absent. In these cases there is a return to the imitative style of the first movements, and the fugal relationships of tonic-dominant are not present in the sequence of the imitations. The third movements of the two sets most resemble each other: the same change of key is at hand (relative minor or major); the same near approach to lyric melody; the same use of triple meter. Only in sonata IX is there an exception: the third movement is in fast duple meter, homophonic in style with parallel thirds and sixths; but it is, like the other third movements, in the related key (C sharp minor in an E major sonata).

Looking at these two groups of trio sonatas together (those ascribed to 1696 and the set of Opus 2), one is struck by the remarkable

[12] Leichtentritt, *Händel*, p. 823, unaccountably lists the third of this set in D minor. Three movements are in F major, and only the third movement is in D minor.

technical skill Handel exhibits in them. Granted that the melodic materials are not exceptional, the total effect produced is one of great maturity in handling the materials. The dramatic moments and the great lyric breadth one finds in the operas are missing for the most part. But those factors are not components of early eighteenth-century chamber music, and one does wrong to look for them here. What one does have is music entirely suited to the trio-sonata instrumentation, music in which every detail is clear and well-proportioned, and music that is delightful to play. One often suspects that Handel improvised on paper in writing his dramatic works, thereby achieving a certain spontaneousness at the cost of well-proportioned forms. These trio sonatas are definitely not improvised; yet, strangely enough, the spontaneity is not lost in the process of composing them. They are not world-shaking, but they are excelled in musical worth only by the really great instrumental works of the period, notably those of Dall'Abaco.

The two sets of trio sonatas examined thus far, the set attributed to 1696 and that of Opus 2, are related to the line of the *sonata da chiesa*, without, however, being so named. The prevalence of counterpoint, the absence of dance rhythms, the fugal second movements —these are all *da chiesa* characteristics. The next set of Handel's works we shall examine, the seven trio sonatas of Opus 5 (1739), are just as obviously related to the *sonata da camera*, again without being specifically so named. One cannot generalize about the form or style of these works; each has several unique features, and no two are exactly alike. Thus only sonata I has five movements; VII has five movements plus a short introductory adagio of five measures before the third movement; IV has five movements, the second containing two different tempos; V has six movements; II has six also, but the fourth is a recapitulation of the second; III, with six movements, contains an alternate version of the second movement; VI, with six movements, includes a variant of the fifth.

In content, too, the sonatas show considerable diversity. It is as though Handel only gradually became reconciled to the idea of writing *sonate da camera*, for in sonata I only the last movement is a dance form, in II three movements are dances, in III and IV, four and three respectively. Then the dances decrease in number, for sonatas V, VI, and VII contain only one each. Nor is there regularity in the order: sonata III's last four movements are a sarabande, an allemande, a rondeau, and a gavotte; sonata IV contains a *passacaile*, a gigue, and a minuet as the last three movements. The *passacaile* is noteworthy in that variations 1–12 and 18–20 are in major, while only 13–17 are in minor, thus contradicting the textbooks which describe this form as being predominantly in the minor mode. The three dances of sonata II are a musette and its *da capo* (separated by a lengthy allegro in duple meter with brilliant passage work for the first violin), a *marche* and a gavotte. A *bourrée*, two minuets and two gavottes are scattered elsewhere in the sonatas. All these fifteen dances are predominantly in homophonic style, with passages in note-against-note or in parallel thirds and sixths. Even the *passacaile* of sonata IV is largely homophonic, contrary to the nature of most dances in this form.

Of the twenty-odd nondance movements remaining, two-thirds are in homophonic style. All seven of the first movements are included in this group (six slow, one fast); here they differ greatly from the corresponding movements of the first two sets of sonatas, for the Lully-like dotted rhythm is present only in a few passages, and the skillful imitations characteristic of the sets of 1696 and Opus 2 are noticeably absent. In many of the nondance movements, slow and fast alike, rapid and brilliant passages for the first violin abound. The virtuoso element is present in these sonatas to a great degree, and the demands made upon the third instrument (bass or cello) are as great as those upon the violins. Finally, the remaining eight movements—the other one-third of the twenty-odd—are fugues of the same quality as those found in the 1696 set. The same completeness as to dominant and subdominant expositions, logical episodes, stretto, and coda is found, and the themes themselves contain much more melodic interest.

This last point is in general true of the entire set of Opus 5. While the contrapuntal technique is as masterful as in the works of a decade or two earlier, there is a happier choice of rhythmic and melodic materials. The examples below will show the kind of melody to which Handel has turned in this set of trio sonatas. The period 1735–

1740 marked the emergence of the organ concertos, the *concerti grossi* for strings, and Handel's shift from opera to oratorio. At the height of his musical powers, he could not help but impregnate these trio sonatas with the dramatic power and lyric beauty of which he was now master. Perhaps such factors as drama and lyricism inevitably bring with them a lessened use of counterpoint. Thus, Handel at this time composes *sonate da camera* instead of the more contrapuntal *sonate da chiesa*. But a glance at the fugal movements of these sonatas will assure one that Handel had not lost his contrapuntal skill. He was, in Opus 5, all that he had been earlier, and much more.

One point remains to be made. The fourth sonata of the Opus 5 set contains an optional part for the viola; in the edition of the Händelgesellschaft, this part is printed in smaller notes than the other parts. But the added part is not in Handel's handwriting in one of the autographs,[13] and there seems reasonable doubt of its authenticity. It happens that the first movement and parts of the fourth of this sonata are used in the overtures to *Athalia* and *Parnasso in festa*, two of Handel's choral works from 1733 and 1734, respectively. In these two orchestral overtures there is, of course, a viola part; the latter agrees, note for note, with the added viola part in the corresponding sections of the trio sonata. It seems likely that some enterprising musician who knew all three works abstracted the viola part from the overtures and added it to the trio sonata, thus making the latter, in effect, a string quartet. While speculation is unfruitful,

[13] According to Walker, in *Cobbett's Cyclopedic Survey of Chamber Music*, I, 508.

since we know neither the name of the innovator nor the date of the innovation, it will be well to keep this point in mind in later chapters, when the origin of the string quartet is discussed.

In this account of chamber music, the works of Johann Sebastian Bach (1685–1750) must seemingly occupy a place of secondary importance. This may be considered strange, for in most other fields of music Bach represents the pinnacle of achievement. In fugal writing, for example, his works summarize and bring to glorious completion a long line of development extending back for more than two centuries; in the field of choral music the *Passion According to St. Matthew* and the *B minor Mass* mark the highest point ever attained in sustained intensity, religious fervor, and musical sublimity. In his cantatas, his keyboard works, and his orchestral suites and concertos, likewise, one encounters a breadth of imagination, a logical power, and a degree of poignancy not found in any other composer. And the many chorales exhibit a depth of feeling that epitomizes the entire Protestant religious impulse. Bach's chamber music must be considered in a category both separate and different from any of the above for two reasons: first, it is small in quantity; second, because of the restricted definition of chamber music we have chosen to adopt for this book, much of even that small quantity cannot be included for discussion here.

There are first the three suites and three sonatas for violin alone; these works, magnificent and musically important though they may be, are not ensemble music, hence cannot be examined in this account of chamber music. It must suffice to point out that they exhibit the forms and characteristics of the *sonata da camera* and the *sonata da chiesa*, respectively. With them must be placed the six suites for cello alone; they too are in effect *sonate da camera*, with, of course, notable deviations from the form as we have seen it thus far. The four orchestral suites or *Overtures*, as Bach called them, and the six Brandenburg concertos likewise, cannot be discussed here. While they are sometimes considered chamber music and are often performed by "chamber orchestras," they are orchestral rather than chamber music: more than one player is needed on each string part to insure proper tonal balance. Finally, the twelve sonatas for one instrument (violin, flute, etc.) and harpsichord must be ignored here. While they are derived from trio sonatas, in that the right hand of the keyboard part is often that which would be given to the second instrument in the trio (and incidentally, in these works the harpsichord part is written out in full), still they are for two players, hence must be placed with those works of Bach that are not to be discussed here. There remain for discussion, then, four works: two isolated trio sonatas, *The Musical Offering* (*Das musikalische Opfer*), written after Bach's visit to the court of Frederick the Great at Potsdam, in 1747, and Bach's last work, *The Art of the Fugue* (*Die Kunst der Fuge*), 1749. The trio sonatas are found in Volume IX of the *Complete Works*,[14] *Das musikalische Opfer*, in Volume XXXI[II], and *Die Kunst der Fuge* in Volume XXV[I].

The two trio sonatas are much alike, except that the first, in G major, is for flute, violin, and figured bass, while the second, in C major, is for two violins and figured bass. Each sonata contains four movements, in the sequence slow-fast-slow-fast, and in each work the third movement is in the relative minor key. All of the eight movements are written in contrapuntal style, with the last movement of the G major sonata and the second movement of the C major appearing as complete fugues. The third movement of the C major is in the form of a strict two-voice canon accompanied by a moving bass line. Here is the greatest difference between these sonatas and corresponding ones of Handel. The latter often abandoned contrapuntal style in the interest of melodic writing; most of Handel's lyric slow movements are in homophonic style. Bach finds this unnecessary; within the framework of the strictest and usually most austere of forms, the canon, he writes a melody as lyric, as expressive, as any. The example below shows the first few measures.

In both sonatas the bass is of equal importance with the upper voices: it takes part in the imitative writing, contains melodic bits, and has very little connection with the old *basso continuo*. Harmonically, the result is that the three voices are complete in them-

[14] Bachgesellschaft (Leipzig, 1851–1894).

selves and hardly require the harpsichord to fill out the chords, as had been the practice up to this time. The growing independence and musical integrity of the bass line in Bach can be seen by taking a side glance at the twelve sonatas for one instrument and harpsichord. In these works the harpsichord part is written out completely, and the sonatas need no bass instrument for support. In most cases, the harpsichord engages in strict two-part writing; there are thus three instrumental lines: solo instrument (flute, violin, or viol da gamba), harpsichordist's right hand and left hand, respectively. So obvious is this three-part writing that a number of arrangements of these accompanied sonatas have been made for string trio, are eminently satisfactory and sound well balanced.[15]

Bach, Trio Sonata, C major

Of completely different quality and stature is the magnificently organized work, *The Musical Offering*.[16] When Bach visited Frederick the Great at Potsdam, in 1747, he was given a "royal theme" upon which to improvise. He must have performed to the King's liking, for the visit was completed by the latter's expressions and tokens of esteem. Upon Bach's return home he employed the royal theme in a series of twelve canons and fugues and one trio sonata, for various combinations of instruments (from two to six) and

[15] Arnold Trowell selected movements from the first and second sonatas for violin and harpsichord, arranged them for two violins and cello as Trio II and I, respectively (published by Augener, London, n.d.). As Trio III, for violin, viola, and cello, he chose movements from the three sonatas for viol da gamba and harpsichord.
[16] In modern edition by Hans T. David.

presented the work to Frederick as a musical offering (*musikalisches Opfer*).

The work is unique in the symmetry and proportion it exhibits, unique even for Bach, whose musical forms in general show strict adherence to a well-laid formal plan. In *The Musical Offering*, the plan is as follows:

I. *Ricercare*, two instruments and bass
II. Five canons, for three instruments
    (*a*) Canon at the double octave
    (*b*) Canon at the unison
    (*c*) Canon in contrary motion
    (*d*) Canon by augmentation and contrary motion
    (*e*) Modulating canon (C, D, E, F sharp, G sharp, B flat, C minor)

> *In these canons the "royal theme" is carried by one instrument, while the other two engage in canonic imitation, in the manner indicated, of original counterthemes.*

III. Trio sonata, two instruments and figured bass
    Largo, allegro, andante, allegro
IV. Five canonic elaborations of the theme, for two to four instruments
    (*a*) Mirror canon, two instruments and figured bass
    (*b*) Crab canon (in retrograde motion) and its retrograde form, two instruments
    (*c*) Contrary motion canon and its inversion, two instruments
    (*d*) Canon in quadruple counterpoint, four instruments
    (*e*) Canonic fugue at the fifth above, three instruments

> *In these canons the "royal theme" itself is made the subject of the canons, while the other instrument or instruments carry the countermelodies.*

V. *Ricercare*, six instruments

Thus, there is symmetry in large and small aspects: the work begins and ends with a *ricercare;* the five canons in the second part are balanced by the five in the fourth part. But there is also a gradual increase in size of the canons: those in the second part, for three instruments, are rather short (nine to forty-nine measures, respectively), while those in the fourth part are considerably longer (thirty-six to seventy-eight measures), thus bringing about, through sheer size, a greater amount of emotional intensity. Furthermore, in the treatment of the "royal theme" there is a growth of interest: in the five canons of the second part the theme is announced by one instrument, while the other two carry on the two-voice canonic writing around it; in the canons of the fourth part the "royal theme" itself is made the subject of the various canonic devices, while the other voices carry the countermelodies. Finally, the six-voice fugue which is the last *ricercare* is considerably more intense, is longer, and rises to a greater climax than the three-voice fugue with which the work opens.

The royal theme itself, as presented to Bach by Frederick, is well adapted to the contrapuntal treatment it receives. Well-defined to-

nality, the characteristic leap of a diminished seventh, and a long chromatic line—these elements testify to the good musical judgment of the King in presenting a fugue theme upon which Bach was to improvise. But Frederick could not have foreseen the wealth of technical invention, musical profundity, and organizing genius Bach eventually disclosed in this "musical offering." Obsolete contrapuntal practices were revived, and contributed to the greatness of this work. Symmetry, balance between parts, well-proportioned climaxes and a gradual ascent in emotional intensity—all these, plus a unique plan that is in itself a stroke of genius, are found here. The work as a whole, particularly the charming trio sonata (Part III), is well worth any amount of study one can give it. As a technical *tour de force*, as a monument to Bach's contrapuntal genius, and as a piece of pure music, *The Musical Offering* is unique in the chamber-music literature.

In speaking of the differences between German and Italian instrumental music, Láng [17] calls attention to the Germans' "tone and their fantastic world, ranging far and wide in the metaphysical beyond.

[17] *Music in Western Civilization*, pp. 488–489.

. . . It is still this same unfathomable and mysterious musical world which is conjured up in Bach's *The Art of the Fugue* and in the last string quartets of Beethoven. The scholar's work ends here, for while the ear still continues to hear, the intellect ceases to function. We feel everything and we know exactly where we are, but the light that burns in our hearts flickers when we attempt to force the intellect to translate into concrete formulae what we are beholding. It is impossible to explain this music in terms of technical, formal analyses, for it is lost in the sea of the irrational; any formal elements are merely particles washed ashore."

The honesty implicit in the above quotation emboldens the present author to give mainly a description of Bach's *The Art of the Fugue*. Any "explanation" of this great work would, through sheer language inadequacy, become either ponderous, trite, or hysterical, and nothing at all would be gained thereby. *The Art of the Fugue*, like *The Musical Offering*, is a unique phenomenon in music; it, more than almost any work in the Baroque period, must be heard, lived with, and experienced fully in order that its scope may be understood and its purpose revered.

The Art of the Fugue, written in 1749 and published posthumously, is Bach's last work. It is included in Volume XXV[I] of the Bachgesellschaft edition [18] and, in a slightly different form, edited by Wolfgang Graeser, as Volume XXVIII[I] of the Neuen Bachgesellschaft set.[19] It is in the latter form that the work first attracted the attention of the musical world (with a performance at Leipzig in 1927), and allowed its colossal structure to be seen. Earlier editions, including the original and six subsequent ones,[20] had rearranged the order of various sections, had omitted others, and in general had given a distorted view of the total plan. Erich Schwebsch, in an exhaustive and highly stimulating account of the work,[21] finds that Graeser's ordering of the sections is correct.

The Art of the Fugue consists, in simplest terms, of nineteen

---

[18] Leipzig, 1851–1894.   [19] Leipzig, 1927.
[20] By Hauptmann, Rust, Riemann, Tovey, etc.
[21] *Johann Sebastian Bach und die Kunst der Fuge.*

fugues, the last of which is unfinished. Although designed for instruments, as is evidenced because its parts are written on separate staves,
the desired instruments are not indicated by name, nor are there any
tempo indications. The separate fugues are called "counterpoints"
and are numbered from I to XIX. Six groups are discernible: Group
A, Counterpoints I–IV; B, Counterpoints V–VII; C, Counterpoints
VIII–XI; D, Counterpoints XII–XV; E, Counterpoints XVI–XVIII;
F, Counterpoints XIX (*a,b,c*). Running through the entire cycle as a
basic subject, but altered considerably on each successive appearance,
is the theme:

Group A, Counterpoints I–IV: Two fugues with the subject in
normal position, two with the subject inverted, all containing some
small but significant rhythmic changes. Group B, Counterpoints V–
VII: One fugue with the subject in normal and inverted positions
simultaneously, one with both positions in regular and halved note
values (i.e., twice as fast), one with both positions in regular, doubled,
(half as fast) and halved note values.

Group C, Counterpoints VIII–XI: Four fugues, but of greater size
and complexity, for here double and triple fugues appear. Be it
remembered that in a double fugue there is a more or less complete
fugue on the first subject, an equally complete fugue on the second,
followed by a section in which both subjects are heard together. In
a triple fugue three subjects are used, and all three appear together
in the final section. Of such nature are the four fugues of Group C.
Counterpoints IX and X are double fugues; VIII and XI are triple.
The first subject of VIII introduces an element of chromaticism
into the cycle; it is an undulating (Schwebsch calls it "snake-
like" [22]) phrase, out of whose chromatic line the third subject of XI
will evolve. The second subject (of VIII) is derived from figurations
found in the first section. At this point, when this fugue's cyclical
unity with the first seven fugues is threatened, Bach introduces a

[22] *Ibid.*, p. 241.

third subject which restores the unity; for the third subject is yet
another version of the cycle's basic subject. Counterpoint XI, again
a triple fugue, contains two transformed versions of subjects heard
earlier in the cycle, and a third subject based on the notes B flat, A,
C, and B natural, which in German terminology becomes B-A-C-H.[23]

Group D, Counterpoints XII–XVI: Four two-voice canonic
fugues whose apparent innocence conceals a wealth of relationships
to earlier fugues of the cycle. The basic subject is present in all four
fugues of this group, yet it is considerably transformed in contour,
rhythm, and style. Devices of augmentation and diminution of note
values in conjunction with normal and inverted position of the subjects appear together. And the B-A-C-H theme tends to be reab-
sorbed into the chromatic line in Counterpoint XII. Group E,
Counterpoints XVI *a* and *b*, XVII *a* and *b*, and XVIII *a* and *b*: these
are single fugues in contrast to the double and triple fugues of Group
C; but they are also mirror fugues. A fugue of this type is actually
two fugues in one, for in addition to the normal fugue there is its
exact inversion. Every interval of every voice and each voice itself
is inverted throughout the whole course of the movement—is "mirrored" from below, so to say. Thus, in Group E, XVI *a* is followed
by its inverted form XVI *b*; XVII *a* by XVII *b*; XVIII *a* by XVIII
b.[24]

Group F: the uncompleted Counterpoint XIX *a*, *b*, and *c*. Containing a first subject (XIX *a*) derived from the basic subject of the
cycle, a second subject (XIX *b*) apparently unrelated to other
themes in the cycle, and a third subject (XIX *c*) on the B-A-C-H
theme, this gigantic movement is a triple fugue of the most profound
type. But Schwebsch, on the basis of the whole cycle's plan, on
internal evidence, and on his own keen insight into Bach's intention,

[23] The German terminology employs the suffix *es* to indicate a flatted note: E flat
becomes *Es*, D flat becomes *Des*, etc. The suffix *is* indicates a sharped note: *Cis*
for C sharp, *Gis* for G sharp, etc. Exceptions are A flat, B flat, and B. The corresponding terms are *As* for A flat, *B* for B flat, and *H* for B natural. B sharp then
becomes *His*.

[24] According to Apel, in *Harvard Dictionary of Music*, these three are the only
mirror fugues known to have been composed.

declares this to be an unfinished quadruple fugue of which a bit more than half was completed. For a fourth subject (XIX *d*) Bach had planned the original form of the basic theme, thus completing the unity of the cycle, establishing a symmetry of the most subtle kind and presenting in a complex musical form a symbol of deep significance.

Seen in its entirety, *The Art of the Fugue* is a work with a plan of thematic transformation unequaled in the history of music. A tabular view of the entire cycle, adapted from Schwebsch,[25] follows:

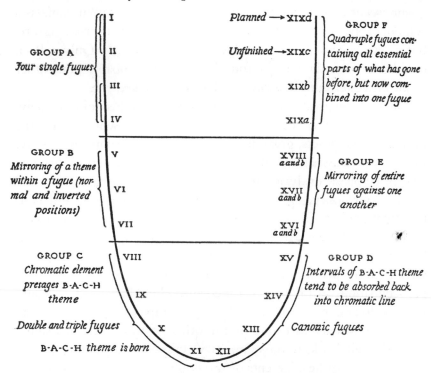

Schwebsch sees the cycle as an esoteric work symbolizing the gradual materialization of the human being's spiritual essence descending out of higher regions (Counterpoints I–XI), the entry of the human ego (B-A-C-II theme in Counterpoint XI, the midpoint of the cycle), and the gradual ascent of the transformed human spirit

25 *Johann Sebastian Bach und die Kunst der Fuge*, p. 123.

back into its spiritual home (Counterpoints XII to XIX *d*). Such an interpretation can come only out of a knowledge of the philosophical and esoteric works of Rudolf Steiner (1861–1925) and a *Weltanschauung* based on these works.[26] As to Bach's participation in esoteric wisdom, Schwebsch points out that Bach was well acquainted with the sermons of the mystic Johannes Tauler (1300–1361) [27] and that the connections between the divine and the human were ever-present in his mind. As his last work, he chose to symbolize the human spirit's incarnation upon earth and its subsequent ascent to a higher existence. Bach's use of his own name as a symbol of the human ego is not to be taken as a light-hearted gesture, but as evidence of his knowledge of his own worth. Only a Bach could have carried out so profound a plan, and probably in no other work in western music is such a plan to be looked for.

Three of the great composers spoken of up to this point, namely, Dall'Abaco, Buxtehude, and Handel, are representative of the dozens of composers, great and small, writing trio sonatas in Italy, France, Germany, and England. In the works of these three men one sees an emphasis on lyric melody and a noble singing style (Dall' Abaco), virtuosity, lightness, and humor (Buxtehude), and contrapuntal perfection and excellence of form (Handel), respectively —although all these elements are found, obviously, in all three composers to a greater or lesser degree. In the many other composers writing in the period roughly from 1700 to 1740, one finds a similar preoccupation with this or that element. Though all of them could write melodies, though all were skilled contrapuntists, and though all were virtuosos at heart, one or the other of these elements shines through their works to the temporary eclipse of the others.

Thus, among the adherents of the noble, singing style best represented by Dall'Abaco we must include the Frenchmen François Couperin (1668–1733) and Jean Leclair (1697–1764) and the Italians Francesco Veracini (1685–1750) and Antonio Vivaldi (c. 1678–

[26] Published in German by Philosophischer-Anthroposophischer Verlag (Dornach, Switzerland), in English by The Anthroposophic Press (New York).
[27] *Johann Sebastian Bach und die Kunst der Fuge*, pp. 137 ff.

c. 1741). Vivaldi is of especial importance in the history of the solo violin concerto (as opposed to the *concerto grosso*); unfortunately, any elaboration of this point would lead too far afield, and we must be content merely to mention the fact. While lyric melodies and fugal movements are present in the works of Giuseppe Tartini (1692–1770), Francesco Geminiani (1680?–1762), and Johann Birkenstock (1687–1733), the main interest of these composers lies in technical brilliance and display. Tartini is remembered especially for highly ornamented violin sonatas, which, while they are lyric and full of noble expression, opened the way for nineteenth-century virtuosity. Among the lesser masters of counterpoint, whose music is typically Italian in its gayety and charm, are Tommaso Albinoni (1674?–1745?) and Pietro Locatelli (1693–1764). The mention of these names by no means exhausts the list of chamber-music composers writing in the period from 1700 to 1740. To be complete, such a list would have to include practically every composer of consequence living at that time. Composers of opera and church music, organists, and harpsichord composers—all would have to be included; for all were interested in chamber-music forms, and all contributed at least a few works to the literature.

Having reached this point, with true sonata form just a step beyond, we have come to the limits of Baroque form. The essentials of that form, be it recalled, were adherence to one mood and one melodic idea per movement, in keeping with the doctrine of the affections. Many composers of the period from 1730 to 1750 were on the edge of violating that doctrine by tending toward a contrasting second theme; in so doing they were in close proximity to the Classical forms of the mid-eighteenth century. Half a dozen important composers after the 1740's still continued to write trio sonatas, but each one came closer to the style and forms we associate with the Vienna of Haydn and Mozart. Among these composers Giovanni Pergolesi, Johann Gottlieb Graun, Karl Philipp Emanuel Bach, and Christoph Willibald von Gluck will be discussed in the following chapter, along with their eminent contemporaries of Vienna and Mannheim.

Thus we close the account of the chamber music of the period from Gabrieli to Bach, roughly from 1600 to 1750. Anyone who gathers from the music discussed that this period was a period of forerunners merely, of vapid experiments which produced no real music, has missed its real significance. Each of the composers in the line from Gabrieli through Frescobaldi, Vitali, Corelli, Purcell, Buxtehude, Dall'Abaco, Handel, and Bach has written music in the style of his times, has clothed musical truth and beauty in the aesthetic apparel of his generation. That we have substituted another style for the style of these composers is in itself no guarantee that ours is superior to theirs. Styles change, inevitably, as the economic, material, and psychological factors of human life change. Anyone who will take the trouble to assume the aesthetic outlook and adopt the psychology of the Baroque man will find in Baroque music a source of great satisfaction. In clarity, freedom from sentimentality, and forthrightness it stands on a level with the best music of the Classical period. In choice of melodic materials it approaches the nobility and the charm of the great Italian vocal tradition. With these elements as characteristics, the music cannot fail to serve the same purpose as music of every other age: to move human emotions and to inspire toward a richer life.

7

THE EMERGENCE OF CLASSICAL STYLE

THE WAYS in which musical style changes come about gradually have been mentioned earlier in this book. During most of music's history several decades have been required to alter the sound and the appearance of the music, decades during which the new style begins to become noticeable in the midst of the old style characteristics, decades in which the latter eventually become submerged in the body of the new style elements. It has been the custom of historians to seize upon a date midway in this transition period, a date at which both styles are clearly defined, and refer to it as a style boundary. We are now confronted with a major change—that from the Baroque style to the Classical; we can for convenience take a date near 1755 to mark the beginning of the latter style. As we shall see below, that date marks the appearance of Haydn's first string quartets.

But the Baroque did not fade smoothly into the Classical; Baroque characteristics did not, in general, persist up to and past 1755. A large quantity of music written from about 1725 to 1760, and many art, architectural, and literary works of the same period show characteristics which, while derived from Baroque elements, are not based on the same aesthetic principles. In France, under Louis XV, a new style of architectural ornamentation arose, based on the use of artificial rock-work, decorated and sculptured shell-work, and extravagance of detail in general. Enthusiastically imitated in Italy and Germany, the new style soon left its mark on other art forms, particularly music and literature, in the shape of delicacy of structure, elaborate attention to insignificant details, and choice of some frivolous subject matter. The new style was called *rococo* (derived from the French *rocaille*, rock-work); we can refer to the Rococo period in discussing the chamber-music works of the decades between 1725 and 1760.

As one of the accompanying phenomena of the new Rococo style (probably the sociologist would put the horse before the cart), the long fight against absolute monarchy, against the domination of one individual by another, flared up afresh. Liberty became a new watchword; enlightenment and reason became ideals. And liberty soon became synonymous with freedom from rules, from conventions, and forms. Inevitably, Baroque music, with its strict rules, its conventional affections, and its monumental forms, became one of the first victims of the new urge. "Back to nature" was the popular cry in theater and opera; capriciousness and entertainment were demanded in instrumental music. Inevitably, lowered standards of taste became general. Music was faced with one measuring stick: entertainment value. Much of the music measured up (or really down) to the new taste level.

The emancipation from rules brought with it a search for new effects. Dignity gave way to frivolity, and a new type of melodic line came into being. The Baroque principle of one mood per movement gave way to the practice of contrasting moods within a movement, and musical forms suited to this different content emerged. Dilettantism flourished; every gentleman played the violin, and every lady the flute. This invasion of music by the amateur in search of diversion required a type of music which was within the technical and intellectual limits of the dilettante and made necessary more detailed directions for playing the music itself. Thus, as more or less immediate results of the Rococo social outlook and trend of thought, the sonata form and the serenade, or divertimento, came into being, along with a new type of expressiveness in the melody, a new type of accompaniment, and the careful marking of dynamic changes in the music. Composers of the Rococo period experimented with these new devices, improved upon them, and in due time passed them on to the great Viennese masters whom we associate with the full flowering of the Classical period.

Among the most obvious of the changes brought about during the Rococo decades were those which had to do with form. Before discussing the changes, it will be well to review the nature of the forms as they existed in the late Baroque. The reader will remember that insofar as chamber music is concerned we have had to do primarily with only two formal types; practically all the single movements in *sonata da chiesa*, *sonata da camera*, and trio sonata (since the period roughly from 1650) have belonged to one of the two types. Either they have been related to the fugal form which resulted from the solidification of the *canzone's* elements into a single movement, or they have been derived from the dance form as found in the dance suite as far back as 1600. Stylistically, of course, the two types differed from the beginning, in that contrapuntal treatment was characteristic of the fugal form, and homophonic treatment of the dance. We have seen above that in the course of time, from about 1675 to 1725, these elements merged, so that by 1725 there was little stylistic difference between the two types.

But each type had had its own formal scheme, a scheme which had remained relatively unchanged during the seventy-five year period under discussion. Thus, the fugal type of movement had begun with a fugal exposition in the tonic key, had contained episodes and additional expositions in other, closely related keys, and had ended again in the tonic. The dance type of movement, on the other hand, had consisted of two parts separated by a double bar, each part designed to be repeated; the first part, beginning in the tonic key, had ended in the dominant, whereas the second part, continuing in the dominant, had modulated back to the tonic. Diagrammatically, the formal difference between the two types may be shown as follows:

Fugal type: I–V–VI–IV–V–I
Dance type: I–V :|||: V–I

Since, in the balance of this chapter our concern will be almost entirely with pieces of music derived from the dance type, let us examine that form a bit more closely.

The melodic materials in a movement of the latter type had consisted in general of rhythmically alive phrases from four to twelve measures long, and with no noteworthy contour or melodic shape. During the course of such a movement several such phrases would be presented, would move toward the mid-point of the movement, and would end in the key of the dominant. After the mid-point, usually marked by a double bar, similar phrases would occur, and the movement would move back to the tonic key. Nowhere could one speak of a theme (defined as the vehicle for a musical thought), and only rarely was a phrase first heard at the beginning of the movement encountered again elsewhere. Thus, any symmetry in the form was confined to the harmony, with the I–V:‖: V–I pattern by far the most common.[1]

In the keyboard sonatas of Domenico Scarlatti (1685–1757) is found the first consistent step toward a solidification of the form from a melodic standpoint. In the great majority of his more than five hundred one-movement keyboard sonatas, the harmonic scheme we have described above applies. But in these works a second scheme appears, this time based on balance of figurations. Scarlatti's practice is to begin with a musical phrase containing some degree of melodic appeal, carry the phrase toward the dominant, and let it dissolve in brilliant figurations in that dominant key; the second part begins with the melodic phrase of the first part, but now in the dominant key, moves toward the tonic key, and ends with figurations similar to those with which the first part ended. There emerges a balance best shown as A–B:‖: A–B, contained within the harmonic symmetry of I–V:‖: V–I; it will be seen that in the second part the melody and figurations appear with the harmonies reversed. Each section is in effect transposed to the key of the other.

Now, the contour or melody of the A section is in general distinctive enough to be remembered and recognized when it returns at the beginning of the second part; hence it can be called a theme. But the material of the B section is usually not distinctive enough to be remembered and recognized; often it consists of figurations, broken chords, and similar virtuoso devices; it rarely shows signs of melodic shape or phrase structure and cannot be called a theme. It remained for other composers, notably Pergolesi, to invest the B section with

[1] I–III :‖: III–I usually appeared in movements in a minor key.

melodic integrity sufficient to justify calling it thematic, and thus to prepare the way for the next important development in this form, namely, the isolation of the first and the second themes.

Giovanni Battista Pergolesi was born near Naples in 1710. Famous during his brief lifetime as a composer of church music, he is best remembered for his *Serva padrona*, usually considered the first comic opera, and his *Stabat Mater*. We are more interested in his twelve trio sonatas, published about 1731, for we shall see in them several innovations which influenced the course of the sonata to a considerable extent. Pergolesi died in 1736.

In order properly to evaluate Pergolesi's innovations in the form of the sonata, we must first examine the structure of the melodies themselves. In Pergolesi's trio sonatas there is a successful attempt to build up long singing melodies in fast tempo, perhaps the first such attempt in instrumental music. The old manner of extending a melody had been to present a motive or short phrase capable of being manipulated contrapuntally. By means of imitations, short extensions, running scale figures, and similar contrapuntal devices, the motive or phrase was expanded, and the section or movement was filled out. The new process is best seen in the first movement of Pergolesi's first trio sonata in G major,[2] a fragment of which is reproduced below.

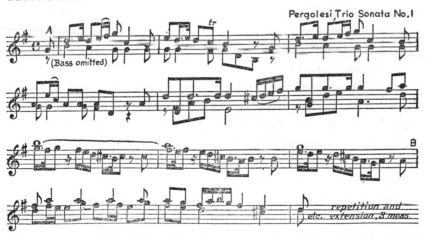

Pergolesi, Trio Sonata No. 1

[2] The first two of Pergolesi's twelve trio sonatas are reprinted in *Collegium musicum*, Nos. 29 and 30. The complete set of twelve, published by Bremner (London,

A two-measure phrase (A in the example above) ending on the tonic is heard, and is immediately repeated with a cadence on the dominant; another two-measure phrase on the dominant follows, which in turn leads to a transitional phrase of three measures ending on the dominant of D major. At this point a new, somewhat contrasting phrase in D major appears (B in the example); this phrase is repeated and provided with a coda (literally, tail), much as the first phrase (A) had been. The facts that all three instruments are essential in the presentation of these themes and that a closely-knit period structure results are noteworthy.

And of great significance for the future development of sonata form is the fact that the second half of the first section (phrase B in the example) now begins to assume melodic integrity, begins to have a recognizable melodic shape, and is no longer merely a broken chord or running scale pattern. The way to an independent second theme, contrasting in contour, style, and key, is now open. Though Pergolesi did not progress so far as an independent second theme, he was consistent, in the majority of his trio sonatas, in giving the section under discussion a definite melody, an advance over the form as Scarlatti left it.

As a consequence of that achievement, other advances are to be noted also. The most immediate one can best be described by recalling (*a*) that composers of the form before Scarlatti had contented themselves with achieving a harmonic symmetry of I–V:‖:V–I, no noticeable formal scheme having been apparent in the choice of melodic materials; (*b*) that in Scarlatti's hands the form achieved a kind of balance based on similarity of melodies in the first section of each part and a similarity of figurations in the second section of each, depicted by the diagram A–B:‖:A–B; (*c*) that now, with Pergolesi's success in establishing a melodic section at the end of each part, a melodic balance of A–B:‖:A–B over the harmonic symmetry of I–V:‖:V–I became possible. This new departure in form is obviously a direct result of transposing the melodies of the first

n. d.), is in the Library of Congress, Washington, D.C.; the Mirabeau B. Lamar Library of the University of Texas contains a photostatic copy.

part to the keys of the second, but that it was of great significance in
the future development of the sonata's first movement may not be
clear at the moment. Its full importance can be realized best in
retrospect, when we examine the sonata form of the late eighteenth
century in the following chapter.

A third innovation tending toward the fully-developed Classical
form is also to be encountered in Pergolesi's trio sonatas; we now
turn our attention to the second part of the first movement. When
once the dominant key had been established and the second part had
begun (in that key) with the melody of the A section, Pergolesi
showed great skill in hinting at the forthcoming B section in the
tonic key, while still concerned with the phrases of the A section. In
several cases in the twelve sonatas, shortly before the B section is
recapitulated in the tonic key, bits of the A, also in the tonic key,
appear. The end result is that finally the whole of the A section, now
entirely in the tonic key, appears between the A (dominant) and B
(tonic) sections of the second part. Thus, the following form appears:

MELODIC SECTION: A — B: ‖: A — A — B
HARMONIC SCHEME: I — V: ‖: V — I — I

And so it is found in eight of the twelve first movements. It may
be remarked that three of the first movements (numbers 6, 9, and
12) are fugal; thus actually eight out of nine movements contain
the form described above. Only in the seventh sonata is a different
scheme to be observed: the movement is in G minor, and the harmonic sections are I–III: ‖: I–VI–I. The second sonata, in B flat,
illustrates the new procedure in detail. The A theme gives way,
after eight measures, to a B theme, of which the two halves total
eleven measures. In the second part of the movement the A theme,
in the expected dominant key, is developed in the direction of the
tonic for thirteen measures. Now a complete recapitulation of the
A theme with a five-measure extension occurs, after which there is
an equally complete recapitulation of the B theme, transposed note
for note to the tonic key. We shall look back upon this movement in

the chapters to follow and shall see it as a beautiful example of sonata form in miniature, but with all the essential details in place.

Nor have we finished with Pergolesi at this point; one more aspect of his works remains to be mentioned. His trio sonatas are characterized by a three-movement form derived from the Neapolitan opera overture. Since about 1700 these opera overtures had had a three-part form in the sequence fast-slow-fast, in distinction to the slow-fast pattern of French overtures. Until well into the eighteenth century most composers of instrumental music made use of the French opera overture's formal pattern and carried out the sequence of slow-fast-slow-fast in the four movements of their trio sonatas (compare the works of Corelli, Dall'Abaco, Handel, etc., discussed earlier). In the trio sonatas of Pergolesi, dating from about 1731, the Neapolitan overture scheme makes probably its first appearance in chamber music, for the three movements are in the sequence fast-slow-fast. This innovation, appearing almost simultaneously in keyboard sonata (Karl Philipp Emanuel Bach), orchestral *sinfonia* (a three-movement overture divorced from the operatic stage and heard simply as concert music), and occasionally in concertos, was also destined to be influential in shaping the newly emerging symphony.

Thus, the twenty-six-year-old Pergolesi left a rich heritage of important and excellent music, introduced significant changes in the structure of the trio sonata and in the form of the single movements themselves, transformed the melodic aspect of instrumental music to a considerable degree, and influenced the course of that music for seventy-five years.

Second and third movements of Pergolesi's trio sonatas do not bring such important innovations with them. In the G major sonata, for example, the second movement is slow, in triple meter, and in E minor. It is largely in note-against-note style, with a lyric melody, very much in the manner of Corelli's slow movements. In the third movement Pergolesi reverts to the old *sonata da chiesa* practice by writing a fugue, but unlike the *da chiesa*, in fast tempo. Likewise in the B flat sonata: the second movement is slow, in triple meter, and in E flat major; the third is a presto in triple meter, and is similar to the first movements in having an A–B:|||:A–B melodic form over a I–V:|||:V–I harmony. In these works, as well as in most of the symphonies, sonatas, and quartets later in the century, the main emphasis is on the first movements. It is there that the composer was most ingenious, took greatest pains, and provided the greatest amount of innovation. The fact that final movements are often lacking in musical values may be ascribed to this emphasis on beginnings.

In the decades following the appearance of Pergolesi's trio sonatas (c. 1731) the majority of instrumental composers adopted the formal plan there set forth. The three-movement form became normal; but the first movement was not always in fast tempo. Indeed, one of the striking characteristics of the form with contrasting themes and a recapitulation, as illustrated by Pergolesi, was its flexibility in all tempos. Many examples of this emerging sonata form in slow tempo exist, along with movements having either theme contrast or recapitulation, but not both devices. Among the best trio sonatas of this period are those of Christoph Willibald von Gluck (1714–1787), a composer more famous for his operas and operatic reforms than for his chamber music.

Seven of Gluck's trio sonatas are available in modern reprints.[3] The first six, originally published at London in 1746, are much alike in that all have three movements, all the first movements are in slow tempo, all the second movements are fast, and all but one of the last movements are minuets (the exception being the first trio in C major, in which the movement is in the form of a fast two-voice canon). In the majority of the eighteen movements of these six sonatas considerable similarity to the form of Pergolesi is seen. Usually there are two contrasting sections (A and B) in the first part, on tonic and dominant, respectively. Usually there is a double bar, after which the second part begins on the dominant. But there the similarity ends. For while it is Gluck's practice to begin the second part with motives derived from the first part, there is no consistent attempt to recapitulate the entire first part on the tonic. A tabular

[3] In *Collegium musicum*, Nos. 32–38.

PERGOLESI

$$\begin{cases} A - B - Coda: \|||: A \text{ developed } - A - B \text{ and Coda} \\ I - V - V : \|||: V - I - I \end{cases} \text{typical}$$

GLUCK

$$\begin{cases} A - A \text{ developed } - Coda: \|||: Development - A - Coda \\ I - V - V : \|||: V - I - I \end{cases} \begin{array}{l} No. 1, C \text{ major} \\ 2d \text{ movement} \end{array}$$

$$\begin{cases} A - B - Coda: \|||: A \text{ developed } - B \text{ (quasi)} - Coda \\ I - III - V : \|||: III - III - I \end{cases} \begin{array}{l} No. 2, G \text{ minor} \\ 2d \text{ movement} \end{array}$$

$$\begin{cases} A - B - Coda: \|||: A \text{ developed } - B \text{ and Coda} \\ I - V - V : \|||: V, VI, etc. - I \end{cases} \begin{array}{l} No. 3, A \text{ major} \\ 1st \text{ movement} \end{array}$$

$$\begin{cases} A - B - Coda: \|||: A \text{ developed } - A - Coda \\ I - V - V : \|||: V - I - I \end{cases} \begin{array}{l} No. 4, B \text{ flat, 1st and} \\ 2d \text{ movement} \end{array}$$

view of Gluck's practice will make his procedure clear. Only once in the seven available trio sonatas of this composer is the formal pattern exactly like Pergolesi's: in the last movement of the seventh. This work is also the only one with a fast first movement. It is almost as though Gluck experimented with all other possible forms of recapitulation before he was willing to adopt Pergolesi's model. The question may arise: Why should one be so eager to trace Scarlatti's and Gluck's deviations from the former's practice? It is largely because the form as seen in Pergolesi's works contains in miniature all the structural elements found in later fully developed sonata form as used by the great masters from Haydn to Brahms, a form in which much of the finest music since 1759 has been written. As such it deserves more than passing reference.

Other composers, both before and after Gluck, adhered even more closely to Pergolesi's scheme, notably the Sammartini brothers (Giuseppe, c. 1693–1770, and Giovanni Battista, c. 1701–c. 1775) and one of the Graun brothers (Johann Gottlieb, c. 1702–1771).[4] In this group of composers one occasionally finds a four-movement sonata, and often the first movement is in slow tempo with the old Baroque imitative devices much in evidence. But the sonata-form

---

[4] All are represented by trio sonatas in *Collegium musicum:* No. 27, Giuseppe Sammartini; No. 28, Giovanni Battista Sammartini; Nos. 24–26, Johann Gottlieb Graun.

movements usually have complete recapitulations of both A and B sections, and the sections themselves are compounded of motives and short phrases, much as Pergolesi's melodies were.

In another group of Gluck's contemporaries and immediate predecessors, on the other hand, we find Baroque formal and aesthetic practices still very much in evidence. One such composer is Johann Fasch (1688–1758), resident in central Germany. Among quantities of excellent instrumental and church music are five trio sonatas and one sonata for four instruments; all reprinted in *Collegium musicum*, Nos. 8–13. The first trio sonata is for violin, viola, and bass; the others are for two violins and bass. All five are compounded of the old polyphonic and new homophonic styles. Sonatas 1 and 2 are in four and three movements, respectively; each movement is a two-voice canon accompanied by the bass. Canonic devices and less strict imitations are present in Sonatas 3 and 4, both of which contain three movements in slow-fast-slow sequence. Sonata 5, in four movements, again shows considerable contrapuntal treatment, extending as far as a complete fugue (second movement) in fast tempo, in the general style of Pergolesi.

But there is an equal amount of evidence that Fasch was sympathetic to new style tendencies. Several of the fast movements are in rudimentary sonata form, whereas others, notably the final movement of Sonata 3, are complete with elaborate developments and regular recapitulations. Even in these sonata-form movements, however, Fasch inclines toward the old way of building melodies: he bases his melodic extensions on repetition or sequence of motives rather than on the introduction of new melodic phrases.

The sixth Fasch work, the sonata for four instruments, is for two violins, viola, and bass without *basso continuo*. While it is impossible accurately to date this work, there is internal evidence that it was influenced by the Mannheim composers about 1755; hence Fasch's omission of the *continuo* is not among the early examples of this practice. We shall see below that two divertimentos of the Viennese Joseph Starzer probably antedate Fasch's work with regard to this innovation. The sonata contains four movements in slow-fast-slow-fast sequence. There is the same mixture of old and new elements; homophonic melodies give way to contrapuntal imitations, and fugal sections contain homophonic episodes. Fasch is conservative in his use of the instruments. Much of the time the viola simply proceeds in octaves with the bass or supplies missing chord notes. The two violins are of equal importance in presentation and development of the musical ideas; thus the predominant solo violin is not in evidence. Fasch stands squarely at the crossroads, and gives evidence that as late as 1755 certain Baroque practices and factors of musical expression were still very much alive.

Another composer with the transitional outlook was George Philipp Telemann (1681–1767). Telemann was the director and producer of opera at Hamburg, was a colleague and friend of Handel's, and was a prolific composer of operatic, instrumental, and religious music. Among his works are about two hundred French suites for combinations of strings and wind instruments and a series of works called *Tafelmusik*, literally table music, or banquet music, written about 1733. Each *Tafelmusik* as a whole contains five sets of movements for various groups of instruments; the sets are always arranged in the order of suite, quartet, concerto, trio, and solo, plus an orchestral conclusion. While the suite, concerto, and conclusion are orchestral, the quartet, trio, and solo are chamber music and deserve to be discussed here. The second *Tafelmusik*[5] is typical and may be examined in detail.

The work begins with an Overture, or suite, for oboe, trumpet, and strings; a French overture (slow-fast) is followed by four airs, each one fast and diverting and in a different meter (vivace 4/4, vivace 3/8, presto 4/4, and allegro 12/8, respectively). Next is a quartet for three flutes and *basso continuo*, similar to works by Dall'Abaco and Handel, for it contains the usual four movements in slow-fast-slow-fast sequence, and the same half imitative and half homophonic style. The third piece is a concerto for three solo violins and string orchestra; it is in the three-movement form (fast-slow-fast) often found in other concertos of the period. Fourth is a

[5] Three of the *Tafelmusik* sets are found in D.D.T., Vols. LXI–LXII.

trio sonata for flute, oboe, cello, and *basso continuo;* it, like the quartet, is in the traditional four-movement form, with a slow first movement, and is characterized by the same texture and style. Then a four-movement solo sonata for violin and *basso continuo;* the same formal structure we found in the trio and quartet, and the same style characteristics, are found here also. The work ends with a conclusion, a one-movement allegro in which the whole orchestra—oboe, trumpet, and strings—comes together again.

There is obviously nothing new in the purpose to which this *Tafelmusik* set is dedicated. Dinner music had existed throughout the previous century, for example, in Schein, *Banchetto musicale* of 1617. Nor is there anything remotely suggesting the formal and stylistic innovations of Pergolesi's and similar works. Two other characteristics may be singled out, however, as pointing toward the future. First are the variety of instrumentation employed in this work, and the placing of large and small ensembles within the framework of one musical composition. It will be recalled that throughout a great part of the seventeenth century specific instrumentation for this or that composition was not called for. *Continuo* parts could be played by cello or bassoon or bass—whichever was available. As late as Handel's trio sonatas Opera 1-5 (1724-1740) the phrase "for violins or flutes or oboes" gives a clue to the flexible concept of instrumentation the Baroque composer employed. During the Classical period, well into the time of Mozart, the instrumentation of the symphony and chamber music became standardized, and a more rigid regard for instrumental color became the rule. In these compositions of Telemann we see a step in that direction. A quartet had a function different from that of a trio, or a solo sonata, or even a full orchestra. In the *Tafelmusik* Telemann combines the existing instrumental groupings, realizing full well that each combination of instruments will carry its own unique message.

And the second characteristic is found in the general mood of the music itself. There are slow and fast movements, as there were in older music also. But the slow movements here are not designed to be profoundly moving as were those of Corelli, Dall'Abaco, and

Handel; nor are the fast movements cast in precise formal or fugal patterns, as was the older custom. Both the slow and the fast movements of Telemann have a common characteristic: they are meant to be enjoyable and enjoyed. The Rococo spirit of diversion is alive in these works; there is no attempt at serious utterance, no attempt to move the listener. Insofar as the music serves that ideal, it is in keeping with the spirit of Telemann's age (be it remembered that Telemann was typical of his time and that his great contemporary Bach was considered old-fashioned even in his day), and is a forerunner, in mood at least, of the serenades, nocturnes and divertimentos of Vienna.

Toward the middle of the eighteenth century a practice long known to suitors and lovers in every land became extremely popular, was seized upon by composers, and gave rise to a new musical literature. It became customary to honor one's friends by engaging a number of musicians to play appropriate music under their windows. Especially in Vienna did this practice flourish, and another step in the evolution of sonata form is seen in the music composed for that purpose. Serenade, nocturne, divertimento, and cassation were the terms used to identify this new music; and the terms at once give clues to its nature. Generally it was performed after nightfall (*sera* = evening) in the streets (*Gasse* = lane; *gassatim* = street-like), and it was light and diverting in character. A few string and/or wind instruments sufficed for the purposes at hand, and generally one player, or at most two, performed each part. Toward 1770 Charles Burney reports that a singer returning to Brescia after a long absence in Russia was serenaded by a band of two violins, mandoline, French horn, trumpet, and cello, "and though in the dark [they] played long concertos, with solo parts for the mandoline." [6]

Various versions of the divertimento [7] differed widely in the number of movements, but all had two features in common: their light, cheerful content, and their derivation from the three-movement

[6] *The Present State of Music in France and Italy,* p. 115.
[7] Let us include in this term all the music of this type, even though there were minor technical distinctions, and some differences in instrumentation, between serenade, divertimento, nocturne, and cassation.

sinfonia. Conservative North German composers adhered to the three-movement form in writing their divertimentos. Many Italian works of this type, on the other hand, contain two movements, one fast and one slow; and at this "sin against the spirit of the *sinfonia*" the North Germans protested vigorously.[8] South German and Austrian composers added one or more movements taken from the suite, usually the minuet. And it is this four-movement version of the divertimento which had the greatest influence on the future symphony and string quartet. The sequence allegro-andante-minuet-finale is known to everyone as the standard form for the Classical symphony and quartet of the late eighteenth century. There it was deepened in content and expanded in form, without a doubt; but its kinship to the unassuming, light divertimento of the period from 1740 to 1755 or so is seen in its adoption of the latter's essential framework. And the divertimento to a considerable degree bridged the gap between the old trio sonata and the soon-to-be string quartet, both in structural details and in instrumentation.

Many divertimentos were just as suited to performance by small orchestras as by quartets and quintets; often, when the resources of the serenader permitted, they were performed by orchestras of fifteen to twenty-five players. It was characteristic of the divertimento type to be considered both chamber and orchestra music. The distinction between the two fields, never too carefully drawn in the early history of instrumental music, threatened to disappear entirely in the period from 1740 to 1760. We shall see in the following chapter that among Haydn's early string quartets, many of which are divertimentos, is one that is reputed to be his first symphony.

Two divertimentos by Joseph Starzer (1726–1787) may be taken as typical of the chamber music of Vienna at that time.[9] Each contains four movements: allegro, minuet and trio, larghetto or adagio, and allegro. Each is for two violins, viola, and bass without the usual *continuo.* Adler points out that these may be among the first works which omit the harpsichord and its function of realizing the figured

[8] Adler, *Handbuch,* II, 802.   [9] Reprinted in D.T.Ö., Vol. XV².

bass.[10] The style is ingratiating, noticeably homophonic, and altogether enjoyable. Sonata form is present in a rudimentary fashion: Starzer does not go beyond the harmonic scheme of Scarlatti, and there is scarcely a trace of a contrasting second theme.

But the works are unique in the responsibility given to the lower instruments of the quartet. The first violin dominates, true enough, in keeping with the *style galant,* of which these divertimentos are good examples. But second violin, viola, and bass all take part in thematic developments, in transitional passages, and all three are far removed from the function of merely supporting the first violin. In the minuet of the first divertimento the viola is actually the leading voice. Throughout the two works the bass engages in figurations much more worthy of a cello than a bass viol; indeed, if Baroque practice were followed here and the bass part were to be read "for bass or cello," we would have two string quartets in the contemporary sense. Unfortunately, there is little possibility of dating these works accurately; a comparison of them with Haydn's first quartets of 1755 with a view to establishing priority would lead nowhere.

It is during these decades of divertimento composition that the German-speaking countries assumed their dominant place in the history of instrumental music. From about 1750 the great composers and the great accomplishments in music are identified with Austria and Germany. Operas continued to be written in Italy and were still performed in France. Italians were still active in London, and for that matter in Vienna and some German cities. But the new accomplishments in the field of keyboard, orchestral, and chamber music are henceforth to be looked for north of the Alps. The long domination of the Italians was over; a century and a half of German supremacy was at hand.

In discussing the works of Fasch and Starzer we have called attention to their occasional omission of the *basso continuo.* The *continuo* principle, as we know, had dominated practically all musical composition since the early 1600's. It had required the services of a keyboard performer to realize the figured bass. It had left the inner

10 In the foreword to *ibid.,* p. xi.

voices of the instrumental group relatively free to take part in imitations, to engage in thematic work, and at times to develop a degree of musical independence. And it had provided a solid harmonic foundation to which the lowest voice was securely bound. Now, in the years between about 1735 and 1750, a new musical idea was born—an idea which grew out of the Rococo desire for display, an idea which led to the speedy decay of the *continuo* principle, an idea which made possible the transfer of the prima donna role to the first violinist.

Now, as one of the characteristics of the *style galant*, came the idea that one instrument was to dominate the musical structure, that the others were to be completely subordinate, both in musical significance and in style. We can best see the nature of this departure by recalling the typical trio sonata of the late Baroque period. Two more or less coequal melodies in the two violins, the alternation of melodic importance between the violins, made unavoidable when the factor of imitative writing was so prevalent, and the parallel motion of the violins in thirds and sixths—these had all been present in the trio sonatas of the early eighteenth century.

In the new style, all musical significance was confined to the solo violin; melodic interest was found only in the uppermost part of the ensemble. The bass line and the inner voices became vehicles for indicating merely the harmonic scheme of the piece, and, possibly because the composers distrusted the amateurs' ability to realize their intentions as expressed in figured bass symbols, all the parts were written out in full. Chords below the dominating melody became complete, and all harmonic changes were adequately indicated in the parts for the lower instruments. As a consequence, the erstwhile *continuo* part, traditionally realized on a keyboard instrument, became unnecessary, and the practice of writing figured basses became obsolete. At first in orchestra music, later in chamber music, and last of all in opera, figured basses and the *continuo* principle disappeared.

The Viennese composers of the divertimento decades were probably among the first to discard the *continuo*. We have just seen in the

Starzer divertimentos two early examples of that practice. Soon the new style became a factor in composing at Berlin, Mannheim, and elsewhere. The orchestra, the string section of which had long since included first and second violins, violas, cellos, and basses, found it expedient to add new wind instruments to the few oboes and trumpets already present and to employ the entire wind choir to sustain harmonies. As a consequence, the violas and cellos were freed from their task of holding out long notes and otherwise providing a chordal background for the melody instruments, were able to take part in a more lively accompaniment for the dominating first violins and achieved a certain amount of melodic self-sufficiency. In chamber music, where the trio sonata was still the most used instrumental combination, the harpsichord was discarded. Since the remaining two violins and bass were not able to supply a melody plus three complete harmony parts, the addition of a fourth instrument was made necessary. The choice logically fell on the viola. About 1745 that instrument made its appearance in chamber music, along with the two violins and the bass. Shortly thereafter, with the emergence of thematic work in all four instruments, the cello was deemed better suited to the combination than the bass had been, and the latter disappeared from the field of chamber music. So the contemporary string quartet, composed of two violins, viola, and cello, was born about 1745.

Periodically attempts are made to ascribe a somewhat earlier date to the founding of the string quartet. For example, several *sonate a quattro* by Alessandro Scarlatti (c. 1659–1725) are often referred to as the earliest string quartets; they were written between 1715 and 1725 and are for *due violini, violetta e violoncello senza cembalo*.[11] We ourselves, in Chapter 6, called attention to a quasi-quartet among the trio sonatas of Handel's Opus 5, 1738, a work in which a viola part had been added to the two violins and bass, thus making the *continuo* unnecessary. Probably other works from the first years of the eighteenth century will be unearthed from time to time, works in which the four string instruments are used without

[11] One in modern reprint ed. by David (Music Press).

continuo, and the date of the quartet's founding will presumably be pushed back again. But we can be sure that such works will be derived from the old *sonata da chiesa*, or *da camera*, and will have no connection with the innovations in form, in style, and in general mood which the Rococo period brought about. In short, they will be Baroque works which happen to be written for four string instruments—the Scarlatti and Handel compositions mentioned above do fall into that style category. As such, they will not be the direct ancestors of the quartet as Haydn first knew it, nor will they contain the formal elements and aesthetic qualities upon which Haydn built so magnificently.

We may mention in passing the six string quartets of Georg Matthias Monn (1717–1750), an important Viennese composer in the generation just preceding Haydn. Monn's significance lies mostly in the field of orchestral music, however, for in a work of his dated 1740 the minuet makes its first appearance in the symphony. Comparatively few of his works have been preserved; among them are seventeen symphonies of various types, several suites and sonatas, and six string quartets. Each of the quartets contains but two movements: slow-fast, in a style reminiscent of the old *sonata da chiesa*. But the fourth quartet of the series is simply a transcription of the first two movements of Monn's first *sinfonia da chiesa* for string orchestra, and the sixth quartet is similarly derived from the second symphony.

Wilhelm Fischer [12] assumes that the other four quartets are likewise fragments of other similar symphonies which no longer exist. He points out that such fragments of orchestral *sonate da chiesa* played an important role in the Imperial Chapel at Vienna well into Mozart's time (c. 1785) and that two other examples of this treatment exist among Monn's orchestral suites. Thus, while these works of Monn are quartets insofar as performing medium is concerned, they are not to be included in the chamber-music literature.

And what of the keyboard instruments in the years after they were forcibly dropped from the field of chamber music? They immediately forced their way back into the field, and became more dominating than they had ever dared be before. The harpsichord, with the newly developing pianoforte, being freed from the duty of improvising accompaniments for orchestral and chamber-music ensembles, went its own ways. On the one hand, it reached new dignity and usefulness in three-movement, completely written out sonatas for keyboard instrument alone—especially in the works of Karl Philipp Emanuel Bach (1714–1788), the oldest son of the great Johann Sebastian Bach. The younger Bach was long active at the court of Frederick the Great at Berlin; his keyboard sonatas, modeled on the trio sonatas of Pergolesi, but exceeding them in quality of invention and refinement, were destined to be of great influence on the long line of Classical composers who succeeded him. On the other hand, the keyboard instrument (and from about the 1760's we can speak only of the pianoforte in this connection, for the harpsichord was soon made obsolete) established a new connection with string instruments in which it now provided the main musical interest: the strings accompanied. Thus, sonatas for piano solo accompanied by violin and cello came into being. In many such cases the violin doubled the upper voice of the keyboard part, and the cello the lower; the subordinate role of the strings was assured, and at times the string instruments could be omitted entirely.

In other cases the violin and cello parts differed to some extent

[12] In the preface to Vol. XIX² of D.T.Ö., in which all these works of Monn are reprinted.

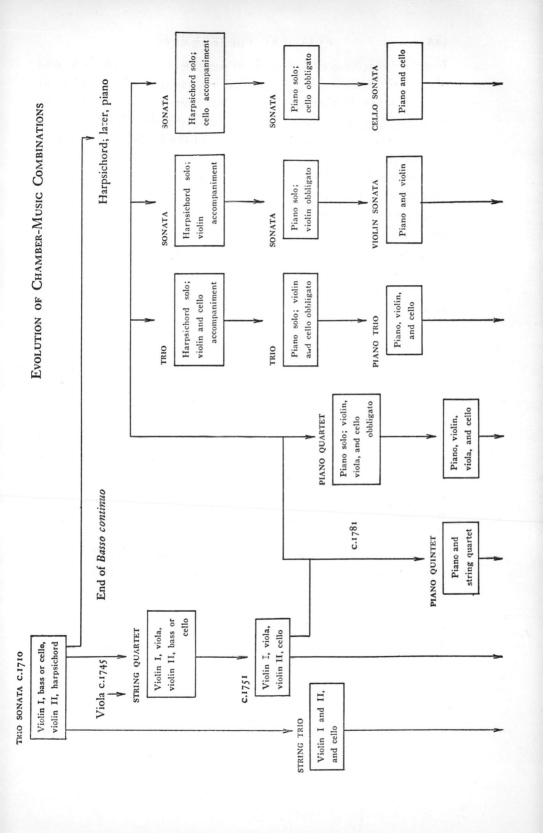

EVOLUTION OF CHAMBER-MUSIC COMBINATIONS

Harpsichord; later, piano

End of *Basso continuo*

TRIO SONATA C.1710
Violin I, bass or cello, violin II, harpsichord

Viola c.1745

STRING QUARTET
Violin I, viola, violin II, bass or cello

c.1751
Violin I, viola, violin II, cello

STRING TRIO
Violin I and II, and cello

PIANO QUARTET
Piano solo; violin, viola, and cello obbligato

Piano, violin, viola, and cello

c.1781

PIANO QUINTET
Piano and string quartet

TRIO
Harpsichord solo; violin and cello accompaniment

TRIO
Piano solo; violin and cello obbligato

PIANO TRIO
Piano, violin, and cello

SONATA
Harpsichord solo; violin accompaniment

SONATA
Piano solo; violin obbligato

VIOLIN SONATA
Piano and violin

SONATA
Harpsichord solo; cello accompaniment

SONATA
Piano solo; cello obbligato

CELLO SONATA
Piano and cello

from the outer voices of the piano part; hence their presence was obligatory. Such works were called sonatas with violin and cello obbligato. In still other cases the keyboard was provided with violin or cello obbligato, or with obbligato parts for violin, viola, and cello. In all these cases the predominant place of the keyboard instrument was clearly maintained. And in these three cases are seen the Rococo forerunners of piano trio, violin or cello sonata, and piano quartet, respectively. This practice of so qualifying the string instrument's function remained in fashion long after the separation into solo and accompaniment roles had been resolved in chamber music. As late as 1797 Beethoven's cello sonatas, Opus 5, appeared with the legend, for piano with obbligato cello.

From a formal point of view, also, those movements of the composition which were in sonata form were changed, enlarged, and deepened. The innovations in melodic construction introduced by Pergolesi were the starting points for experiments to heighten the contrast between first and second theme groups, to construct themes out of melodies cast in regular period forms (as opposed to melodies growing out of short motives through repetition and imitation), and to construct transitions between themes out of thematic fragments. The end result of these successful experiments was a lengthened exposition section consisting of (*a*) first theme group of phrases, (*b*) transition, (*c*) second theme group, (*d*) coda—the total often reaching the respectable number of 75 to 100 measures. The development section, too, was broadened to some degree by the use of thematic fragments, characteristic portions of melodies heard earlier in the exposition, and sequence modulation. But its ultimate destiny did not develop for thirty years or more, until Haydn's quartets, "composed in an entirely new manner," appeared, in 1782.

Finally, and perhaps most important, the aesthetic content of sonata form was radically altered: subjectivity made its appearance, and dynamic changes introduced purely as expressive devices became new factors in musical composition. Since the early decades of the eighteenth century many composers had taken steps away from the single-mood movement of the Baroque, and steps toward the contrasting-mood movement (brought about through the use of contrasting first and second themes) of the Classical period. By 1745 such contrasts were well established, but in a diffident and refined manner. In the works of composers at Mannheim, of whom Johann Stamitz is the foremost representative, we have an orchestral and chamber-music literature which is largely subjective, contains extreme contrasts between thematic groups, hence is in keeping with the new aesthetic practices, and makes use of all the important changes and innovations in sonata form which had been accumulating during the previous twenty-five or more years.

In the years from 1720 to about 1750, Mannheim, in central western Germany, rose from a modest existence as a provincial town to a place in the musical sun. The transfer of the courts of Düsseldorf and Heidelberg to Mannheim and the presence of the music-loving Elector Karl Theodore at the head of the court—these were the external stimuli which led to the establishment of an orchestra renowned in all parts of Europe, to the assembling of a group of capable composers with Johann Stamitz (1717–1757) at their head, and to a new style of performance. The discoverer of the Mannheim school, Hugo Riemann,[13] evaluated its contributions to the rise of the Viennese Classical school in terms so enthusiastic that a lively controversy arose between him and the spokesman for the early Viennese composers, Guido Adler. Riemann credited the Mannheimers with creating all the musical factors for which they were famous in their day, namely, abruptly contrasting dynamics in sharply contrasting melodic fragments, expressive crescendos and diminuendos, and the form of the symphony itself. Adler [14] points to Monn, Starzer, Wagenseil, and others of the Viennese generation from c. 1740–1760, emphasizes their inclusion of the minuet in the symphony, their abandonment of the *basso continuo*, their reseparation of orchestral and chamber music, and considers them the true

13 In the forewords to Vols. III¹, VII², VIII², XV, and XVI of D.T.B.
14 *Handbuch*, II, 774 ff.

forerunners of Haydn, Mozart, and the early Beethoven. Opinion is still divided as to the exact place of the Mannheimers in music history.

Johann Stamitz had secured his positions as Karl Theodore's concertmaster (1743) and director of instrumental music (1745) by virtue of his excellent violin playing. His principal works are six orchestral trios, Opus 1, and a number of symphonies. The orchestral trios, which Riemann considers the starting point of the new style, may be taken as typical of Stamitz's works.[15] Dating from about 1751, each of these works contains four movements, in the sequence we had seen in a few Viennese compositions a decade earlier: fast, slow, minuet, fast. They are for two violins and bass with *basso continuo*, thus are typical of earlier eighteenth-century practice. But several other features set these trios apart from contemporary compositions.

There is first the use of extreme differences of texture which provide for musical as well as psychological contrasts, to a degree unknown before. The example on page 169, drawn from Stamitz's Trio Opus 1, No. 4, is seen to begin with a loud, forceful unison passage; this is immediately followed by a restrained, thin-textured section which contrasts with the first in style, tonality, texture, and mood. The forceful passage returns, and the restrained one likewise—all within a space of twenty-two measures. Such treatment of contrasting moods naturally brought with it a new use of dynamic changes. Let us review briefly the status of dynamics up to this point properly to appreciate the extent of Stamitz's innovation.

Dynamics in instrumental music up to about 1750 had been confined largely to alternations of loud and soft. Based on echo effects centuries old, used consistently in antiphonal choral works before 1600 (cf. the two Gabrielis), and forming an important expressive element in all seventeenth-century trio sonatas, this tradition of loud-soft (the so-called "terrace dynamics") was characteristic of practically all Baroque music. Numerous works based on this tradition are

---

[15] Reprinted in *Collegium musicum*, along with a trio in E major, Opus 5, No. 3, as Nos. 1–7. The opus number by no means indicates that the orchestral trios were Stamitz's first works; publishers were prone to assign opus numbers in the order in which the works reached their publishing houses, not in the order of composition.

well known: the sonata *Pian e forte* of Giovanni Gabrieli, the *Echo Song* of Lasso, the chorus "In Our Deep Vaulted Cell" from Purcell's *Dido and Aeneas*, and the closing chorus of Bach's *St. Matthew Passion* are some of the most famous. But in all these cases the softer phrase was simply a repetition of one heard previously; the alternate dynamic level had done nothing to change the form or style of the music. Indeed, in the Baroque period it could not have been otherwise. By the doctrine of affections, only one mood per movement was permitted in music; and a Baroque musical phrase, whether played loudly or softly, was tied to the phrases which surrounded it by the requirements of the single affection being exploited, and was indifferent to dynamic levels.

In the music of Stamitz, on the other hand, the alternate dynamic level was not used to bring about a modified repetition of a previously heard phrase. Rather, the musical contrast, embracing style, texture, and mood, was so complete that it inevitably required a different dynamic level as well. And so it appears in the above example from Stamitz's Opus 1, No. 4. The contrasting phrases (beginning in measures 9 and 17) by their very nature must be played softly. Their unassuming and intimate appeal, the fact that they carry on after virtually all the bombastic thematic motion has ceased for the moment—such characteristics assure the musician that a lower dynamic level is made necessary. In this and countless other cases Stamitz at once gave dynamics a new function by making them organic parts of musical composition. With this one set of six orchestral trios he showed for all time that a new music was at hand, a music in which emotional contrasts were achieved by dynamics as well as by tones.

The restriction of "terrace dynamics" was applied, in the Baroque period, primarily to instrumental groups. Such groups, always under the thumb of the keyboard performer realizing the *basso continuo*, knew of no other way of performing music than to engage in alternations of loud and soft; intermediate nuances were unknown in their activity. But not so with singers and violin soloists; they, in distinction to instrumental groups, had long since employed dynamic levels between loud and soft, had employed gradually increasing and decreasing volumes of tone in moving from one tonal level to another, and made full use of the conventional signs for a swelling tone ($<\ >$). It remained for Stamitz, and to an even greater degree to later adherents of his style, to make use of the terms "cresc." and "decres." [16] and to develop an orchestral discipline which made this refinement possible in performance. So simple an effect as that seen in the following example (measures 8–10) from Stamitz's Opus 1, No. 2, was a great innovation in his day, and the Mannheim crescendo became famous throughout Europe.

The innovations and style elements of Johann Stamitz were widely imitated by his colleagues at Mannheim, by his successors, and by composers geographically removed from that center. The "Mannheim style," with most of its elements derived from the founder of the school, became characteristic of a great amount of orchestral and chamber music by dozens of composers. Nicknames, such as the

[16] Riemann, *Handbuch*, II³, 146.

"Mannheimer sigh" (an accented suspension or an appogiatura) and the "Mannheimer rocket" (a melody based on chord tones ascending at great speed) testify to the amount of attention the style attracted. Countless examples of these and other Mannheim devices in the works of Mozart and Beethoven give evidence of the style's lasting influence on the great works of the Classical and Romantic periods.

Stamitz, Opus 1, No. 2

Returning now to the orchestra trios of Stamitz—those of Opus 1, as well as later works—we must recognize that they are not chamber-music works, even though only three voices (plus *continuo*) are indicated. On most occasions they were doubtlessly played by string orchestra and harpsichord; on others, wind instruments were added to reinforce the strings in the loud passages. Indeed, the earliest preserved edition of these Opus 1 trios, one published at Paris, includes in its title *ou à trois ou avec toutes l'orchestre.*[17] For true chamber music we must turn to other Mannheim composers and to non-Mannheimers influenced by the style of Stamitz. Vol. XVI of the *Denkmäler der Tonkunst in Bayern* contains a bibliography and thematic index of forty-seven Mannheim composers, many of whom were prolific in the field of chamber music. None attained to the level of Johann Stamitz's musical ideas, nor to his degree of originality. Several, however, stand head and shoulders above their colleagues, and their music may profitably be examined. Among them are Franz Xaver Richter (1709–1789), Ignaz Holzbauer (1711–1783), Johann Baptist Wendling (c. 1720–1797), Giuseppe Toëschi (c. 1724–c. 1800), Ernst Eichner (1740–1777), Wilhelm Cramer (1745–1799), Karl Stamitz (1746–1801), Anton Filtz (c. 1730–1760), and Christian Cannabich (1731–1798). We shall confine ourselves largely to a discussion of Franz Richter, the oldest of the group, and in a sense the best musician among them.

Richter seems by nature to have been more conservative than some of his younger associates. There is first of all, throughout most of his works, a contrapuntal element which one seeks vainly in Stamitz and in the majority of the other Mannheim composers. Richter's contrasts are achieved by changes in melodic contour, by changes in key, and to some extent by changes in texture. Almost never does he employ the abrupt changes of style, psychological as well as musical, that are so characteristic of Stamitz. In dynamic contrasts, too, Richter is more conservative than the latter. Sudden fortes or pianos and overwhelming crescendos are both foreign to his manner of writing—even though on a few occasions such dynamic contrasts do appear.

In formal scheme, also, Richter leans on past decades. Of the more than forty of his chamber-music compositions listed in the *D.T.B.* thematic index, the six string quartets of Opus 5 may be singled out.[18] Each of the six quartets contains three movements, and only

17 Riemann, *Handbuch*, II³, 133–134.
18 Reprinted in Vol. XV of D.T.B.; originally published in 1767 according to Rie-

two of the movements (the finales of Nos. 3 and 4) are minuets. This point becomes important when one recalls that the six orchestra trios of Stamitz had all contained minuets as third of four movements and that the inclusion of a minuet was decidedly an innovation in the decade from 1750 to 1760. As a matter of record, Stamitz was almost unique among the Mannheimers for his regular use of the minuet. Throughout the chamber music of these composers no regularity of form seems to have been established. Of the twenty-nine trios, quartets, and quintets by various Mannheimers in Vols. XV and XVI of the *D.T.B.*, eleven have two movements, sixteen have three (in seven of these the minuet is the last movement), and only two contain four movements. Still more noteworthy, only one of these last two—a wind quartet by Franz Danzi (1763–1826), Opus 56, No. 2 —contains movements in the order fast-slow-minuet-fast. The two-movement works are evenly divided between slow-fast and fast-slow; twelve of the sixteen three-movement works are fast-slow-fast. Thus, only in the very first works of the Mannheim school is the model for the soon-to-be Classical period's four-movement form consistently to be seen: the six orchestral trios of Stamitz's Opus 1, in which all are in the order fast-slow-minuet-fast. We shall see in the following chapter that Haydn, whose first quartets are roughly contemporary with Stamitz's Opus 1, adopted a similar form.

But we have digressed again; let us return to Richter. In his choice of forms he is conservative. But in another characteristic he is well in advance of his contemporaries: the great responsibilities given to the viola and the cello. Only rarely does the first violin dominate in the six string quartets of Opus 5. The lower instruments are equal in importance to the upper, and the cello in particular is entrusted with running passages and figurations not seen in chamber music— except in the Starzer divertimento mentioned above—since the trio sonatas of Buxtehude. The two following examples, drawn from the first movement of Opus 5, No. 3, will serve to show how the parts are divided among the four instruments and how this type of writ-

---

mann, in 1765 according to Eitner, *Quellen-Lexikon,* but quite possibly written much earlier.

ing, which the Germans call *durchbrochene Arbeit*, leads directly to the genuine "quartet style" of the later Classical period.

Anton Filtz (c. 1730–1760) was another of the enthusiastic but uninspired disciples of Stamitz. In none of his numerous works (Eitner's *Quellen-Lexikon* lists about thirty) did he rise beyond the level of primitive apprenticeship.[19] But one innovation must be credited to him: the establishment of the string trio for two violins and cello without *continuo*, a combination which became one of the standard groupings of the Classical period. Filtz's Opus 3, No. 6, reprinted in *D.T.B.*, Vol. XV, is one of the few four-movement chamber-music works to be found in the entire Mannheim stock, and is perhaps the first work in which three string instruments, unaccompanied by *continuo* and with a degree of equality among themselves, are employed.

We now leave the Mannheimers at Mannheim, but come to one of their disciples far removed from his spiritual home. With the mention of Johann Schobert (c. 1720–1767) we touch upon one of the contemporaries of Haydn, and a composer whose chamber music with piano opened up new paths which lead directly to the giants of the Classical period. Little is known of Schobert's life, except that he was either Austrian or Silesian by birth, that he was

19 Riemann, D.T.B., XV, xii.

engaged as chamber musician to the Prince of Conti at Paris, and that he—with his entire family—died of mushroom poisoning. A selection of his works is reprinted in *D.D.T.*, Vol. XXXIX; the chamber-music compositions found there include five sonatas for piano and violin, two piano trios, and two quartets for piano, two violins, and cello.

In Schobert's music we find, possibly for the first time, the Mannheim style transferred to the piano. Here are the same type of melodic line, the same Mannheimer "rockets" and "sighs." But along with Mannheim characteristics is an impulsiveness, a power, and a degree of force that even Stamitz's music lacks. Schobert makes considerable use of thunderous tremolos, of rapidly moving figures in the left hand, of unexpected melodic turns—all of which combine to give his music an air of virtuoso brilliance. He must be reckoned as one of the founders of modern piano music; many devices we associate with the mature Beethoven are first found in Schobert.

But the string parts of these sonatas, trios, and quartets do not bear out the promise given by the piano parts. In the truest sense of the word, the strings accompany. In the trios and the quartets, for example, the cello doubles the bass notes of the piano part; in those works, as well as in the sonatas, the violin part contains a few small countermelodies, progresses in thirds with the piano melody, or adds a bit of rhythmic vitality to the harmony notes. Occasionally the violin is entrusted with the theme for a few measures, but then lapses into its accompanying role again. Two exceptions to this practice may be seen in four minuets: those of the trios Opus 16, Nos. 1 and 4, and of the quartets Opus 7, No. 1, and Opus 14, No. 1. In the first two cases the violin and the cello progress in thirds and sixths, and alone provide melodic interest. In the two latter cases the two violins are similarly employed; here the cello is again relegated to a bass role. In all four cases the piano engages in a modest figured accompaniment which shows admirable restraint. The conclusion can be drawn that minuets were still newcomers in the sonata's framework and hence deserved to be treated somewhat as they were treated in the dance suite of the Rococo period. At any rate, these four minuet movements give the only available evidence that Schobert was ever diffident in writing his piano parts.

Schobert's piano trios and quartets testify to the new place of the piano in chamber music. Its old place as realizer of the *basso continuo* now gone, that instrument assumed the dominant role in one branch of chamber-music literature. As we have seen in these works, the strings either accompanied or were obligatory. Indeed, Schobert sometimes designated his string parts as "ad libitum," and his publisher often furnished a second keyboard part in place of the strings.[20] But in spite of this characteristic, Schobert must be credited with systematically establishing a chamber-music literature in which the piano part is fully written out and with laying the groundwork for the important contemporary media of piano quartet and piano quintet.

A number of composers yet remain unmentioned, notably two sons of Bach: Karl Philipp Emanuel (1714–1788) and Johann Christian (1735–1782). The first, who was briefly discussed above in connection with the development of the keyboard sonata, must take a minor role in chamber music. String trios (from 1756) and string quartets (1773) bearing his name remain cool, conservative North German works distinguished only by their grace and their use of well-contrasting second theme groups. Johann Christian, on the other hand, was in all essentials a follower of the Mannheim composers. Among his most important works are the six quintets of Opus 11, published about 1776; [21] these quintets are even dedicated to Karl Theodore, the Elector Palatine, head of the court of Mannheim. They are for flute, oboe, violin, viola, and cello; the second, third, and fifth quintets contain two movements, the others three— again a Mannheim characteristic. Much of the time the quintets are in the form of dialogues between two pairs of instruments: flute and oboe opposite violin and viola, with the cello providing an old-fashioned bass, figured to some extent. The figuring indicates that Bach desired a *continuo* accompaniment in these works; but such

20 Moser, *Geschichte der deutschen Musik*, II¹, 344.
21 Reprinted in *Das Erbe deutscher Musik*, Vol. III. A trio in D major is found in *Collegium musicum*, No. 19.

accompaniment is by no means necessary. The harmonies are complete even without the realized bass; there are ample motion and rhythmic vitality in the string and wind parts to insure a satisfactory performance even without the keyboard accompaniment.

8

FRANZ JOSEPH HAYDN

FRANZ JOSEPH HAYDN was born in 1732 at Rohrau, a little Austrian village near the Hungarian border; he was the second of twelve children, six of whom died in infancy. His parents were industrious, honorable people in humble circumstances; they came from a line of artisans and farmers. Franz Joseph's father was a wagon maker; his mother had been a cook. Although neither parent was trained in music, the elder Haydn was fond of singing and music-making of all sorts.

In his early years Franz Joseph was consigned to the care of his relative Matthias Franck, in a neighboring village. There he attracted the attention of the choirmaster of St. Stephen's Cathedral at Vienna, and was promptly engaged for the choir of that church. At the age of eight he set out for Vienna. He remained in the choir until his voice broke, and at the age of seventeen, in 1749, he was cast adrift.

His musical instruction had been perfunctory; a few lessons on the violin and harpsichord, a few voice lessons, and rudimentary instruction in Latin and other subjects. But Haydn's interest and keen observation had enabled him to go far beyond the bounds of formal teaching. The experience at St. Stephen's gave him a practical insight into the problems of music and a knowledge of choral repertoire. What more he needed to know he found out for himself. To the end of his life he was his own teacher.

At the time Haydn was thrown upon his own resources, Vienna was probably the most musical city of Europe. No festivity was complete without music; serenaders roamed the streets; everyone composed. Haydn's cheerful, equable disposition found some satisfaction, and a meager livelihood, in joining groups of serenaders; he played with them and wrote for them. But such an existence was not to be endured forever. Good fortune placed Haydn in the path of several influential friends, among them Metastasio, the court poet, and Porpora, renowned composer and teacher. Through them he met his first employer, von Fürnberg, about 1755.

This Austrian nobleman, as fond of music as most of the aristocracy were, engaged Haydn as violinist to assist in his chamber-music evenings, to which cultivated amateurs and professionals alike were invited. Haydn remained with von Fürnberg less than a year, for in 1756 he was again without regular employment. About 1759 he was engaged by Count Morzin, with the title of composer and director of music. Morzin's musical resources were somewhat greater than von Fürnberg's had been, for at the former's estate Haydn found himself in charge of twelve or more musicians. Two years later Morzin was obliged to cut expenses (the rumor is that his impending marriage made the step necessary), and the small orchestra was disbanded. But Haydn was immediately engaged by Prince Paul Anton Eszterházy in the employment of whose family he remained until death. Thus, in 1761 began the long association with the wealthy and sympathetic Eszterházys, who provided the external means to make Haydn's enormous musical output possible.

Prince Paul's main residence was the huge old moated castle of Eisenstadt, some thirty miles from Vienna. There the prince maintained an elaborate establishment which included some fifteen or twenty musicians, instrumentalists as well as singers. Haydn was placed second in command of these musical forces, for Joseph Werner, appointed musical director in 1728, was still active in 1761. Little less than a year after Haydn's appointment Prince Paul died; his brother Nicholas became heir to all the extensive Eszterházy estates. And Nicholas, familiar with the palace of Versailles, immediately made plans to build a comparable residence on the Hungarian plains. Still farther from Vienna than Eisenstadt had been, the new palace, which Nicholas called "Eszterháza," was completed in 1766. Shortly before the household moved to the magnificent new estate, Werner died; Haydn succeeded him as musical director and composer to Prince Nicholas.

At Eszterháza, Haydn lived and worked for twenty-four years, until the death of Nicholas in 1790. Encumbered by a shrewish, unsympathetic, and selfish wife, far removed from the stimulation regular contact with other composers and other music might have given him (his friendship with Mozart did not begin until 1781), isolated, except for winter visits to Vienna, burdened by a mass of administrative and disciplinary detail—in spite of these handicaps Haydn remained serene, joyful, and good-natured. His creative activity during these years was enormous; we shall give fuller accounts of its scope below.

Nicholas's heir, in 1790, was another Paul Anton Eszterházy. The latter had little interest in music, however. Immediately upon taking possession of the estates Paul disbanded the orchestra and retired Haydn, after increasing the handsome pension Nicholas had willed to his faithful friend and composer. Haydn, free for the first time in three decades, and well provided for, returned to Vienna. Almost immediately an enterprising concert manager from London, Johann Salomon, prevailed upon him to go to that city, to compose an opera, six symphonies, and a number of other works—for a handsome fee. Late in 1790, at the age of fifty-eight, never having been more than a short distance from Vienna, Haydn embarked upon his first visit to England.

It is interesting to note that Haydn had become much better known and was much more highly respected abroad than in Austria and Germany. As early as 1764 a Parisian publisher named Venier issued a number of Haydn's early quartets, together with works of other composers (Beck, Pfeiffer, and Schetky, among them), with the legend, "Unknown names which it is well to know." [1] By 1785 Haydn had received a commission to compose for the Cathedral at Cadiz, and his works were regularly performed at Paris and London. Yet as late as 1793, after Haydn's enormously successful London

[1] Strunk, "Haydn's Divertimenti for Baryton, Viola, and Bass," *Musical Quarterly* (New York, April, 1932), p. 227.

visit, the Bonn correspondent of a Berlin paper wrote that "one begins to allow Haydn to be grouped with Cannabich, K. Stamitz, and their consorts." [2]

Haydn's visit to London lasted almost two years, and was eminently successful in every respect. His musical fame secure, his compositions universally admired, Haydn returned to Vienna with the applause of all London ringing in his ears and the degree of Doctor of Music, conferred by Oxford, in his pocket. After some eighteen months of resting in Vienna, Haydn returned to London for a second time, again through the urging—and financial guarantees—of Salomon. The second visit, lasting from February, 1794, to August, 1795, was as successful as the first had been.

But Haydn had aged during the London visits. The hundreds of pages of music, the dozens of large and small works, the strain of constant activity had begun to wear down the industrious composer. From 1795 composition became more difficult for him, although songs, quartets and the two great oratorios *The Creation* and *The Seasons* were written. In his last years he found refuge in his friends and his memories. Increasing weakness made public appearances impossible; increasing age dried up the stream of compositions which had flowed so copiously for almost sixty years. In 1809, at the age of seventy-seven, with Napoleon's armies beginning the bombardment of Vienna, Haydn died.

One can best understand some aspects of Haydn's style after realizing the conditions under which he worked. Haydn's position with the Eszterházy family was typical of scores of similar positions in great and small aristocratic households throughout Europe. Musicians placed at the heads of such private establishments were conductors, composers, disciplinarians, administrators, and musical men-of-all-work. They wore livery, dined with the servants, waited upon their noble employers for detailed instructions concerning this or that assignment, and in general were upper-class menials.

On the positive side one can point out that such musicians had relative security, were sure of having their works performed, and

² Riemann, *Handbuch*, II³, 151.

were given ample opportunity to compose—even though they did compose to order. At a time when public concerts were rare, when performance royalties were unthought of, when plagiarism was the order of the day, when a livelihood for the independent composer did not exist, the relationship of musician to patron was a wholesome one. Many of the aristocrats able to maintain private orchestras were themselves cultivated and sincere music lovers.

The twenty-nine years of active association between Haydn and the Eszterházys were on the whole pleasant ones. Haydn worked early and late at his various duties: composing and rehearsing operas in preparation for some noble guest's visit, writing new symphonies as they were called for, producing new masses for festivals and holy days, having available new quartets for regular and special occasions. That Nicholas Eszterházy was for so long pleased with these new works speaks well for his musical taste.

But Haydn suffered greatly from the enforced isolation which residence at Eszterháza brought with it. Again, as in his teens, he was thrown upon his own resources. He was compelled to develop his own style in solitude, to experiment, to invent. His own self-criticism, his innate sense of what was right in music, kept him from deteriorating into just another craftsman. What in another situation would have acted as a stimulant and corrective—namely, contact with other music and other musicians—was, in his early years at Eszterháza, almost entirely missing. He knew the works of Karl Philipp Emanuel Bach and other contemporary composers; later he was to know and admire and learn from Mozart. But live association with the great world of music, with performances of old and new works, with professional shop talk, was denied him to a great extent in the first twenty years at Eszterháza, in the years when his style was developing its personal characteristics.

It is not surprising, in the light of the above, to find that much of Haydn's work is uneven. In the stress of constant composition, usually against a deadline, many pieces issued from his pen which were unworthy of him. But having once erred, he seldom repeated the bad judgment. The works show a gradual improvement up to the point where he felt his style had reached its full development. When that point had been reached, Haydn did not regress. One has only to listen to his London symphonies, to his last quartets, to *The Creation*, all written in his sixties, to realize how firmly Haydn retained control of his musical faculties.

The conditions under which he wrote did not lend themselves to an orderly indexing of his works. Some pieces were written to be performed once. Many were designed for publication, and were better cared for. Most of them found their way into the private library of the Eszterházys, and were brought out as the occasion demanded. As a consequence, fewer works of Haydn have reached the general public than of any other major composer. The complete edition of his works, begun in 1908, was planned to embrace some eighty volumes. To date only eight or ten have been issued.[3] But the scope of the project gives us an insight into the enormous quantity of Haydn's compositions. About thirty works for the stage, including operas, operettas, and pieces for marionettes; twelve or more masses; three oratorios; almost two hundred songs, airs, catches, and vocal canons; a number of motets and fragments of other sacred music—this vast amount of music for and with voices. Among the instrumental works are found between one hundred and four and one hundred and forty symphonies;[4] five or six dozen pieces for groups of wind and string instruments, including serenades, divertimentos, and allied forms; fifty or more concertos for various instruments; almost two hundred pieces for the baryton;[5] more than fifty sonatas for keyboard instrument and several more for violin and piano. And finally, among what we have defined as chamber music are about thirty trio sonatas, thirty-five piano trios, and eighty-three string quartets.

A fearful list! One does not envy the editors of the *Complete Works* their task of arranging it for publication, discarding spurious

[3] By Breitkopf & Härtel (Leipzig, 1908).
[4] The presence of some spurious works and some doubtful ones makes the exact count uncertain.
[5] The *viola bordone*, an eighteenth-century string instrument upon which Nicholas Eszterházy was proficient.

works, removing duplicates, and tracing relationships in this vast accumulation. That many of these works have been lost goes without saying, and that many are mediocre or worse is equally plausible. No composer has yet succeeded in writing only masterpieces; even the greatest geniuses slip from their lofty perches at times. We are made happy, for this serves to remind us that they, too, are human. And Haydn was human indeed.

This cold statistical listing can perform only one service here: to show us weaker mortals what a lifetime of industry can bring forth. The curious reader may estimate the number of separate movements contained within the total works of Haydn. He will find some twenty-five hundred. Apportioning these to the fifty years of Haydn's creative activity, roughly from 1750 to 1800, he will arrive at an approximation of one movement a week for half a century! The equivalent of one symphony a month for two generations; of a quartet every four weeks, of a sonata per fortnight—and sustained throughout a lifetime! And composing was only one part, almost a minor part, of Haydn's work: rehearsing, performing, and administering took up equally large segments of his time. One never ceases to marvel that so large a proportion of Haydn's available compositions are of masterful quality, that he so seldom repeated himself, that he was never at a loss for worthwhile, characteristic musical ideas.

The vocal portions of this mass of music lie outside our interest here, as do the concertos, sonatas, and smaller pieces. The symphonies will engage our attention only as they demonstrate a point not made in the chamber music. And even in the latter field will we restrict ourselves. The trio sonatas probably would offer nothing that we have not already seen in earlier examples by other composers. Two or three of Haydn's trio sonatas are available at present writing; if they may be taken as typical of the larger bulk—and only the issuance of the *Complete Works* can determine that point—one may draw parallels between Haydn's trio sonatas and those of Gluck, Sammartini, and other mid-century composers. Likewise the piano trios; here again little would be gained by a detailed discussion of those works. While many of them are excellent, and some contain Haydn's finest musical inspirations, they are essentially piano sonatas with violin and cello accompaniment. No harm is done if the string instruments are omitted in performance.

But the eighty-three string quartets are another story. These works loom so large in a survey of Haydn's compositions that a detailed account of them alone would give a true picture of that composer's total style, development, and importance in music history. Haydn and the string quartet are so closely linked together in the chamber musician's mind that concepts of Haydn and the piano trio or Haydn and the trio sonata cause something of a jolt. Finally, some twenty or thirty of the quartets are among the most important part of the string quartet's repertoire; they can best be evaluated and appreciated if their relationships to the remaining quartets are seen in detail. For these reasons the balance of this chapter will be concerned only with the eighty-three string quartets of Haydn.

Several points must be kept in mind in reading this account of Haydn's early quartets. First, that no real distinction was made between orchestral and chamber music in the middle of the eighteenth century. The terms "symphony," "divertimento," and "trio" were rather freely bandied about; one has only to recall the Stamitz "trios" for orchestra, the many "simphonies" for three to five instruments, and the indiscriminate instrumentation of compositions of the divertimento class. Titles can serve no purpose here; one must look to the content of the works themselves. Second is the fact that *divertimentos* usually contained minuets; symphonies in general did not. Often one's only clue to the genre of a work is the number of its movements—at least in the early decades of the Classical period. And third, that the real test of whether a work is modern—in the sense of 1750 or thereabouts—is whether or not it includes a *basso continuo*.

During the course of Haydn's first employment, as violinist and chamber musician to von Fürnberg in 1755–1756, he wrote twelve works; we know them today as the two sets of string quartets, six in each, labeled Opus 1 and Opus 2. But these twelve works were not all quartets in their original version. Opus 1, No. 4, is Haydn's first symphony, and was not at first included in the quartets. Opus 2, Nos. 3 and 5 were originally sextets with two horns. Both sets were at first known as divertimentos, and appeared in the early catalogues as being for two violins, viola, and *basso*. To complete the list of characteristics which sets these works apart from later ones, we may mention that all but Opus 1, No. 4 (the symphony), contain five movements: a minuet appears both preceding and following the central slow movement. The one feature which establishes these works as belonging to the future is that there is no trace of a *continuo* part or need of a *continuo* performer. The evidence is strong that as late as the London visits, 1790 and 1794, Haydn accompanied his symphonies at the keyboard, amplifying the harmonies and strengthening the bass in the good old traditional manner. But not in the chamber music; even in the earliest works that practice has no place.

The texture of these quartets is homophonic in the extreme. Thematic material is based largely on broken-chord patterns whose repetitions and naïve elaborations are confined to the first and second violins. Indeed, in distribution of melodic materials the two violins come off as well as they did in the old trio sonatas. Viola and cello (we may read the *basso* as "cello or bass," with the certainty that the cello was employed more frequently than the bass) are confined to harmony notes and to animated pedal points.

In Chapter 7 we discussed the preliminary steps leading toward sonata form. That discussion may have left the impression that with Haydn all stumbling toward that form ceases, and that from 1755 we have the real thing. Far from it! The quartets of Opus 1 and Opus 2 exhibit hardly any advance over the simple two-part forms we found in the late Baroque and Rococo periods. A typical first movement begins and ends in the tonic key; its middle part gravitates to the dominant and ascends again toward the tonic. But there is yet little trace of growth in the themes, of comment upon them, of subtle contrasting of their component parts—elements which characterize the form as it appears from 1781 onward.

But three features which Haydn's music carries throughout his lifetime are present even in these youthful works: dramatic utterance in a compact and harmonically simple form; a masterful handling of phrase lengths, resulting in typical phrases five, seven, or any other number of measures long; an ingeniousness and boundless inspiration in minuets. And wherever the mood of the music permits—notably in the last movements—an effervescent humor, a light-hearted play with comic elements, is the rule. If music is a reflection of a composer's temperament, Haydn must have been a delightful person to know: never stodgy, never conventional for the sake of convention, never trite. Even these early works give us the picture of a man to whom morbid gloom was virtually unknown.

We might ask what significance may be attached to the fact that eleven of these twelve works contain five movements instead of the four movements of the old trio sonata. A brief review of the latter's content may clarify the picture. The trio sonata's four movements, it will be remembered, were slow-fast-slow-fast; we have traced their origin back to the contrasting slow and fast sections of the sonata of the 1620's. The innovations of Pergolesi, however, had taken place not in the four-movement form thus arrived at, but in the three-movement form taken from the Neapolitan opera overture—even though Pergolesi's works were also called trio sonatas. And the latter's sequence of tempos was regularly fast-slow-fast. One does well to keep in mind this duality of trio-sonata types. We had seen, some decades later, that the Viennese divertimento composers had chosen the Neapolitan-Pergolesi three-movement version for their vehicle, and had built upon it by adding additional movements. There was no limit to the number of movements that might be so added. Entrance and exit marches appeared at either end of the set of three, and minuets were interspersed between other movements. Haydn, in adhering to the tradition of the time, wrote his first works in the divertimento manner, both as to content and as to exterior framework: two minuets seemed appropriate, and two minuets were written.

Not until the six quartets of Opus 3 appeared—and the dates are

variously reported from 1755 to 1765—did the *modern* four-movement form achieve some degree of regular employment. These quartets, along with those of Opus 1 and Opus 2, seem to have filled a
great need, for they were published in many parts of Europe: all
eighteen quartets were published at Leipzig in 1760 and at Paris in
1764–1769; Opus 1 was published at Amsterdam in 1765.[6] And
with Opus 3 the quartets of Haydn begin to find a place in the modern repertoire. Here we come in contact with music that may be
heard on the concert stage today.

Almost every major composer has written at least one piece which
touches the popular heart. Brahms's "Lullaby," Beethoven's "Minuet
in G," and Rachmaninoff's "Prelude in C sharp minor" are typical
examples. For Haydn the piece is the famous "Serenade"; and that
piece is the slow movement of Opus 3, No. 5. It is a good example of
the song-like style of Haydn's early slow movements: a lyric or
dramatic melody played by the first violin, surrounded by a large or
small amount of embroidery and other ornamentation and a discreet
and subdued accompaniment of pulsating repeated notes or (as in
the case of the "Serenade") pizzicato chord tones—these two elements are found in at least nine of the first eighteen slow movements.
Dramatic moments are present in abundance, and the change of pace
upon which drama depends likewise. But a distribution of the more
important (or at least the more obvious) musical details among all the
instruments is lacking in these early works.

The six quartets of Opus 9, probably written about 1769, mark
another step forward in Haydn's musical development. That they
were musically superior to the first eighteen quartets was known to
Haydn himself. August Artaria, a son of the Artaria who published
most of Haydn's works from 1780 on, often heard his father say that
in later years Haydn wished his early quartets to be ignored and to
have the numbering begin with the nineteenth quartet (the work we
know as Opus 9, No. 1). The elder Artaria conformed to the composer's wish and drew up a thematic catalogue of the quartets, omit-

6 Pohl, *Joseph Haydn*, I, 333–334.

ting the first eighteen.[7] Still later, when the early works of Haydn were reprinted by Artaria, the quartets we know as Opus 9 and Opus 17 were reprinted as Opus 1 and Opus 2.[8]

It is difficult to call attention to certain details and demonstrate that one quartet is superior to another. We shall have to be content with pointing out that the themes of Opus 9 are no longer so firmly tied to the tonic triad, but are full of imaginative little melodic bits, that they are, in general, shorter and more amenable to working over, and that the quartets are more perfectly formed, more appealing— in a word, better. One must hear these quartets and immediately thereafter the earlier ones; then and only then is the superiority of Opus 9 revealed.

A parenthetical remark is in order here. The work of the musical historian and analyst resembles the function of milestones and road markers. The analyst, having gone before, is in the position of pointing out details, of directing the reader's attention to this or that musical fact. But everyone must do his own traveling; he must arrive at his destination under his own power. To depend upon analysis or historical description to the exclusion of personal acquaintance with the musical works themselves is to negate the purposes of both music and musicology. There is no substitute for hearing the music; and in these days of inexpensive editions, innumerable recordings, and inexhaustible musical enthusiasm there is no excuse for not hearing it.

Haydn's next set of quartets, Opus 17, written in 1771, presents several new features. First, it is as though the violinist for whom Haydn was writing had suddenly achieved a virtuoso brilliance. During his many years at Eszterháza, Haydn enjoyed the friendship and the sterling musical qualities of Luigi Tomasini, the Prince's first violinist. There can be no question but that the excellence of Tomasini's playing influenced Haydn in his quartet writing;[9] it seems likely that the latter wrote with the violinist actually in mind. The

[7] Artaria and Botstiber, *Joseph Haydn und das Verlagshaus Artaria*, p. 87.
[8] *Ibid.*, p. 99.   [9] Pohl, *Joseph Haydn*, I, 262.

first violin had always dominated in Haydn's quartet writing; now he begins to dazzle even his colleagues. Double stops, arpeggios, string crossings, passages which ascend to the violin's stratosphere— in short, all the traditional virtuoso devices are there in abundance. Along with this increased brilliance in the fast movements is an increased thoughtfulness—perhaps "expressiveness" is a better word— in the slow ones. Dramatic tension is temporarily lost sight of in the interests of greater melodic beauty and more equable distribution of melodies among all four instruments. Haydn seems to have become aware of viola and cello as musical individuals in the quartets of Opus 17. Their long apprenticeship as supporters of the melody, as providers of the harmonic foundation, now over, the lower instruments are entrusted with running passages, discreet tunes, and, occasionally, with the principal melody, to a degree unknown in the early quartets. Viola and cello must now begin to practice, to prove themselves worthy of being in the company of the brilliant first violin and the competent second.

Also in these quartets is an unevenness that is surprising when we look back upon the quartets of Opus 3 and Opus 9. Along with movements of outstanding beauty, charm, and wit are dull and stodgy ones. We have come to expect more of Haydn than the minuet of Opus 17, No. 1, gives us. The movement is adequate, but nothing more; one waits for something striking to happen, and nothing does. The finale of Opus 17, No. 2, likewise; the theme is abrupt and angular and is paced neither to provide a sense of inexorable motion toward a climax nor to elevate one through sheer joy at the rapid movement. Several times Haydn threatens to break out into an accompanied fugue—which would have been a decided novelty in this set—but fails to do so. Similarly, two or three other movements are disappointing and below the standard Haydn has set for himself thus far. But, on the whole, unevenness of quality should not condemn the whole set; Opus 17, in its brilliance, marks a considerable advance over the quartets of Opera 1, 2, 3, and 9.

The six quartets of Opus 20, although written only a year after the Opus 17 set, namely, in 1772, mark a real milestone in Haydn's path of development. The two sets are roughly contemporary; but Haydn made giant strides in his progress toward complete mastery between the writing of the two series. Having achieved the brilliance typical of the earlier set, Haydn now moves in other directions. From Opus 20 it is no longer feasible to treat a whole set of quartets together (but we shall probably continue that type of treatment if only for reasons of convenience); no one quartet is typical of a set, and individual differences are greater than formal similarities. Each of the twenty-four movements of Opus 20 bears some mark of Haydn's genius, be it in the direction of melodic contour, of formal innovation, or of technical competence—and in almost every case the mark is a different one. From the very first quartet of this set Haydn shows a new regard for tone color, for the melodic possibilities of the cello. Quartet style, one factor of which is musical equality of all four instruments, is well on the way to completion through this new use of the cello.

The best evidence of the newest development is seen in the first few measures of Opus 20, No. 2. The cello announces the theme while the first violin actually has six measures rest. This simple fact is world-shaking when one realizes how completely the first violin had dominated in the first thirty quartets. In the one hundred and twenty-seven movements of those quartets, there are only three which do not begin with the first violin's announcement of the theme at the very outset of the movement; and in all three of the exceptions the second violin, which is in a sense the first playing in a lower octave, temporarily takes over the dominating role. Now, suddenly, the picture changes. In Opus 20, No. 2, the cello sings out the theme, the second violin ambles along in thirds below the cello, and the viola provides the bass. Later in the same movement, the viola announces the theme for a single measure, the first violin accompanies, and the second provides the bass.

These are small beginnings, it is true; but the ice has been broken. Haydn seems a bit uncertain of the new technique at first, for the following quartet begins with viola and first violin announcing the theme in octaves. Does he not trust the new method? His confidence seems quickly restored, for in the last movement of the same quartet the second violin, bravely and alone, presents the melody upon which the movement is based. And in the trio of the following quartet's minuet the cello is given the theme. So it goes: at first, tentatively and with some doubts; later, definitely and in full confidence. A true four-voice texture gradually appears, a texture in which each instrument has something to say, after which it is relegated to the background. It must be said that even so, the first violin's background is considerably in front of the other instruments' foreground. The former's domination, while more discreet and less consistent, is not so easily canceled entirely.

Meanwhile, consequences of the new method, consequences of great import, are being realized by Haydn. Having once broken away from the *galant* characteristic of a single melody always in the uppermost instrument, Haydn is in a position to carry the new freedom to its logical conclusion. He is faced with a medium employing four equal instruments, a medium in which concepts of solo melody and group accompaniment may at times be disregarded. And the logical consequence of this freedom is—counterpoint. At this moment Haydn returns to a device ignored by a generation of Rococo composers and writes contrapuntally. The final movements of three of the quartets (Opus 20, Nos. 2, 5, and 6) are four-voice fugues. Haydn labels them with four subjects, two subjects, and three subjects, respectively, depending upon how many countermelodies accompany the principal subject throughout the fugue.

This is not the place to give an account of the habits of textbook writers. One point very much needs to be made, however, a point which concerns everyone who reads textbooks on music. Almost invariably one finds references to the "fugue form"; the authors of that fiction, following ancient authority, purport to describe a fugal structure so regular that its formula can be set down. Any careful examination of a considerable number of fugues by Baroque masters will convince the interested reader that such is not the case. Fugue is not a form; it is a mode of treatment—a style. As such it has its laws, its dramatic tensions, and its factor of harmonic unity; as such it was treated by Bach and other Baroque composers, and as such we find it in Haydn.

Textbooks tell us that the "fugue form" consists of a number of sections or expositions, each in a key closely related to the key of the fugue itself: a section in the tonic, one in the subdominant, one in the dominant, and so forth. These sections are separated by others called episodes, in which the theme and its countertheme are imitated freely. A stretto, in which theme and countertheme overlap in a climax of contrapuntal fury, ends the fugue. The books often go further and give exact description of length and sequence of sections, number of entrances, and the like.

If that be true, then Bach was ignorant of the rules, or broke them with impunity, for almost every fugue by that master establishes its own form, goes its own harmonic way. One thing is constant: the type of treatment, the contrapuntal nature of the exposition, episode, and stretto. But Bach goes no further in establishing formal regularity; it would be well for textbook writers to be equally restrained. These writers invent a form which they call "scholastic fugue" and point out that every great fugue departs merely in some details from their invention—that the latter represents the "average" course of a fugue. And precisely what does one gain by averaging a number of great fugues and calling the result a musical form?

The reader may have gathered that fugue is not a form, but a style of treatment. From this point of view one can realize the importance of the fugues of Opus 20 to Haydn's total style development. Seen in conjunction with a backward glance over the earlier quartets, they represent the logical fulfillment of Haydn's desire to develop a texture made out of four equally important instrumental parts. Seen as fugues *per se*, they mark a return of the contrapuntal element to instrumental music, a return devoutly to be wished for ever since the Baroque gave way to the early Rococo (c.1730). But seen with a look into the future, they enable Haydn to employ all the contrapuntal resources of the past in combination with the melodic and formal developments of his own time. What use is he to make of them?

Melody has been defined as a succession of musical tones which together convey a musical thought. In the thirty-six quartets from Opus 1 to Opus 20, Haydn has written hundreds of melodies. The typical melody up to this point has a beginning, a middle, and an end; it has a contour and a rhythmic shape, so that it may be perceived as a unit; and it generally appeals to our sense of either lyric beauty or dramatic tension. In almost every case it is accompanied by a more or less elaborate harmonic substructure. Thus, melody and accompaniment, being composed of different musical materials, are on different planes of musical thought; their interaction has produced a texture quite similar to that of the Rococo period's *style galant*.

Now, fugues contain melodies too. But fugues differ from other musical styles in that there is no separation into melody and accompaniment; all voices are engaged in simultaneous melodic utterance, and all voices are on the same musical plane. Hence the application of the term "polyphony" to fugal style, for polyphony is the art of employing two or more melodies simultaneously. One further characteristic of fugal style may be noted: usually the first or principal melody is heard together with another melody which differs from the first in contour, rhythm, and place within the metrical group (or measure).

Does Haydn write only fugues from this point on? Scarcely that, for this would have meant reverting to late Baroque style. He does something much better, and vastly more important for the future of music. He finds a way of combining homophonic melodies and polyphonic textures; or, in a better phrase, he employs a polyphonic texture in forms whose content had been largely that of the homophonic Rococo period. That he was fully aware of his innovation is proved by his propaganda for the next set of six quartets: Opus 33, written about ten years after the Opus 20 set. In his announcement of the Opus 33 quartets, first published early in 1782,[10] he proclaims quartets "written in an entirely new manner." The new manner contains two factors.

First, the melodies contain a greater variety of distinctive intervals

[10] Artaria and Botstiber, *Joseph Haydn und das Verlagshaus Artaria*, pp. 21, 93.

and a more elaborate rhythmic scheme. They are more loosely held together, and are in fact composed of a number of short contrasting motives. The phrases below give examples of both old and new types; the new are, of course, those found in Opus 33 and later.

Second, when Haydn begins to construct a musical piece out of a melody of the new type, he proceeds to dissect it, to break it down into its motives, and to reassemble the fragments with all the contrapuntal arts of which he is now master, but of which he had given

virtually no hint before the fugues of Opus 20. The best example
of the new manner is seen in the first movement of Opus 33, No. 2,
the principal theme of which has been quoted immediately above.
A fragment of that movement's development section is given also.
To make the point still clearer, it will be well to compare the old
style; the following is drawn from Opus 17, No. 2, whose theme
was quoted on page 195.

At this late date, when music of the Classical period is spread before us in wholesale lots, when generations of composers after Haydn
have appropriated his "new manner" and have made us thoroughly
familiar with applications of it, one can only with difficulty realize
the importance of the innovation. At the moment when Haydn realized the implications of the new manner and made it an element of
his mature way of life, the quartet was completed and quartet style
was an accomplished fact. A new principle had been given to the art

of music: the principle of thematic development based upon contrapuntal devices and employed in a homophonic context. From this
point on the quartets of Haydn become deeper or lighter or more
lyric or more comic—in a word, they become individual works of
art, bound together by adherence to a common style, but bound no
longer by type characteristics.

At first the new manner is used tentatively. A few measures here,
a few there, suffice. Large sections of these works are still in the style
of Opus 20, with one notable exception: the minuet movement becomes faster and receives the name *scherzo*. This Italian word implies
playfulness or a joke-like character and gives a clue to the changed
content. The fifty or so minuets Haydn has written up to this point
are astonishing in their great variety of mood. Some are full-bodied
and severe; others, light and flowing; many are gleeful; others merely
gay. But almost all have some semblance of dignity reminiscent of
the courtly dance out of which they came. The scherzos of Opus 33
have lost some of their dignity and gained a great deal of humor.
But it would be a mistake to place them in the same category with the
enormous movements to which Beethoven gave the same name a few
decades later. The latter, as we shall see in due course, transferred
the principle of thematic development to the scherzo and confided
to it some of his most dramatic ideas. Complete sonata-form movements are found among Beethoven's later scherzos—a phenomenon
we do not find among Haydn's. We must be satisfied that Haydn
invested the minuet with a new content, accelerated its tempo and
provided moments of real humor in 3/4 meter. It is noteworthy that
Haydn did not use the word "scherzo" after the Opus 33 movements, even though several "minuets" among his last quartets are
marked presto and are very similar to the movements now under
discussion.

Here is an appropriate place to mention a point which, as far as
I know, has never been adequately examined: the location of the
minuet-scherzo type within the quartet's four-movement structure.
If we omit for a moment any consideration of the quartets of Opus
1 and Opus 2 (for there we have to do with a five-movement form

in which a minuet is placed on each side of the middle movement—probably with no more significant purpose than symmetry), we find a rather regular placement of the minuet as second movement in the early quartets, but as third movement in the later ones. The chart of Haydn's eighty-three quartets on page 199 shows both the regular location and the exceptions.

It is far too easy to assert that the minuet's location doesn't matter, that it happens to be where it is because of accident, coincidence, or even willfulness. A great artist does not give way to willfulness, nor is he subject to such neat coincidences. He is conscious of what he is doing, and he does his work with full realization of its aesthetic effect. Nor may one say that the balance of a quartet, or its drive toward its end, is not altered if the sequence of movements is altered. Even superficial reflection will convince one that a dramatic slow movement provides more effective contrast if placed just before a fiery or humorous presto finale than it does if placed before an ambling, moderately paced minuet, or that a first movement of a certain type may better set the stage for a minuet than it does for an adagio. The sensitive listener will have heard too many examples of cumulative pace in sonatas, symphonies, or quartets to have any doubts on that score.

We begin to ask, then, what kind of music surrounds the minuet when it is placed second in the series of four movements? What kind when it is placed third? The answers are disappointing, for in both cases fast, moderate, and slow movements precede, and fast, moderate, and slow movements succeed, the minuet. We look for differences in texture, and are disappointed again; all kinds are found, irrespective of the minuet's location. We try again, from the standpoint of enjoyment this time; both arrangements are equally enjoyable. There remains an examination of the harmonic content of movements. Let us try that approach.

One principle which every composer of Haydn's day kept in mind was overall unity of tonality. No piece dared wander too far from its tonic key, and no piece in a four-movement form dared to present a tonality not closely related to the key of the whole series. A study of

TABULAR VIEW OF HAYDN'S STRING QUARTETS

m minuet   s scherzo   * instances of chromatic usage (see pp. 207–208)

Blank spaces represent the normal arrangement of fast first and last movements and slow middle movement; the exceptions are marked

PRE-MOZART QUARTETS

1755 Opus 1

	I	II	III	IV	V
1		m		m	
2		m		m	*
3	Slow	m		m	
4		m		(symphony)	
5		m		m	
6		m		m	

1755 Opus 2

	I	II	III	IV	V
1		m		m	
2		m		m	
3		m		m	
4		m		m	
5		m		m	
6	Var.	m		m	

1755–1765 Opus 3

	I	II	III	IV	V
1		m			
2	Var.	m			
3			m		
4					
5			m		
6			m		

c.1769 Opus 9

	I	II	III	IV	V
1		m			*
2		m			
3		m			
4		m			
5	Var.	m			
6		m			*

1771 Opus 17

	I	II	III	IV	V
1		m			
2		m			*
3	Var.	m			*
4		m			
5		m			
6		m			*

1772 Opus 20

	I	II	III	IV	V
1		m			
2			m	Fugue	*
3		m			
4	Var.		m		**
5		m		Fugue	
6			m	Fugue	

1782 Opus 33

	I	II	III	IV	V
1		s			*
2		s			
3		s			**
4		s			*
5			s		
6			s		

1768–1783–1785? Opus 42

	I	II	III	IV	V
	Slow	m			*

MOZART-INFLUENCED QUARTETS

c.1785 Opus 50

	I	II	III	IV	
1			m		*
2			m		*
3			m		*
4			m	Fugue	*
5			m		
6			m		*

1785† Opus 51   "The Seven Last Words"

1788–1790 Opus 54

	I	II	III	IV	
1			m		****
2			m		*
3			m		

1788–1790 Opus 55

	I	II	III	IV	
1			m		***
2	Slow		m		**
3			m		**

1790 Opus 64

	I	II	III	IV	
1		m			
2			m		***
3			m		
4		m			*
5			m		**
6			m		*

POST-MOZART QUARTETS

1791–1793 Opus 71

	I	II	III	IV	
1			m		
2	Introd.		m		
3			m		*

1793 Opus 74

	I	II	III	IV	
1			m		*
2			m		
3			m		

1797 Opus 76

	I	II	III	IV	
1			m		
2			m		
3		Var.	m		
4			m		
5			m		
6	Fantasia		m		

1799 Opus 77

	I	II	III	IV	
1			m		*
2		m			*

1803 Opus 103

	I	II	III	IV	
			m		*

† arranged 1787–1794?

the key relationships existing among the movements of these quartets will give ample evidence that Haydn adhered very closely to the second half of that principle: with the exception of the so-called quartets of Opus 51, which will be discussed below, only one quartet exhibits an unorthodox key relationship among its several movements: Opus 76, No. 6, in E flat, contains a slow movement in B minor and major; but that movement is labeled "fantasia." No other movement goes further than to subdominant or dominant, to relative major or minor, to tonic major or minor, or to mediant or submediant. The great majority progress to the most closely related keys of all, namely, subdominant or dominant. And it is always the slow movement, regardless of its place in the series, that presents a contrasting key; the minuet, like the first and last movements, is always in the tonic key. Thus we have in the minuet a stabilizing force, a movement which, through its clarity and unpretentiousness, is well suited to recalling a quartet to its harmonic senses should it threaten to depart too far from its tonal center.

One possibility of discovering the reason why the minuet wanders around within the framework remains. A hypothesis may be established: when Haydn feels that he has violated the principle of harmonic unity in his first movement, he places the minuet second, firmly to re-establish the tonality before departing on his second excursion into the tonality of the slow movement. And when he feels that the first movement is normal harmonically, and the second is merely a dip into a closely related key, he is happy to put the minuet in third place in order to develop sufficient momentum toward the rapid last movement. I suggest that as Haydn achieved full maturity during the writing of the Opus 33 set and became less fearful of violating harmonic unity, he tended more and more toward favoring the climax of tempos achieved by placing the moderate minuet between the slow second and fast final movements. The chart on page 199 shows that with only two or three exceptions, the last thirty-six quartets contain the minuet in third place. But I am not completely satisfied with this hypothesis and suggestion. Only a careful analysis of all the harmonic vagaries of all the movements will throw final light upon this problem. And that study has not yet been undertaken.

The single quartet of Opus 42, in D minor, seems to have puzzled commentators more than any similar work. Pohl, Haydn's best-known biographer, feels it to be one of the composer's early works, contemporary with Opus 9, that is, about 1768.[11] Altmann, in his edition of the eighty-three quartets published by Eulenberg, gives the date as 1768, thus agreeing with Pohl. Tovey [12] points out with considerable conviction that it could not have been written earlier than its place in the opus numbers indicates, namely, a year or so after 1782 which marks the publication of Opus 33. Karl Geiringer refers to the original manuscript as bearing the date 1785.[13] Thus we have a typical musicological problem: 1768, about 1783, or 1785? And the question is not an academic one (in the worst sense of that phrase), for this quartet Opus 42 contains features that are still noteworthy in 1785 and would decidedly be innovations in 1768. The slow movement is a lyric gem, with a long, singing melody such as is virtually unknown in the early quartets. The finale is in imitative, almost fugal style reminiscent of Haydn's Opus 20 (1772), and certainly not found earlier. And yet the work as a whole is unassuming and does not have the air of brilliance one finds in almost all the quartets from Opus 33 onward.

About 1784 or 1785 Haydn wrote the set of six quartets in Opus 50; they were published in 1787 with a dedication to Frederick William II (1744–1797), king of Prussia from 1786 to 1797. The dedication becomes significant when one glances at the cello parts of these quartets. Frederick William, a nephew of Frederick the Great, was a capable cellist and took delight in playing chamber music. Haydn, to please his noble patron, took full advantage of the cello's lyric, dramatic, and technical possibilities and wrote cello parts far richer (and more interesting to the cellist, one might add) than any had been previously. We shall see later that Mozart's procedure was

---

[11] Pohl, *Joseph Haydn*, II, 43. Here he labels it Opus 8.
[12] In *Cobbett's Cyclopedic Survey of Chamber Music*, I, 540.
[13] Geiringer, *Haydn*, p. 253.

identical in his "Frederick William" quartets; he, too, provided the King with ample material.[14] Returning to Haydn, we find that the cello had paved the way to a more brilliant utterance, and therefore the other parts are increasingly filled with sparkle, with touches of deft humor, or with romantic melancholy. A much greater variety of material is found in the Opus 50 quartets; they range from extreme delicacy, as in Opus 50, No. 1, to the great forcefulness of No. 6, and they include one of the finest quartets of all: No. 4, with a masterful fugal finale.

It is necessary to cast a backward glance over the forty-three quartets we have discussed in the preceding pages, for in one respect Opus 50 exhibits formal characteristics not found in the previous quartets. We must even, for a moment, exhume the musical form of Pergolesi and his successors. In that form we saw three sections on tonic, dominant, and tonic, respectively, but confined within a two-part form.

$$\textit{Exposition} \quad \textit{Development} \ \textit{Recapitulation}$$

$$\text{A} - \text{B}: \|\!|\!|\!: \text{A} - \qquad \text{A} - \text{B}$$
$$\text{I} - \text{V}: \|\!|\!|\!: \text{V} - \qquad \text{I} \ \underline{\quad\quad}$$

The factors labeled A and B, we had indicated, differed in contour and rhythm; they were not sufficiently contrasted, however, to justify calling them first theme and second theme, nor did their interaction contribute essentially to the development section. That lack of real contrast in style, as we noted in Chapter 7, was typical of the many divertimento composers in the generation before Haydn. And that same lack of contrast, we may now point out, was typical of Haydn himself, in the quartets of Opera 1, 2, 3, 9, 17, and 20. A group of phrases in the tonic key sufficed for the A part; a different group for the B, but, of course, in the dominant. Development consisted largely of sequential modulations, derived phrases, figurations, and other embroidery—all of which led back more or less regularly to the recapitulation, in which both A and B parts were in the tonic key.

[14] Beethoven likewise, in his two cello sonatas of Opus 5.

From Opus 33, then, comes the great innovation: the use of thematic development, the fragmentation of the phrases, and contrapuntal development of those fragments. The extent of the innovation and the results directly traceable to it have been described. But even in the quartets of Opus 33, the symmetrical form had not been altered appreciably. The three large parts—exposition, development, and recapitulation—were still in the same relationship to each other that they had been previously.

From Opus 50 onward, the picture changes. Donald Tovey has made a generalization about the new procedure which is well borne out by the facts.[15] He points out that in the works of Haydn it is difficult to speak of first and second "subjects" (we would have called them "themes"); rather must one speak of first and second theme-groups: collections of phrases in tonic and dominant keys, respectively. The generalization, with detailed examples to demonstrate its correctness, follows: "Haydn invented a brilliant type of coda à la Beethoven, and used fully-developed codas instead of recapitulations. . . . From Opus 50 on, there is no dealing with Haydn's first movements except by individual analysis."

By this Tovey indicates that the principle of thematic development, which in Opus 33 had been confined largely to the development section, had in Opus 50 and thereafter also become active in the recapitulations. Key relationships in the recapitulation had remained; indeed, the symmetry of tonality was a reality from which Haydn almost never broke away. But exact return of first and second theme-groups was now a thing of the past. To what extent Haydn differed from Mozart in this respect, and anticipated Beethoven, will be seen in Chapters 9 and 10, respectively.

Haydn's Opus 51 is a strange work, with an unusual history. Discussion of the work is in order here for two reasons: it appears in the authoritative Peters edition of Haydn's complete quartets, and it is included in the numbering whenever Haydn's "eighty-three" quartets are mentioned, as we have included it thus far in the interest of conforming to general usage.

15 *Cobbett's Cyclopedic Survey of Chamber Music*, I, 541.

About 1785 Haydn accepted a commission to compose appropriate music for a Good Friday service commemorating the seven last words of Christ, for the Cathedral of Cadiz. The result was a series of seven slow movements: largo, grave, grave, largo, adagio, lento, and largo, respectively; the whole is preceded by an adagio introduction and followed by a presto "Earthquake." It is an orchestral piece; its instrumentation is that of the symphony of the time. Because of its "singularly expressive character" and its suitability as a "vocal Passion piece," [16] an obscure church musician in Passau named Joseph Friebert added, in 1792, a set of vocal parts and a sacred text, and performed the work on many occasions. Haydn heard such a performance in Passau on his second trip to England (in 1794), was pleased with the result, but felt that "he could have done the vocal parts better." Subsequently he did make alterations, but retained considerable portions of Friebert's vocal additions as well as short recitatives the latter had seen fit to add at the beginning of each movement. Some years earlier, Haydn had arranged the orchestral version of the work and published the seven slow movements for string quartet, allowing them to be included in his series of quartets as Opus 51.[17]

The work is undoubtedly effective in its orchestral version; there is evidence that Haydn was greatly pleased with the arrangement for chorus and orchestra. But the quartet version leaves much to be desired. The several movements are stripped down to bare essentials. Contrapuntal treatment, which had become so essential a factor in Haydn's style from Opus 33 on, is noticeably absent. What remains is a series of dramatic, passionate, and exquisitely beautiful melodies, with an adequate accompaniment in the lower instruments. The final "Earthquake," when heard in quartet guise, verges on the comic—

[16] Geiringer, *Haydn,* p. 305.

[17] According to Artaria and Botstiber, *Joseph Haydn und das Verlagshaus Artaria,* pp. 35 and 94, the quartet version was published in 1787, almost simultaneously with the original orchestral version. Geiringer, *Haydn,* p. 270, agrees with them. Thus, the latest authority differs from Adolf Sandberger ("Zur Entstehungsgeschichte von Haydns sieben Worte des Erlösers am Kreuze," in his *Ausgewählte Aufsätze zur Musikgeschichte,* pp. 266 ff.), who asserted that the quartet version was made after the vocal version of about 1795.

so inadequate are the tremolos and the *tutti forzi* to carry Haydn's great programmatic intentions. One remains puzzled by Haydn's questionable judgment in including these seven works among his quartets, and it is well to attribute to him, not eighty-three, but seventy-six.

Returning to the line of true quartets, we encounter three in Opus 54 and three in Opus 55; both sets were written about 1788 or 1790. Having spoken of earlier quartets as great works, as dramatic or light-hearted or profound, I am embarrassed at the thought of describing the later ones in the same phrases, but one cannot do otherwise. The quartets of Opus 54 and Opus 55 are all that the earlier ones were; they are also written with contrapuntal development, with freer forms, and with greater melodic charm. Moreover, where the earlier quartets sparkle, the later ones glisten. Where the earlier are moving, the later are poignant. Where the earlier make much of a new device or a new treatment, the later are so closely identified with the new device or new treatment that they are unthinkable with a single detail changed. In a word, they are musically greater in every respect. It is a continual source of amazement to see (or to hear) in how many ways Haydn can be humorous, or how many gradations of humor are possible. One never ceases to marvel at the number of ways a lyric phrase can be turned in order to lead to a mood of resignation, or to a mood of dramatic abandon, or even to a continuation, across a long period, of the lyric mood. And it is precisely this enormous variety that gives the quartets of Haydn's their eternal freshness, their spontaneity, and their everlasting charm.

Formal descriptions of the quartets beyond Opus 55 would lead nowhere. Each one is unique in the way it disposes of its musical materials, to the great advantage of musical literature. Each one gives us the composer in a new light and fills us with gratitude for the creative power of a genius. Each one provides a new experience in the field of emotionally moving and aesthetically stimulating music. There is no substitute for hearing, playing, and living with these works. A bare catalogue of them must suffice here.

Six quartets, Opus 64, written about 1790, follow upon the Opus

55 set. One of the former, Opus 64, No. 5, has become famous under the nickname "The Lark"; it, along with the two quartets which surround it, are among Haydn's most popular works. Three quartets in Opus 71, presumably written at London about 1791, but published in 1795, are next in order. Opus 71, No. 2, contains the only slow introduction to a fast first movement in all of Haydn's quartets. Slow introductions were characteristic of Haydn's symphonies; their noteworthy omission in the quartets points to Haydn's feeling that a quartet is not a miniature symphony and does not require a pretentious introduction. Indeed, such introductions stand in the way of the intimate, essentially cheerful mood he is at great pains to establish. Three quartets of Opus 74, written about 1793 and published in 1796, include the favorite G minor (No. 3), nicknamed "The Rider" because of its prancing first theme.

If words fail one in approaching the previous works, what is one to do when the six quartets of Opus 76 are reached (written about 1797 and published in 1799)? I shall resolutely refrain from attempting even the most fragmentary analysis and shall be content to point out that Opus 76, No. 2, is "The Quinten": its descending fifths in the first movement give a clue to the origin of the nickname. No. 3, "The Emperor," contains the famous variations on the hymn, "Gott erhalte Franz den Kaiser," a tune which Haydn had composed a short time before, and which remained one of his favorites even on his deathbed. No. 4 is "The Sunrise"; the aptness of the nickname can be appreciated only by those who know the quartet. No. 5 contains the marvelous largo in F sharp major, possibly one of the most sublime creations of this or any other composer. Finally, No. 6, with the slow movement marked fantasia, a unique piece in B major modulating to B flat, A flat, and back to B (in a quartet whose other movements are in E flat), and one which presents the only movement so remotely related in all the seventy-six quartets.

About 1799, after the two London visits, after Haydn had withdrawn into semi-retirement, the two works of Opus 77 were written. At first for flute and piano, they were later transcribed by Haydn for string quartet, and were published in 1802. In these quartets the highest point of Haydn's creative activity is reached. Hearing the works and knowing them is all that is needed; talking about them would be futile. Finally, in 1803, Haydn wrote a slow movement and minuet, Opus 103, for what was evidently designed to be a quartet in D minor. The slow movement is in B flat, the minuet in D minor; consequently the quartet is referred to (in *Cobbett's* and elsewhere) as in B flat. But it was Haydn's consistent practice to place the minuet in the key of the first and last movements. Hence, if there had been two more movements, they would undoubtedly have been in D minor.

Two final points must be mentioned here before bringing this survey of Haydn's quartets to a close. The full significance of the first will not be seen until Mozart's chamber-music works have been discussed. A glance through the many pages comprising Haydn's quartets up to Opus 42 reveals an astonishing lack of passages made out of chromatic scale fragments. The diatonic scale, with its neighboring tones, provides the material out of which almost all the melodies and figurations are constructed. But a similar inspection of the quartets from Opus 50 through Opus 64 discloses, suddenly, a marked use of the chromatic line. Finally, the group from Opus 71 to Opus 103 contains very few such passages.

The statistics may prove interesting to those for whom no detail is unimportant. In the group from Opus 1 to Opus 42—forty-three quartets in all—there are actually fourteen instances of the use of chromatic melodies four or more notes in length.[18] In the eighteen quartets from Opus 50 through Opus 64 twenty-four instances are to be found. And in the fifteen quartets from Opus 71 to Opus 103, five instances. In the first group there is, on the average, one chromatic instance in every three quartets; in the second group, four instances in every three quartets; in the last, one in every three again.

Now what is the significance of this? It happens that Haydn and Mozart met about 1781 and began their mutually fruitful influence

---

[18] A chromatic line of less than four tones indicates merely the filling-in of two neighboring diatonic scale tones; as such, it is of little emotional interest. When the line persists for four or more tones in the same direction, the peculiar richness and pathetic appeal of the chromatic scale are made evident.

upon each other shortly thereafter. In 1785 Mozart dedicated his six great quartets (written about 1783) to Haydn; it was after hearing these works that Haydn made his famous remark to Mozart's father about Wolfgang's being the greatest composer of whom he had any knowledge.[19] From about 1785 Haydn was strongly influenced by Mozart; we shall see in Chapter 9 what form that influence took. Of importance here is the fact that before 1785, that is, up through Opus 42, the quartets show no appreciable use of chromatic lines, that during the rest of Mozart's lifetime, up to 1791, the chromatic line is much in evidence in Haydn (the quartets from Opus 50 through Opus 64 fall in the years 1785 to 1790, and that after Mozart's death Haydn reverted to the diatonic scale formulas (in the quartets Opus 71 to Opus 103, between 1791 and 1803) as consistently as he had in the pre-Mozart quartets. The chromatic scale in Mozart's work forms an important aspect of his style, as we shall see below.

The last point has to do with the incompleteness of the available Haydn quartet repertoire. Throughout the Haydn literature one finds references to quartets which are not included in the generally accepted list of seventy-six (or eighty-three, if one includes the *Seven Last Words*) or in the thematic indexes of his works made by various publishers. A few such items may be mentioned here.

A divertimento appearing as a string quartet about 1765 is mentioned by Pohl.[20] This work was not included in Haydn's own thematic catalogue, nor, according to Haydn himself, was it ever published. Two similar quartets appeared in Breitkopf's catalogue about the same time, but Haydn ignored these works. Yet when the six quartets of Opus 9 first appeared, about 1769, they were numbered, presumably by Haydn, as quartets 21–26.[21] We know of eighteen quartets in Opera 1, 2, and 3; Opus 9 should, accordingly, have been 19–24, not 21–26. Where are the others? Possibly the quartet we know as Opus 42 (which Pohl called Opus 8) is one of them; possibly not. And in connection with the two quartets of Opus 77, published

[19] Jahn, *W. A. Mozart* (4th ed.), II, 11.   [20] Pohl, *Joseph Haydn*, I, 258.
[21] *Ibid.*, II, 43.

in 1802, Botstiber mentions a "third and last quartet in B flat" dedicated to Count Fries and published by Artaria in May, 1807.[22]

In recent years a quartet in E flat major, called "No. 0," has been found. Originally included in Haydn's Opus 1, it disappeared from later editions and was replaced by the "symphony," Opus 1, No. 5. Haydn himself listed the quartet among his divertimentos, where it was discovered independently by Karl Geiringer and Marion Scott about 1932.[23]

The Haydn authorities throughout the world assure us that all of the seventy-six quartets are authentic. They imply that certain other quartets which circulated under Haydn's name, even during his lifetime, may be spurious.[24] And they hold out the hope that if and when publication of the *Complete Works* of Haydn is resumed, some of these questions will be answered and the world may have even more Haydn masterpieces to enjoy. Let us hope that a few choice works will be added to the quartet literature from the pen of this sincere, profound, and human genius.

[22] Artaria and Botstiber, *Joseph Haydn und das Verlagshaus Artaria,* p. 100.
[23] Geiringer, *Haydn,* pp. 194–195.
[24] Cf. Geiringer's remarks (*ibid.,* p. 208*n*) about the E major quartet which is attributed to Haydn.

9

WOLFGANG AMADEUS MOZART

WHAT IS the source of Mozart's style? Whom can one single out as having provided him with his musical models? Concise answers to these and similar questions are difficult to give, for the whole world of music lay open to Mozart, and the source of his style is that world itself. For any given period the teacher or the model was a different one; yet Mozart is more than the sum of such teachings. Throughout his lifetime he was extremely sensitive to musical impressions. Each new work, each new style, left its mark upon his mind. And during his extensive travels he had ample opportunity to hear new works, possibly the greatest opportunity that any composer has ever had. Mozart's style is so largely the result of his many journeys that the style cannot be considered without the journeys.

Joannes Chrysostomus Wolfgangus Theophilus [1] Sigismundus Mozart was born at Salzburg in 1756. Of his parents' seven children, only he and his sister Maria Anna ("Nannerl") survived infancy. It need hardly be mentioned that both were child prodigies, so well known are the many anecdotes concerning the concert tours of the young Mozarts. At the age of three, Wolfgang began serious and organized musical studies with his father, a competent musician in his own right.

The older Mozart (1719–1787) was employed from 1743 at the court of successive archbishops of Salzburg as composer, court violinist, and, later, as vice-chapelmaster. His famous work, *Versuch einer gründlichen Violinschule*, published in the year of Wolfgang's birth, was highly regarded by contemporary musicians, was issued

[1] Sometimes Amadeus, sometimes Gottlieb. See Jahn, *W. A. Mozart* (4th ed.), I, 19*n*.

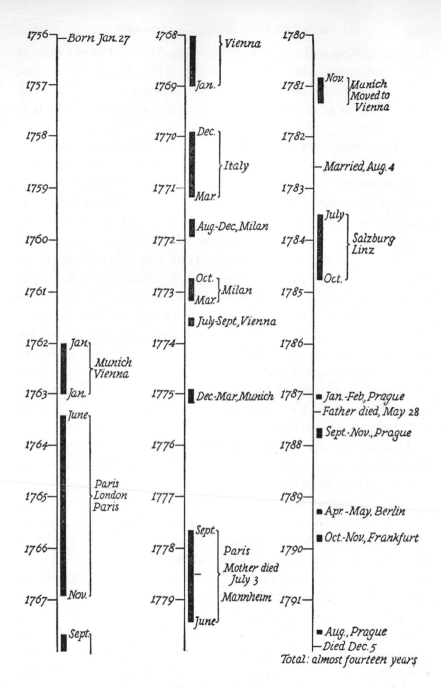

1756 — Born Jan. 27

1757 —

1758 —

1759 —

1760 —

1761 —

1762 — Jan.⎱
                ⎰ Munich
                    Vienna
1763 — Jan.⎰

1764 — June⎱

                Paris
1765 —   ⎱ London
                Paris
1766 —

1767 — Nov.⎰

        Sept.⎰

1768 —   ⎱ Vienna

1769 — Jan.⎰

1770 — Dec.⎱
                ⎰ Italy
1771 — Mar.⎰

1772 — Aug.-Dec., Milan

1773 — Oct.⎱
        Mar.⎰ Milan

        July-Sept., Vienna

1774 —

1775 — Dec.-Mar., Munich

1776 —

1777 —

1778 — Sept.⎱
                ⎰ Paris
                    Mother died
                    July 3
1779 —   ⎱ Mannheim
        June⎰

1780 —

1781 — Nov.⎱ Munich
                ⎰ Moved to
                    Vienna
1782 —

        — Married, Aug. 4

1783 —

1784 — July⎱
                ⎰ Salzburg
                    Linz
        Oct.⎰

1785 —

1786 —

1787 — Jan.-Feb., Prague
        — Father died, May 28
        Sept.-Nov., Prague

1788 —

1789 — Apr.-May, Berlin

        Oct.-Nov., Frankfurt
1790 —

1791 —

        Aug., Prague
        — Died Dec. 5
Total: almost fourteen years

MOZART'S TRAVELS

in many editions and several translations, and was for some years the only fundamental violin method in use. Thus, Wolfgang at once fell into the hands of an experienced musician and teacher, well qualified to foster and develop—and exploit—his young son's enormous talent.

In his earliest years at Salzburg, Mozart's father supplied him with music of all sorts: works of his own, music by great and small contemporaries, and music of past generations. The young student heard contrapuntal pieces (old-fashioned even then) and pieces in the new *galant* style. And from his sixth year on, when the long series of concert journeys began, he heard remote and foreign music as well.

The first tour was modest enough: a one-year visit to Munich and Vienna. But the scope of the journeys soon widened; a three-and-one-half-year visit to Paris, London, and Paris again, 1763–1766, was the most extensive of all. There Mozart learned to know the music of Johann Schobert and Johann Christian Bach, echoes of which appeared in his own music as much as twenty years later. On his return to Salzburg he studied the *Gradus ad Parnassum* of Fux, one of the great contrapuntalists of the Baroque period. Then followed one and a half years in Vienna, 1767–1769, and three separate trips to Italy between 1770 and 1773.

At first the tours followed a uniformly successful pattern. Extended stops were made at each city on the route. Public concerts and private performances for the nobility were quickly arranged. Wolfgang played the violin, the harpsichord, and the organ, read the most difficult compositions at sight, and presented programs of his own new works. Maria Anna carried her share of the musical burden as well. Both children delighted their hearers by their charm and unspoiled natures, and many valuable gifts were showered upon them. The receipts at the public concerts more than covered the family's expenses, and each stop was a financial as well as a musical success. The reputation of the famous prodigies often preceded them and made their next appearance eagerly expected. Each stop brought with it opportunities to hear the music of local and regional composers. And for Mozart, to hear was to remember. All the mannerisms of good and bad composers, all the formulas and clichés of the *galant* style, became material for Mozart to use, to transform in the light of his own taste, or to discard. In Italy he became familiar with the operatic music and spirit of that country; in Germany and Austria, with the solid counterpoint of the serious composers and the diverting melodies of the Rococo.

But even dazzling reputations, even unique accomplishments, could not forever attract audiences and win patrons. As Wolfgang grew older and became less of a child prodigy, interest in his talents and accomplishments waned. His father persisted in his sincere desire to let the world share in his son's great musical abilities and, incidentally, to procure a court appointment for him; he did not become discouraged. His employer, the Archbishop of Salzburg, had finally grown weary of repeated requests for leaves of absence, and in 1777 he forbade the elder Mozart to take another journey. The latter pressed his wife into the role of traveling companion to her son, and the journeys began again. In 1778, while on a two-year visit to Paris and Mannheim (1777–1779), Mozart's mother died. In his twenty-second year Mozart was on his own, for the first time in his life.

The countless musical experiences Mozart had had during his adolescence had done much to influence his own style. But in many cases the influences appeared decades after the impression was made. The dark colors, the passionate fire of Schobert's music deeply impressed Mozart as a child of eight; not until the middle 1780's, when Mozart was almost thirty years old, did these characteristics become a part of his style. On the other hand, the gracefulness of Johann Christian Bach and the lyric flow of Italian music, to both of which he was exposed between his ninth and his fifteenth years, were more immediately apparent. It could hardly have been otherwise. A boy in his adolescent years, even if he be a prodigy, cannot be expected to feel dark thoughts, to paint in dark colors; but even a boy can sing, and sing gracefully. Thus, we find that Mozart's early works are full of *galanterie* and charming melody, carried on the surface of the music, much in the style of the "London" Bach and his spiritual relatives, the Mannheim and Italian composers.

Mozart was now twenty-two. His childhood accomplishments had long since been forgotten by the world at large. There remained only his prestige as a performer and his solid achievements as a composer. Commissions for operas and other works had always come his way; successful as the results usually were, they never endured. The one thing both father and son longed for, namely, a permanent post as court or opera composer, was still denied Mozart, as it was denied him throughout his lifetime. The best he was able to achieve was the post as concertmaster and organist to the Archbishop of Salzburg, a post that was offered and regretfully accepted in 1779. And from that position he was forcibly separated two years later, in Vienna. His marriage to Constanza Weber took place during the summer of the following year (1782) and resulted in the Mozarts' making Vienna their permanent home.

Innumerable engagements came to him during the next few years, and Mozart presented many concerts of his own works. But income was uncertain, and his wife was, if possible, even less capable in financial matters than her husband. Always in debt, always pressed for money, always living in the vain hope of receiving a regular position, Mozart's life from 1782 to his death was full of great discouragement and grinding poverty.

The successes of the *Marriage of Figaro* (1786) and *Don Giovanni* (1787) did much to add to Mozart's prestige, but did little to alleviate his financial troubles. Debts continued to mount, and it was in the hope of bettering his financial condition that he paid a visit, in 1789, to the court of Frederick William II, at Berlin. And when finally a worthwhile offer was made to him there—the post of chapel master to that Prussian king—Mozart refused it out of misguided loyalty to his Emperor, the man who had so deliberately neglected him. One tangible result of the visit was a commission to compose some quartets, of which we shall speak again.

In the last year of his life several commissions came his way, notably those which gave rise to *La Clemenza di Tito, Die Zauberflöte,* and the unfinished *Requiem.* The first, composed for the coronation of Leopold II at Prague, was coldly received. Mozart had traveled to that city for rehearsals and the performance; his disappointment in the court's reaction was great. The second, composed for a small theater in Vienna, found equal disfavor in the minds of its first audience; only later did it grow in popular regard. The disappointment at the "failure" of these two works, plus the constant worry over finances and livelihood, contributed to the complete undermining of Mozart's health. When he died, in December, 1791, a few months after the apparent fiascos, a few friends accompanied the body part way to the cemetery. Mozart lies in an unmarked pauper's grave. He was not quite thirty-six when he died; his journeys had begun at the age of six. In the almost thirty years from January, 1762, to December, 1791, Mozart had been away from home for a total of fourteen years.

Seen in the light of a normal span of years, Mozart lived only half a lifetime. He had certainly attained the height of his musical powers in 1791; presumably he would have retained or exceeded those powers had longer life been granted him. But Mozart began his creative activity at an age earlier than most composers. Leaving out of account the half-dozen minuets from his fourth year, his first large compositions—six sonatas for violin and piano—were written about 1763, when Mozart was seven. From that day until his death he composed; his activity embraces twenty-nine years. In that sense he was given almost as full a life as many other composers: thirty-five years elapsed between Beethoven's Opus 1 and his last work; Brahms had had scarcely forty years of composing when he died. And Mozart's activity was continuous during his twenty-nine years of writing.

The quantity of his work, while not as great as Haydn's, is considerable. Among the works are some twenty operas, operettas, and similar works for the stage; fifteen masses, seventeen trio sonatas, and numerous other sacred compositions; more than a hundred airs, songs, choruses, and vocal canons. The instrumental works include almost fifty symphonies, more than three dozen serenades, divertimentos, and shorter pieces for orchestral and other ensemble combinations, about fifty concertos (of which more than half are for piano and orchestra), seventeen piano sonatas, a number of short pieces for piano, forty-two sonatas and many smaller pieces for violin and piano. The chamber music consists of twenty-six string quartets, eight string quintets (two of them with one wind instrument), seven piano trios, two piano quartets, and almost a dozen larger or smaller works for various combinations.

A word must be said about the numbering of Mozart's works. Mozart rarely used opus numbers and left few clues about the chronology of his many compositions. About the middle of the nineteenth century Ludwig von Koechel, an Austrian naturalist, musician, and, later, nobleman, began the process of collating the compositions with Mozart's letters, contemporary newspaper accounts, internal evidence supplied by the quality of paper and ink, and similar information. The result was the publication, in 1862, of Koechel, *Chronologisch-systematisches Verzeichniss*, listing all Mozart's works. Better known as K. or K.V., it furnishes accurate chronological data on the origin of Mozart's works; reference to those works customarily includes the K. item numbers. We shall follow custom by referring to those numbers. A revision of the *Verzeichniss*, which removed certain inaccuracies and attained a greater degree of completeness, was made by Alfred Einstein in 1937.

Mozart's earliest chamber-music work was written during the first of three visits to Italy. It is a string quartet (K.80) in G major; the manuscript is dated: Lodi, March 15, 1770, 7 P.M. In its original form it contained three movements: adagio, allegro, and minuet with trio. A rondo, as fourth movement, was added late in 1773. This quartet is not a distinguished work, nor does it differ greatly from similar works written by Mozart's Italian contemporaries. The violins move in thirds and sixths much of the time, the lower instruments are confined to an accompanying role, and kinship with the old trio sonata is not remote. While the formal details are well handled and the writing is clear and precise, the general effect is not one of maturity. The work is influenced by Italian love of melody; one short tune follows another, transitions between themes are composed of new material, and one is reminded of a potpourri. The prevailing style is homophonic; the few contrapuntal passages serve only to remind one that Mozart was a well-educated young musician, trained in all styles.

After two successful trips to Italy, Mozart returned to Salzburg. His stay at home, from December, 1771, to October, 1772, was the longest since his travels had begun, almost ten years earlier. Among the fruits of this stay at home were three quartets or, as they are called on the manuscript, divertimentos (K.136–138). But these are not the usual kind of divertimento, for they are three-movement works without minuets; a divertimento of this time almost always contained at least one minuet.

The Italian influence prominent in K.80 is here noticeably absent. In its place one finds the ingratiating qualities and clichés of the Rococo period. Broken chords and scale passages give rise to a feeling of restlessness. Rapid pulsations in eighth-notes, usually carried by either the viola or the cello, are characteristic throughout these three quartets and serve to disguise lack of harmonic movement. But even in these early works there are premonitions of the genius Mozart was to show in later life; they are best seen in the sonata-form movements, at the transition from first to second theme in the recapitulation. In that section (the recapitulation) the musical intention is to present both themes in the tonic key, but to approach the second theme as though it were still in the dominant, as it had been in the exposition. The problem of balancing exposition and recapitulation sections, one containing themes on I and V, the other on I and I, was apparently a fascinating one for Mozart. Nowhere did he show his genius so clearly and so often as in these transitions. An early example of that skill is seen in the first movement of the B flat quartet (K.137); a series of chromatic bass sequences leads to the return of the second theme in a highly original way. In other respects these quartets are not noteworthy. Developments are short, and the typical Mozartean device of introducing a new subject in the development is seen (K.138). The first violin dominates in these quartets; the second has the dual role of accompanying the first violin in thirds or in imitations and of adding its voice to the purely harmonic accompaniment provided by the viola and the cello.

A few months after these quartets were written the Mozarts were again on the road to Italy, to remain from October, 1772, to March, 1773. On the way to Milan, Mozart composed a quartet (Jahn hints at boredom during a stop-over at Bozen [2]); before returning home he wrote five more. These six quartets (K.155–160), although written within a few months of the K.136–138 set, show again with what giant strides Mozart approached artistic maturity. Each of the six contains three movements, but there all similarity with the earlier set ceases.

There is first of all a greater degree of freedom in Mozart's handling of the lower voices. In K.155 the second violin emerges with a charming melody; in K.159 it announces the first theme, while the first violin rests. The cello is given a part in imitative developments in K.157, and in K.158 all three lower instruments share honors with the first violin. Formal details, also, are treated with comparable freedom. Transitions hint at forthcoming themes; a second theme on occasion (K.155) modulates throughout its entire course; an increasing competence in contrapuntal technique is recognized (K.158).

Mozart has also grown wiser in his choice of themes. First and second themes contrast to a greater degree than they do in the earlier quartets and, for that matter, than they do in many of the Haydn quartets up to Opus 20. The consequences of thematic contrast were not yet realized by Mozart; the vivid interplay of diverse dramatic and lyric bits, as we find it twenty-five years later in Beethoven, was seldom to become a factor of Mozart's style. Perhaps we do the latter an injustice in pointing out the absence of this useful and expressive device in the early works. We should be content that Mozart wrote these cheerful works and be glad that they pave the way for the great quartets of the following decade.

There are evidences of growth, of changes leading toward a mature style, in almost every major composer. A late work, when compared with an earlier one, reveals how the composer has acquired a more sensitive feeling for melody, has found a new use for counter-

[2] Jahn, *W. A. Mozart*, I, 355.

point, has changed his rhythmic habits, or has altered his style in general. Such growth is typical of Mozart, too, as we have seen above. But what sets Mozart apart from other composers is the rapidity with which major changes in style take place. Almost a decade was required for Haydn to progress from counterpoint to imitative development; seven years went by before the Classical Beethoven became the Romantic Beethoven. Comparable changes took place in Mozart after a few months had elapsed. He too suffered the growing pains which are the lot of every composer, be he child prodigy or not, but his rate was much faster than anyone else's. His year encompassed another man's decade.

A case in point is provided by the next set of six quartets (K.168–173), written in 1773, the year which also saw the writing of the K.155–160 set. Mozart spent the summer of that year in Vienna, where he became acquainted with Haydn's quartets of Opus 20 (published in 1772), those in which Haydn rediscovered counterpoint and wrote fugues. What is the result? Mozart discovers that counterpoint is admirably suited to quartet writing, and composes fugues: two of the quartets (the first and the sixth) contain fugal last movements, and for the first time he employs the four-movement form, a form found in Haydn ever since his Opus 3, about 1755–1760.

Nor does the resemblance end at this point. K.168 begins with a nine-measure period composed of one three-measure phrase and three of two measures—an irregularity typical of Haydn. The second movement begins with the intervals found in Haydn's Opus 20, No. 5. Likewise in the others of this set; the fugal finales, mentioned above, and the first movement of K.170, which is an andante with variations, as in Haydn, give further evidence of direct influence. Einstein, in his account of these quartets,[3] lists several other similarities, and points out how directly and unashamedly Mozart leaned on his older contemporary. It could not have been otherwise, Mozart being what he was. Throughout his lifetime he was the perfect assimilator: he borrowed, to discard after one use or to refine on a higher level, from every composer with whom he had any feeling

[3] Einstein, *Mozart*, pp. 175–178.

of kinship. His genius shows most clearly in the uses he made of other men's innovations. Having once seen or heard a new device, a new texture or style, or even a new melody, Mozart was able to estimate its worth accurately, alter it to conform to his needs and make it an element of his style. Thus, his music becomes in a sense the synthesis of all he heard and experienced, but purified and brought into order through his immaculate taste and musical perception.

Mozart left Salzburg only once between the fall of 1773 and September, 1777: a four-month trip to Munich in the winter of 1774. For the first time since early childhood he stayed at home long enough to taste the real flavor of his native city. He had never liked Salzburg; he found its society dull and his court duties boring. And of especial significance here, he found little interest in string quartets, and he received no commissions to write for that medium. Being a practical musician, he wrote none.

Nor did he write string quartets on the almost two-year visit to Mannheim and Paris, September, 1777, to June, 1779, during the course of which his mother died. He did compose four quartets for flute and strings: K.285, K.285a, K. Appendix 171, and K.298. The first three were written at Mannheim as the result of a commission. Several facts indicate that Mozart considered these works off the beaten path: the first contains only three movements, the second and third only two; Mozart had adopted the four-movement form for his string quartets several years earlier, in the K.168–173 set. Again, the flute predominates to a large extent, while the strings merely accompany. The first quartet, in D major, is on the whole a charming work, typically Mannheim in its graciousness, melodiousness, and absence of deeply felt sentiment. The second and third, K.285a and K. Appendix 171, not being included in the *Complete Works*,[4] are not available. Einstein reports that "they are in good style and 'tender,' nothing more." [5] The fourth of the flute quartets (K.298), written at Paris in 1778, is, again according to Einstein, a parody. Exuberant, perfunctory, at times almost insipid, it is not among the important works of Mozart.

[4] *W. A. Mozarts sämtliche Werke.*   [5] Einstein, *Mozart*, p. 178.

After the Paris-Mannheim visit, Mozart returned home for a year and a half. Salzburg offered no more stimulation than it had earlier, and he felt no compulsion to compose string quartets during that stay. Late in 1780 Mozart went to Munich, and there, early in 1781, the quartet for oboe and strings (K.370) was written. Unlike the flute quartets, this work deserves a high place in the music of that period. It embodies many of the stylistic elements that were later to become so characteristic. The oboe is treated in general as one of four equal instruments; it no longer dominates as the flute had done in the earlier works. And while it too contains only three movements (the minuet is omitted), the quartet provides for great contrasts of expression. A graceful yet sturdy first movement is followed by a moving adagio in which the oboe is given full opportunity to exhibit its possibilities. The final rondo, in 6/8 meter, contains a unique passage in which the oboe proceeds with an embellished melody in 4/4 while the strings continue in 6/8, a device most unusual in Mozart.

In 1781 came the eventful move to Vienna. Mozart, summoned from Munich by his archbishop employer, arrived in a resentful mood, was greatly dissatisfied with the conditions of his employment, and succeeded in breaking away from the disliked archbishop. He was free, without prospects, without funds, and he was twenty-five. Secure in the knowledge of his own gifts, confident of his future, and glad to be rid of Salzburg, Mozart decided to remain in Vienna. From that time, from June, 1781, his activities were centered in that most musical, therefore most stimulating, of cities. But still no string quartets!

At about the same time Haydn was completing his Opus 33 quartets, those written "in an entirely new manner." In the winter of 1781 Haydn came to Vienna to supervise the performance of the quartets at the Austrian court; there is a strong likelihood that Mozart met the older man during that winter.[6] Here began the ten years of friendship and mutual esteem, years full of reciprocal influence and stimulation. Mozart modeled his works on those of

[6] *Grove's Dictionary of Music and Musicians* (4th ed.), III, 293.

Haydn; yet Haydn "learned from Mozart how to compose quartets." With the stimulation provided by Vienna, the encouragement and respect offered by Haydn, and the Opus 33 quartets available as models, Mozart returned to the path he had left almost ten years earlier. He began to write quartets again in December, 1782.

It was not Mozart's custom to compose without an external reason. A great number of his works were written to complete his commissions. Many were designed to demonstrate his fitness for a particular position. Others he wrote as material for his own concerts; with some Mozart hoped, through appropriate dedications, to influence prospective employers. Only a few seem to have been composed for inner reasons, to fill some need in Mozart's life. The six quartets written at Vienna between December, 1782, and January, 1785, fall into the latter class. They were not commissioned, Mozart had no professional need for them, nor were they directed toward a particular nobleman. They arose solely out of the desire to write for musical Vienna, to demonstrate his prowess in the long-neglected field of quartet writing, and to pay homage to Haydn. The six are: K.387, in G major; K.421, in D minor; K.428, in E flat; K.458, in B flat ("The Hunt"); K.464, in A major; and K.465, in C major. These six, together with four later quartets, which will be discussed below, are usually published together as the "ten famous quartets."

The first three were written within a year of December, 1782; the last three between November, 1784, and January, 1785. Published in September, 1785, they carried a dedication to Haydn in which Mozart spoke of them as being the "fruit of a long and laborious work." But no trace of effort appears in the music; only the autograph gives evidence of how Mozart altered, erased, discarded, and substituted. And the results are models of perfection: not a false gesture; not a faulty proportion. The six quartets stand as the finest examples of Mozart's genius.

We have seen that Mozart had been greatly influenced by Haydn's quartets of Opus 20 a decade earlier; he had imitated the older man's style, his counterpoint, and even his melodies. He was, perhaps, even more strongly influenced by Haydn's Opus 33, with which he became acquainted in 1782; but this time he was stimulated to go in other directions. With Haydn's Opus 33, the quartet's structure and style were virtually completed; the "new manner" of Haydn had provided the bridge between *galant* melody and "learned" counterpoint, and sonata form was fully established. Mozart, ever willing to build on another man's achievements, immediately seized upon that new manner and made it his own—with what difficulty the autographs and the dedication give evidence.

If one is to characterize the Mozart of these quartets, one must use the terms "restraint" and "subtlety." On a fabric that is in turn gloomy, pensive, resigned, and gay the designs, usually in the darker shades, are laid in a variety of patterns that defies description. Mozart does not brood, although he is aware of life's sternness; his gloomier moments are subtly lightened by contrasting passages which restore one's optimism. He does not laugh uproariously, although he is gay by temperament; his humor is always tinged with the knowledge that comedy and tragedy are a short step apart. His sunlight carries with it the promise that it will soon be cloudy, but, miraculously, one is glad to accept whatever weather Mozart ordains. Therein lies one of the great delights of these quartets. We are in the hands of a great guide, seeing through his eyes the components of human emotion. And though we may look into the darker pools, we are not plunged into them—as we will be by Tschaikowsky. Though we may observe the unrestrained humor of peasants, we do not ourselves take part in it—as we did with Haydn. Mozart in an impersonal way shows us what exists, reflects upon it with us, and returns us, moved but unimpaired, to our own worlds. That is the essence of Classical music.

It is one thing to point out the restraint and impersonal nature of these quartets; it is quite another to describe the musical means whereby they are achieved. One could quote this passage and trace the subtle overlapping of phrases; one could quote that passage and compare its effect with a similar one. One could point to a sequence of chords, to this turn of a melody, to that combination of motives. All this would be true and relevant, and yet it would not "prove" anything. A sensitiveness to untheatrical music, an appreciation of musical refinement, and an awareness of the myriad facets of human life and emotion are necessary properly to evaluate these six quartets.

One technical detail may be singled out, however: the chromatic scale or, more accurately, the fragment of chromatic melody. Mozart had often used chromatics before 1782; after that date they became characteristic. From the G major quartet (K.387) of that year to the *Requiem* (K.626) of 1791, they are almost constantly in evidence. The half-poignant, half-resigned tone of Mozart's late works is due in no small part to the use of short chromatic lines.

For two centuries before Mozart, composers had turned to chromatic melody to depict intensities of emotion not easily achieved through the diatonic scale. Purcell, in *Dido and Aeneas,* and Bach, in the *B Minor Mass,* surrounded some of their most pathetic utterances with chromatic lines. But Mozart found that intensity need not be restricted to pathos. He arrived at a concentration of emotion in fast-moving passages and in minuets as well. The presence of a series of half-steps lends a conciseness, a weight, and a drive to melodic passages that a diatonic series cannot always supply. Mozart

uses the chromatic line most often in transitional passages where contrast is needed or where a change of mood is anticipated; the first movement of the G major quartet is an example. The device is used subtly to intensify a moving bass line, as in the minuet of the D minor. And in one of the most masterful of all passages, the introduction of the C major (see example above), it brings a mood of despair and resignation unequaled in all of Mozart's works. Chromatics appear numberless times in the six quartets; often they are concealed, but their effect is felt nonetheless. Several themes in the E flat quartet are based upon chromatics; the A major, despite its bright key, is melancholy in part, and chromatic passages are largely responsible.

In Chapter 8 [7] the place of chromatics in Haydn's quartets was touched upon. One finds a noticeable lack of chromaticism in the quartets before 1785 and in those after 1791, but finds the device used extensively in the period between those dates. And that is precisely the period during which Haydn and Mozart were mutually influential, and Haydn learned to know the six quartets of his younger friend. Between 1785 and 1791 Haydn wrote his quartets from Opus 50 through Opus 64; in them he made use of the chromatic elements whose effectiveness Mozart had demonstrated. But Haydn was not by nature as intense or as pensive a man as Mozart; the concentrated style was not natural to him. Small wonder, then, that during his London visits and in his later years, after Mozart's direct personal influence was no longer available, Haydn returned to the direct, expansive and open style which was innate. The element of intensity, introduced by Mozart, was to await further use at the hands of Beethoven.

A second difference between the quartets of Mozart and those which influenced them comes to light when the element of subtlety is examined. Haydn, a simple man, was honest with himself and his listeners. His music is a reflection of a mind that was serene and strong in religious faith. Mozart, during the last ten years of his life, gave us music in which unrest, a degree of pessimism, and some concern over the prospect of death are reflected, however faintly. Even in the minuet, in the form which Haydn had filled with sly wit or outspoken humor, Mozart remained aloof, dignified, and reflective. Haydn's finales are full of boisterousness and unrestrained animal spirits. Mozart's are occasionally gay, as in the B flat quartet, or serene, as in the C major; but the humor and the liveliness are seen as though from a distance.

[7] Pages 207–208.

Finally, a basic difference between the character of the two men is seen when formal aspects of the quartets are examined, notably the recapitulations of the sonata-form movements. Haydn was a master of the unexpected. His themes often recur in an unorthodox fashion; occasionally, when their return has been prepared for in the usual way, they do not reappear at all. Mozart was not given to shocking or surprising his listeners. The expected thing takes place, but in ever new and interesting ways—therein lie the surprises in Mozart. The transitions between development and recapitulation and the transitions between main themes best show his genius and marvelous subtlety. It is fair to say that Haydn had his listeners in mind when he composed, that he chuckled at the thought of their reactions to this effect or to that, but that Mozart remained divinely aloof from the world, preferred to write music that expressed what was in his mind and heart, and concerned himself only slightly with the reactions of individual listeners. In that sense Mozart was an aristocrat.

In variety of mood, quality of workmanship, and musical excellence the six quartets of 1785 are among Mozart's great works. The composer had taken all possible pains with them and felt that they were quartets to be proud of. Haydn, as we know, was enthusiastic about them; the playing of the last three occasioned his famous remark about Mozart's being the greatest composer of whom he had any knowledge. But public reaction to them was not satisfactory; they attracted no great attention, nor did they lead to commissions. More than a year elapsed before Mozart again tried his hand at quartet writing: a single quartet in D major (K.499) was the result. The work was published about 1788 with a dedication to Franz Anton Hoffmeister, publisher and Mozart's friend. Jahn surmises that in this quartet Mozart tried to approach public taste without lowering the standards of quartet style.[8] But there is no trace of such popularizing in the music.

It is first of all a gracious work, clear and direct in its first movement, strong in its minuet, and deeply moving in its adagio. Only in

[8] *W. A. Mozart*, II, 217.

the last movement are there traces of the melancholy tone which pervades so many works of these years. And even there it is manfully concealed under the outward signs of brightness: D major tonality, bustling vitality in the themes, incisive pauses between phrases. Perhaps this general restlessness contributes to the feeling that all was not well with Mozart when he wrote the quartet.

The *Adagio and Fugue* for string quartet (or string orchestra), K.546, has an interesting history. In December, 1783, Mozart completed a fugue for two pianos, one of the only two works which he wrote for that pair of instruments. About a year earlier Mozart had first become acquainted with the music of Johann Sebastian Bach. Deeply impressed with the grandeur of that music, he had arranged some of Bach's music for string groups, had written other works in the style of that master, and finally, according to his established custom, had made elements of that style his own. The fugue for two pianos (K.426) is one of the results. In June, 1788, he arranged that work for strings and added a prelude. In the latter form it is known as K.546. The prelude, appropriately enough, is somewhat like an old French overture. A slow, stately section with dotted rhythms, in the style of Handel and Bach, alternates with quiet lyric bits typical of the pensive Mozart. The fugue is a masterpiece. The style, in a technical sense, is that of Bach: all the contrapuntal arts of inversion, expansion, and overlapping of phrases are present. Yet the piece is unmistakably by Mozart. Sinuous chromatic lines, characteristic melodic figures, and Mozartian phrase structure provide the trademarks. In all respects the piece is worthy of a high place in Mozart's works.[9]

In the spring of 1789 Mozart visited at the court of Frederick William II, king of Prussia, the sovereign to whom Haydn had dedicated his Opus 50 quartets two years earlier. One result of the visit was a commission to compose some quartets—apparently the first time that an actual request for quartets had come to Mozart. The

[9] The Adagio and Fugue, along with K.155–160, K.168–173, the two flute quartets, and the one for oboe, are contained in an American edition published by Kalmus (New York) as Vol. II of Mozart's Quartets.

commission seems to have pleased him greatly, for the first quartet was completed and sent to the King during the month following his return to Vienna. Financial worries arising out of dire poverty hindered the completion of the commission: the two remaining quartets were delayed almost a year, until May and June, 1790. Mozart's letters of that year indicate his troubled state of mind and his serious concern for the future; but no traces of that worry and gloom are found in the music. The three quartets are in D major, K.575; in B flat, K.589; and in F major, K.590. They were published late in 1791, a few weeks after Mozart's death.

Few late works of Mozart's are as unburdened and free from doubt as these three quartets. If reserve and pensiveness are characteristic of the six "Haydn" quartets of 1785, then sheer beauty and serenity describe the three of 1789–1790. Hardly a single moody passage is found anywhere in the quartets; the few turns into minor and the few excursions into darker keys only serve to emphasize the optimism present everywhere else. One melody flows out of another and gives way to a third—all under an unbroken, cloudless sky. Not that Mozart loses his dignity and becomes merely tuneful. But the inner soul-searching, the reflective moodiness so characteristic of the 1785 set is no longer present.

And a new element appears in these quartets: virtuosity. Frederick William was a competent cellist; as Mozart's patron in this instance, he deserved richer cello parts than the chamber music of that time usually afforded. And Mozart provided them. Themes are about equally divided between first violin and cello, and occasionally the cello is given a solo, as in the trio of the D major quartet's minuet. Nor is the cello spared in the figurations and passage work with which these quartets are replete. Brilliant scale passages, rapid string crossings, and a full share of development episodes fall to that instrument—all without destroying the balance of the four instruments. Mozart achieves this quite simply by first raising the cello to a dominating position and providing it with glorious melodies, then lifting the other instruments proportionately high and restoring the balance. As a consequence, the whole level is raised, and new standards of brilliance are set. Only in one or two movements, notably in the minuet of the F major quartet, does Mozart forget that his cello part is for a king of Prussia. There he writes in the accustomed simpler vein.

The line of string quartets which began in 1770 with K.80 breaks off with the F major quartet (K.590) of 1790. We have in these twenty-six works a complete record of changes in Mozart's style. Italian characteristics, the warm sentiment of Johann Christian Bach, the mannerisms of the Mannheimers and the benign influence of Haydn—all appear in turn. Changes in Mozart's temperament, or rather in his outlook, are observed, and the development of his genius is laid down for all to see. The other series of chamber-music works, notably the string quintets and the piano trios, are not nearly as complete; they illustrate now one, now another aspect of Mozart's style. Only in the quartets has he left a complete record of his growth as a chamber-music composer.

The majority of string quintets contain a part for second viola added to the usual string quartet.[10] Exactly who first contrived this instrumentation is not known. There are several quintets among the works of the Mannheim composers, but most of these include two or three wind instruments. Some of Mozart's early symphonies contain parts for two violas; perhaps the idea of string quintet originated there. The quintets of Luigi Boccherini (1743–1805) were known to Mozart in the 1770's; Michael Haydn (1737–1806), Mozart's fellow townsman and friend, wrote several quintets during those years. But no composer before Mozart had invested the medium with such a wealth of musical ideas, profundity, and charm. The obvious rejoinder is that Mozart was the first major composer to be interested in that medium. Only one or two of Mozart's eight quintets are believed to have been ordered; various other reasons contributed to his choice of the quintet medium. The first, in B flat (K.174), written late in 1773 at Salzburg,[11] may have been modeled upon the quintets of Michael Haydn.

[10] Einstein (*Mozart*, p. 189) believes that Boccherini's 113 quintets with two cellos are actually for two violins, two violas, and one cello; the "alto violoncello" part is written in viola clef throughout.
[11] Jahn, *W. A. Mozart*, I, 357, states that the work was written following Mozart's return from Vienna in the fall of 1773; Einstein, *Mozart*, p. 188, declares that it was

The year 1773 had seen the writing of the six string quartets K.155–160, those in which Mozart progressed far beyond Rococo mannerisms; it had seen also the emergence of the K.168–173 set, in which Mozart made use of Haydn's rediscovery of counterpoint. And the very next work was the quintet. But the contrapuntal treatment, which Mozart had so wholeheartedly appropriated a short time before, is noticeably absent in the quintet. Except for a few bits of imitation in development sections, the music goes on for page after page in a melodious, homophonic style. Only in the finale, a long, fast, sonata-form movement, does Mozart allow himself to write contrapuntally; yet even there extended passages based on busy-work in the middle voices tend to remove the piece from the category of pure counterpoint. On the whole, the quintet is a diverse work, full of episodes of orchestral weight, of others replete with virtuoso brilliance, and still others which are in the tradition of chamber music.

Fourteen years elapsed between the writing of the B flat quintet and the two following ones, in C major (K.515) and G minor (K.516), respectively.[12] In the interval, Mozart had written the moody "Haydn" quartets and the ingratiating "Hoffmeister" quartet (K.499). The intensity and charm of those works are found again in the quintets of 1787.

written in the spring of that year (i.e., before Mozart became acquainted with Haydn's Opus 20), and was revised in December.
[12] K.515 is unaccountably missing from the list in *Cobbett's Cyclopedic Survey of Chamber Music*, II, 151.

The C major quintet begins with a rising arpeggio figure in the
cello, a graceful lyric comment in the first violin, and a light, pulsating accompaniment in the inner voices. These simple elements, plus
a scale fragment in broken thirds, are enough to enable Mozart to
construct a movement unequaled for strength, dramatic concentration, and excitement. And the stage is set for three other movements
equal to the first, but in contrasting directions. A sturdy minuet is
followed by a charming slow movement with beautifully ornamented
lyric melodies. The quintet ends with a finale whose deceptive simplicity conceals a wealth of contrapuntal subtleties and imaginative
developments.

The following quintet, in G minor, is a direct antithesis of the C
major work. Here all is dark and hopeless; the resignation of the
"Haydn" quartets has turned to despair. The concentration of mood
in the first movement is scarcely duplicated anywhere in the litera-

ture. A short phrase with the inevitable chromaticism and a downward inflection, another phrase which rises and falls—these are the
elements out of which this most pathetic of movements is created;
both themes appear in G minor, and the piece ends in that key. The

minuet gives the impression of one stumbling in the gloom: the adagio is a rich movement in which the stumbling is replaced by groping—but still in the darkness. After three such intense, almost desperate movements, the final rondo is disappointing. It does not measure up to the others, either in content or in style.

In September, 1789, a short time after the first quartet for the King of Prussia was written, Mozart composed a quintet in A major for clarinet and strings (K.581). It was designed for his friend Anton Stadler, an excellent Viennese clarinetist. The combination of wind and string instruments in chamber music was not new. We have seen dozens of trio sonatas for flute and violin; we have mentioned Mozart's own quartets in which flute and oboe, respectively, are used; we shall shortly hear about his trio, quintet, and sextet for combinations of winds and strings. What is new in the K.581 quintet is the way in which the five instruments are combined. Mozart was faced with the possibilities of treating the clarinet as a solo instrument, thus writing non-chamber music, or of ignoring its special characteristics and treating it as just another voice in a five-voice texture, thus writing dull chamber music. He made neither mistake, but evolved a texture in which the beauties of the wind instrument shine through, in which no instrument is slighted, and in which tonal balance is achieved perfectly. First violin and clarinet alternate in the first announcement of the themes; but lest that practice seem too ordinary, Mozart writes so that all the instruments share in subsequent thematic statements. The result is a piece of music whose charm and delicacy are difficult to duplicate in the literature for strings and winds.

Two more string quintets were written during the last year of Mozart's life: the D major (K.593) in December, 1790, and the E flat (K.614) in April, 1791. The feeling of oppression, so characteristic of the G minor quintet and the six "Haydn" quartets, is completely missing in both the D major and the E flat quintets. Such darker moments as exist are full of noble sentiment and great feeling rather than pensiveness or gloom. The fast movements incline toward Haydn's type of humor. Light, bustling figures are characteristic, and an air of openness and naïveté takes the place of subtle turns toward dark moods. Both quintets are alive and sparkling, in a manner reminiscent of the Prussian quartets of 1789, and are on the same level of brilliance and virtuosity.

There remain for discussion four works in different categories and in different styles. About 1782 Mozart wrote an octet for wind instruments (K.388): two each of oboes, clarinets, horns, and bassoons. In that form it is one of his finest works; the title "Serenade" is misleading, for this is no occasional piece to be performed out of doors, even though it was commissioned for such a purpose. The work contains the four movements usually found only in the more serious quartets and symphonies. Its dark color, its many gloomy moments, the contrapuntal genius shown especially in the minuet, the flares of passion—all these make it unsuited as a serenade. Why Mozart later arranged the work for string quintet is not known with certainty. Einstein assumes that the four quintets of 1787–1791 (K.515, 516, 593, 614) were written with an eye to dedicating a set of six to Frederick William II (hence the prominence of the cello part in several of these works), and "to hasten the achievement of that goal he even arranged one of his own wind serenades as a quintet —surely against his artistic conscience." [13] The quintet version, known as K.406, can hold a place with any of the regularly conceived chamber music. The slight loss of instrumental color is more than compensated for by the greater expressive flexibility of the string version.

The Peters edition of Mozart's quintets contains several other works in addition to the seven quintets discussed above. Vol. II of that edition begins with two quintets labeled K.S. (supplement?) 515 and K.46, respectively. Now, Einstein declares that K.46 is spurious.[14] But K.46 consists of four movements which Mozart used in a divertimento for thirteen wind instruments, K.361, written in 1780 or 1781. The latter work consists of seven movements; there is, in the minds of the authorities, no question of its authenticity. The editor of Mozart's *Complete Works*, Vol. IV[1], says of this work:

[13] Einstein, *Mozart*, p. 190.   [14] *Ibid.*, p. 473.

"movements 1, 2, 3 and 7 are arrangements of a string quintet composed in 1768." Obviously, if the content of K.361 is genuine, then
K.46 must be. To a lesser degree this is true also of the quintet
labeled K.S.515 in the Peters edition. This work, of four movements,
contains a first and a third movement which are identical with the
fifth and sixth, respectively, of K.361 again. The second and the
fourth movements of K.S.515 do not appear in the latter work, nor
is their original status made clear elsewhere. It would appear, then,
that K.361 is composed of all of K.46, two movements of K.S.515,
and one movement all its own. Questions of priority and arranger
remain; but if K.361 is Mozart, then K.46 and at least half of K.S.515
are likewise.

Vol. II of the Peters edition includes an arrangement of the clarinet
quintet K.581, which has been discussed above, and of a quintet for
horn and strings, K.407. The latter three-movement work in E flat,
written about 1782, is for violin, two violas, horn, and cello. It is an
unassuming piece which is part serenade, part concerto for horn, and
part chamber music. The overweight of low-register instruments
accounts for a certain lack of sprightliness, to which the general
emptiness of melody and figuration contributes.

Before discussing the seven piano trios and the two piano quartets
of Mozart one does well to recall the place of the keyboard instrument in chamber music in the decades before 1770. The trio sonata
was a vehicle dominated by the two violins; the harpsichord (later,
the piano) supplied missing chord tones, provided a degree of
rhythmic movement, and augmented the musical structure in general. And the bass or cello merely amplified the keyboard instrument's lowest voice. Thus the piano served only in an accompanying
role. With the emergence of the string quartet the piano was cast
out of its relationship with the strings, only to develop its own solo
literature in the field of the piano sonata. Then arose the strange
medium of piano solo accompanied by violin and/or cello. And
out of these grew the modern violin sonata, cello sonata, and piano
trio.

In the early years of the piano trio's life, notably in the works of Haydn, the concept was retained that the piano should dominate. Many of the Haydn trios can dispense with violin and cello without great loss to the performance. Were we to investigate the almost three dozen violin sonatas of Mozart, we would find that the violin is, in the main, really unessential—at least in the early works. In the later ones, of course, this is not true.

In the first of the Mozart piano trios, in B flat (K.254), written in the summer of 1776, when Mozart was twenty, a similar concept prevails. The violin part in the first of the three movements contains nothing more than a few accompanying figures and a few doublings of the piano's upper voice; the cello is tied to the bass line throughout. In other movements the violin is used more individually. Seen as a balanced trio, the work is at an elementary stage. As a piece of music, on the other hand, it holds its own with other works of that period. The first movement is light and entertaining; the last is graceful. The slow movement contains an aria-like, broad melody over a running accompaniment, in Mozart's most romantic vein.

Ten years elapsed before Mozart again turned to the piano trio. (One work, K.422, in D minor, begun about 1783, had remained unfinished.) In 1786 he composed three in quick succession: one in G major, K.496; one in E flat for clarinet, viola, and piano, K.498; one in B flat, K.502. Two years later, in 1788, three more issued from his pen: the E major trio, K.542; the C major, K.548; and the G major, K.564. Taking them in order, one feels a rising level of quality when approaching the E major trio and a rather quick falling off afterward. The first G major (K.496) is no longer of the type which K.254 represents. The violin and the cello are responsible individuals; they are no longer confined to accompanying roles, but have important parts to play in the creation of the musical structure. And near the beginning of the first movement one realizes that a new texture is about to be born: a texture composed of two dissimilar tonal bodies. Violin and cello, working together, are opposed by the piano; a duality of intention results. This division of textures becomes important in Beethoven and reaches its peak in Brahms. But without doubt it begins with Mozart.

The G major trio is an excellent and satisfying piece of chamber music in all respects. But it is overshadowed by the unique tone color, peculiar charm, and complete perfection of the E flat trio, K.498. The choice of instruments is unusual: both clarinet and viola are on the dark side, and both are essentially in the alto range. These facts, coupled with the fact that the trio's first movement is an andante, should go far to establish a melancholy mood in the music. But, miraculously enough, a mood of well-being, of melodic serenity, pervades all three movements. The final rondo is a marvelous example of musical sensitivity and takes a place high among Mozart's finest works.

The rising level of quality continues in the B flat trio, K.502, of 1786. That work contains everything that Mozart had achieved up to this point: an air of gentle brooding, combined with moments of brilliant display; perfection of form with daring and unexpected turns of phrase; sublime melodies with roughly dramatic contrasts. The trio as a whole is a great musical achievement and is perhaps equaled only by the E major trio, K.542, written in the summer of the year (1788) that saw the three great symphonies come to light —the E flat, the G minor, and the "Jupiter." If the E major trio seems more brilliant than the B flat, it is only because of its brighter tonality. If it seems richer, it may be because of remote and colorful modulations. Drama, lyric beauty, charm, repose, fire—everything is there. One cannot choose between these two masterworks; they remain among the great music of the Classical period.

Quite differently placed are the two remaining trios of 1788: the C major, K.548, and the G major, K.564. The C major trio has about it an air of reserve, of seeming unwillingness to be brilliant or dramatic or even lyric. It is "correct," and moves along in expected, traditional fashion. But beyond that, it leaves one unenthusiastic, and it provides a good example of the untutored layman's idea of "classical music." The G major trio was, according to Einstein,[15] originally a piano sonata, "obviously intended for beginners." Although it contains charming movements and would undoubtedly

15 Einstein, *Mozart*, p. 263.

rank high among the piano sonatas, the trio version leaves much to be desired. The texture is rather thin; the string instruments add nothing really essential to the structure. If these two trios are disappointing, we must remember that "the yardstick of perfection against which we measure these two works was put into our hands by Mozart himself." [16]

Two piano quartets, in G minor, K.478, and in E flat, K.493, were composed in 1785 and 1786, respectively. These are among the first examples of a vehicle that was to become important in the nineteenth century. It may be recalled that Haydn wrote no piano quartets; that when the Mannheim composers (among whom we may include their spiritual brother, Johann Christian Bach) wrote for piano and other instruments they turned out either piano concertos or *galant* pieces in which the piano dominated. The G minor piano quartet is completely different from such earlier works; it is a piece of true chamber music, making virtuoso demands upon the pianist, but allowing the strings full responsibility in establishing a real ensemble texture. The E flat quartet is like its companion except for the differences brought about by the tonality. Where the G minor is pensive, dark, or morbid, the E flat is energetic, dramatic, and straightforward. Einstein calls attention to the influence on the latter work of a quartet by Schobert which Mozart had first heard two decades earlier and whose sweeping power "enriches Mozart's fantasy years later." [17] Such other piano quartets as are attributed to Mozart are arrangements: the quintet for piano and winds, K.452, and the string quintets K.581 and 593.

The last two works to be discussed are completely different from each other. The sextet, K.522, for string quartet and two horns, written in 1787, is a *musikalischer Spass*—a musical joke. Full of wrong notes, structural defects, uncalled-for cadenzas, and the like, the piece represents a playful, practical-joking vein in Mozart of which his biography gives ample evidence, but which his music seldom exhibits.

The divertimento in E flat, K.563, for violin, viola, and cello, is

[16] *Ibid.*   [17] *Ibid.*, p. 115.

a serious and profound work. Again the title is misleading. For while this trio contains six movements in the manner of a divertimento (allegro, adagio, minuetto and trio, andante, minuetto and two trios, allegro), it is not music written to be merely diverting. This is sincere, heart-felt, and deeply moving music, whose variety of effects is astounding. That Mozart was able to draw so many different textures and so great a variety of colors from three instruments is a never-ending source of astonishment. No feeling that an instrument is missing, no feeling of incompleteness or of hampered resources exists. Rather one receives an impression of intensity and concentrated power; seldom does a work achieve so much with such limited means. The contrasts between the powerful first movement and the beautiful adagio, between the comfortable andante with variations and the happy finale—these are only part of the picture. Moments of concentration and dramatic power, details of counterpoint—all these add to the completeness of the work and make it one of Mozart's most satisfying chamber-music compositions.

IO

LUDWIG VAN BEETHOVEN

THE STORY of Beethoven's life has been told so well, so often, and in such detail by so many writers that nothing would be gained by attempting yet another version. It is a fascinating story, if only as an example of how a strong-willed person—and Beethoven was one of the strongest—can master the events which shape the course of his destiny. Seldom does a great composer allow external affairs to influence the content of his music; nor did Beethoven. Yet seldom has a composer so completely transformed his personal difficulties into the difficulties of all humanity and made them in turn the background out of which he writes. There is in that sense a close relationship between Beethoven's biography and his music. Crises in his personal life made their mark upon his musical style; three distinct series of happenings are largely responsible for the three periods into which his music is usually classified. In order to have available a brief sketch of the principal events of Beethoven's life so that certain style changes may directly be related to those events, a condensed biography is appropriate at this point.

Ludwig van Beethoven was born at Bonn, on the Rhine, in December, 1770. He was the second child of his parents; the first, also named Ludwig, had died in infancy a year before the composer's birth. His brothers Karl and Johann were born in 1774 and 1776; a sister Maria was born in 1786, but lived only a year. Ludwig's musical heritage came largely from the paternal side: two generations of Beethovens were employed at the court of the Elector in Bonn. His grandfather held the honored post of chapel master until his death in 1773; his father, a lesser person in all ways, sang in the choir.

His mother's father had been chief cook at the famous castle of Ehrenbreitstein, known to every Rhine traveler.

Ludwig grew to adolescence amid the musical influences of the ecclesiastical court whose seat had been removed from Cologne to Bonn in the thirteenth century. Musicians were numerous in Bonn, and his early teachers were his father's professional friends or local church organists. But his studies were desultory, his father's discipline harsh, and home life anything but well-ordered or conducive to quiet growth. With the example of the Mozarts so lately before his eyes, the elder Beethoven sought to exploit Ludwig's talent, much as Leopold Mozart had Wolfgang's. But great as Ludwig's talent was, it was not that of a child prodigy; nor had his instruction been as thorough as was Wolfgang Mozart's.

In about 1781 Ludwig came into the hands of Christian Neefe, organist, well-trained musician, and excellent person. Under Neefe's guidance Beethoven made rapid progress and began to compose. Hardly a year later Ludwig was able to substitute for Neefe at the organ when the latter was away from Bonn. Neefe's influence on Ludwig was strong, and the boy was well aware of its quality. Two years later, about 1784, Ludwig was officially appointed assistant court organist—this in addition to his duties of playing viola and harpsichord in the Elector's orchestra. In both positions he had opportunity to learn new music of all sorts: church music, operas, and other theater music—and even dinner music. In taking part in chamber music at the homes of wealthy amateurs, he learned to know that field also.

That existence, in which the teen-age boy successfully discharged a grown man's professional duties, was interrupted in the spring of 1787. Beethoven was enabled to go to Vienna, the lodestone of all musicians of that day. There he met and played for Mozart, who was greatly impressed by Ludwig's achievements and talent. And he received a few lessons from the master whom he had always admired. A few months later he was recalled to Bonn by his mother's serious illness. The long series of deprivations and neglects to which she had been exposed culminated in tuberculosis. She died in July, 1787.

Ludwig was deeply affected by his mother's death. She alone had shown any understanding of her son's talent, any sympathy with his problems. Without his mother, he was forced to assume full responsibility for his two brothers and his drunken father. Throughout his lifetime he keenly felt his obligations to look after members of his family, most often in spite of violent disagreements and other unpleasantnesses.

Ludwig returned to his position in the Elector's orchestra. His many loyal friends smoothed his pathway wherever possible and provided a substitute for the home life he could not enjoy under his own roof. He faithfully discharged his orchestral duties, composed a great deal—we shall hear more of these compositions of the Bonn period below—and made the most of every opportunity to improve and educate himself.

In 1790, and again in 1792, Haydn passed through Bonn on his way to and from London. The orchestra entertained him on both visits, and Ludwig took advantage of the occasions to become acquainted with the famous composer. Haydn, for his part, was sufficiently impressed with the boy's accomplishments to agree to accept him as a pupil in Vienna. Arrangements were made, Ludwig was granted a leave of absence by the Elector, and the trip was made. In November, 1792, Ludwig bade a last farewell to his Rhenish homeland and set out for the Mecca of all musicians.

Personal troubles, Beethoven's constant companions throughout his lifetime, followed him to Vienna. A few weeks after his arrival his father died in Bonn; money set aside to care for his brothers had been squandered. Remittances from the Elector ceased early in 1793, when the French invasion of Bonn put an end to the court. And political affairs in Vienna itself were confusing. Conditions for launching a new career at that time were anything but propitious.

But Beethoven's quality as a performer and the genius of his improvisations stood him in good stead. He quickly came into demand as a piano virtuoso and teacher. His pupils were drawn mainly from the aristocratic circles of Vienna, circles whose love of music and generous sponsorship of musicians were sincere. Beethoven's ability to move in those circles had been demonstrated at Bonn. At Vienna it grew; he soon numbered among his loyal friends and stanch supporters some of the noblest families of the Empire. But he did not cringe before them or cater to their tastes. He accepted them on his own terms, and they respected him for his independence.

Along with the career as performer and teacher came the lessons with Haydn. But Beethoven proved himself a difficult pupil, and the lessons soon became mutually unsatisfactory. Haydn's second London visit, early in 1794, provided an opportunity to end the arrangement. Beethoven began to study with Albrechtsberger, a famous contrapuntalist, and Salieri, court composer of operas. Within a year or two those lessons, too, had ceased, and Beethoven became his own teacher. Little academic schooling, a succession of minor music teachers, and short terms of study with two excellent teachers and three eminent composers—such is the extent of Beethoven's formal instruction. But education went on; he read, studied, experimented, and became his own severest critic.

The years to the turn of the century passed uneventfully enough. Beethoven was highly esteemed as a pianist and a teacher and earned a fair income from these sources. As a composer he was attracting favorable attention; his first symphony was well known, his dozen or so piano sonatas were accepted, and a number of his chamber-music works were played in wealthy homes. Beethoven's career as a virtuoso performer in the salons of Vienna seemed assured.

In the last year of the century Beethoven became increasingly aware of a deterioration in his hearing. By June, 1801, he realized that his deafness was increasing rapidly, that a cure was unlikely, and that his performing career was over. He saw himself cut off from normal social relationships and living in a world of hideous silence. At first plunged into despondency and contemplating suicide, he forced his enormous strength of will to come to the rescue. He would compose in spite of the deafness; he would "take Fate by the throat" and master it, helped, presumably, by a young countess with whom Beethoven had fallen in love. Her marriage, in 1802, to someone else brought back the despondency. Not until the winter of that year was some measure of balance restored.

The next dozen years, from 1803 to about 1815, passed quietly enough. A succession of great works, including the third to the eighth symphonies, a dozen sonatas of various kinds, nine chamber-music compositions, and dozens of larger and smaller masterpieces, occupied Beethoven. A series of love affairs, all coming to the same heartbreaking conclusion, raised him to the heights and plunged him to new depths. And always the increasing deafness and the never-ending hope for an eventual cure.

In 1815, then, came another crisis. Beethoven's older brother Karl died. In his will the latter appointed Ludwig as guardian of his nine-year-old son, Karl junior, and specifically mentioned his desire that the son not be taken away from his mother. Beethoven thoroughly despised his sister-in-law, considered her unfitted to care for her own son, and immediately took steps to remove her from the scene. Early in 1816 he was awarded sole custody of his nephew. For the next four years Karl was a constant source of worry and anguish; Beethoven was continually torn away from his music to look after his ne'er-do-well nephew. Karl's mother made determined efforts to have her son restored to her; Beethoven was equally determined to retain him, and in the end succeeded. But at what a price to the world! The steady stream of great works all but dried up. Litigation and heartsickness over his nephew, the deafness that had become almost total, the continuing series of fruitless love affairs—these are among the external reasons for the small number of compositions ascribed to the years 1816–1818. And when Beethoven began to compose again, about 1818, his style had changed completely.

The following years were devoted mainly to the production of a few works of such grandeur that all reporting of external happenings seems trivial. Indeed, one could only report on this escapade of Karl's, on that disagreement with friend or publisher, on a move to Baden or some other suburban town, and on a return to Vienna. But two things there are: the ever-increasing reputation of Beethoven as the greatest living composer, and the deterioration of his general health. In 1826 the final blow came: Karl, made aware of his unpleasant position and possibly overcome by the difficulties he had caused his uncle, attempted suicide. The hateful business passed over, but at the cost of much of Beethoven's remaining strength. He aged suddenly and declined rapidly. The winter of 1826–1827 was one long illness: pneumonia, dropsy, and cirrhosis of the liver.

In his last months he was haunted by fear of poverty; he had set aside the bulk of his modest resources for Karl and refused to touch it for his own needs. Unable to compose, neglected by his surviving brother, he was maintained only through the help of his loyal friends. Nevertheless, he still planned new works and looked forward to renewed health and activity when spring came. But fate decided otherwise. Late in March, 1827, Beethoven died.

Various commentators have noticed that the lives of composers divide themselves into three well-defined periods. There is first a time in which the composer imitates his teachers and the models around him. Then, having acquired full maturity, he gives full sway to his own artistic impulses; his thoughts turn toward the world, and the world becomes mirrored in his works. Finally, having grown old and his passions having cooled, he becomes introspective and interprets his own soul.

Within certain limits, Beethoven's life supplies a striking example of this generalization. His earliest works, those written at Bonn as well as those written during the first years at Vienna, disclose a kinship with works of Mozart and Haydn, with Schobert and with the Mannheimers. But they are not imitations of those works. From the first they have a forthrightness, a degree of originality, and a powerful quality not often encountered in the works of the composers which they resemble most closely. The compositions of Beethoven's second period, falling roughly between the years of the two great crises in his life—1800, with its first intimation of deafness, and 1816, with the litigation over his nephew—are not subject to a generalization, however wide its terms may be. In that period Beethoven departed from the concise, transparent form and content of the Classical period, true enough; but he did not abandon strict form nor give way to the other excesses that characterize many newly matured composers. His second-period works exhibit a logical power, a feeling of inevitableness, and a discipline that hardly any other music possesses. Then, beginning about 1816, came the series of legal and emotional disturbances, and with it a break in the steady flow of compositions. About 1818, when intensive work was resumed, Beethoven had again changed his style radically: the third period discloses a reversal of the intents shown in the second. He turned inward; his music cast off the last traces of interest in external events, and became stark and severe. A torso remained, a torso characterized by the greatest of contrasts in emotion—and consequently in dynamics and tempo—but also by a profundity matched nowhere in musical literature.

Throughout Beethoven's lifetime chamber music remained one of his major interests. Among his very first works are three piano quartets; a string quartet movement was his last completed composition. Leaving out of account a number of fragments and duets, there are forty-seven works in all categories. A summary discloses the following: twelve piano trios, three piano quartets, and one work which was issued simultaneously as a piano quartet and as a piano and wind quintet, seven trios (five for strings, one for winds, and one for strings and winds combined), one string quintet, and one fugal fragment for the same combination, a sextet, an octet, and a one-movement rondino (all for wind instruments), a sextet and a septet for strings and winds in combination. Finally, there are seventeen string quartets which form the backbone of chamber-music literature. Other works are arrangements, some by Beethoven and some not, of certain of the above works.

In previous chapters it has been possible to discuss works more or less in chronological sequence. In the works of both Mozart and Haydn, composition and publication dates have coincided rather well; an orderly account of the style-development of those composers emerged when their works were discussed in the order of publication. With Beethoven, a similar procedure is impractical. Several works written in his earliest years were not published until decades later and were then supplied with high opus numbers. Other works, finished at one time, were completely rewritten before publication. And it was Beethoven's habit to work on several compositions at once. The end result is that reference of compositions to specific years is in most cases only approximate. Furthermore, in no one category of Beethoven's chamber music are all phases of his style changes to be observed. Piano trios, for example, were among the first works written; but the line of trios ends on the very border of the third period. Conversely, while the string quartets include his last compositions, there are no quartets representative of the first period. With these chronological difficulties in mind, the following order will be followed in the present account: the seven compositions of the Bonn period; the nine piano trios from Opus 1 through Opus 121a; the thirteen miscellaneous works from the wind octet, Opus 103, to the C major string quintet, Opus 29; finally, the seventeen string quartets from Opus 18 to Opus 135 and the fragmentary string quintet labeled Opus 137.

In 1785 Beethoven was a well-established member of the Electoral orchestra in Bonn. His duties as organist, harpsichordist, and violist could not have been too formidable, for he found time to compose three piano quartets. The works were published posthumously in 1832, in the sequence of E flat, D, and C major. The C major was the first to be written, however, and hence may be recorded as Beethoven's first chamber-music composition. The composer was fifteen at the time; but because of his father's falsification of the son's birth date—hoping to make the prodigy seem even younger than he was—Beethoven wrote the quartets in the belief that he was thirteen years old.

The question immediately arises, what were Beethoven's models for these works? It will be remembered that Haydn wrote no piano quartets, that works for that combination by the Mannheim composers were essentially piano sonatas with minor string accompaniments, and that Mozart's only two piano quartets were written during the winter of 1785–1786, namely, after Beethoven's quartets were composed. It is not likely that Mozart's were modeled upon Beethoven's, for Mozart remained firmly planted in Vienna from October, 1784, to January, 1787. Conversely, Beethoven's quartets in manuscript could hardly have been circulating in that city. The conviction grows that the two composers, one a boy of fifteen, the other a mature master of thirty, developed the new medium almost simultaneously and quite independently of each other. Mozart's piano quartets were among the first piano and string combinations in which a true ensemble texture appeared in the string parts. But Beethoven's are also characterized by that treatment. Themes are given to violin and viola with great frequency, and all three string instruments take equal part in contributing figurations and development episodes. The conclusion is inescapable that even in his very first chamber-music works Beethoven was an innovator.

Stylistically, however, the works are not significant. They are in general full of Mannheim mannerisms, of Mannheim dynamic contrasts, and of Rococo figurations and ornaments. One theme, that of the C major quartet's slow movement, was used again ten years later in the piano sonata Opus 2, No. 1. Each of the three quartets contains three movements, as do all of the Mozart chamber-music works with piano. Beethoven did not employ the four-movement form in works with piano until he had moved to Vienna and adopted Haydn's forms.

About 1786 Beethoven wrote two trios: one in G major for flute, bassoon, and piano,[1] and one in E flat for violin, cello, and piano.[2] The latter is usually included in complete editions of Beethoven's trios, hence is known to some extent; the G major trio is known hardly at all. Although the trios are roughly contemporary, there is little similarity between them.

The G major is a long diffuse work with enough themes for sev-

[1] In Vol. XXV of *Ludwig van Beethovens Werke.*
[2] According to Thayer, *The Life of Ludwig van Beethoven*, I, 136, who quotes from a contemporary catalogue: "composed *anno* 1791, and originally intended for the three trios Opus 1, but omitted as too weak by Beethoven."

eral compositions. An extended allegro in sonata form is followed by a loosely constructed adagio. The trio concludes with a set of eight variations on a moderately paced theme. The E flat trio, on the other hand, is a concise work; transitions are developed out of thematic fragments, and an air of economy prevails throughout. The second movement is noteworthy. Although it is a fast minuet, it is labeled "scherzo," just as similar fast minuets in Haydn's quartets of Opus 33 are given that name. This is not yet the presto movement in sonata form that we shall find later in Beethoven, but its content points in that direction. A rondo in the style of Mozart's violin sonatas concludes the work. The trio was published posthumously in 1830.[3]

A series of variations in E flat, for piano, violin, and cello, was written about 1792 and published in 1804 as Opus 44. The theme is a well-ventilated melody based on rising and falling chord tones; the fourteen variations are concerned with slight rhythmic modifications of the theme. One or two of the variations have real emotional interest, but the work as a whole is merely pleasant. Also belonging to the music of the Bonn period is a single movement for an octet of wind instruments, in E flat. Written about 1792 and published posthumously in 1829, this *Rondino* is not an important work; it is mentioned solely in the interests of completeness.

Thus, three piano quartets, three piano trios, and a short octet for wind instruments are known to have been completed before Beethoven's twenty-second year in Bonn.[4] Many other chamber-music works were begun in that city, but were carried to Vienna by Beethoven in 1792. There they were completed or rewritten, supplied with opus numbers and published. Those works will be discussed below.

Among the works begun in Bonn were three piano trios. During his first months in Vienna, Beethoven continued work on them, and he performed them at Prince Lichnowsky's in the fall of 1793;

[3] Nottebohm, *Beethoven: thematisches Verzeichniss.* Thayer, *The Life of Ludwig van Beethoven,* I, 136, gives the date 1836.
[4] Scott, in *Beethoven* (2d ed.), p. 296, lists an additional trio in E flat, composed in 1792. I have been unable to find this work listed elsewhere, nor is it included in the *Werke*.

Haydn was present. The trios attracted considerable attention, were played often in Viennese aristocratic circles, and contributed to the ever-growing reputation of Beethoven as a promising composer. But not until the summer of 1795 did he allow them to be published; with them he made his debut as a professional composer, for he numbered them Opus 1. At least three years of polishing and perfecting went into these three trios in E flat, G major, and C minor, respectively.

That they are modeled upon contemporary works is evident in the general transparence of their style, in the contour of their melodies, in their four-movement form, and in their adherence to other formal restrictions. But there the similarity ends. At the very outset of the first trio Beethoven employed a device which he retained throughout his lifetime: the theme is constructed out of repetitions of a short motive. In this case the motive is a rapidly ascending series of chord tones, similar to the "Mannheim rocket" of earlier decades. It appears in transitions, and it creates almost a second development section out of the elaborate coda. Many of Beethoven's fast movements are constructed largely out of similar motives. It is the consistent use of this device that made possible his great contribution to musical form: the extension (one might almost say the development) of the development principle, perhaps the outstanding musical achievement of the post-1755 era.

Other examples of originality abound throughout the trios. Among the most important are Beethoven's expansion of the harmonic scheme. Sudden modulations, especially to the keys a third above and below the tonic, became characteristic. The G major trio's slow movement and the C minor's finale provide cases in point. An example, given on page 250, will illustrate the practice.

We shall see that similar modulations served Beethoven throughout his lifetime. They influenced later composers so strongly that in the Romantic period they became stock items. Here, in Opus 1, they immediately widened Beethoven's harmonic horizon far beyond that of his contemporaries. It was, indeed, significant that they appeared in the works with which he began his Viennese career.

With these trios Beethoven established himself as an original and powerful composer.

The trios grew in popularity in the years following their publication. More than twenty years later, about 1817, an unauthorized and very poor arrangement of the C minor trio for string quintet appeared in print. Beethoven, greatly incensed at the mediocre quality of the arrangement, made one of his own. It was performed publicly

in 1818 and published the following year as Opus 104 with the following whimsical description: "an arranged terzett as a four-voice quintet by Mr. Goodwill, brought from the illusion of five voices into the light of day with five real voices and lifted from the greatest miserableness to a degree of respectability by Mr. Well-wishing. Vienna, the fourteenth of August, 1817. *N.B.* The original three-voice quintet score has been consigned to the gods of the underworld as a festive burnt offering."

In October, 1798, a trio for clarinet, cello, and piano, Opus 11, was announced by Beethoven's publisher as "wholly new." The trio was written for an obscure clarinetist whom Beethoven knew, but who apparently did not inspire the composer to his best efforts. The first movement is merely pleasant; its contrasting melodic fragments are developed at length, but to no real purpose. The second is a highly ornamented adagio, superficially beautiful, but lacking in true sentiment. The finale, a set of ten variations on a little tune drawn from a contemporary opera, is a perfunctory movement; its variations do little more than modify the theme. On the whole, Opus 11 is a minor work; Beethoven was subject to better inspirations in 1798 than this work exhibits.

In the years after 1798 Beethoven passed through one of his great personal crises: the deafness he feared became actual. He realized that it was progressive and probably incurable. A period of despondency, of near-suicide, lasted for several years. In about 1802 the despondency gave way to resignation and an outpouring of feeling. The somewhat restrained (for Beethoven) transparence of his style gave way to an intense, subjective manner. Personal expression became the goal. The works of this second period show, in general, more heightened contrasts, greater harmonic freedom, more concentrated power. The two piano trios of Opus 70, in D and E flat, respectively, were written ten or more years after the Opus 11 work; they are typical of that period. Their publication took place in 1809.

The D major trio is a unique work. Its first movement is probably one of the most tightly knit pieces Beethoven had written up to that time. Two contrasting motives, one powerful and fast, the other lyric and sustained, appear at the very outset and provide the material out of which the entire movement is constructed. It is essentially a long development section, even though it contains contrasting harmonies and a recapitulation. Emotional contrasts are achieved by extreme changes in texture: a driving passage in unison or octaves gives way to tight contrapuntal imitations; a brief lyric movement is interrupted by a savage outburst of sound. The second movement, full of mysterious tremblings and passionate cries set opposite fragments of sublime melody, of thunderous chord progressions opposite delicate ornaments, has given the work its popular nickname: the "Ghost Trio." Like the first movement, it is constructed out of a minimum of materials; but here the effect is awe inspiring. The finale, a large piece in sonata form, is neither concentrated nor intense; the same inner compulsion to make much out of little is seen, however. Again the development principle steps out of its normal place and takes possession of the entire movement. The D major trio is one of the most passionate of all Beethoven's chamber-music compositions.

It was typical of Beethoven to provide startling contrasts within the same opus number. The second trio of Opus 70, in E flat, differs from the first in every essential respect. It begins with a slow, sustained introduction. The first movement proper contains graceful melodies and a well-defined form in which elements of the introduction appear. The second is a quiet set of six variations in C major and minor; here Beethoven's boundless imagination is given free play. And then the four-movement form, missing in his piano trios since the Opus 1 work of 1795, returns: the third movement is a minuet. It is a quiet, unassuming piece with broad melodies; it contains a type of passage that Schubert was to employ a decade later. In the finale the impetuous Beethoven returns; rushing scale passages give way to reflective moments, bustling figures are succeeded by short recitations for each instrument in turn. The movement is outstanding in its climaxes and in the quality of its developments. It forms a fitting close to one of Beethoven's truly great works.

The trio in B flat, Opus 97, marks one of the highest points reached by Beethoven in his chamber music. In breadth, sublimity, and originality, it is scarcely exceeded by any work in the nineteenth century. His sketch books of 1810 give evidence that the trio was in his mind during that year. The theme fragments set down in sketch form were not utilized at once, however. Not until March, 1811, and then within a period of three weeks, was the trio written.[5] Publication was deferred until the summer of 1816, when the work appeared with a dedication to Beethoven's patron of long standing, Archduke Rudolph of Austria. The nickname of the "Archduke Trio" derives from this dedication.

The first movement is unique in the originality and the logic of its development. We have come to expect striking new departures in Beethoven; here are devices yet unthought of. Pizzicato string figures combined with staccato passages in the piano; phrase extensions leading to unexpected changes of mood; new textures and new types of emotional contrast. Yet the entire movement is pervaded with an air

[5] Thayer, *The Life of Ludwig van Beethoven*, II, 199.

of nobility and a unity of expressive purpose unmatched in the literature. The second movement is a fast scherzo cast in a highly imaginative form. A sixteen-measure melody is presented; the first phrase of that melody returns four or five times, each time leading in a new direction. It is developed; it modulates; countermelodies grow out of it. The trio combines mysterious phrases made of syncopated chromatic lines and heavy-footed phrases of a coarse bucolic dance. The movement as a whole is one of Beethoven's most original and enjoyable scherzos.

But even this inspiration is overshadowed by the slow movement which follows. Formally, it is a theme with five variations and a coda; musically, it is one of the noblest pieces ever composed. The theme,

of great beauty and haunting simplicity, is not so much varied as transformed. The variations are based on successively smaller note values: triplets, sixteenths, sextuplets. The harmonic framework remains, and the melody is recognizable throughout. But the content of the theme is refined, given new life and spirit. No description can hope to do justice to the sublimity of this movement. The spell it engenders is rudely broken by the finale which is connected to the slow movement. Here is a lively, energetic, and humorous rondo, of a size and quality that only Beethoven ever achieved. It is said that Beethoven often ended his most moving improvisations with a loud chord and a louder laugh, in order to bring his listeners down to earth again. A similar device is employed here, and succeeds admirably in restoring the listener's balance.

In June, 1812, Beethoven wrote a single movement for piano trio, in B flat. The autograph is inscribed, "to my little friend Max [Maximiliane] Brentano, for her encouragement in piano playing. Vienna, June 2d, 1812." The trio was subsequently laid away; it was found by the Brentanos after Beethoven's death, and published without opus number in 1830. The movement is in sonata form, with themes and development laid out on a small scale. But characteristic modulations and a masterful coda, longer than the exposition and in effect an additional development section, distinguish the work. Even in his miniatures Beethoven's sense of pace and expressive feeling are evident. While not a great work, it is a charming bit of music.

Beethoven's visitors at Baden in the summer of 1823 heard what they reported as "a new manuscript trio." [6] This work, a set of variations on a naïve tune from a contemporary opera, was published in 1824 with the title, *Adagio, Variations, and Rondo—Opus 121a.* No information about the reason for writing the work exists. The theme, "Ich bin der Schneider Kakadu," is insignificant; but all else in the trio is of fine quality. A long adagio in G minor, serving as an introduction, is essentially a fantasy or improvisation on the first phrases of the variation theme. Dramatic movements are plentiful, and an air of brooding hangs over the whole. After so profound an introduction, the theme comes as a great shock. The ten variations are based on subdivisions of the note values: variations in sixteenth notes are set between variations in triplets, in thirty-second notes, etc. An adagio, in minor, provides a moment of repose before the final fast, major variation. A large and elaborate movement labeled "rondo," but having the character of a development, concludes this fifteen-minute work. The proportions of the three sections are unusual. The introduction itself, quite apart from its musical weight, is five minutes long; the listener is prepared for an equally large main movement. But the light, almost child-like theme is heard instead;

[6] Thayer, *The Life of Ludwig van Beethoven*, III, 135.

one sees the introduction in retrospect and realizes its greatness. This is third-period Beethoven in many respects.

We must now retrace our steps and return to Beethoven's first years in Vienna in order to discuss another category of his works. His interest in chamber music during those years was not exhausted with the writing of a few piano trios. Beethoven also experimented, while catering to the Viennese love for outdoor music or completing commissions; he wrote a number of works for unusual combinations of instruments. Thirteen compositions are in that category; they represent the tentative side of Beethoven's chamber-music activity. These works have left the Bonn style far behind, but they have not yet ascended to the richness and power of the second period; in a word, they are typical of the style represented by the piano trios of Opus 1. Exact dates of writing cannot be attached to these works: some of the thirteen were begun during Beethoven's last year at Bonn and completed later; others saw the light of day in Vienna. All, however, were worked on and finished in the latter city between 1792 and 1801.

Probably the first of these works is the octet for pairs of oboes, clarinets, horns, and bassoons, in E flat, written about 1792. Beethoven must not have thought too highly of the octet; it was not published during his lifetime. Not until 1834 did it receive publication, and then it was given an irrelevant opus number, namely 103. But within a few years of its completion, about 1796, he rewrote the work for string quintet with two violas. It was published in that form about 1797 as Opus 4.

Opus 4 is in no sense an arrangement of the octet. External similarities between the two versions exist, true enough; the first themes of the four movements agree in most particulars. But secondary themes are completely different, developments are more carefully worked out in the string version, and its modulations roam much farther afield. The very phrase structure of one is unlike the other. Two words characterize the second version: expansion and maturity. Opus 4 is at least half again as large a work as Opus 103; the former's minuet contains two trios in place of the one in the latter. Developments are expanded, elaborate transitions grow out of previously heard phrases. Yet the string version is a more concise work than the original octet; with all its greater length it seems to move along tightly without any waste motion. Here is one example of Beethoven's increase in maturity in the period 1792–1796. Another example is seen in the greater harmonic freedom of Opus 4. Modulations to the mediant, virtually unknown in Opus 103 and the earlier Bonn works, are characteristic in the quintet, as they were in their contemporaries, the piano trios of Opus 1. It is altogether fitting to regard Opus 4 as an original work on a level with other first-period compositions. One cannot raise Opus 103 to that level.

Contemporary with Opus 103 is the trio for violin, viola, and cello, also in E flat, also begun at Bonn in 1792. But the trio is far superior to the octet, and cannot be considered a juvenile work in any sense. A first movement in sonata form, with a masterful development and a highly original coda, gives way to a charming andante. A minuet is followed by one of the most moving works of Beethoven's youth: an expressive and dramatic adagio, like the first movement in sonata form. Again one is astonished at Beethoven's skill in handling development and transition details. A second minuet, with the trio built over a drone bass, intervenes between the adagio and the lively rondo finale. Thayer gives evidence [7] that this work was played from manuscript in England in 1793 and thus was probably the earliest of Beethoven's compositions to be known abroad. It was published in 1797 as Opus 3.

But not all of his early instrumental works were in sonata form; Beethoven also tried his hand at writing serenades. Two trios, roughly contemporary, resulted; both are in D major. One is for violin, viola, and cello; the other for flute, violin, and viola. The exact time of their writing cannot be determined; Thayer believes [8] that both were composed about 1795–1796. The date is probably correct, for both trios are full of a light-heartedness and a secure mastery that were not always present in earlier years. At any rate, the string

[7] *The Life of Ludwig van Beethoven*, I, 134.   [8] *Ibid.*, p. 208.

trio was published in 1797 as Opus 8; the trio with flute was delayed until 1802, when it appeared as Opus 25.

The string trio contains seven movements, the last one being a repetition of the march with which the trio begins. Three of the movements are quite regular: an adagio, a minuet, and an andante with variations. But the fourth movement is unique: essentially a poignant adagio, it also contains two bright and sparkling sections called scherzos. The contrasting bits appear alternately, in the form ABABA. Beethoven was to use that form to great advantage in his string quartets in later years. In that form the principle of contrasting themes within a movement is carried to its farthest limits, for here is a contrast of tempos as well. A considerable number of works later in the century, notably certain of Brahms's compositions, make use of the device seen in Beethoven's Opus 8. To return to the trio: the fifth movement, a sprightly dance "alla Polacca," is distinguished by a daring episode for the cello, high and awkward. Thus, Beethoven's

habit of ignoring the instrumentalist's comfort and convenience was shown very early in his career. Here is probably the first example in his chamber music. The trio as a whole is not profound; but is it wrong to expect entertainment from a piece cast in the old divertimento form?

The seven movements of the Opus 25 trio are equally light and diverting. But here the presence of the flute and the absence of the cello add a note of daintiness to the ensemble. Charm and delicacy characterize the work; one has the impression of hearing a full-size miniature, if that be possible. The flute's graceful voice is not overly assertive, yet the work is conditioned, in style and content, by that instrument. The trio deserves more performances than it receives.

The three string trios of Opus 9 also belong roughly to the same years, 1796–1797. Nothing is known of their genesis other than that they were given to a publisher early in 1798 and were published in the summer of that year. They are dedicated to Count Brown, a Russian officer who had given Beethoven a horse. In these trios the diverting content of Opus 8 and Opus 25 is missing, for these are serious works. They are in G, D, and C minor, respectively. Each of the trios contains four movements; the first trio has a slow introduction in addition.

In the G major trio one is struck first of all with the richness of texture. Sonorities such as a string quartet brings forth are everywhere evident. One does not feel that this trio, like so many trios, is merely an incomplete quartet. Particularly in the E major slow movement, with its pulsating figures and florid melodies, does the impression of completeness prevail. The scherzo, although fast and brilliant, is not a cheery piece. The finale, a long movement in sonata form with imaginative developments and beautifully contrasted themes, is the finest of the four.

The D major trio, the second of the set, is less successful. It is a long work, and for the first time in Beethoven's trios one feels that the composer was handicapped by having only three instruments. Although there are moments of interest and charm, a general impression of dryness in the writing remains.

Perhaps the finest of all Beethoven works written up to this time is the third trio of Opus 9. Beethoven's affinity for the key of C minor is well known; the dramatic tensions and powerful emotions that key inspired in him are everywhere present in this trio, as they are later to be in the C minor symphony, in the slow movement of the "Eroica," in the piano sonata Opus 111, and in the "Coriolanus" overture. Darkness dominates all but a few passages in the first movement, along with a degree of concentration not found earlier in Beethoven. The scherzo is in minor; its trio provides a moment of repose in a major key. The finale, an intense and passionate movement, is in sonata form; both themes are in minor. But the great moments of the trio are found in the magnificent second movement, an adagio. Here, in C major, is a piece of music with repose, with noble sentiment, with dramatic utterance, and with reckless abandon. It alone would have been enough to lift the C minor trio to a high position among Beethoven's early works.

Three other compositions from these productive years may be grouped together, for they are neither good nor bad. Probably the first of the three to be composed was the sextet for string quartet and two horns, in E flat major, written about 1795 and published in 1810 as Opus 81b. Here we encounter a three-movement form again, a decided rarity in Beethoven's chamber music: allegro, adagio, rondo. The problems of texture that a mixed ensemble offers are neatly solved in this sextet. The horns are given the themes on occasion; at other times they accompany the quartet, play in thirds, or engage in imitations. And their ability to play lyric melodies is taken into account. Throughout the work their essential characteristics are kept in mind. An excellent blend of colors results.

Another sextet in E flat major, but this time for pairs of clarinets, horns, and bassoons, belongs to the same years: 1795–1797. It was first performed in 1805 (one need not wonder at the delay), and was published in 1809 as Opus 71. Here the four-movement form returns. A slow introduction is followed by a discursive movement in sonata form. A florid adagio, an orthodox minuet, and a march-like rondo follow in due course. The themes are appropriate to wind-instrument style; they are in the main composed of short melodic fragments with breathing spaces between fragments. The form is clear, each instrument is given its share of melodies, and the tunes are suited to the medium. More one cannot say. All the conventional devices appear, and the composer's good taste is in evidence. What Beethoven hoped to accomplish with this work is not clear.

A similar work is the trio for two oboes and English horn, in C major. It, too, belongs to the prolific years of 1795–1797; it, too, was delayed in publication, for it appeared in print in 1806. Later, the irrelevant opus number 87 was attached to the work. The usual four movements occur. The first is rather too long for the quality of its themes; the second is overly sentimental. But the trio gains momentum as it progresses; the finale is a good, workman-like piece of music. Charming and light-hearted moments are found often. On the whole, Opus 87 is a better work than either of the sextets, possibly because Beethoven's resources were more limited in this trio and he was inspired to do more with less.

And now the piano returns to his chamber music. A quintet for oboe, clarinet, bassoon, horn, and piano, in E flat, was written before 1797; it was performed in April of that year. It was published in 1801, together with an arrangement, made by Beethoven himself, for violin, viola, cello, and piano. Both versions were given the same number: Opus 16. The piano quartet piece is an arrangement in the truest sense; Beethoven made only such changes as the new instrumentation required.

A stately introduction precedes the first movement. Rich sonorities and an air of largeness are characteristic. The following allegro is in fully developed sonata form and contains three themes; the development is exciting and does full justice to the contrasting melodic groups. The andante is a long, melodious piece in large rondo form. Beautiful themes, delicious counterpoints, and delicate embroideries make it a charming movement. The finale (there is no minuet) is again a rondo: brilliant, fast, and full of humor. In a sense, Opus 16 is the most Mozartean of Beethoven's early chamber-music works. Its transparent quality, its beautifully clear lines, and its general perfection are reminiscent of Mozart. But its vigor, humor, and size remove it from direct comparison with that master. It is the young Beethoven at his best. Straightforward in its emotional purposes, perfect in form and texture, richly endowed with satisfying melodies, it represents all that is best in first-period Beethoven.

When Beethoven's C major symphony received its first performance, in the spring of 1800, the program included a septet for violin, viola, cello, bass, clarinet, bassoon, and horn, in E flat. In succeeding years the septet became enormously popular, so much so that Beethoven complained about its obscuring the fact that he had also written other works. It was published in 1802 as Opus 20. He arranged the work for piano trio some years after its completion; in that form it is sometimes included among his trios. A version for string quintet was done commercially, without his approval. But the original is the only version worth considering.

It was not a new departure, even in Beethoven's time, to combine string and wind instruments into a chamber-music ensemble. Many works of Mozart, of the Mannheimers, and of earlier composers were for mixed instrumentation. But employing wind instruments in a work of large dimensions, treating them as integral parts of the structure, and lifting them out of their erstwhile orchestral anonymity had been done only rarely, notably in Mozart's clarinet quintet. And even there only a single wind instrument was added to the strings; the problems of manipulating three diverse colors is enormously more difficult. Beethoven's septet marks possibly the first successful attempt to write so skillfully and in such size for a mixed instrumental group in chamber music.

This work is a composite of several styles. Its six movements, including an adagio, an andante with variations, a minuet,[9] and a scherzo, point to a revival of the divertimento. Slow, dignified introductions to first and last movements are reminiscent of the Mozart of about 1780. The dominance of the first violin, plus an occasional cadenza for that instrument, bring the Rococo *style galant* alive again. Against such old-fashioned (even in 1800) characteristics one may place three sonata-form movements with large development sections, a true ensemble texture, and a general feeling of modernity. Beethoven's sense of pace and feeling for drama, present even in his less successful works, play important parts in lifting the septet well above the level of much wind-instrument music. Opus 20 is one of the truly great works of his first decade in Vienna.

The septet is no mere resurrection and expansion of the divertimento. It is a composition embodying everything Beethoven had

[9] The theme of the minuet was used later (1802) in the piano sonata, Opus 49, No. 2.

learned up to his thirtieth year. It brings to an end the period of experimentation in chamber music. Gone was the vacillation between string- and wind-instrument works; gone, even, was all desire to include the winds in chamber music. With the exception of one work which is contemporary with the septet, and which will be discussed in the following paragraphs, Beethoven's chamber-music activity after 1802 was confined almost entirely to piano trio and string quartet.

A string quintet in C major was begun about 1800 and published in 1802 as Opus 29. Even though it was written after the string quartets of Opus 18 were well on the way to completion and was indeed published after the quartets, the quintet retains certain of Beethoven's early characteristics. But it also quite definitely points to the future and gives an indication of what is to come after 1802. This is one of the transitional works which lies squarely across style boundaries.

Few of Beethoven's works flow as smoothly and easily as the quintet's first movement; its melodies move from cadence to cadence with a quality of repose that is delightful. The lyric, florid adagio, with its recitative-like middle section and its wealth of contrapuntal detail, is a charming inspiration worthy of comparison with the best works of Mozart. These two movements, taken together, are probably as closely akin to the mature Salzburg master as anything Beethoven wrote. But these beauties are echoes of the past.

Then the picture changes; at once we enter a new tonal world. The third movement, a pungent and concentrated scherzo, is generations removed from Beethoven's immediate predecessors. Its dominant feature is a one-measure motive, repeated ceaselessly in every instrument and on every scale step. This is a late Beethoven characteristic: the reiteration of a single figure (see page 263). The scherzo moves forward relentlessly, and clearly anticipates certain of the great scherzos of later decades. And the finale is a surging, restless piece containing probably the most advanced contrapuntal passages Beethoven had composed up to that time. The form itself is enlarged; it includes three complete themes plus a codetta, and, in the development section, an entirely new theme which prepares for and justifies the final coda. Transitional details and modulations in this finale deserve careful study; the whole movement is a masterwork. In this fragmentary description of the third and fourth movements we see the Beethoven of the future.

In what respects, then, is the C major quintet a transitional work? In what sense is it merely anticipatory of second-period works and not one of them? The question cannot be answered fully until Beethoven reveals his later characteristics in the string quartets. But a phrase comes to mind, one that indicates in which direction the answer will lie: the generating power of the individual motive. We shall see in the pages to follow that Beethoven, in his post-1802 compositions, became able to endow his motives with life of their own. An organic growth, logical and controlled, and virtually unknown in music previous to that date, is disclosed. In Opus 29 that organic growth was not attained, even though other characteristics of the second period were. Thus, the quintet came to the very border of the new style without crossing it. With all its qualities, it is essentially a first-period work.

He who knows only the nine symphonies of Beethoven can nevertheless acquire a deep understanding of that composer's art. Humor, power, drama, poignancy, majesty, great depth of feeling, and utter abandon—all are present in those compositions. Likewise, to one knowing only the thirty-two piano sonatas the secrets of Beethoven's music are very largely revealed. The symphonies, extending from about 1799 to 1823, embrace all three of his style changes; the sonatas, from 1795 to 1822, do likewise. A composer whose musical thought is called "orchestral" by some, who is described as "keyboard-minded" by others, could not help but disclose his innermost feelings in either or both of these categories.

Yet the strange fact remains that *all* of Beethoven is not to be found exclusively in symphonies and sonatas. Neither category embraces the subtleties and stark contrasts of post-1823 works. Nor is there in them the degree of intimacy or even the religious feeling one finds in other works. In only one series of compositions does one find all of Beethoven; in only one series is every shade of emotion, every technical refinement, every significant expressive musical purpose to be looked for. That series begins with works written in Beethoven's first maturity; it concludes with works written during his last months of life. The seventeen string quartets, from Opus 18 to Opus 135, form that series.

The quartets are variously described. They are the New Testament of music, or, more inclusively, they are its Bible; they are the backbone of musical literature; they are the first really modern music. Such characterizations, by sincere and thoughtful musicians, deserve recognition. They serve to show how highly regarded the quartets are; to how lofty a place the feeling of musicians has raised them. Generations of quartet players have marveled anew, with each replaying, at the greatness of these works. Informed contemporary opinion agrees that the seventeen quartets form a whole unmatched in the literature.

Beethoven was fully aware of his worth as a composer, even in his early Vienna years. But he was equally aware of his limitations; self-criticism and complete objectivity in self-appraisal were strongly developed. He knew and admired the quartets of Haydn and Mozart; he had received a commission to compose some quartets in 1795. But with every incentive to do so, with great interest in the field of chamber music, he wrote no quartets until he was almost thirty. It seems plausible that only his high regard for quartet writing and his unwillingness to turn out mediocre works kept him from working in that medium until he felt himself to be ready. Beginning in 1799, he spent almost a year in polishing and perfecting his first attempts in that field. The results, six of them, were published in sets of threes in July and October of 1801 as Opus 18. They are in F, G, D, C minor, A, and B flat, respectively.[10]

The six quartets give ample evidence of the "generating power of the individual motive," which was mentioned above as finding employment in the post-1800 works of Beethoven. Possibly the most illuminating examples are found in the F major, the very first quartet of the set. The first movement opens with a concentrated motive:

Beethoven, Opus 18, No.1

Easily recognizable, rhythmically characteristic, and harmonically clear, it dominates the entire movement. Out of it the first theme is constructed; in that theme's first twenty measures the motive appears eight times. The theme in the truest sense is generated out of the motive. But a single manifestation of growth is not enough for Beethoven; a small melodic strand occurring in the seventh and eighth measures of the theme is preserved for future use. Pages later, the strand is used extensively in the recapitulation. And as though that were not enough, the strand there gives rise to another short melody which in turn becomes a transition based on the original motive. The cycle is complete and nothing has been wasted.

[10] Beethoven's sketch books give evidence that the quartets were not written in their published order. The first and sixth, in D major and C minor, respectively, were placed third and fourth in the published version.

The scherzo is even more revealing. Usually the second of the scherzo's two parts is roughly twice as long as the first part. In this case it is almost eight times as long; extensive development of four fragments heard in the first part account for the unusual proportions. And furthermore, a small detail—an octave leap in the lower instrument, coupled with a grace note in the first violin—quite incidental in that development, becomes the generating motive out of which the passionate trio grows. In the following example the fragments are shown; reference to a score will disclose the use to which they are put.

This method of basing musical construction upon organic growth became Beethoven's life-long characteristic. The great majority of his works after 1800 disclose a similar method. And even in the largest works, those containing dozens of melodic ideas—for example, the first movement of the "Eroica"—each idea, one might almost say each fragment, is exhaustively cultivated, is made to yield its full crop of derivative tunes.

Side by side with movements based on this type of organic life are movements built out of series of tunes, similar to many first-period works and similar to many works by Haydn and Mozart. Slow movements and rondos in general are less susceptible to motive manipulation, since their appeal is primarily a melodic one. Thus, three of the slow movements in Opus 18 are traditional, and one, the andante of the A major quartet, is a set of variations. But in the adagio of the second quartet, in G major, occurs the kind of extreme tempo contrast we saw in Opus 8: two slow and broad sections are separated by a sprightly allegro fragment. Here, again, is a premonition of third-period works, since such startling tempo contrasts became characteristic in the 1820's. And the slow movement of the C minor quartet is labeled "scherzo." Built upon fugal expositions, but in sonata form nevertheless, it is a light and deft movement. It is difficult to see why Beethoven called the movement what he did, for there is not the slightest point of resemblance between this andante scherzoso and a true scherzo. Perhaps that is the joke.

The third quartet, in D major, is one of Beethoven's happiest inspirations. Pure joy and great beauty permeate the entire work. Joy and liveliness also dominate in the sixth quartet, in B flat, particularly in the marvelous syncopated scherzo. But here the joy is abruptly terminated; the fourth movement is prefaced by a moving adagio labeled "La Malinconia," which serves to restrain the finale to a great extent.

Taken together, the six quartets of Opus 18 are charming, beautifully proportioned, and at times noble and moving. What distinguishes them from first-period works is their craftsmanship, their new techniques, and their emotional subtleties. They are six unrelated works which happen to share the same opus number. Their emotional content varies from movement to movement; only their consistency of style and their key relationships connect one with the others. But they are not profound. Not until Beethoven had passed through the crisis brought on by his deafness, with its great depression and subsequent moral victory, did he develop the profundity and largeness of vision which are so uniquely his contributions to music. Those attributes appear in his chamber music with the writing of the three quartets of Opus 59. Begun in May, 1806, they were completed in the same year and were published in January, 1808, with a dedication to Count Rasoumowsky, the Russian nobleman who had commissioned them. The quartets are in F, E minor, and C, respectively. But no longer are they unrelated, as the quartets of Opus 18 had been; they are tied together in several ways.

The most obvious connection is furnished by the Russian element. Folk songs in the F and E minor quartets and a brooding slow movement in the C major (said by Scott [11] to be a transformed folk song) provide external links. Whether Rasoumowsky specified the inclusion of the Russian tunes or whether Beethoven employed them out of deference to the former's nationality is not known. But a connection of that sort is scarcely a subtle one. A profound connection of an inner sort exists also, one that has so far not been generally recognized.

The F major quartet begins tentatively and in a restrained manner. Doubt is felt from the very beginning: the first phrase begins on the

fifth note of the scale, returns to it time and again, and ends on an incomplete six-four chord—all of which provides a feeling of uncertainty. The recapitulation is unprepared; the theme returns shyly and a measure too soon. And the movement contains no real climax. The allegretto, which serves as a scherzo, is not joyful. With its hesitant style, its second theme (the movement is in sonata form) in minor, and its long development of the down-to-earth rhythmic motive, the movement does not generate momentum. It leads to tragedy, for the F minor adagio is, perhaps, the most tragic movement in all of Beethoven's works. Its gloom is not resolved; almost

[11] Scott, *Beethoven* (2d ed.), p. 256.

every moment of its eleven minutes is bathed in the deepest, most expressive pathos. Nor does it find relief in the Russ-tinged finale which is directly attached to the adagio: the quartet ends, not triumphantly, but with an air of resignation.

The first movement of the E minor quartet is intense and questioning: two abrupt chords, a short, doubting phrase in E minor, and,

after a pause, a repetition of that phrase a half-tone higher—thus the beginning. The doubtful chords, the many short pauses, the strange shifting rhythms all strengthen the feeling of uncertain wandering, of indecision. Only in the final coda is a decision reached. The E major adagio which follows is sublime and full of divine beauty. The deepest inspiration and celestial repose characterize this movement; one can well believe Beethoven's remark that he conceived it while contemplating the starry sky. Uncertainties are laid to rest; the movement is strong and clear. But it is not written on a note designed to relieve personal tragedy; the F minor adagio is not yet completed. The third movement, again tentative, with its shifting rhythms and abruptly contrasting trio (based on a Russian folk song), is moody and impulsive. And the finale, an unrestrained, march-like movement, is like a false dawn of hope. The very harmonies are false: a reiterated C major in an E minor movement. He who finds only humor in this movement has forgotten how Beethoven shouted raucously at the close of his tenderest improvisations—if only to conceal the depth of his feeling. So has he done here.

With the C major quartet the gloom lightens. A diminished chord (related to the final E minor chord of the previous quartet) intro-

duces a series of shifting harmonies in which rhythm is virtually negated. The transition to C major requires thirty measures. The first movement proper, with crystal-clear themes, with pace and straight-forwardness, prepares for an excursion into a kind of retrospective melancholy. This second movement contains none of the anguish of the F minor adagio, but rather a gentle reflective mood. The third movement, a minuet, bridges the gap between the andante and the enormous fugal finale. And then all creation breaks loose. The finale of the C major is the culmination of the whole of Opus 59, the crowning glory of the entire Rasoumowsky set. Its confidence, its unrestrained joy, its dramatic climaxes, and its sheer *joie de vivre* make it one of the most exciting pieces in the literature. The tragedy of the F minor adagio, transfigured by the heavenly repose and the sublime detachment of the E major slow movement, is here resolved, at the very end of the C major quartet. The uncertainty, tragedy, and questioning are answered and evaluated by light from above; renewed strength is found, and creative activity is again made possible. There lies the emotional connection between the three quartets of Opus 59.

Consider Beethoven. Filled with misgiving at signs of deafness; beset with the greatest tragedy a man such as he could suffer; plunged to the depths of despair and contemplating suicide; restored to balance through sheer strength of will and divine guidance; emerging from the valley of the shadow and restored to creative sanity in spite of his terrible affliction; composing all the more intensely and profoundly and joyously after the soul-searing experience. The parallel lies open to view: the quartets of Opus 59 are Beethoven's autobiography.

A single quartet in E flat was written in 1809 and published in 1810 as Opus 74. Its nickname, the "Harp Quartet," is derived from two short passages in the first movement; pizzicato arpeggios ascend through the three lower parts, in one case to lead to the recapitulation, in the other to form the coda. The unfortunate nickname has drawn more attention to those passages than they deserve. Many other details of the quartet are much more worthy of being singled out.

A slow, dreamy introduction leads into the first movement. A dramatic moment in the latter is the brilliant coda featuring a virtuoso passage for the first violin. It serves to rescue an otherwise placid movement from the threat of monotony. The high points of Opus 74 are supplied by the two middle movements. The romantic and intensely beautiful adagio, with its expressive, exquisitely ornamented melodies, realizes the perfect balance between sentiment and restraint. The diabolical scherzo, full of hammering figures and breathless scale passages, is a masterpiece. Its concentration and rhythmic drive are unmatched, even in Beethoven. The finale is a set of six variations based on a graceful theme. An increase in the speed of the variations provides the only dramatic note in the movement. On the whole, the quartet, in spite of its many intense and beautiful moments, does not compare to the works which surround it.

The eleventh quartet of the series, in F minor, is in quite another class. Composed late in 1810 and published in 1816 as Opus 95, it is one of the great works of Beethoven's second period. But it also stands at the very gateway to the third; many features of the F minor relate it closely to the six quartets of his last years. The work is labeled "Quartet serioso," and a more terribly serious composition Beethoven never wrote. The first movement stands as a tonal incarnation of grim earnestness; its powerful, rough-hewn phrases, its extreme drive and compactness, and its sharp contrasts of mood are unique. The second movement contains a quiet, brooding first theme and a mournful, undulating second; the latter is introduced fugally. The themes are held together by a descending melody given to the cello. Indeed, the whole movement is inflected downward, with a resulting air of pensiveness. The third movement is a scherzo in form only; a curt rhythmic figure and a chorale-like trio are combined in a movement of restlessness and dissatisfaction. The agitated finale, prefaced by a short, poignant introduction, is magnificent in its concentration. To cancel out the quasi-morbidity of the previous movements, an extreme contrast is required; and this Beethoven supplies in the coda. A boisterous new theme in major appears in the light and fleeting fragment with which this most intense and possibly briefest of Beethoven's quartets closes.

Fourteen years elapsed before Beethoven again turned to quartet writing. In the interval he had been brought low by family trouble, litigation, and the consequent emotional turmoil. A period of relative barrenness had set in, to be followed by renewed creative activity. But during the period of lessened productivity Beethoven had altered his position toward his fellow men: he learned to despise humans and to love humanity. The changed attitude resulted in marked changes in his musical style. Subjectivity disappeared, to be replaced by a spiritualization, by an objectivity which defies verbal description. Musical forms were expanded, extreme contrasts became characteristic, and a new world of stark, bare tonal lines was revealed.

It is almost impossible to describe the last Beethoven quartets. Music is a matter of moods, of emotional states; to such states must be attached labels which are in common use. Quartets of the first and second period have been gloomy or joyful, pensive or abandoned, light-hearted or somber. But those are all personal, subjective labels. Here, in the works from Opus 127 onward, such labels are no longer adequate. There is no poignancy or sentiment in these quartets, nor even gayety or charm. Rather is there the spiritualized equivalent of those moods. The subjective, merely human emotions have been transformed into their objective, almost disembodied counterparts. Great strength becomes inexorable force; charm becomes austere beauty; extreme joy becomes divine abandon. Beethoven's last quartets become understandable, become one's own, only when one can go beyond everyday emotional experiences and ascend to the world in which he dwelt during his last six years of life. Sensuous beauty has no place in that world, nor has adherence to external forms. Everything in the quartets is flowing, plastic, newly formed; rigid concepts of harmony, form, or melody do not apply. To the extent that one can accept such fluidity, the works reveal themselves as the most divinely inspired music in the literature; by ordinary standards they are cold and unintelligible. Beethoven makes great demands upon his listeners in these quartets. One can meet them only with an open mind receptive to spiritual truths. It is not Beethoven who is being judged here, but we.

From this point of view, no attempt at a musical description of the works between Opus 127 and Opus 135 can make them understandable. It can only disclose the technical means whereby Beethoven achieved his results. But that, in turn, may be a step on the path toward that understanding. It is worth making, if only for that reason.

Six quartets were written between 1824 and Beethoven's death in 1827, namely, Opera 127, 132, 130, 131, 133, and 135. The first three were dedicated to the man who had commissioned them in 1822, the prince Galitzin; [12] the quartets so dedicated would seem to belong

---

[12] Galitzin's commission from St. Petersburg was for "one, two, or three quartets"; Beethoven's acceptance is dated "January, 1823," according to Thayer, *The Life of Ludwig van Beethoven*, III, 87.

together. Actually, however, Opus 127 stands alone. The two others, Opus 132 and Opus 130, respectively, are linked thematically with Opus 131, which is not one of the Galitzin quartets. For this reason we shall ignore the external connection provided by the dedication and discuss Opus 127 as a separate work.

That quartet, in E flat, was written during 1824, received its first performance the following year, and was published in 1826. Its subtleties obscure the fact that its form is as regular and clear as any work of Beethoven's. The quartet begins with a few impersonal and majestic measures. The flowing first movement is in sonata form, with orthodox themes and recapitulation. But the introductory measures twice appear in the development section and thus seem to divide the movement into three unequal parts. They serve really to unify and to stabilize its very free harmonic scheme. The second movement, a perfect example of Beethoven's depth of feeling even in the midst of this most objective work, is a set of five variations. The theme is born out of darkness, proceeds to grow and undergo transformation, and dies away in the light of its new life. It is a plastic, vital movement, yet its quiet impersonality can be described only with the word divine. The stammering, fitful scherzo is combined with a swift, impulsive trio; abrupt changes of mood, tempo, and dynamics provide a feeling of unrest in this movement, a wavering between order and chaos. The clarity of the finale restores the order; it supplies, perhaps, the only personal note in the quartet; the earlier movements are pervaded to a large extent by austerity, by a feeling of remoteness.

The four (or five) following quartets must be considered in the order of their writing; opus numbers obscure the proper sequence. The A minor, Opus 132, was begun in the winter of 1824–1825. Work on it was interrupted by Beethoven's serious illness in the spring of 1825, but the quartet was ready for rehearsal the following September. The B flat quartet, Opus 130, begun shortly after the A minor, was completed late in 1825 and performed early in 1826. Its gigantic fugal finale was felt, by publisher and friends, to be too long for the work. Beethoven accepted their judgment, withdrew it from the quartet, and allowed it to be published separately as Opus 133. Meanwhile, before the B flat was completed, work on the C sharp minor quartet, Opus 131, was well under way. It was finished by early summer of 1826, by which time the F major quartet, Opus 135, had been begun. The latter was completed in October. Finally, during those same summer and fall months the new finale for the B flat quartet, Opus 130, was written. Finished about November, 1826, it was destined to be Beethoven's last completed composition.

One must not suppose that Beethoven had lost control over his thematic material, that tight chronology alone was responsible for thematic similarities between these last quartets. It was quite possible for him to compose half-a-dozen works simultaneously without letting tunes from one leak into the others. In this case it was Beethoven's plan to connect the works through the use of a basic motive. The resulting cycle of three quartets and one fugue will be a perpetual monument to his genius.

The introduction of the A minor quartet presents the motive in its pure form:

The development section of the quartet's first movement and the fugue theme of Opus 133 make use of the motive in that pure form. But dozens of modifications appear throughout the four works. The characteristic intervals of the motive are, of course, a half step at either end and a sixth in the middle. Those intervals are altered, expanded, inverted; new motives and phrases grow out of them. The example on page 276 will show a few of the developed forms.

Beethoven's severe illness in the spring of 1825 and his consequent recovery were the inspiration for the slow movement of the A minor quartet. Entitled "Holy Song of Thanksgiving to the Divinity by a Convalescent, in the Lydian Mode," the movement contains two contrasting sections: a chorale-like and prayerful passage and a more vigorous section, in which the invalid, according to the superscription, "feels new strength." The prayer is repeated, along with the vigorous passage, after which the prayer is heard again. During the course of the three prayerful sections the figurations become more syncopated, hence less definite. One has the feeling that the prayer gradually rises and dissolves, like a cloud high in the sky; indeed, the chorale melody played by the first violin appears in successively higher octaves on each return. The movement, beginning upon earth, becomes more and more filled with divine light as it progresses.

The five-movement scheme of the A minor is expanded to six in the B flat quartet. The first movement, with its duality of adagio and allegro tempos, is followed by a fleet and meaningful scherzo. A slow movement, willful and sublime in turn, leads to a German dance, which, originally designed for the A minor quartet, was shifted to the B flat to make room for the "song of thanksgiving." Then follows a fifth movement: an expressive cavatina filled with heavenly repose and superhuman pathos. The finale is a deceptively naïve movement whose wealth of melody and contrapuntal detail conceals certain subtle connections with the main motive of the cycle [13] in spite of the fact that it was written later and has in general no organic connection with the quartet as a whole.

It is in the original finale of the B flat quartet, namely, the "Great

[13] The interested reader is referred to the A flat major section, between measures 109 and 145, and to the E flat-B flat section, measures 353 to 400, notably in the violin parts.

Fugue, sometimes free, sometimes sought for," Opus 133, that one must look for the culmination of the ideas contained in Opus 132 and Opus 130. This massive movement, possibly the most complex of Beethoven's compositions, deserves a full analysis. Lacking space for a complete account of its intricacies, only a brief description will be attempted. The movement begins with an *Overtura,* in which several versions of the cycle's basic motive are passed in review. Then follows a fugue (allegro, ¼) in which the motive becomes counter-subject to a leaping and rhythmically forceful theme new to the

cycle. After a stupendous development a quiet section (meno mosso, ¾) intervenes; the leaping theme is completely altered, and the motive theme disappears. Suddenly a fast and furious version of the motive (allegro molto, ⁶⁄₈) is introduced, is expanded (A flat major) to several times its normal length, and is virtually developed out of existence; it dissolves until only a few trills remain. The leaping theme (E flat major), restored to some semblance of its original form, returns, as does the quiet section (meno mosso, ¾) containing yet another version of the motive theme. This time it is the latter that remains; the leaping theme dissolves. The following section (allegro molto, ⁶⁄₈) presents an early version of the motive theme again; now the development transpires quietly and confidently. A few retrospective measures, recalling the very beginning of the movement, are heard. The final section (allegro molto, ⁶⁄₈) presents the expanded version of the motive, with the now subdued, erstwhile leaping, theme serving modestly as countermelody.

The whole movement is an example of thematic conflict unsurpassed in the literature. It is the kind of conflict in which a theme, though beaten to earth, rises to fulfill its destiny; it is the conflict disclosed in the G major piano concerto, but raised to an intensity and profundity undreamed of in that work. In short, it is the kind of conflict Beethoven himself lived in; he, too, though beaten to earth, rose again to fulfill his destiny. No description can hope to do justice to the power, to the overwhelming conviction of this movement. A quality of growth, of organic development, pervades the entire work. Beethoven here reveals the actual life processes of music —truly a stupendous achievement, even for a Beethoven.

The C sharp minor quartet, Opus 131, is tightly constructed; its seven movements are designed to be played without a break, for one connects with the next. The first is a slow fugue in C sharp minor. From the example above one sees how the cycle's motive is inverted to form the fugue theme. The fugue's somberness and detached air contrast greatly with the second movement, in D major, a movement full of restrained gayety. A short recitative in B minor leads to the fourth movement, an inspired set of variations in A major whose theme, divided between the two violins, again suggests a transforma-

tion of the motive. Then follows a long scherzo, full of humor; its thematic connections with the motive are obvious. The sixth movement is short; its prayerful melodies lead directly into the finale, an involved movement in sonata form whose thematic material is in large part based upon further transformations of the motive.

The relationship of the melodic material of the quartets Opera 132, 130, 133, and 131 to the four notes with which the cycle begins (in Opus 132) is open to every observer. Not so obvious is the very largest expansion of which the motive is capable. Consider the keys of the first four movements of the C sharp minor quartet [14] and compare this key relationship with the original form of the motive.

Beethoven missed nothing. The three quartets together with the Great Fugue form a related whole whose full significance cannot easily be grasped. This cycle, in its spiritual depth as well as in the technical mastery it discloses, represents the culmination of Beethoven's creative activity. It places him on a plane of musical achievement that perhaps only Bach, with *Die Kunst der Fuge*, attained before him.

There remains one work [15]—the quartet in F major, Opus 135, the seventeenth of the series. Begun in the summer of 1826, it was completed by October of that year; thus, it is contemporary with the new finale for Opus 130.[16] Despite a few faint echoes of the previous cycle in the present quartet,[17] there is no thematic connection between this work and Opera 130–133. The F major quartet stands alone.

It is a relatively short work of four movements. The first begins, strangely enough, in B flat minor, but quickly becomes established in F major. That harmonic fact sets the mood for the entire movement; a somewhat dark and pensive tone predominates. The scherzo is an impulsive, syncopated piece with a powerful and relentless trio. The music of the lento which follows is pure repose. The fourth movement bears the famous superscription, *der schwer gefasste Entschluss*. Beethoven's biographers have discussed long and vainly the

---

[14] Adapted from Scott, *Beethoven* (2d ed.), p. 272, who in turn quotes d'Indy.

[15] One other chamber-music work, published in 1827 as Opus 137, is a fragmentary fugue for string quintet, in D major. It occupied Beethoven briefly in 1817, but was laid aside with other fragments for the same combination—notably a piece beginning in C major, never to be completed.

[16] In the interest of filling the gap in the opus numbers involving the quartets, namely, Opera 130, 131, 132, 133, 135, it may be mentioned that Opus 134 is an arrangement for piano (four hands) of the Great Fugue. Some doubt exists that the arrangement was made by, or even authorized by, Beethoven.

[17] Compare measures 17–18 of the last movement's allegro with measures 3–4 of the first movement of Opus 131.

meaning of this "resolution reached with difficulty" and of the cryptic phrases which follow it: "Must it be? It must be!" It has not yet been determined to everyone's satisfaction whether the phrase refers to Beethoven's need for paying his bills or to his knowledge that death was inevitable. A slow and dramatic introduction ("Must it be") precedes the main allegro ("It must be"); it appears again in heightened form in the movement's development section. Again a conflict of themes results, as in the Great Fugue. In the present case the "must be," with its air of jauntiness, prevails. Whatever Beethoven's problem, it is solved bravely and with a light heart. If the movement really embodies his awareness of death's approach, it is quite in keeping with his character and moral greatness that he met death with a gay tune upon his lips.

I I

SCHUBERT AND THE ROMANTIC PERIOD

AT CERTAIN times in the history of music a close relationship develops between musical ideas and the principles under which the ideas are organized. During those times the ideas—melodies, harmonic types, rhythmic patterns, textures, and all the other factors of expression— develop characteristics which allow them to be utilized in accord with well-established aesthetic principles: proportion, symmetry, contrast, and variety. The great composers living during those times succeed in writing expressive and meaningful music while giving full recognition to the validity and force of the organizing principles. In their work they achieve a perfect balance between the ideas and the principles, between musical content and musical form. One is not separated from the other; a particular content is seen to require a particular form, and a certain form specifies its own content. Such a period is called classical; there have been several such periods in the history of music and the other arts.

During the course of a classical period, its music may also achieve characteristics of transparence, clarity of purpose, perfection of detail, and complete objectivity. Minor composers, following in the path of the masters, may succeed in implanting those characteristics in their music; a pseudo-classical style arises, a style built upon detail, objectivity, and clear textures. But the essential element in classical style, namely, the interdependence of form and content, is missing; a sterile, empty period may result. Formal principles turn into rigid forms and musical expression becomes burdened with mannerisms; all becomes hard and stylized, and the fluid life of true classicism becomes mere formalism.

Subsequently, a period of reaction sets in; the rigid concepts of pseudo-classicism are abolished, great freedom is permitted, and the very nature of the musical content is changed. New organizing principles—forms—are established, lyricism and free melody substitute for conventional modes of expression, youthful enthusiasm takes the place of tradition, and a general air of liberty pervades the musical scene. Such a reaction from extreme classicism is called romanticism; the history of music is in one sense the history of the alternation between the two opposing styles. That alternation may be summarized as follows: a balance between form and content is first achieved, then misunderstood; a reaction against the dry formalism takes place, a reaction stressing lyricism and freedom, and develops into a new style. In time the romantic characteristics of the new style develop their own classicism, the worship of the new classicism leads to new formalism, and the cycle is repeated.

Thus, every cultural period may have its romantic beginnings, its classical maturity, and its pseudo-classical or formalistic decline. In some cases the mature section of the period seems most noteworthy; thus, we speak of classic Greece. In others, the beginnings attract the historian's eye; consequently, the romantic Middle Ages are emphasized. Closer to our own time, we speak of the Classical period of the late eighteenth century and of the Romantic period of the early nineteenth.

We are now concerned with the first half of the nineteenth century. The full flower of Classicism, represented by Haydn and Mozart, had faded. Beethoven, who in one sense bridged the gap between the periods and in another sense stood apart from them, was pursuing his own isolated way. The empty formalism of the rank and file of composers surrounding these giants had evoked the usual reaction. Adherence to traditional forms and worship of traditional musical content quickly became a thing of the past. A new expressiveness, new organizing principles, and a new aesthetic philosophy gave rise to the Romanticism of the decades between about 1820 and 1860. In its development the works of Schubert led the way, and those of Mendelssohn and Schumann became its outstanding examples.

The Romanticist, in his reaction against the formalized aspects of Classicism, looked around for new worlds to conquer. He discovered the world of the past and the world of nature; he became interested in the Orient, he read the mythology and folklore of all humanity, he rediscovered the chivalry and romance of the Middle Ages. Filled with youth and enthusiasm, he loved everything and tried to bring everything into his own life. He strove to master other art forms and to combine them with his own. Thus arose the fusion of drama and music which culminated in Wagner. Thus arose the preoccupation, in opera, with mythology and superstition. Thus arose, for the Romantic musician, the interest in activities other than music. Schumann was an editor and a critic; Wagner thought of himself as a dramatist who composed; Mendelssohn was an accomplished linguist. A movement so rich in interests and so alive with enthusiasms could not keep within bounds; indeed, it recognized no bounds. Enthusiasm became fanaticism, friendship became undying love, and noble sentiment eventually became sentimentality. To the Romanticist, the world was a wonderful place; everything in it had inherent nobility, and the great variety of experience it offered him affected him vitally. Out of that feeling grew the intense subjectivity which is the outstanding characteristic of Romanticism. Out of the all-embracing love for the world grew the lyric expressiveness which is its musical counterpart.[1]

Evidence that definite boundaries cannot be set to style periods has been presented in earlier chapters. We have seen how periods overlap, how great composers have often produced their greatest works long after the style they represent has begun to decay in the world

[1] In a larger sense, however, Romanticism is not merely a reaction against Classicism. It is also a positive realization of ideas and ideals which had lain dormant or forgotten during the last decades of the eighteenth century. For a full account of those phenomena, with a complete analysis of the parts literature and philosophy played in their unfolding, see Láng, *Music in Western Civilization*, pp. 734–750, 801–809.

at large. So it is with the nineteenth-century shift from Classicism to Romanticism. At the time when Beethoven was composing his most Classical works, a number of poets, along with composers such as Weber, were concerned with the artistic principles which led to the Romantic movement. And during the decade when Beethoven was creating his terse, epigrammatic, third-period quartets, Schubert was establishing his own rules for Romantic expression. Thus, the period from about 1815 to 1828 presents a mixture of several style tendencies. Minor composers occupied themselves with the formal shell of Classicism, Schubert laid the foundations of a style which the Romantic composers were unconsciously to follow, and the great Beethoven went his own way.

And for perhaps the first time since instrumental music began, major composers appeared who showed no interest in chamber music. Such great Romanticists as Berlioz, Chopin, Liszt, and Wagner will not be mentioned in these pages; they were too concerned with the piano, the orchestra, or the opera to write significant quartets or trios. Only Schubert, Mendelssohn, and Schumann can be singled out for their important contributions to the chamber-music literature.

A sketch of Schubert's life must by its very nature be unsatisfactory; nothing of vital importance took place during his brief span of years, and one can report only a few external happenings. But three factors make that life of great importance to music history: Schubert's musical genius, his great zeal in composition, and his complete freedom from family responsibility.

Franz Peter Schubert was born at Vienna in January, 1797. He enjoyed few educational advantages during his early years. The family situation was humble to an extreme degree; his father, a schoolmaster, was handicapped by a small income, long hours of work, and a large family. Schubert was taught the rudiments of violin, piano, organ, voice, and harmony at an early age. In his eleventh year he entered the Vienna court choir, where he remained until his voice broke in 1813. In order to avoid the compulsory military service to which he was subject, he became an elementary teacher in his father's school. He remained in that position until 1816, his nineteenth year. But Schubert was not destined to be a teacher; indeed, he was not fitted for any "practical" activity. The teaching was drudgery; he was bored with his students and his subjects. About 1817 he left his home; during the remainder of his life he enjoyed the meager hospitality of his friends in various parts of Vienna.

He had begun composing about 1811. Literally hundreds of songs, many masses, piano pieces, and works for the stage were written before he was twenty. But the compositions were no source of income. Publishers, when they deigned to notice his works, exploited him shamefully. Always dependent upon his friends for financial assistance, never able to secure regular employment, he remained at the edge of destitution throughout his life.

Many of his friends were aware of his genius. Certain of his songs had attracted favorable attention and had been accepted. And from about 1826 his smaller instrumental compositions gained in popular esteem—to the extent that in 1828 he was able to give a concert of his own works. That concert was an artistic and financial success; but public recognition came slowly. When the quality of Schubert's compositions finally became known to the musical world, it was too late to profit the unfortunate composer.

Moving from friend to friend, from room to room, as financial circumstances warranted, Schubert's physical existence was desultory. He lived only to compose, and he composed incessantly. But the irregular existence, coupled with the complete freedom from responsibilities, contributed to the undermining of his health. A serious illness early in 1828 was followed by an attack of typhus later in the same year. Schubert died in November, 1828, at the age of thirty-one. Mourned by the friends who appreciated his musical qualities, cherished his cheerful disposition, and admired his excellent character, he was almost unknown to the musical public at large. And he was one of the most prolific composers of all time. He composed more than six hundred songs, eight or more symphonies, two dozen piano sonatas, scores of smaller pieces for piano and for vocal groups, operettas and masses, and finally about two dozen chamber-music works.

The great excellence of the majority of Schubert's compositions must be attributed to the quality of his musical instinct and to his keen awareness of aesthetic and dramatic values. His general and musical education was incomplete and unsatisfactory. Actually untrained in counterpoint and not too thoroughly grounded in other aspects of music, he depended largely upon the inspiration of the moment. But that inspiration never failed him. Gifted far beyond any previous composer as a creator of melodies, and writing with an ease and surety given to few more studied musicians, Schubert's outstanding characteristic is the charm of his lyricism.

Possibly the most formative musical influence in Schubert's early life was exerted by the chamber-music activity in his own household. Under that influence he made his first contributions to the literature. Six string quartets [2] and a one-movement sonata for piano trio [3] were written for the family group between 1812 and 1813, when Schubert was in his teens.

If Schubert intended to model his first efforts on the works of Haydn and Mozart, he fell considerably short of the mark; there is little trace of the proportion, texture, or even the self-discipline of those masters in the quartets. But if, as seems likely, he was experimenting to produce a style based upon his innate feeling for drama and color, he succeeded admirably. One has but to compare them to the great chamber-music works of 1824–1828. Long, forceful passages rising to great climaxes of sound are present in the very first quartet of 1812, as they are in his last works. Orchestral effects of tremolo, sonorous unison, and widespread chordal writing are typical of early and late compositions alike. Schubert's apparently aimless harmonic wandering in the early quartets is merely a prelude to his lifelong preoccupation with colorful harmonies. The first quartet, for example, begins with a long introduction in C minor, D minor,

[2] All fifteen of Schubert's quartets are in Vol. V of the *Werke*.
[3] Discovered about 1922.

and G minor, although the quartet as a whole is in B flat. The first movement proper, beginning in G minor, contains long sections in D major and minor; other movements are in F and B flat. This extreme harmonic variety, extravagant as it is, served to develop in Schubert the surety of touch and the fertile harmonic imagination that are such large factors in his later style.

One must not dismiss these experimental works on the grounds that their form is faulty. True enough, they are over-abundantly supplied with melodies, they ramble, and their proportions are obscure. But it was not Schubert's aim to restrict himself to formal patterns here. That he was able to discipline himself is seen in the single movement for piano trio, the 1812 work mentioned above. Here the clarity of form, the transitions, and the balance of themes all testify to the acuity of his formal perceptions. And in the first movement of the C major quartet of 1813, the form grows naturally out of the thematic content—as it did in earlier Classical works. That it is not the concise form of Mozart or the logical form of Beethoven is no defect. Schubert was not striving to imitate Classical form; his efforts were directed toward an expansion of color possibilities, toward a discovery of new textures and a warm lyricism. In short, Schubert was a Romanticist in the making, a composer breaking away from Classical models in his search for subjective expression.

The year 1813 also saw the writing of *Eine kleine Trauermusik*, for pairs of clarinets, horns, bassoons, and trombones plus a contrabassoon, and a minuet and finale for pairs of oboes, clarinets, horns, and bassoons.[4] They are mentioned here only as examples of Schubert's early interest in instrumental color.

We return now to the line of string quartets. The six of 1812–1813 were followed by one ascribed to a period between late 1813 and 1817 and two written in 1814. The three are, respectively, in E flat, known today as Opus 125, No. 1; in D, without opus number; and in B flat, published as Opus 168. And now Schubert's mastery of sonata form is disclosed, for the E flat quartet's first movement is as well balanced and beautifully proportioned as one could wish. The middle

[4] Both are published in Vol. III of the *Werke*.

movements are reminiscent of early Beethoven, and the sparkling, pulsating finale is a model of formal clarity. The D major quartet is less successful; it represents a return to the experimental style of the earlier quartets.

In the B flat quartet of Opus 168, however, Schubert's progress toward a solution of his own formal problem is outstanding. The problem may be stated simply: to reconcile his essentially lyric themes with his feeling for dramatic utterance, within a form that provides the possibility of extreme color contrasts. The solution, in the B flat quartet's first movement, takes the form of a sectional structure; the contrasting sections, well marked by sustained notes, by pauses, and by holds, present in turn a melodious theme or an imaginative modulation or an exciting rhythm. The final synthesis of these diverse elements, brought together under the influence of a Romantic melancholy, is not found until the last great works after 1824; but here, in 1814, the solution of the problem is appreciably nearer. The slow movement is an early example of Schubert's sustained lyricism; the minuet is not unlike Haydn's. In the presto finale a single motive supplies the entire thematic material and provides the basis for a kind of harmonic development that only Schubert fully mastered; we shall see other examples of that process later in his chamber music.

Also belonging to 1814 is a quartet for flute, guitar, viola, and cello. Having been discovered in 1918, it is not included in the *Complete Works;* not being available at present writing, one must depend upon Kahl's account of the piece.[5] The instrumentation, not especially unique at the time, gives further evidence of the Romanticist's interest in tone color. The quartet is cast in serenade form: five movements have been found, and there may have been a sixth. But that form, or more especially its content, has been raised to a dignified level; the quartet is distinguished by its "delicate harmonies and sound effects, its clear thematic work and ingenious instrumentation."

Schubert's tenth string quartet, in G minor, a one-movement string

[5] Kahl, in *Cobbett's Cyclopedic Survey of Chamber Music,* II, 355.

trio and an adagio and rondo for piano quartet were written during 1815–1816. Despite several dramatic and powerful themes, the G minor quartet marks no real advance for Schubert; Haydn casts a pale shadow over much of it. Nor is the fragment for string trio [6] an important work.

The piano quartet is on a higher level. The introduction—for the adagio serves in that capacity—is highly imaginative and succeeds in building up suspense and anticipation. The rondo is a brilliant piece, but it is not at all in the form we associate with that term. Instead of an alternation of thematic material (ABACA is a typical rondo diagram), Schubert presents a series of contrasting themes in various keys; a pattern of ABCD-development-ABCD-coda results. Again one may assume that his aim was not to imitate the old masters, but to create a new form for the expression of his harmonic color interests. In that aim he succeeded admirably. In these early works of Schubert's, thematic material is of secondary importance and strict form falls by the wayside. The works must be evaluated from a different standpoint entirely, a standpoint that recognizes Schubert's lifelong search for color variety—both harmonic and instrumental.

A four-movement string trio [7] in B flat was written in 1817, along with the eleventh quartet, in E major; the latter is known today as Opus 125, No. 2. The publisher who caused the E flat quartet of 1813–1817 to be paired in the same opus number with the present quartet was an excellent judge of values. For just as the E flat (Opus 125, No. 1) discloses Schubert's mastery of sonata form, so the E major stands as the finest example thus far of his mastery of texture. Schubert's goal had never been precise four-part writing, nor did he often achieve it. He was much more concerned with a search for textures which were made attractive by the warmth of their instrumental color. In the E major quartet such a texture appeared for the first time in his works. At times, violins are set opposite the lower instruments; at others, violin and viola appear in octaves against second violin and cello accompaniment. The resulting alternations

[6] Published in Vol. VI of the *Werke*.   [7] Published in Vol. XXI of the *Werke*.

of instrumental color must have satisfied Schubert, for they became characteristic in later compositions. The E major quartet is a brilliant work; its sparkle is in no wise lessened by the rapid shifts of interest from one instrumental line to another. On the contrary, the texture is so alive and flowing that a real vivaciousness pervades the whole quartet.

In 1818 Schubert was engaged as music teacher to a branch of the Eszterházy family in nearby Hungary. Away from Vienna for the first time and confined to the plains of Zelész, he was not stimulated to write quartets; the year marks the first break in Schubert's chamber-music composition since 1812. But he returned to Vienna at the year's end, and quickly regained his old interests. His first major chamber-music work was written in the summer of 1819: the famous *Forellen Quintet,* later published as Opus 114. The quintet, in A major, is for piano, violin, viola, cello, and bass. An acquaintance of Schubert's had suggested the work and asked that variations on the composer's song *Die Forelle* (The Trout) be included in it. Schubert acquiesced and composed a work in five movements; the added movement, inserted between scherzo and finale, is a set of six variations on phrases from that song.

At first sight, the instrumentation of the quintet is unique. One finds no similar work in Haydn, Mozart, or Beethoven; piano quintets by the minor Mannheimers usually include one or two wind instruments. But a possible model exists in the quintet [8] arrangement of the septet for piano, three wind instruments, and three string instruments, Opus 74, by Johann Hummel (1778–1837). The Hummel arrangement and Schubert quintet are alike in instrumentation, and there is a strong likelihood that Schubert knew the older man's work.

Even though his choice of instruments may have been suggested by Hummel's quintet, Schubert's use of them is original. For the bass does more than double the cello; it is largely an independent

[8] According to Láng, *Music in Western Civilization,* p. 935, a quintet by Hummel (possibly the same work) appeared on the very first program of the Philharmonic Orchestra of New York, in 1842.

voice which provides a foundation for the piano as well as for the string instruments. It is open to question whether the presence of the bass enabled Schubert to dispense with the usual six-octave range of the piano or whether the nature of the piano part made the bass necessary. At any rate, the piano plays in a high range throughout the quintet; only rarely are its two lowest octaves employed. The end result is that a new tone color is given to chamber music: octave passages and a general two-voice texture, both in the piano's upper range, are typical. Schubert's ceaseless preoccupation with color is again in evidence; now, in addition to colorful harmonies and textures, he employs characteristic instrumental ranges. And the experiment is successful. Hardly any work of Schubert's, or of many another composer, is as brilliant, as sparkling, and as alive as the *Forellen Quintet*.

A fresh lyricism pervades the entire work. The second movement, a songful piece in Schubert's finest Romantic vein, provides an excellent illustration of his harmonic methods and may briefly be analyzed here. Three related sections, one lyric, one melancholy, and one restrained, are heard in F major, F sharp minor, and D major, respectively; but the last section ends in G major. The three sections are then repeated note for note, but a minor third higher: A flat major, A minor, and F major—with the insertion of only a single measure (the eighteenth from the end) in the last section to make possible the retention of F major in that section. Thus, the themes are presented in different colors, are thrown into sharp harmonic contrast, but are otherwise unchanged. These are Romantic characteristics; yet the external tonal symmetry of Classicism is maintained, in that the piece begins and ends in F major.

In the following year, 1820, Schubert turned to quartet writing again. But the single chamber-music work of that year remained unfinished: a first movement in C minor (the so-called *Satz-Quartett*, which is bad German for *Quartettsatz*) and a fragment of a second movement are known. Here a new Schubert stands before us. The inner joy and vivacity which filled the earlier works is gone; a restlessness and concern with more serious expression appear. A tortured, twisting chromatic theme is passed about from instrument to instrument over rapidly shifting harmonies. The second theme, more songful, offers but little relief from the dissatisfaction expressed by the first. With this C minor quartet movement, peace of mind and joy of spirit ceased to be typical components of Schubert's chamber music. When they reappear in later works, it is in company with darker moods.

After 1820 Schubert turned his thoughts to the writing of a "Grand Symphony." In a letter written in 1824 [9] he declared that chamber music had for him become a means of developing a larger style in preparation for symphonic writing. It is true that the seven great chamber-music works written between 1824 and Schubert's death in 1828 are constructed on a larger scale than heretofore, and contain many orchestral effects. But those works are not embryonic symphonies; they are merely more sonorous, more colorful, and more lengthy than earlier works, and are still based on intimate, economical chamber-music techniques.

The first of these works is a string quartet in A minor—the thirteenth of the series. Written early in 1824, it was performed in March of that year and published in 1825 as Opus 29—the only one of Schubert's fifteen quartets to appear in print during his lifetime. The A minor is a gentle and modest work throughout; an occasional mild outburst in the first movement is quickly subdued and serves but to outline the prevailing melancholic serenity more clearly. The beautiful slow movement, employing a fragment of Schubert's own "Rosamunde" music, is at once lyric and resigned; it is as perfect in its way as any work of Mozart's—without the intensity that characterizes so many of that master's andantes. The minuet is restrained; its charm lies largely in its rich modulations and its deceptively simple phrase structure. The finale is in regular sonata form, with a development section that approaches Classical perfection; in spite of its brilliant key of A major and its third theme in E, it is a delicate movement. The minor keys and subdued colors of the earlier movements are here beautifully transformed into brighter shades, but wistfulness

[9] To Leopold Kupelweiser, dated March 31, 1824.

and restraint are maintained to the very end. The quartet as a whole ranks as one of Schubert's finest achievements.

Contemporary with the A minor quartet is an octet for wind and string instruments in F major, written in February, 1824, and known today as Opus 166. The work is in some respects similar to the Beethoven septet. It is written for string quartet, clarinet, horn, bassoon, and bass; in the Beethoven there are all these but the second violin. Like the Beethoven, it contains six movements, with slow introductions to first and last movements, a centrally placed slow movement with variations, and both a minuet and a scherzo; in the Schubert, however, the scherzo is placed third and the minuet fifth. Again like the Beethoven work, it exudes a general air of well-being. But there all similarity ends; the octet is typically Schubertian in its internal organization and Romantic color.

Now one may believe Schubert's remark about preparing for a "Grand Symphony," for the octet is laid out on orchestral lines. Forceful themes, brilliant figurations, and a wealth of instrumental detail characterize the work. A large and stately introduction leads into the impulsive first movement. The lyric, dreamy adagio contrasts with the solid, almost heavy scherzo. The andante, with eight variations on a simple theme, follows the usual course of Schubert's variation sets; concern with color and variety substitute for an interest in theme transformation, for nothing beyond figurations and embroideries is attempted. The minuet, with its delicacies, subtle phrase structure, and charming melodics, is one of the finest movements in the octet. It contrasts strikingly with the powerful and dramatic introduction to the last movement. The finale itself recaptures the drive and force of the first movement and brings this long work to a brilliant conclusion.

The octet represents in many ways a reversion to Schubert's pre-1820 manner. Melodious, brilliant, and forthright as it is, it contains few of the soul-searching qualities that began with the C minor fragment of 1820 and developed so poignantly in the works of his last years. The resignation of the A minor quartet is not apparent here, nor any sign of the dramatic conflicts which occupied Schubert's mind after the spring of 1824. One has but to contrast the octet with another work, written within a month of the former's completion, to realize how wide is the distance which separates the melancholy Schubert from the vivacious one. That work is the fourteenth string quartet, in D minor.

Schubert's choice of a theme from one of his songs as the basis for the slow movement's variations has given the D minor quartet a nickname: "Death and the Maiden." The subject of that song—death—plus the fact that a few phrases in the last movement are quotations from his *Erlkönig*—again a preoccupation with death—have inspired commentators to dwell on the inner unity of the quartet and to assert that death provides that unity.[10] Such an interpretation is pure speculation, even though it is made to sound plausible. Need the powerful and dramatic first movement be considered a struggle with death? Can it not also be seen as depicting Schubert's struggle with a refractory motive? What real evidence exists that the scherzo's theme is "Death, the demon fiddler," as Heuss has it,[11] or that the andante "dwells on death's words," or that the last movement is a "dance of death"?

It is both misleading and indefensible thus to attach an external program to so profound and pure a work as the D minor quartet. One may appropriately discuss the emotional effect of a movement, or bring to light the contrasting moods which underlie a series of movements, or even describe the composer's state of mind at the time of writing, but not to the extent of attaching external phenomena to the music, of burdening the music with a "program." It is much more to the point to indicate the nature of Schubert's handling of an obstinate motive in the first movement and to describe his success in creating a plastic, living development section in the finest Classical tradition—even though Romantic color and drama abound—and to call attention to the poignant slow movement, with its new technique (for Schubert) of transforming the simple theme in successive varia-

[10] Cf. Kahl, in *Cobbett's Cyclopedic Survey of Chamber Music*, II, 359. Kahl in turn quotes Heuss, *Kammermusikabende*, pp. 85–90.
[11] Heuss, *Kammermusikabende*, p. 89.

tions so that a series of contrasting moods is called up. Likewise the scherzo has no need of a program, but stands on its own feet as a wonderfully wrought example of rhythmic intensity. The finale provides perhaps the finest of all illustrations of relentless drive and controlled power. In organization, expressive quality, and sheer emotional strength the D minor quartet is one of Schubert's greatest works.

The fifteenth quartet, in G major, published as Opus 161 many years after Schubert's death, was written in 1826 within the space of ten days. It is in many ways the most orchestral of all his chamber music; tremolos, forceful unisons, and quantities of sound give the impression that the quartet is about to burst its bonds. Except for a few melodic fragments in the adagio and the tuneful trio, there is virtually none of the lyricism of the earlier—and later—Schubert. In place of the songfulness is a harmonic unrest, a ceaseless shift from one key to another. The quartet as a whole offers perhaps the most striking example of Schubert's departure from the lines of true Classicism. The clear part-writing of earlier decades is almost nonexistent here. A preoccupation with the composite sound of the individual chord, or measure, or harmonic progression replaces the concern for linear clarity. The result is a degree of harmonic freedom that Schubert never again attained. The G major quartet points the way to the vertical conceptions of post-Romantic composers; it is generations in advance of Schubert's own time.

In 1827 Schubert became associated in friendship with three musicians who had formed a piano trio: Ignaz Schuppanzigh (1776–1830) and Joseph Linke (1783–1837), members of the Rasoumowsky Quartet and friends of Beethoven, and Carl von Bocklet (1801–1881), an excellent pianist. Inspired by that friendship and moved to expand his newly achieved harmonic skill still further, he wrote two trios for piano, violin, and cello in the fall of 1827. The first, in B flat, was published in 1836 as Opus 99. The second, in E flat, performed at the only concert of his own works Schubert ever organized (early in 1828), was published a few months before his death; it is now known as Opus 100.

Never before had Schubert revealed himself as completely as he did in the two trios. All that is essentially Schubertian is found there: noble melodies, piquant rhythms, persevering figurations, Romantic melancholy, harmonic variety—and great length. The first movement of the B flat trio might be taken as a model of Schubert's formal practices: themes and theme fragments are not so much developed as repeated—but always in different keys and with different color effects. The second movement's theme contrasts greatly with the naïve and reiterated figures which surround it; a more serene piece is difficult to find anywhere in the literature. The buoyant scherzo and the delightful final rondo are pure joy. The E flat trio is more virile throughout. Schubert's practice of establishing contrasting tonal groups (strings opposed to the piano, in this case) here results in a general thickening of the texture and a certain heaviness of style. A march-like slow movement and a canonic scherzo are followed by one of the longest movements in the literature.[12] In the

[12] The following solution of the formal problem offered by this movement may be of interest. It illustrates the kind of sonata form in which Schubert was most eloquent.

	Measure Number	Key	Meter	Content
EXPOSITION	1	E flat	6/8	1st theme
	73	C minor	2/2	2d theme
	125	B flat	6/8	2d theme modified
	163	C minor	2/2	2d theme developed
	193	B flat	6/8	1st theme developed
	275	B minor	6/8	3d theme, derived from second movement
DEVELOPMENT	315	B minor	6/8	
		D minor	2/2	
		D minor	6/8	development of 1st and 2d themes, with suggestions of 3d theme
		B minor / F major	2/2	
		E flat minor / B minor / E flat minor	6/8	
RECAPITULATION	441	E flat	6/8	1st theme
	519	F minor	2/2	2d theme
	551	E flat	6/8	2d theme modified
	593	F minor	2/2	2d theme developed
	623	E flat	6/8	1st theme developed
	693	E flat	6/8	3d theme and coda; end in meas. 748

hands of a Beethoven such a movement might have achieved colossal stature; Schubert, a repeater of sections rather than a developer of themes, here gave full scope to his vivid harmonic and tonal color senses, but at the expense of listener interest and effective climax.

It is seldom given to a composer to produce his most perfect work at the very end of his life. The C major quintet, for two violins, viola, and two cellos is such a work. Written in September, 1828, two months before Schubert's death, and published in 1854 as Opus 163, it has taken its place in chamber-music literature as one of the finest compositions of any period. In nobility of conception, beauty of melody, and variety of mood it is without equal. Instrumental color effects unknown in the earlier literature are scattered about in rich profusion. The presence of an added cello refines the texture and makes possible a quality of lyricism that a string quartet can seldom achieve.

The first movement of the quintet contains two lyric themes and a few derivative melodies. Out of them Schubert creates music of indescribable beauty and gentle pathos. Moments of dramatic tension are resolved with a degree of refinement and a technical skill that are truly wonderful. All possible groupings of instruments in two's and three's are employed; the variety of tonal effects results in a quality of texture no other work possesses. Probably nowhere else in chamber music are drama, serenity, and melancholy combined as they are in the recapitulation, whose beginning is shown on page 298: one of the most eloquent passages in nineteenth-century music—and its technical means are of the simplest. If ever inspired genius was shown in music, it is in those few measures.

The contrasts afforded in the slow movement are extreme: a sublime melody in E major is suddenly interrupted by a violent passage in F minor full of complex rhythms and dominated by a soaring melody of great emotional intensity. After a restrained transition the E major theme returns, now transformed by the addition of stumbling, uncertain passages in the lowest voice. According to some commentators, it may have been Schubert's intention to express in this movement his emotional states before and during his severe illness of 1828, with its premonition of approaching death. The scherzo presents a similar set of contrasting moods. All is power, energy, and activity in the first section; the trio is dark, brooding, and altogether

Schubert, Opus 163
1st movement

resigned. The finale has about it an air of false gayety, of restless haste; perhaps Schubert knew that his time was short.

Schubert would have been assured of a high position as a chamber-music composer had he written only the C major quintet. The two quartets of 1824 and the two piano trios of 1827, together with the quintet, mark him as one of the truly great. Departing from the Classical forms which resulted from the relationship between organizing principles and content, and faced with the need of creating new forms to encompass his enormous melodic gifts, he added a new element to musical form. The chief principles had been emotional contrast in clear and symmetrical forms, proportion, and organic growth. To them Schubert added the principle of harmonic and instrumental color contrasts. In most cases his works are held together by the unifying force of sustained lyricism. The world of music is a better place for having had Schubert dwell in it, even if briefly. A fresh, ever-youthful melodic quality, adorned with the most subtle color perceptions, will be his enduring monument.

Jacob Ludwig Felix Mendelssohn [13] was born at Hamburg, 1809. The son of wealthy and cultured parents, he enjoyed every advantage in education, environment, travel, and associations with famous people. The Mendelssohn home in Berlin, to which city the family moved about 1812, was a center of musical life; small orchestra concerts were a feature of that life, and eminent musicians considered it a privilege to attend the bi-monthly performances. The young Mendelssohn, a capable pianist from about his ninth year, began to compose in his twelfth. Many of his earliest compositions were written for and performed at the family concerts. There he had every opportunity to conduct and hear them and to profit from the expert criticisms he received.

By the time he had reached his sixteenth year Mendelssohn had achieved considerable fame for his improvisations at the piano and had dozens of worthwhile compositions to his credit. His maturity as a composer dates from about that time, for the famous Overture to *A Midsummer Night's Dream,* the string octet, Opus 20, and similar works in which his style developed its later characteristics were written within a year or two of 1825. From about 1826 his style underwent little significant change. Confirmed in his espousal

[13] The surname Mendelssohn-Bartholdy was adopted by the family when they renounced the Jewish faith and entered the Protestant church.

of a sweet lyricism, secure in his mastery of form in all details, he composed steadily.

The years from about 1827 to 1835 were filled with constant activity. Famed as a pianist and a conductor, known as a composer, and enjoying a wide acquaintance with great men in all fields, he traveled widely. Several trips to England established him in the affections of that country; his fame on the Continent increased from day to day. Among his great achievements were two performances of Bach's *St. Matthew Passion,* at Berlin, in March, 1829—the first since Bach's death. With those performances began the modern recognition of Bach as one of the greatest of composers. The enthusiasm engendered there eventually led to the founding of the Bachgesellschaft and to the publication of that master's complete works; in that endeavor, as we shall see below, Schumann shared wholeheartedly.

In 1835 Mendelssohn accepted the directorship of the Leipzig Gewandhaus Orchestra; in 1842, he was largely instrumental in organizing the Leipzig Conservatory, which began its sessions in April, 1843, with Schumann as one of the faculty. The joint activities, carried out with the broad vision and attention to detail that were typical of Mendelssohn, soon made Leipzig the brightest spot in the musical sun. In addition to those responsibilities, he made many concert tours, appeared as guest conductor, and composed unceasingly.

But Mendelssohn was also in constant demand at the court of Frederick William in Berlin. Performances, compositions, and the organization of festivals kept him occupied to such an extent that he was forced to relinquish a portion of the Leipzig responsibilities. Continued travels to England and about Europe, along with masses of correspondence and administrative work, kept him busy from morning to night. The years to 1847 were filled with such intense, almost feverish activity; the resultant strain gradually undermined his rugged good health. Late in 1847, prematurely aged and completely exhausted, Mendelssohn died. His sterling moral qualities, his accomplishments as a musician, linguist, painter, and simple, unaffected human being had endeared him to all the musical world.

Richly endowed, fortunate in his education, and warm in all his friendships, he stands for all that was noble in the Romantic period in which he lived.

Robert Schumann, a year younger than Mendelssohn, was born in Saxony in 1810. The literary influences to which he was subjected in his formative years turned his attention to the works of the Romantic writers, particularly to those of Jean Paul Richter (1763–1825). The sentimental, effusive, extravagant style of that writer left its lifelong mark on Schumann. Much of the latter's activity as a spokesman for the Romantic movement later in his life can be traced to the youthful fixation on Jean Paul.

Schumann's mother was opposed to his undertaking a career in music, in spite of his youthful accomplishments as a pianist and composer. She persuaded him to enter the University of Leipzig as a law student in 1828. But the free and attractive life there gave Schumann ample opportunity to work in music. He neglected his law studies, practiced piano assiduously—laming his hand with an ill-chosen mechanical device of his own invention—and steeped himself in Romantic literature. About 1830, having obtained his mother's grudging consent, he left the University, with the intention of embracing a musical career; Frederick Wieck became his piano teacher. Intimacy with the Wieck family led to an acquaintance with Wieck's daughter, Clara, a girl nine years Schumann's junior and already a remarkable pianist. Clara Wieck later became one of the finest pianists of Europe, a lifelong champion of Schumann's music and, in 1840—after determined opposition from her father, which required a lawsuit to circumvent—Schumann's wife.

About 1833 Schumann and a group of like-minded friends made plans to establish a music paper, critical in purpose and designed to combat the bad taste and "Philistinism" then prevailing. Schumann became the editor, and for ten years, from 1834 to 1844, wielded an ever-increasing power over the cultural standards of Germany. His critical discernment and his literary skill made the paper, *Neue Zeitschrift für Musik,* a real influence in the musical life of the time.

And his championship of new composers, of new ideas, and above all, of a higher standard of taste was, perhaps, his most important contribution to the musical scene up to that time.

When Mendelssohn moved to Leipzig in 1835 a long friendship between the two men began, one which was terminated only by Mendelssohn's death in 1847. The two men, so unlike in externals, temperament and training, shared a great admiration for Bach. Mendelssohn's crusade to make Bach better known stimulated Schumann's interest in a project to republish all the works of that master. The founding of the Bachgesellschaft, together with the subsequent issuance of Bach's *Complete Works,* beginning about 1850, were in large part the result of Schumann's activity. Thus, the latter deserves equal credit with Mendelssohn for initiating the present-day interest in Bach.[14]

In the years following the Schumanns' marriage, in 1840, Clara undertook extensive concert tours; Schumann often accompanied his more famous wife to distant parts of Europe. Within a short time the exertion of travel, the editorial responsibility, and the intense musical life of Leipzig had combined to affect Schumann's nerves. Never sociable, always preoccupied and introspective, he became irritable, absent-minded, and aloof. In 1844 the Schumanns moved to Dresden in an attempt to restore his health. The quieter life at Dresden, it was hoped, would bring about a change. The move turned out beneficially; Schumann was restored to creative vigor and apparent good health.

In 1850 he accepted the post of conductor of a singing society and within a few months, that of musical director at Düsseldorf. But Schumann was not a capable conductor. His withdrawn manner, his absent-mindedness, and his strange inability to communicate his ideas verbally made him entirely unsuited for the post. In 1853 retirement was forced upon him. And in that year he met Johannes Brahms, then twenty years old, and prophesied for him a brilliant future. Schumann's negative characteristics grew stronger, and uncertainty concerning his health returned. In 1854 he attempted suicide and was

14 Schauffler, *Florestan,* p. 180.

placed in a private asylum near Bonn. Periods of lucidity alternated with fits of great depression; the melancholy moods grew stronger, and finally clouded his whole consciousness. In July, 1856, at the age of forty-six and in a state of complete mental collapse, Schumann died.

Mendelssohn's interest in chamber-music composition revealed itself at the very beginning of his career: his first attempts (and they are scarcely more than that) took the form of three piano quartets, Opera 1, 2, and 3, written between 1822 and 1824. The precocious Mendelssohn, hardly in his teens, here disclosed his awareness of musical form and his innate good taste. But the works as a whole give little evidence of the technical mastery and vivid imagination which were to illuminate later compositions. Themes are amenable to development to some extent, and mildly contrasting harmonies are in evidence. The three quartets are pale imitations of Classical formalism—except in one important feature. That feature, marking a definite departure from the earlier period, is the scherzo in duple measure. It is interesting to recall the eventful history of that form.

The minuet, it will be remembered, had been introduced into the sonata structure by the Viennese predecessors of Haydn in the divertimento decades, about 1740, Haydn faithfully wrote minuets until about 1781, when the famous quartets of Opus 33, those "written in an entirely new manner," were composed. In that set of works, possibly to balance the new seriousness of their first movements, Haydn increased the speed of the minuet and labeled the form "scherzo." In Beethoven's hands the speed was retained; but a light, deft, and humorous content drove out what was left of the minuet's courtly dance characteristics. It was also expanded, occasionally, almost to the size and proportions of sonata form. The scherzo's trio, at first merely a contrasting section in a style similar to the scherzo proper, now became a section in contrasting meter: the trio of the ninth symphony's scherzo is in duple measure—but still in fast tempo. In Schubert the contrasting trio had undergone further change; the C major quintet, Opus 163, exhibits the most extreme contrast between a brilliant scherzo in triple measure and a somber andante in duple—the latter serving as a trio. Now, finally, in Mendelssohn further modifications are at hand: a new form results, bearing the name "scherzo" and containing somewhat the same style characteristics as the earlier form, but now distinguished by the use of duple measure throughout. The last trace of relationship with the minuet will be seen to have disappeared when, later in these pages, subsequent scherzos of Mendelssohn reveal themselves in large rondo form—the trio and *da capo* features having disappeared entirely.

We return now to the survey of the works of Mendelssohn. A sextet for piano, violin, two violas, cello, and bass was written about 1824. Like the piano quartets, the sextet is a naïve work and exhibits no real originality. For even though the minuet is notated in 6/8 instead of 3/4 no significant musical difference results. Evidence of cyclical form exists in the finale: extended quotations of the minuet's theme are heard in that movement, without any real inner reason. The two movements are thus "unified" in an external way, but one is not convinced of the need for that unity. The odd instrumentation must be looked upon as experimental. The presence of two dark-toned violas and the doubling of the bass line by bass and cello make real tonal balance impossible. Schubert might have manipulated such a combination; indeed, the *Forellen Quintet* is somewhat similar in instrumentation. But the Mendelssohn of 1824 was not yet a Schubert. The best clue to the sextet's quality is given by its publication date: the work appeared, as Opus 110, in 1868, decades after Mendelssohn's death. Had it been successful, or had the composer thought highly of it, he would have seen to its publication during his lifetime.

Hardly a year after the sextet's composition, Mendelssohn suddenly stood at the very threshold of greatness. An octet for four violins, two violas, and two cellos, in E flat, was written in 1825 and published as Opus 20; that work is altogether of different quality. First of all, it differs greatly from the antiphonal double quartets of Louis Spohr (1784–1859), the first of which is roughly contemporary with the octet and is among the last flowerings of pseudo-Classical formalism. Mendelssohn's work is truly eight-voiced and shows his great skill in handling a large tonal body. The first violin dominates to some extent; the virtuoso brilliance of that instrument's part sets the mood for the whole work. The octet is conceived on orchestral lines; development sections are concerned in part with rhythmic modifications of themes, in part with their lyric transformations. The scherzo, played softly and swiftly throughout, is perhaps the finest movement. As a whole, the work suffers from too orchestral a treatment: important thematic lines are sometimes obscured by the mass of tone. Nevertheless, in general content and effectiveness it ranks as one of Mendelssohn's masterpieces.

The first of Mendelssohn's string quartets,[15] in A major, was written in 1827; the second, in E flat, in 1829. They were published together in 1830 as Opus 12 and Opus 13; the E flat quartet, however, received the earlier number. In these two works the mature composer stands revealed. All the melodic charm, all the perfection of detail, all the deftness of touch we associate with the later works are present in these quartets from about his twentieth year. The first movement of the E flat quartet is melodious throughout. Its second theme partakes of the rhythmic nature of the first; no conflict of thematic materials, hence no drama, is possible. In the absence of thematic conflict—one of the essentials of true Classicism—Mendelssohn substitutes a lyric mood of great charm. The second movement is the well-known "Canzonetta." It occupies an important place in the long line of light, fairy-like pieces which represent Mendelssohn's greatest contribution to music. Evidences of cyclical form are present: the impetuous finale contains quotations from the first movement's themes and concludes with a coda based on that movement. In the quartet of Opus 13, also, a similar attempt to achieve unity is seen; the quartet ends as it began, with material from one of Mendelssohn's own songs.

A string quintet (with two violas) in A major was begun in 1826, rewritten in 1832, and published in 1833 as Opus 18. In this work Mendelssohn's power of invention seems weak. The themes in gen-

[15] An earlier effort, in E flat, and dating from about 1823, remained in manuscript until 1879; publication took place without an opus number. This quartet is not included in the thematic index of Mendelssohn's *Werke*. See Altmann, in *Cobbett's Cyclopedic Survey of Chamber Music*, II, 133.

eral are not distinguished, in spite of their rather cheerful mood. Nor does the dramatic slow movement, with its detailed accompanying figures, flow with the ease and charm we have learned to expect from Mendelssohn. The contrapuntal scherzo is by far the finest movement—an observation one makes repeatedly in discussing Mendelssohn's music. A rather pretentious finale concludes a work which, on the whole, is not one of his great compositions.

The three string quartets of Opus 44, in D major, E minor, and E flat, respectively, were begun in 1837, finished during the following year, and published in 1839. During the ten years or so which intervened between the writing of the Opus 12 quartet and those of Opus 44, Mendelssohn had grown more impetuous (perhaps nervous is a better word); the first and last movements of the D major quartet are models of enthusiasm and brilliance. But he had also gained in repose; the two middle movements are among the best representatives of that quality in all of his compositions. The E minor is a melodious work, distinguished by one of the most original and enchanting of all scherzos. Fleet, dainty, and lyric at once, it is Mendelssohn at his very best. Other movements stand in the shadow of this delightful piece.

With the E flat quartet Mendelssohn reached new heights of strength, surety of purpose, and technical perfection. From start to finish the work is perfect. The vibrant allegro is followed by a lively scherzo, by a deeply moving slow movement, and by an impetuous, brilliant finale. The quality of Mendelssohn's counterpoint had been improving through the years; in the quartets of Opus 44 we see its finest manifestation. Rich fugal passages, delightful imitations, and luscious countermelodies flow smoothly from his pen. And with the greater worth of his contrapuntal writing comes an increased clarity of form.

Mendelssohn's two piano trios, Opus 49, in D minor, and Opus 66, in C minor, were composed in 1839 and 1845, respectively. Neither conceived for the orchestra nor dominated by the piano, they represent the most enjoyable aspects of Mendelssohn's writing. Laid out on a large and flowing scale, full of beautiful lyric melodies and refined to the utmost degree, they are pure Romanticism. The scherzo of the D minor trio is one of his great inspirations, as is the lovely and serene andante. Seldom did Mendelssohn attain the level of technical perfection he reached in the first movement of the C minor; scarcely ever did he equal the tempestuousness of its finale. The exquisite finish and satisfying form that were Mendelssohn's outstanding characteristics are present throughout these two masterworks.

But with all their charm and beauty, they reveal Mendelssohn's weaknesses as well. Vigorous they may be, and impetuous; but there is little real strength or passion in them. Mendelssohn permits no harshness or driving emotion in his works; he is always refined, possibly a bit effeminate, even in his most striking moments. The depth of emotion, the ability to feel strongly, the reflection of significant experience—those characteristics are seldom found in his works. And it is precisely this lack of profundity that makes Mendelssohn fall short of being one of the eternal masters. All else was his: taste, technique, temperament, and imagination. To the extent to which those qualities shine through his works, we can enjoy them.

The second string quintet, Opus 87, in B flat, dates from 1845. In other categories Mendelssohn showed a steady growth in expressive power, in melodic invention, and in formal perceptions. In the string quintets the opposite is true: Opus 87 is even less distinguished than its predecessor, Opus 18. Orchestral tremolos, which here indicate a certain paucity of invention, characterize the quintet; the first violin, in its efforts to save the work, dominates with an air of bravado. Only in the rich adagio does Mendelssohn show that he has not regressed too far; that movement is outstanding in the beauty of its melodies and the quality of its figurations. The finale, except for several excellent contrapuntal passages, is rather weak.

Mendelssohn's last completed string quartet, Opus 80, in F minor, was written in 1847, the last year of his life and nine years after the quartets of Opus 44. It is a somber work throughout; even the scherzo and fast finale have about them an air of gloom. The adagio is subdued and dark in mood, in spite of its restful moments. The whole work is weakened by many orchestral effects; the exquisite polish and perfection of earlier works is seldom in evidence. It is the least satisfactory of all his chamber-music compositions.

Four single movements for string quartet were found among Mendelssohn's papers after his death: the two middle movements of what was to be a quartet in A minor, from 1847, a capriccio from 1843, and a fugue from 1827. The four were assembled and published as Opus 81, in 1850. There is obviously no connection, in key or in content, between them: andante, E major; scherzo, A minor; capriccio, E minor; fugue, E flat. But individually, they are purest Mendelssohn. The variations of the andante are highly imaginative; the scherzo is again one of the typical light, fairy-like pieces. The capriccio, consisting of an introduction and a fast fugue, is more dramatic than Mendelssohn's fugues usually are; certainly it is a more successful piece than the moderate fugue which serves as this uneven work's finale.

Schumann's habit of concentrating on one musical medium for an extended period is well known. The years up to 1839, for example, saw only the composition of piano music; in 1840 Schumann was preoccupied with songs. With the same enthusiasm he showed for these categories, he turned to chamber music in 1842. Six of his ten compositions in that field were written in that year: three string quartets, Opus 41; the piano quintet, Opus 44; the piano quartet, Opus 47; and the *Fantasiestücke* for piano trio, Opus 88.

The three quartets of Opus 41 were written within a few weeks' time in the summer of 1842. They are in A minor, F major, and A major, respectively. From the very outset, Schumann disclosed himself as a master of the gentler moods. Dreamy introductions to the first and third quartets, fervent or tender melodies in the slow movements, and an occasional introspective passage in the allegros—these all testify to his Romantic temper.

But, the adagio of the A minor quartet is a model of eloquence—until it is broken off by the uncertain agitation of the middle part; the adagio of the A major flows smoothly and richly—until interrupted by a pulsating dramatic episode. And these typify another of

Schumann's characteristics: sudden contrasts of mood, impulsive changes of heart that bespeak the dual personalities with which he clothed himself. The Eusebius and Florestan personalities, creations of his imagination though they were, reveal themselves in almost every work of Schumann's. The dreamy Eusebius vein contrasts with the forthright Florestan on many a page. The moments of lyric tenderness in fast, rhythmic passages, the sharply accented or bois- terous sections in melodious movements—both indicate that the per- sonalities have momentarily changed places. But seldom does either achieve complete dominance within a single large movement. Acting on impulse or on inspiration, Schumann contrasts the most diverse elements in an episodic manner. Often unexpected, not always justi- fied musically, these flights of undisciplined imagination give his music the great variety and charm it so often discloses. And it is the failure of performers to recognize this duality of moods that contrib- utes to a certain misunderstanding of the real nature of Schumann's music.

Individual movements of the quartets are masterworks. The finale of the A minor, for example, is an exciting piece filled with boundless energy. The first movement of the F major gives us the soaring, pas- sionate, and warm Schumann; the finale represents the youthful, ex- uberant young Romanticist. The A major quartet's second move- ment, cast in variation form, is in a sense the most imaginative piece in the entire set. The theme undergoes subtle emotional transforma- tions in successive variations, but ordinary variation techniques are noticeably absent. Forceful, agitated, and somber at once, the move- ment, with its Eusebius strains in the coda, represents a synthesis of Schumann's finest qualities.

A few months after the quartets were finished, Schumann con- ceived the idea that a string quartet might well be combined with the piano. The piano quintet in E flat was the result; begun about Sep- tember, 1842, it was published, in 1843, as Opus 44. It is the first in a notable, if short, line of piano quintets by nineteenth-century com- posers and exhibits many features which were to influence subse- quent works for this combination.

Scarcely any work of Schumann's is so noble, exuberant, and vital. The first movement is a model of formal clarity and perfection. The vigorous first theme—divided into six related phrases—is followed by a lyric second and by a short codetta based on phrases of the first theme. The development, in sectional form, is concerned entirely with material heard in the exposition; the recapitulation is regular in structure. Thus, a Classical sonata form results—an unusual achievement for Schumann. The second movement has about it the air of a funeral march; the scherzo is based on rapidly ascending scale passages. In the finale Schumann attained new heights of imagination and technical skill and created a kind of double sonata form; [16] here also is seen evidence of his adherence to the principle of cyclical form.

In many evaluations of this quintet one finds references to its or-

[16] Up to the 224th measure the finale is in regular sonata form, but is distinguished by great harmonic freedom; at that point a new theme is introduced. A second development section follows; in it, themes from the finale are combined with phrases from the first movement in a masterful way. A recapitulation of the new theme and a final coda conclude the movement. The following table will clarify the above description.

EXPOSITION	C minor Theme I 42 measures	G major Theme II 34 measures	B minor Codetta 19 measures
DEVELOPMENT	Theme I and Theme II 40 measures		
RECAPITULATION	C sharp minor Theme I 42 measures	E flat Theme II 34 measures	G minor Codetta 12 measures
NEW EXPOSITION	E flat Theme III 24 measures		
SECOND DEVELOPMENT	Elements of Theme I and a theme derived from the first movement by expansion 130 measures		
RECAPITULATION	E flat Theme III 24 measures		
CODA	E flat, based on Theme I 25 measures		

chestral quality, to the dominance of the piano, and to other factors which are taken to be defects. It is true that a large number of sonorous doublings occur and that the piano part is worked out in fuller detail than are the string parts. But a criticism that considers the piano as merely *one* of five equal instruments is wide of the mark. As a matter of fact, the piano opposes, or balances, or contrasts with, the quartet as a unit; it represents not one fifth but one half of the entire tonal body. From this point of view the quintet takes its high place among true chamber-music works and provides a sonority and effectiveness unmatched in the earlier literature. It is in every sense a unique work; the quality of its themes, the forms which result from their manipulation, and the instrumentation itself all contribute to making it one of Schumann's outstanding compositions.

The last months of 1842 saw the completion of the piano quartet in E flat, published in 1845 as Opus 47. In this work the piano is again accused of dominating the texture, and now the charge is more justified. Here the piano is but one of four instruments rather than being an entity opposed to the entity of the three string instruments; in that role its voice is too prominent. Rich accompaniments, unnecessary doublings, and a general thickness of texture in the piano part contribute to a loss of balance in the work as a whole. But that is a minor defect, after all; the quartet has its full share of musical beauty and significance.

It begins with a slow and solemn introduction which anticipates the motive of the first theme. Imitating a device employed by Beethoven in his E flat quartet of Opus 127, the introductory material appears in the development section; thus, the theme is heard in slow and fast tempos, is seen in different lights, as it were. The scherzo is a large piece with two greatly contrasting trios. The expansion which results from this extreme contrast represents one of Schumann's real contributions to the development of Romantic forms. The slow movement employs a dreamy, almost sentimental melody in Schumann's finest Eusebius vein. The finale, while containing some excellent contrapuntal writing and large melodic sections, is less successful; it seeks out the lower ranges of the instruments, thus achieving a darker color than the nature of the themes requires, and produces a general effect of restlessness and fragmentation.

The last chamber-music work written in the prolific year of 1842 was a set of four pieces for piano, violin, and cello. It was published in 1850 as Opus 88, with the title *Fantasiestücke* (Phantasy Pieces). The work begins with a Romanza, a short piece based upon sequence repetitions of a single theme. The second movement, the Humoresque, is a long, loosely constructed movement containing four or five unrelated parts, each of which undergoes a certain amount of development. Then follows the Duet: cello and violin engage in mutual imitations of a lyric theme over a subdued accompaniment. The set ends with the March. The whole is one of Schumann's minor works; in spite of many delicate and songful moments, it discloses few of his finer qualities.

Similar in quality to the above work is the set of *Märchenerzählungen* (Fairy Tales), composed in 1853 and published a year later as Opus 132. This work is for an unusual combination: piano, clarinet, and viola. Even in this, the last of Schumann's chamber-music compositions, his Romantic interest in new tonal combinations is disclosed. But the rather dark tone color inherent in the combination is not reflected in the music. The first of the four pieces is lively; fanciful themes and a light, airy accompaniment create a real fairy-tale atmosphere. The second, almost as lively, suffers from considerable repetition of a short motive; no real continuity is established —and even a fairy tale must have continuity. In the third piece a charming duet between the clarinet and the viola over a freely flowing accompaniment creates an air of gentle nostalgia; it is written in Schumann's best narrative style. The fourth, again lively like the second, suffers from the same fragmentation. The four movements, taken together, give a good picture of Schumann's lighter side, a side not often disclosed in his larger chamber-music works. The composer was often most charming when talking to children; there was then no need to be anything but natural. And so he is in the *Märchenerzählungen*.

Between the two sets of miniatures just discussed lie three full-size piano trios: Opus 63, in D minor, and Opus 80, in F major, were written in 1847; Opus 110, in G minor, in 1851. The first two reveal that the impulsiveness of Schumann's 1842 style has developed into vagary. The sudden changes of mood, employed diffidently in the string quartets of Opus 41, become characteristic in the trios. The first movement of the D minor trio, for example, begins in a veiled and subdued manner; the mood engendered by the opening is rudely broken off by a few measures of sharply accented rhythms, after which the veiled mood returns. An ebb and flow of the tempo, too, is characteristic of the movement; *ritardandi* and *a tempi* occur at frequent intervals. Again in the F major trio's first movement: a rugged, well-defined passage of great intensity is interrupted by a few dreamy, meditative measures in which rhythmic motion virtually ceases. And in the last movement a similar situation occurs.

But the impulsive dreamer is absent in other portions of these works. Side by side with movements that can best be described as vague and fragmentary are others whose vitality and straightforwardness do not fail. Of such quality are the finale of the D minor, a vigorous movement in Schumann's most robust style, and the third movement of the F major, whose delicacy and beauty of color are superb. A further characteristic may be noted: Schumann's extensive use of syncopated and compound rhythmic figures—at times employed so ineptly that the formal lines are obscured. The slow movement of the F major trio provides a case in point; sections of that piece are so written that the rhythmic beat is lost for measures at a time. The resultant effect is formless, or at best impressionistic. That characteristic, of course, grew out of Schumann's preoccupation with effects of sonority and tone color. But, like a number of his devices, it was sometimes used to excess, and merely made the music unclear.

The G minor trio of 1851 is an uneven work. Along with moments of genuine Schumannesque humor and energy are irrelevant sections which wander aimlessly. As in so many of Schumann's works, many an inspired detail loses its effectiveness by being overdone. The first movement's undulating chord motive is heard throughout that movement; changed hardly at all on subsequent appearances and having within itself no power of growth, it succeeds only in creating an impression of fragmentation. The middle movements suffer from the same lack of fertile imagination.

Let us now review the principal characteristics of Classical music in order to appreciate the departures of Schubert, Mendelssohn, and Schumann from those characteristics. (1) The Classical composers accepted the validity of the development principle. To be amenable to the demands of that principle, a musical theme had to be rhythmically characteristic, had to have within itself the power of growth, and had to be concise so that it could be perceived in its entirety. Beethoven recognized those demands to a greater degree than any previous composer; his solution took the form of motive manipulation, whose supreme manifestations are seen in the fifth and the ninth symphonies and in the last quartets, Opera 130–133. (2) An essential of Classical sonata form was the conflict between two opposing elements, technically represented by the conflict between two contrasting themes. This conflict took place in the development section of the form, indeed became the *raison d'être* for that section; and in turn it justified the recapitulation, for in the latter section the contrasting themes were reviewed in the light of their revealed opposition. (3) The requirement of unity loomed large in the minds of the great Classical composers. Unity was achieved by adherence to a basic tonality within a movement—with only such deviations as the thematic conflict made necessary—or by an emotional connection between several movements. The three characteristics, then, of organic growth of the material, of dramatic conflict, and of inner unity, determined both the content and the form of the greatest Classical music.

Schubert made little use of motive-laden themes. He was more concerned with large lyric melodies which, when they were manipulated (i.e., developed), broke into fragments. Nor is there often in his works the dramatic conflict between themes; the drama in Schubert arises out of chance encounter, not out of calculated contrast. He reveals his melodies in various lights, in different harmonic colors, but leaves them essentially unchanged. And, having presented them in the exposition and illuminated them in the development, he has no real need of recapitulating them. When he does so—and most often he does—the themes return, not as aesthetic necessities, but as surfeits of beauty. Finally, his larger works are seldom connected within themselves. Movements stand side by side in isolation; only rarely, as in the E flat trio, is one piece organically bound to another.

Mendelssohn's chamber music conforms much more closely than does Schubert's to Classical principles. His solid education and musical background made him aware of the inner significance of musical form at an early age. At first in imitation, later from conviction, he chose Classical formal models and made Classical principles his own. This admiration for the formal practices of the past could easily have degenerated into rigid formalism. That it did not do so speaks highly for the vitality of Classical principles and for Mendelssohn's understanding of them. Hampered neither by slavish adherence to sets of rules (as many pseudo-Classicists were) nor by undisciplined imagination (which sometimes became an occupational disease among Romanticists), he remained true to his educational ideals and his sense of fitness. Only in the quality of his emotion did he fall below his models. Great depth of feeling and an awareness of the powerful tensions of human life were foreign to his temperament, nor are they reflected in his music.

Schumann, in his chamber music, reveals himself as a man of uncertain convictions caught between two opposing tendencies: not strong enough to make a complete break with the past; too strong to give way to every wayward impulse. One senses in Schumann the conflict between form and content—the conflict which was resolved by the great Classical composers and ignored by the typical Romantics. In his songs and his piano music he was as free as the wind; in chamber music, where he was subject to the restrictions imposed by the medium, he was thwarted. In miniatures and unpretentious works he was at his best; his inspirations were heaven-sent. But endurance, in a musical sense, was not in him. His inspirations were of a moment's duration; when he set to work on them, they vanished. Not as melodically gifted as Schubert, not as formally perceptive as Mendelssohn, Schumann represents to perfection one aspect of Romanticism. That period, seen now in retrospect, was concerned with the fleeting moment. It contained enthusiasm, feeling, humor, charm, exquisite taste—but no staying power. Its music was enjoyable, but not significant. And it remained for a later composer to add the ingredients of staying power and significance to the colorful, stimulating mixture which is Romanticism at its best: Johannes Brahms.

I2

BRAHMS AND THE DECLINE OF ROMANTICISM

IN EARLIER chapters it has been possible to show, with due regard for overlapping, how one historical period flowed into the next. Each period has been seen, more or less accurately, as a self-contained unit concerned with its own musical problems and finding its own solutions. And it has been possible, through the admission of sufficiently large generalizations, to characterize one composer near the beginning of the period as the standard bearer for the new, and one near the end as the great exponent of the old (in the sense that the new became old as the period ran its course). Baroque, Rococo, Classical, and early Romantic periods differed sufficiently from each other to make the selection of their representatives simple.

Very probably the historian of the future will have little difficulty in naming "the" composer of the last half of the nineteenth century. By emphasizing one of its aspects, he will see that half-century as a self-contained unit; but in so doing he must necessarily minimize or ignore certain sub-aspects. We, being closer to it, are confronted with at least three concurrent sets of characteristics, each set individual enough to compose a separate aspect, and we see several significant composers representing each set of characteristics. Whom, then, shall we name as "the" composer of the period? What, first, are the various aspects?

1. The middle years of the nineteenth century were characterized by a growing amount of social unrest. The abortive revolution of German liberals against the Confederacy in 1848, the interest in Socialism as a form of government, the definition of the new science of sociology, the Communist Manifesto of Karl Marx—all these in-

dicate the temper of the time: the common man was being discovered. And in that discovery lay one of the contributing causes to the decline of Romanticism. Romantic ideals, somewhat removed from everyday life, perforce became practical; realism, in art and literature as well as in music, was a logical consequence. Composers, in an effort to be as realistic as their brother artists, sought new means of expression, means which would accurately mirror what they had to express. Thus arose the preoccupation with story-telling in music, with extramusical devices, with messages or pictures which could be laid down in compositions—in a word, with program music. In the development of program music Hector Berlioz (1803–1869) and Franz Liszt (1811–1886) were outstanding. And they, together with Richard Wagner (1813–1883), were too concerned with the overall scene to give any thought to chamber music.

2. In another group of composers the search for new means of expression led elsewhere. Possibly as a result of the Napoleonic Wars, a new awareness of national differences and a desire for national recognition arose in many parts of Europe. The establishment of the German Empire and a united Italy (both of which were achieved about 1870) strengthened those feelings; artists turned their attention to the folklore, customs, and cultural heritage of their own people, and a period of Nationalism in the arts developed. In music that development resulted in the use of folk music, national dances, and musical idioms, to the extent that Romantic music lost its universal characteristics (insofar as Europe can be considered the universe) and became Russian or Bohemian or Scandinavian music.

3. Thus Romanticism, transformed into realism, had developed along two parallel (but also intersecting) paths. Program music, concerned with the delineation of literary programs and unconcerned with "music for its own sake," eschewed traditional forms and methods and developed its own. The tone poem, the *idée fixe*, and the characteristic piece ("Butterflies," "The Mill," "The Last Spring," etc.) were among the new phenomena. National music, on the other hand, turned to folk songs, rhythms, and dances, and superimposed them upon forms and a type of expression which were not essentially

different from Romantic musical practices. But not all composers could hold with the new tenets. Some, too weak to overcome the inertia imposed by tradition, maintained the lyric content and idealistic aims of Romanticism; such composers were swallowed up in the rush of new events and contributed nothing of great value. Others, however, through temperament or aesthetic philosophy, were drawn strongly to the past. Equipped with contemporary techniques, affected by contemporary developments, but largely influenced by the works of earlier generations, these anomalous composers struggled against indifference or a feeling of loneliness throughout their lifetimes. With those words one has characterized César Franck and Johannes Brahms, the two greatest exponents of that aspect of the nineteenth century which is characterized neither by program music nor by Nationalism.

Johannes Brahms was born at Hamburg in 1833. His father, a bass player, taught him the rudiments of music at an early age; the quality of the boy's talent soon made itself evident, and Johannes was placed with Eduard Marxsen, an excellent local musician. In his fourteenth year, when he made his debut as a pianist, he had gained local renown for the excellence of his playing. In 1853 he became the accompanist for a Hungarian violinist, Eduard Reményi. During the course of the tour Brahms met Joseph Joachim, who became his lifelong friend, and Robert Schumann, who hailed him as the hope of the future after seeing some of his compositions.

For parts of three years (1857–1859) Brahms served as pianist and choral conductor at the court of Detmold. In 1860 he returned to Hamburg for further study, and in 1862 accepted a position as conductor of a singing society in Vienna. Between 1864 and 1869, becoming increasingly well known as a pianist, he made several successful concert tours. In the latter year he returned to Vienna, and he served for three years as conductor of the Friends of Music concerts.

Brahms's life was enriched by many beautiful and significant friendships. Joseph Joachim and Hans von Bülow were representative of the scores of musicians with whom he corresponded, whom he misunderstood, and whom he forgave through the greater part of his lifetime. His early acquaintance with Schumann soon ripened into friendship with the latter's entire family, particularly with his wife Clara. As an artist (Clara Wieck Schumann was one of the finest pianists of her generation) and as a woman she exerted a strong influence on him until her death. Brahms's love affairs with younger women usually came to the same unhappy conclusion: when he was all but committed to marriage, he broke off the relationship in the fear (sometimes expressed to the girl in question, sometimes not) that domestic entanglements would deter him from the composing which had become the sole reason for his existence. The emotional turmoils into which Brahms plunged himself, plus his essentially reserved temperament, impelled him to adopt a mask of gruffness in most of his social encounters; which, in turn, estranged him, at one time or another, from all who held him in highest respect and sincerest friendship. Lonely, misunderstood by many, Brahms was not a happy man. Much of his most deeply felt music is a reflection of that unhappy state.

His fame as a composer gradually extended to all parts of the musical world; he played or conducted performances of his own works in Holland and in Switzerland, as well as in all parts of Germany and Austria. Invitations to visit England were declined out of fear of the Channel crossing. Each year saw Brahms's reputation growing; it became customary to hold festivals devoted entirely to his works. This fame was established in the face of Wagner's domination of the musical scene, of the preoccupation with program music and with Nationalistic elements—to all of which Brahms remained indifferent.

Clara Schumann's death in the spring of 1896 marked the beginning of Brahms's own decline. A summer of rest in the country under the care of physicians brought no improvement. Brahms returned to Vienna, which had been his permanent home since 1878, and attended a few concerts. Unable to maintain the active life he had led for decades, he sank rapidly. When he died, on April 3, 1897, all Europe was affected. Thousands marched in the funeral cortege, distant cities and foreign countries sent representatives, and musicians mourned the passing of a great master.

Brahms's contributions to instrumental ensemble literature total twenty-four works. Seven sonatas for piano and one instrument— three for violin, two for cello, two for clarinet or viola—fall outside our definition of chamber music. The remaining seventeen ensemble compositions, each one a masterpiece, include five piano trios, three piano quartets, one piano quintet, three string quartets, two quintets, two sextets, and one quintet for strings and clarinet. But that short list gives no indication of how prolific a composer Brahms actually was. He felt no regrets at destroying a completed work if it did not measure up to his own standard. Almost two dozen string quartets were written; three remain. Other works were ruthlessly altered, transposed, or written for other media: the D minor piano concerto, originally designed as a symphony, passed through a two-piano phase before it emerged in its final form. Other examples of that practice will appear below. And in one notable case an early work was completely transformed late in Brahms's life: the B major trio, Opus 8, the first of his chamber-music compositions. We may begin our account with that work.

The trio, for piano, violin, and cello, was written in 1854. It was a large, extravagant work. The first movement contained five complete themes; after the adequate development section a second development in fugal style appeared in the recapitulation; the slow movement included a large section in fast tempo. In 1890, when the need for a second edition of the trio arose, Brahms undertook to revise it. But the revision took the form of extensive rewriting, so complete that a new work appeared having only its first themes and the scherzo in common with the earlier version. It is the 1890 version that is known today; the 1854 edition has all but disappeared from the repertoire. The later work is scarcely two-thirds as long as the earlier; its mood is much more concentrated and restrained.

Even in its condensed version the B major trio is a monumental work. The series of phrases which constitute the first theme require some forty measures for their unfolding, and they rise to a great climax of sonority; later sections are laid out on an equally massive scale. The scherzo is at once light and boisterous; deft and fleeting passages alternate with thunderous outbursts of exuberance. The adagio is a sustained, intense movement filled with the richness of de-tail and clarity of purpose that are so uniquely Brahmsian. And the work as a whole discloses a texture which is typical of all Brahms's chamber-music works with piano. In those nine works a duality of tonal bodies is established: the piano is set opposite the two, three, or four string instruments (and woodwinds, in the case of the horn and clarinet trios), and carries half of the tonal burden. Thus, a great number of string passages in unison, octaves, thirds, and sixths occur, or passages in two- or three-part counterpoint—all set opposite a full and magnificently written piano part. The resultant division of the tonal mass into two equally complete components, seen to some ex-tent in the later Beethoven trios, provides Brahms with ample op-portunity to develop a massive, multi-voiced medium capable of carrying a detailed contrapuntal texture.

During his relatively happy sojourn at Detmold, about 1857, Brahms began work on a sextet for two violins, two violas, and two cellos, in B flat. The work was completed about 1859–1860 and was published as Opus 18. The storm and stress characteristic of the B major trio are no longer in evidence; the sextet is one of Brahms's most cheerful and most Classical compositions. From the first tran-quil melody to the humorous coda of the finale, the work is serene and placid, except in those passages where Brahms's vitality and enthusiasm find expression.

The first movement's pairs of themes unfold with an air of Classical repose. Never is one in doubt as to Brahms's harmonic or rhythmic intentions; all is transparent and intelligible. The variations of the second movement, lyric or dramatic in turn, make full use of the sextet's color combinations without becoming unduly extravagant in tonal variety. The scherzo is small, but packed full of Beethoven-esque energy. And the final rondo is a movement any of the great Classical composers might have written. Each phrase grows out of the previous one, short developments take the place of transitions, and masterful modulations are characteristic. In the importance given to the first cello throughout the work, the sextet takes its place with those quartets of Haydn and Mozart which bear dedications to Frederick William II of Prussia.

Two piano quartets, in G minor and A major, were published as Opus 25 and Opus 26, respectively. Brahms began the G minor in 1857, and both were performed in Vienna in November, 1862; no more exact information about their origin is available. With these works Brahms made his successful Viennese debut as a pianist. They are among the most expansive of all his chamber-music compositions.

The large scale which is characteristic of the first version of the B major trio is here again in evidence. Whole groups of melodies, in contrasting tonalities, of course, appear in place of first and second themes. The several movements disclose the power of invention and breadth of lyricism that were among Brahms's outstanding characteristics. Yet many of the themes are in themselves not lyric melodies: the G minor quartet's first theme is founded upon a one-measure motive; a two-measure figure is employed in a similar capacity in the A major. It is Brahms's consummate contrapuntal skill which enables him to derive ever-new melodies from these motives, to base transitional passages upon them, and to invest them with dramatic power or gentle pathos at will.

Richness of thematic material such as is disclosed in the first movements of these quartets might have led to diffuseness and disunity in the hands of a less capable composer. Brahms, even in his twenties, was equal to the task of organizing the material, keeping it under control, and developing it in whatever direction his powerful imagination dictated. The charm and rich color content of the G minor quartet's intermezzo provide a fine contrast to the noble, full-bodied slow movement. The latter includes an animated, martial section in which new levels of sonority are established in chamber music; the vital, enthusiastic, almost orchestral Brahms is in evidence throughout the movement. But the climax of the quartet is reserved for the finale: "Rondo alla Zingarese." Brahms's fondness for Hungarian tunes finds here its first expression in his chamber music; Hungarian temperament pervades the entire piece, yet the melodies and texture are all of his own making. The coda, with its cadenzas, is magnificent. The A major quartet is an equally fine work; certain passages, notably those based on the first movement's short motive, illustrate to a high degree Brahms's contrapuntal skill. The slow movement's serene melodies, the flowing scherzo, with its trio written in canon, and the finale's sustained power are unsurpassed.

During the years which witnessed the writing of the two piano quartets, Brahms completed a string quintet (with two cellos) in F minor. After 1862, convinced that the work was lacking in some respects, he rewrote it as a sonata for two pianos. But now the sustained lyricism which only string instruments could supply was gone; again Brahms recast it, this time for string quartet and piano. In that form, completed in 1864 and known today as the piano quintet in F minor, Opus 34, it was successful. It has since taken its place in the literature as one of Brahms's most characteristic works.

Built on broad lines similar to the piano quartets, the F minor quintet's first movement includes pairs of first and second themes and several derivative melodies which are almost thematic in character. And again, as in the quartets, both motive manipulation and lyric melody are fundamental to the themes' development. The slow movement, a shy yet characterful piece, contains moments of real inspiration, particularly in its coda. There, a melodic fragment heard near the end of the first section is employed at the close of the movement (during the last nine measures) with particularly magical result. In the example on page 325 a portion of that passage is given. The powerful, intense scherzo reveals a miniature sonata form in its first part: two contrasting themes are developed and in part recapitulated. The trio is a short, solid piece in Brahms's most eloquent vein. And in the finale his characteristic practice of modifying form to meet thematic requirements (a Classical characteristic, be it noted) is exemplified. A slow, emotionally rich introduction leads into a sonata-form movement which contains no development section as such, but which in effect is a long development from beginning to end. The climax of the whole work is reserved for the coda, in which a masterful contrapuntal development of both themes simultaneously rises to heights of emotional intensity and musical significance.

A second string sextet, in G major, Opus 36, was written in the winter of 1864–1865, the winter in which Brahms's mother died and in which he began to work on *Ein deutsches Requiem*. At the same time, the last memories of one of his most serious love affairs—that with Agathe von Siebold—flared up afresh and caused Brahms to re-live many happier moments. Under the influence of contrasting moods, alternately moved by deep sadness and youthful joy, Brahms worked at the sextet. Essentially filled with sunshine, it has its moments of pathos and heartfelt emotion.

The massiveness and intensity of the F minor piano quintet, completed in the previous summer, are no longer present, nor is the great sonority which characterized the first sextet of 1860. In place of these are an ethereal quality and a mood of poetic restraint. The turbulence of Brahms's emotion is here transfigured; a delicate melancholy suffused with moments of deeply felt but quiet gloom pervades the work. His feeling for Agathe is reflected in the first movement, where her name is called out several times:

(measures 162-168, 509, 525-530)

With the G major sextet Brahms left the tempestuousness of his youth behind. He began to draw around himself a veil of reticence. In later works he was as passionate, he felt as deeply, and he was moved as much by joy as in earlier works; but his emotions were restrained and somewhat concealed. It is as though an invisible barrier stood between composer and listener; only rarely was the barrier lifted entirely, and then only briefly. The essential loneliness of the man began to be reflected in his music.

About 1865, Brahms wrote a trio for piano, violin, and *Waldhorn* (the natural horn, without valves), in E flat, published as Opus 40. The trio, when published, included an optional part for cello (to replace the horn); two decades later an optional viola part was added at Brahms's suggestion. But in his own mind, either of the substitutions "sounded horrible"; only with the original instrumentation could his subtle color intentions be fully realized.

With this work certain of Brahms's suppressed Romantic feelings were disclosed: the inclusion of the wind instrument, the free forms characteristic of the trio, and the general air of Romantic melancholy. For virtually the only time in his larger instrumental first movements, Brahms departed from sonata form. In its place he created a symmetrical five-part form in which two contrasting themes alternate. A unique characteristic of the movement is the subtlety of its cadence structure; one phrase flows into the next, cadences are hinted at, and basic harmonies are only half revealed. The end result is a fluidity and a mysterious quality seldom encountered in Brahms. But the scherzo is as vigorous and straightforward as anything in his works and reveals one of Brahms's later characteristics: the expansion of a phrase by the insertion of measures:

The adagio, in E flat minor, is a sustained, intense movement pervaded by the deepest sentiment. It contains one of the finest of Brahms's recapitulations; the movement's second theme, transformed in the light of what has taken place in the development, returns in a radically modified form, and in a form which enables it to prepare the way for the finale. Seldom is the inner connection between two contrasting movements revealed more subtly and more surely than here.

Eight years elapsed before Brahms turned to chamber music again. Two string quartets, in C minor and A minor, respectively, were written in 1873 and published as Opus 51. Thus, finally, in his fortieth year, after having written and destroyed almost two dozen quartets, Brahms achieved what he felt to be satisfactory results and allowed those results to be published. It is in general true of Brahms that we do not witness his gradual steps toward technical mastery; his self-criticism and his habit of destroying preparatory works deprived us of the opportunity to observe his tentative, stumbling approach to musical heights. In all categories we are at once presented with mature masterworks; particularly is this true in the field of the string quartets.

The C minor is characterized by a sonority and a richness of tone seldom found in string quartets. Many double stops and a degree of elaborateness in the figurations provide a tonal framework well suited to the largeness of the quartet's musical ideas. But with all its richness, the work is not merely a condensed orchestral piece. Its details never serve as mere padding, nor do they in a single instance obscure the clarity of expressive intention. Brahms's feeling for dramatic utterance is in evidence on every page, as is the melancholy air which pervades so many of his works.

The A minor quartet, on the other hand, is a delicate and tender composition. Moments of lyric sweetness contrast with introspective passages; passionate cries are set opposite refined bits of melody, and an air of reserve is seldom absent. The charm of the quasi-minuetto is matched only by the serenity which pours out of the slow movement in a gentle stream. Only in the finale does Brahms give way to a robust and forceful expression of energy.

An account of the next work must begin with the events of 1854–1856. Those years were marked by the complete breakdown of Robert Schumann's health; they culminated in his insanity and death. During those years Brahms spent considerable time in the company of Clara Schumann; while hoping for his friend's recovery, he was filled with love for his friend's wife. The emotional turmoil and moodiness engendered by such unhappy circumstances found reflection in a piano quartet in C sharp minor which Brahms began about 1855. A first and second movement, in C sharp minor and E major, respectively, and a finale were completed, when he laid the work aside. Almost twenty years later, namely, in 1874, Brahms became interested in the work again. But following his usual custom, he revised ruthlessly. The finale was discarded; the first movement was altered and transposed to C minor, and a scherzo and new finale were written. In that form, as the piano quartet in C minor, Opus 60, the work was published in 1875.

Like the B major trio, the C minor quartet reflects both the impulsive youth of twenty-two and the restrained, poised master. The first movement offers striking contrasts between a dark, moody first theme and a lyric second (remarkable in a technical sense for being a short set of variations). Wild sections in remote keys alternate with strong passages crystal clear in their delineation of anguish. The scherzo is dramatic, fitful, and intense; only in its last few measures does it give way to a powerful abandon. The E major andante takes a high place among Brahms's slow movements. Glorious melodies accompanied by exquisite counterpoints soar to heights of Romantic expression. In the finale all is dark again; alternations of restraint and fury characterize a movement which closes one of the most despairing compositions in the literature.

A year or two after the piano quartet emerged, Brahms composed a third string quartet, in B flat, published as Opus 67 about 1876. And for virtually the first time since the A major piano quartet of Opus 26 (about 1862) a work of lightness, charm, and deft humor appeared among the chamber-music compositions. One need not look for the pensive, melancholy Brahms in this delightful quartet; this is the work of a good-natured, straightforward, and healthy composer. The first movement is characterized by changes from 6/8 to 2/4 meter; passages in the one are bustling with activity, in the other are delightfully matter-of-fact. The slow movement is an appealing piece and contrasts well with the piquant, agitated third movement. The fourth movement's set of variations provides moments of great charm, particularly in its last section, in which phrases from the first movement are woven into the variation texture in a masterful way.

It is significant that the B flat quartet, in a sense the lightest of all Brahms's chamber-music works, was written during the time in which the first symphony, Opus 68, approached completion. The tragic mood and monumental scope of that great work made enormous demands upon him from 1874 to 1876; composing the quartet, so different in mood and intensity from the symphony, must have provided the needed moments of repose and relaxation. And in the following years some of the greatest of Brahms's works were written: the second symphony, about 1877; the violin concerto, 1878; the two overtures, 1880–1881; the B flat piano concerto, from 1878 to 1881. During this extremely productive period, about 1875–1881, Brahms found no time for the composition of chamber music. Not until 1882 did he complete a piano trio in C major, Opus 87, whose first movement had been begun two years earlier.

In that trio Brahms reached new heights in mastery of thematic development, in the economical use of material. Virtually every scrap of melody gives rise to other melodies; every motive suggests new motives. The result, in the first movement, is a conciseness which borders on austerity. Terse and objective, the movement is also characterized by dignity and reserve. The second, a set of five variations, is an outstanding example of Brahms's skill; not lyrically inspired nor dramatically contrasted, the variations present different phases of the theme's character. The scherzo is turbulent in a mild way; the finale, in spite of its few outbursts, is essentially cool and reserved.

In the same year (1882) Brahms wrote a string quintet in F major, Opus 88. As so often in his music, these two consecutive works differ completely in mood and content. Where the trio is austere, the quintet is ingratiating; where the trio is calculated, the quintet is alive with inspiration. The latter's tuneful first movement is filled with sunshine; its highly imaginative developments serve but to throw the general lightness of mood into better relief. And for the only time in Brahms's chamber music (the sonatas, of course, excepted) we meet a three-movement form. The second movement of the quintet contains alternating sections in slow and fast tempo and thus combines the functions of slow movement and scherzo. And the finale begins with a fugal exposition—again most unusual in Brahms. Modeled, perhaps, on the fugal finale of Beethoven's Opus 59, No. 3, it exhibits similar combinations of melodic developments and contrapuntal intricacies. The movement discloses an exuberance we have not seen in Brahms's chamber music since the A major piano quartet; a similar exuberance filled Beethoven's heart toward the end of the Opus 59 set. What is more natural than that Brahms should have made use of the free quasi-fugal style to give expression to his enthusiastic state. But the result is not as successful as Beethoven's.

A piano trio in C minor, Opus 101, was written during the prolific summer of 1886, which also saw the composition of the F major cello sonata, Opus 99, and the A major violin sonata, Opus 100. The first movement of the trio illustrates to an even greater degree than does the C major trio (Opus 87) Brahms's great economy of means. A three-note motive and a fragment of lyric melody are the materials out of which he constructed this most concise of movements. The second movement, light-hearted and melancholy at once, serves as the scherzo; although marked "presto," it is essentially a reflective piece. The charming andante, with its mixtures of 3/4 and 2/4 measures, exhibits an unusually thin texture; the string instruments are heard without the piano much of the time, and thus contribute to the great variety of tonal color the movement contains. The finale, beginning brusquely and in a restless mood, settles down to a rollicking gait in its last section. Short phrases, many cross rhythms, and abrupt modulations give the movement a dissatisfied air; it is not the finest of Brahms's finales.

In the summer of 1890, following a delightful visit to Italy, Brahms wrote a string quintet in G major, Opus 111. Full-bodied, strong, and cheerful, it is essentially a happy work. The first movement, with its energetic theme and bustling accompanying figures, is reminiscent of a younger Brahms. The wonderfully moving adagio, on the other hand, is one of the richest and most dramatic movements of his late period. The scherzo, filled with naïve charm, conceals a wealth of contrapuntal details and masterful craftsmanship. In the finale the power and energy of the first movement are repeated, but on a lower level of sonority. Altogether, the G major quintet vigorously belies Brahms's age: fifty-seven. All the youth and enthusiasm of the earlier Brahms are here, without the extravagance.

On so cheerful a note Brahms had planned to end his creative activity. Rather than fall below the level he had attained, he would forego further composition—such was his intention. But a visit to Meiningen early in 1891 caused him to postpone his retirement. For in the Meiningen orchestra he heard a clarinetist, Richard Mühlfeld (1856–1907); so accomplished was that artist and so beautifully did he reveal the possibilities of the clarinet that Brahms resolved to employ the instrument in chamber music. Two works were written in the summer of 1891: the trio for clarinet, cello, and piano, in A minor, Opus 114, and the quintet for clarinet and string quartet, in B minor, Opus 115. Two sonatas for clarinet and piano, written in 1894, may be mentioned here; for with those compositions Brahms's life work was virtually finished.

By comparison with his other works, the trio is somewhat dry. Technically, all is on as high a plane as ever; the clarity of form and contrapuntal workmanship disclose no lessening of creative skill. But the melodic charm of earlier works, which has shown a certain falling off since the C major trio of 1882, is present to a smaller degree. In its place has come a preoccupation with rhythmic development, to the advantage of structural interest, but at the cost of lyric beauty.

In the B minor clarinet quintet, Opus 115, the picture is changed radically. Imaginative details, variety of texture, inspired developments—all these are there, along with a beauty of melody and air of nobility that even Brahms did not always achieve. The gentle melancholy of the first movement, undisturbed by a full sonority and a mass of figurations, is appealing to a high degree. The shy, reserved adagio, with its rhapsodic middle section, full of rich tremolos and richer harmonies, is a deeply felt, imaginative piece of exquisite music. The third movement contains two related parts: a melodious andantino and a bright, deft presto, thematically related to the first part. And the variations of the last movement bring to expression a variety of mood and color virtually unknown in earlier chamber music. The coda combines the theme of the variations with that of the first movement in a passage whose economy, reserve, and sheer beauty are unmatched in the literature.

It may have been Brahms's purpose here to display the clarinet to advantage. Certainly every opportunity is given that instrument; lyric melody, dramatic figuration, rhapsodic utterance, delicate passage work, and complete range are employed. But the quintet is in no sense merely a virtuoso display piece; it is an example of perfectly conceived, lovingly planned chamber music of the highest quality. Exquisite restraint, great variety of textures, and subtle changes of tone color characterize the musical content of the four movements. The clarinet is treated as one of five equal instruments throughout; but its essential lyric character finds reflection in the work as a whole and inspired Brahms to create one of his greatest masterpieces.

It is appropriate at this point to cast a backward glance over
Brahms's forty years of chamber-music writing. One is impressed by
changes in the nature of his melodic line and in the quality of the
rhythmic element. Earlier works, roughly those written before the
horn trio of Opus 40, were characterized by long, sustained lyric
melodies disclosing Brahms's kinship with Schubert. Melodies of that
type are largely missing in the works after 1865 (the sublime melody
of the slow movement of Opus 60, be it remembered, was present in
the first version from about 1855 and is not typical of the later
Brahms). Beginning about that year, a new type of melody was introduced: one which begins lyrically, but which after a few measures
dissolves into the contrapuntal structure or undergoes rhythmic development. Seldom does the melody of the later type have a definite
cadence; it melts into the following passage, thus has a beginning,
but no ending.

With the change in melodic type came a greater preoccupation
with rhythmic details and rhythmic complexities. As Brahms approached his fifties, he concerned himself less with bar lines and clear
rhythmic patterns than with thick textures in which rhythmic detail
was piled upon rhythmic detail. Such polyrhythms as

become typical. Melodic lines such as those found in Opus 51, No. 1
(third movement),

dot Brahms's pages in increasing numbers. Rarely does he shift bar

lines to agree with phrase structure, the most notable example being
the C minor trio of Opus 101 (third movement), immediately above.

Most often he is content to ignore bar lines and to write phrases across the measures.

A third point has to do with the inclusion of two contrasting tempos within a single movement. This device, found nowhere in the chamber music through the sextet of Opus 36, appears eight times in the eleven works which follow that sextet.[1] In several cases the second tempo's melodies are developed out of those of the first; in a sense they may be regarded as highly imaginative variations. In that connection must be mentioned the fact that sets of variations appear with somewhat greater frequency in the later works of Brahms than they do in the earlier.

What is one to conclude from these observations? First, in his early works Brahms was inspired to write long, lyric melodies of the kind we have seen in Schubert's music. Such Romantic outpourings of true lyricism as we find in profusion in the B flat sextet, the G minor and A major piano quartets, and the slow movement of the C minor piano quartet have much in common with Schubert: sturdy grace, rhythmic flow, and an air of gentle nostalgia. Second, Brahms's melodic inspiration failed him to some extent in his middle period and a greater amount of rhythmic variety took its place. This stage is seen in the C minor and A minor string quartets, in which a kind of rhythmic development of melodies substitutes for purely lyric utterance. Finally, in those movements in which rhythmic development is not appropriate, a duality of tempos results (as in the third movements of the Opus 51 string quartets and in the first movement of the B flat, Opus 67).

In later works such rhythmic manipulation of melodic fragments became a characteristic element of Brahms's style. The rhythmic profundity and great freedom of phrase structure which are so typically Brahmsian are seen in the first movement of Opus 87, the finale of Opus 101, and throughout Opus 111 and Opus 115. But occasionally even Brahms's mastery of rhythmic developments, usually so amazingly subtle, becomes a bit obvious. One is enabled to peer be-

[1] In Opera 40, 51 (Nos. 1 and 2), 67, 88, 101, and twice in Opus 115.

hind the scenes and see the mechanism at work; for a brief moment
the passage loses its charm.[2]

May one conclude that inspired pure lyric melody is essentially a
young man's concern? That it was only the power, the depth, and
the energy of Brahms's musical intellect which enabled him to overcome the handicaps that increasing years brought with them? If a
generalization about Brahms's life work may be made, it must recognize the dominant position of intellectual activity in his music. And
that is not in the least incompatible with emotional significance,
warmth, charm, humor, or strength. One may approach Brahms as
one would any other major composer; one may revel in the manifold
beauties and moving passages his music contains. But one may appreciate his full stature only when one takes into account the nature
of his musical activity. Intellect, too, may be inspired, as it was in
Brahms to a tremendous degree.

French instrumental music had suffered an almost total eclipse
toward the middle of the nineteenth century. French musical culture, falling under the spell of an eloquent Wagnerianism, was dominated by the opera. Scores of operatic works from the pens of
Massenet, Gounod, and their lesser imitators became enormously
popular; a welter of music which was merely lyric or dramatic, entertaining or sentimental, overwhelmed the more serious composers.
It remained for a native Belgian to become the leader of a group of
musicians who succeeded in restoring the integrity of instrumental
music in France. César Franck (1822–1890), born at Liége, but educated in France, was doomed to a life of obscurity for the most part.
For more than forty years he taught piano and organ in Paris; for
more than fifty years he composed and found recognition, until late
in life, only in a small circle composed of his pupils and friends. His
music is characterized by a measure of contrapuntal excellence,
formal innovation, and religious idealism; such characteristics found

[2] Such lapses one finds, for example, in Opus 87, I, measures 80–89 and 258–267;
in Opus 101, II, measures 89–94; and in IV, measures 191–212.

no favor among the opera-loving Frenchmen of his time. Yet his influence upon the course of French music was considerable. In proof,
one has but to mention the names of a few of his pupils: Vincent
d'Indy (1851–1931), Ernest Chausson (1855–1899), and Gabriel
Pierné (1863–1897).

Franck's achievement is not reflected in a large quantity of works;
he was among the least prolific of major composers. His one symphony and one violin sonata are well known; his contributions to
chamber music include only one piano quintet and one string quartet,
in addition to four early piano trios, one of which has some slight
historical significance.

Three of the trios were written in 1840 and were later published as
Franck's Opus 1. The first trio, in F sharp minor, bears within itself
the seeds of cyclical form, the form which Beethoven had introduced
so magnificently in the quartets of Opera 130–133, and the form
which became the trademark of the nineteenth century's last decades.
Themes presented early in the first movement are heard again, somewhat transformed, in later movements; other themes are in turn derived from them, and a high degree of unity is thus attained. In other
respects the F sharp trio and its two companions in Franck's Opus 1
are not important works; but Franck was only eighteen at the time
of writing.[3] Nor is the one-movement fourth trio, Opus 2, of great
importance; that trio was originally planned as the finale of Opus
1, No. 3, but was published separately at the suggestion of Liszt.

Almost forty years elapsed before Franck turned to chamber
music again: the quintet for piano and strings, in F minor, was written in 1878. During the long interval Franck had slowly been developing his unique harmonic style, characterized by rich modulations and chromatic wandering. A restless, colorful, but somewhat
loose harmonic structure resulted. The quintet to a high degree
contains such a structure.

But insofar as economy of thematic resources is concerned, few

[3] D'Indy points out (in *Cobbett's Cyclopedic Survey of Chamber Music*, I, 420)
that Franck's use of two contrasting trios in the scherzo and Schumann's first employment of the same device—in the B flat Symphony—occurred in the same year:
1840.

works are so tightly knit. The cyclical principle is carried to its utmost limits. One theme, the cyclical theme of the entire composition,
appears in various guises throughout the work: as second theme and
coda theme of the first movement, in the development section of the
slow movement, and as the theme of the finale's extended coda—
each time appropriately altered in tempo and considerably modified
rhythmically. That theme, playing so important a part in providing
inner unity between the contrasting, shifting sections of the various
movements of the quintet, is in turn derived from one of the cyclical

themes of the F sharp minor trio of 1840. Truly an example of
thematic economy, to utilize in so masterful a fashion what had only
been touched upon four decades earlier!

Outwardly, each of the three movements (there is no movement
to correspond to the scherzo) is in sonata form, with exposition, development, and recapitulation, plus introduction and elaborate coda
in the outer movements. Yet so emphatically does Franck reiterate
certain of his style characteristics throughout the work that one receives the impression that the quintet is episodic. Theme transformations accompanied by abrupt changes of tempo and mood, sequence
modulations of melodic fragments, theme announcements in remote
keys (E, G, F sharp minor, A and D flat are some of the keys dwelt
upon in the F minor first movement), an abundance of *molto ritardandi* and *molto crescendi*—all these features contribute to an ebb and
flow of the music, to a lack of continuity, to an absence of that sense
of direction which was so strong a characteristic of Franck's contemporary, Brahms.

To the degree in which the quintet exhibits the same cyclical form
principles which Beethoven employed in his last quartets, it testifies
to Franck's avowed indebtedness to that composer. But in the sense

that the harmonic scheme, the instrumental color, and the entire emotional content are so purely Franck's own, there is little relationship between this work and earlier ones. The quintet is a unique composition in its combination of outward adherence to formal models and its complete subjection to the peculiar nature of Franck's musical gifts. It has earned a place in the repertoire as one of the most popular of piano quintets.

With Franck's single string quartet of 1889 we are, in the words of Vincent d'Indy, "surveying the most astonishing conception of the mind of this genius in tonal architecture." [4] The astonishment arises when the form of the first movement is examined; two separate yet related musical structures, one inscribed within the other, constitute the movement. A fully developed sonata-allegro is inserted between the parts of a slow, stately monothematic song form, with quasi-trio and recapitulation; each structure is in itself completely unified and satisfying. A diagram may clarify the relationship between the six sections.

	SECTION		TEMPO	KEY
	Theme		Lento	D major
	Exposition		Allegro	D minor and F major
	Quasi-trio		Poco lento	F minor and B flat minor
	Development		Allegro	Various
	Recapitulation		Allegro	D minor and major
	Modified recapitulation		Lento	D major

(Song Form brackets Theme, Quasi-trio, and Modified recapitulation; Sonata Form brackets Exposition, Development, and Recapitulation.)

The slow, soaring theme of the first song form, along with its veiled, fugal transformations in the quasi-trio, provide great contrast to the moderately fast, intense themes of the sonata form. Yet the contrasts, along with the great emotional variety the movement affords, are wonderfully balanced; the inner unity of the movement is never threatened.

Magnificent in structure and completely enclosed within itself,

---

[4] In *Cobbett's Cyclopedic Survey of Chamber Music*, I, 426. Our analysis is based on that of d'Indy's, which follows the quotation just made.

the movement is closely connected with those which follow. The second is a charming scherzo containing a short quotation of the first movement's song-form theme. The sublime slow movement discloses less organic connection with earlier ones; rather is it an eloquent testimony to the depth of Franck's musical feeling and a perpetual monument to the essential nobility of his musical ideals. The finale begins with an introduction which reviews the themes of the two previous movements (much as Beethoven had done in his ninth symphony) and presents a new, contrasting, and agitated theme. The main movement begins with another transformation of the first movement's song-form theme, which thus becomes the cyclical theme of the entire quartet. And more evidence of cyclical structure is yet to be presented: the finale's second theme is based upon a short connecting motive which played an important part in the first movement; the coda contains a masterful passage in which melodies from the first are combined with the scherzo's theme; and finally, the slow movement's theme returns to pronounce a benediction at the very end of the quartet.

In all respects the quartet is a major work, probably one of Franck's finest compositions. In it Franck's rich but meaningless modulation and his sometimes aimless chromatic wandering are kept at a minimum. In technical mastery, nobility of conception, and wealth of color the quartet represents one of the highest points yet attained by French music in the nineteenth century. All the concomitants of cyclical form—the *idée fixe*, the *Leitmotiv*, theme transformation—are employed probably more consistently than in any chamber-music work since Beethoven; thus the validity of that formal principle in nonprogram-music works is conclusively demonstrated. Berlioz, Wagner, and Liszt had, of course, conclusively demonstrated its efficacy in program-music contexts.

Camille Saint-Saëns (1835–1921) was contemporary with Franck and Brahms. But he remained singularly unaffected by the rich, Romantic expression of those men. In his chamber-music works one encounters a late flowering of Classical elements. His music exhibits a contrapuntal excellence, a clarity of form, and, in general, a restrained utterance that were more typical of composers a century before his time. Saint-Saëns, during his long life—much of which was spent as a virtuoso pianist and organist—attempted almost every standard chamber-music combination. A piano quintet, Opus 14, was composed about 1855; a piano quartet, Opus 41, twenty years later. Two piano trios, Opus 18 and Opus 92, appeared in 1863 and 1892, respectively; a septet for string quartet, piano, trumpet, and bass, Opus 65, was published about 1881. His first string quartet, Opus 112, was written in 1900; his second, Opus 153, in 1919, when he was eighty-four years of age. Interspersed between these works are about a dozen others for odd combinations or for piano and one instrument.

The eighteen works, written across the sixty-six-year span, 1855 to 1921, testify to Saint-Saëns's technical mastery of counterpoint, to his perception of delicate proportions, and to his great competence in all matters of musical composition. But they also disclose a lack of real inspiration in melodic writing, a certain sameness of style—indeed, the overuse of one accompanying figure throughout a movement is one of his chief characteristics—and a paucity of profound feeling. If music were to be measured only by its cleverness and originality, or even by its brilliance and effectiveness, the works of Saint-Saëns would hold a high place. Technical competence and fluency of expression are not enough, however, to insure a lasting place in the literature. The essential elements—emotional depth and musical significance—are for the most part lacking in the music of Saint-Saëns.

At the beginning of this chapter, three parallel tendencies which characterize the music of the late nineteenth century were noted. The discussion of the music of Brahms, Franck, and to a lesser degree Saint-Saëns was designed to illustrate how that music had its strongest roots in the great Classical past and thus exemplifies one of the tendencies. The remainder of this chapter will be concerned with music illustrative of a second tendency: that which gave rise to the term Nationalism. The works of Russian, Scandinavian, and Bohemian composers will be discussed, in that order. The third tendency, to make use of literary programs as a basis for musical composition, finds no expression in these pages; the great exponents of that device, namely, Berlioz, Liszt, and Wagner, were not chamber-music composers.

Musical life in Russia before the early years of the nineteenth century had been largely influenced by imported musicians; Germans and Italians, for the most part, dominated the musical scene in the few centers where music was actively cultivated. When, in the 1830's, Michael Glinka (1803–1857) turned to Russian folk song as a source of musical inspiration, the seed for a "National school" was planted. Within a few decades Russia made up for her late arrival upon the European musical stage. Glinka was followed by composers who dipped deeper into the fount whose musical treasures he had revealed; such composers, making a feature of the folk-song elements in their music, were consciously Nationalistic. But other composers appeared who eschewed folk material for the most part; yet so closely were they related to the general stream of Russian expression and style that no great distance separates them from the avowed Nationalists. In the field of chamber music, Tschaikowsky's name looms large. But Borodin, Arensky, and Glazounow are to be reckoned with also.

Peter Ilyitch Tschaikowsky was born (in Russia) in 1840. His early education included music study, but his first positions were various government clerkships. In his early twenties he resumed the study of composition, wrote several large works, and in 1866 became a faculty member of the new conservatory which Nicholas Rubinstein had founded in Moscow. About 1878 he retired from teaching, having become the recipient of a generous pension offered him by Nadejda von Meck, a wealthy widow who was enamored of his compositions. Tschaikowsky spent much time in Switzerland, Italy, and elsewhere, and visited the United States and England as a conductor of his own works. He died in St. Petersburg (Petrograd or Leningrad, to our younger readers) in 1892, the victim of a cholera attack.

Tschaikowsky's chamber-music compositions are few in number: three string quartets, one piano trio, and a single string sextet. The first quartet, in D major, Opus 11, was completed in 1871, and became the work which first carried Tschaikowsky's name outside Russia. The first movement is filled with syncopated rhythmic figures, with a great amount of running passage-work, and with unrelieved sonority. The second movement, the famous "Andante Cantabile" which every café habitué knows in dozens of arrangements, is in its original setting a charming piece, well suited to contrasting with the sonorous first movement as well as with the piquant scherzo which follows. The finale, like the andante, suggests a Russian atmosphere through its irregular phrases and its somewhat sturdy rhythms.

In many ways the D major is the best of Tschaikowsky's chamber-music works, for in later works one must admit to the presence of long arid stretches. The ability to write interestingly at all times seems to have been a characteristic of all major composers before Tschaikowsky. In the latter's music, that ability ceases to be a characteristic; we are faced with the fact that he was not always able to penetrate into the real nature of his themes deeply enough to make their developments significant. Had he restricted himself to the smaller forms, as many earlier Romantic composers had done, his lack might have escaped notice; in the larger forms the paucity of inspiration is sometimes painfully evident. Technically, all is well in these development sections; the fault was not an intellectual one. But real, detailed inspiration of the kind Brahms was exhibiting so profusely at the very time Tschaikowsky was writing, is conspicuously absent.

The second quartet, in F major, was written early in 1874 and was published as Opus 22 in 1876. Three of its movements are typical of Tschaikowsky in his more restrained moods; themes are somewhat dry, transitions and developments are orthodox, and the workmanship throughout is excellent. But the qualities of real charm or real emotional power or even of real musical interest are largely missing. In the scherzo, however, Tschaikowsky succeeded in writing an enjoyable piece of music. Phrases which combine duple and triple measures to produce seven-beat melodies are typically Russian; the scherzo's trio is repetitive, as are so many of his shorter pieces.

The third quartet, in E flat minor, Opus 30, was written early in

1875. Planned as a memorial to his friend Ferdinand Laub, a violinist and colleague of Tschaikowsky's at the Moscow Conservatory, and dedicated to Laub's memory, the quartet is funereal in tone. A slow, elegiacal introduction precedes a sad, introspective first movement in which march-like rhythms vie with great climaxes of sonority. The scherzo, rather subdued in its lightness, does no violence to the prevailing mood of the quartet. The third movement is outspokenly descriptive: elements of a chant are set between phrases of a chorale in a mirroring of the funeral service. After three movements, morbid, restrained, and elegiacal in turn, the bright finale in a major key comes as a relief.

Nicholas Rubinstein, Tschaikowsky's teacher and friend, had died in 1881. Wishing to commemorate that artist as he had commemorated Laub, Tschaikowsky turned to chamber music again. Not to the string quartet, however; Rubinstein had been a remarkable pianist (not to be confused with his more famous brother Anton), and a work with piano seemed more appropriate. The piano trio in A minor, Opus 50, written in 1882 and dedicated "to the memory of a great artist," resulted. In spite of its great length (about fifty-five minutes) the trio contains only two movements.

The first movement contains four main themes and a number of derived motives. Each theme is developed to some extent after its announcement, an elaborate development section occurs in the usual place, and the recapitulation is as extended as the exposition. Noble or impassioned or lyric themes notwithstanding, the movement does not escape a certain amount of the dryness noted above in connection with the quartets. Orchestral sonorities, involved contrapuntal passages, and brilliant virtuoso writing throughout—especially in the piano part—cannot conceal its essential musical weakness.

The second movement, a massive set of eleven variations (two of which are traditionally omitted in performance) plus an equally massive "Finale e coda," is more successful. Tschaikowsky's boundless imagination and technical fertility enable him to present the charming theme in a number of contrasting guises. Each variation assumes a characteristic form: mazurka, waltz, fugue, and scherzo are among the forms presented. The finale is a *tour de force* unlike anything else in the literature. The variation's theme is developed forcefully, at great length (Tschaikowsky himself authorized the omission of almost two-thirds of that development), and toward great climaxes. In the closing section of the movement the main theme of the first movement is reintroduced in the company of thunderous chords and flashing arpeggios; only in the last few measures is a degree of restraint and deep feeling introduced. There, as in the comparable section at the end of the first movement, a dirge-like march restores an air of solemnity to this otherwise brilliant and sentimental trio.

A sextet for strings in D minor, Opus 70, was written between 1890 and early 1892. Bearing the title *Souvenir de Florence*, the piece recalls some of Tschaikowsky's pleasant memories of a stay in Italy early in 1890. It is one of his weakest works and deserves little serious attention.

Alexander Borodin (1834–1887), one of the avowed Nationalists who called themselves "The Five," [5] wrote two string quartets (in A, 1884; in D, 1887) and contributed separate movements to various omnibus quartets composed as a joint venture by several colleagues. On the basis of the two quartets alone, Borodin's place as an esteemed chamber-music composer is assured. The A major, influenced by a theme from Beethoven's B flat quartet, Opus 130, is remarkably free of Russian atmosphere, of Nationalistic mannerisms. One or two phrases suggest native folk songs; but in the main the quartet is one of the most Classical of late nineteenth-century compositions. Throughout the work Borodin's lightness of touch and technical mastery—surprisingly great when one recalls that he was by profession a chemist—are revealed.

In the ever-popular D major quartet, as in his *Sketch of the Steppes,* Borodin imbues the music with a spaciousness reminiscent of the vast plains of his native land. That effect, plus a rhythmic energy in the fast movements, may be considered as Nationalistic

[5] Nicholas Rimsky-Korsakov, Cesar Cui, Mily Balakirev, and Modeste Moussorgsky were the others.

elements. For the rest, the quartet contains charming music, elegantly and effortlessly worked out in a mood of purest lyricism. The slow movement, the famous "Nocturne," remains a favorite of audiences and performers everywhere, in spite of its merely tuneful nature.

With the mention of Anton Arensky (1861–1906) one comes to one of Tschaikowsky's numerous disciples, one who made use of Nationalistic elements, who wrote somewhat sonorous chamber music, but who contributed nothing essentially significant to the literature. Two string quartets, Opus 11 and Opus 35, two piano trios, Opus 32 and Opus 73, and a piano quintet, Opus 51, were written between 1889 and 1905.

Alexander Glazounow (1865–1936), somewhat more prolific in the field of chamber music (seven quartets, a string quintet, several short pieces for quartet) than his contemporary, began writing under the influence of the Nationalists; his earliest works, from about 1882, disclose themes based on Russian tunes. Later works show Glazounow turning away from the Nationalists and adopting a more traditional expression.

The earliest significant composer among the Scandinavians was a Dane: Niels Gade (1817–1890). Gade's numerous chamber-music works—a quartet, a quintet, a sextet and an octet for strings, and two piano trios, all published between 1846 and 1890—have much in common with the works of Mendelssohn, even though Gade was popularly called "the Chopin of the North." Elegance of form and ease of expression are characteristic of his works; their lyric quality and sweetness of mood are agreeable, but hardly moving. One must demand that music be more than sweet if it is to endure past its composer's lifetime.

Edvard Grieg (1843–1907), Norwegian by birth, but German by training, attained a degree of originality that has permitted his music to outlive the works of his Danish and Swedish (and some of his Norwegian) contemporaries. Educated largely in Leipzig, Grieg succeeded in freeing himself, after his return to Norway, from the somewhat saccharine influences which emanated from that seat of

Mendelssohnian tradition. He turned to native folk tunes and dances, much as his Russian and Bohemian contemporaries were doing, and developed a manly, robust style of writing which embodied Norwegian melodic idioms and rhythms. Grieg's chamber-music compositions are few: one string quartet, in G minor, two movements of another quartet, and two or three fragments for other combinations.

The G minor quartet was published in 1879 as Opus 27; thus it is contemporary with Franck's piano quintet. Like that quintet, Grieg's quartet is an embodiment of the cyclical-form principle; but with that the similarity between the works ends. The quartet begins with a slow introduction; the phrases heard there appear again and again throughout the work. The first movement's second theme, its coda, and large portions of the finale are based upon the introductory phrases, and the latter's lyric breadth permeates the slow movement. Grieg, almost to a greater extent than any other nineteenth-century composer, succeeded in creating an individual style. His melodic mannerisms, his extensive use of sequences of short phrases, and his characteristic rhythms appear almost without alteration in the great majority of his works. The quartet is typical of that style. Nor do the orchestral doublings and the somewhat pretentious expression detract from the value of the work. It is filled with beautiful melodies, great exuberance, and much poetic feeling.

For generations before 1850 Bohemia had sent her best musicians to the larger musical centers of Europe. One has but to recall the names of a few: Stamitz at Mannheim, Jiranek at Dresden, Gassmann at Vienna. In all cases, these and other Bohemian musicians similarly placed wrote in the generally prevailing style; their music conformed to international patterns. Toward the middle of the nineteenth century the series of events mentioned earlier in this chapter, which culminated in Austria's granting Bohemia political independence (in 1860), caused Bohemian composers to follow the trend current throughout large parts of Europe. Many of them turned to their own national culture for inspiration and for musical content. Among the leading figures in the National school which developed was Smetana.

Bedrich Smetana was born in 1824. Largely self-trained as a pianist and composer, his first professional ventures were in the field of private teaching. In 1856 he became conductor of the Philharmonic Society's concerts in Gothenburg and produced his first symphonic poems there. The political events in Prague led to the founding of a National opera there about 1860–1862. Smetana, in his desire to contribute to the new movement, returned to Prague from Sweden, composed several operas for the new establishment (among them *The Bartered Bride*, 1866), and shortly thereafter became its chief conductor. But political opposition and severe criticism of later works undermined Smetana's health. In 1874, totally deaf, he resigned and returned to the composition of symphonic works. The cycle of tone poems *Ma Vlast* (My Country), depicting in music Bohemia's castles, woods, rivers, and mountains, was written between 1874 and 1879; of this cycle, the tone poem "The Moldau" has become universally known. Two string quartets were written about the same time; they, with an earlier piano trio, are Smetana's only chamber-music works. The intensive writing did little to improve his health. When he died, in 1884, it was in a state of insanity.

The piano trio, in G minor, Opus 15, was written about 1855, when Smetana was under the influence of his young daughter's death. It is characterized by great variety of mood. The rather free and rhapsodic first movement is at times gloomy or pensive, at times vigorous and straightforward. The scherzo, with its two contrasting trios, tender and majestic in turn, is essentially reserved. The finale (there is no slow movement) begins brightly and with energy; during the course of the movement a chorale and a funeral march are heard. With so many contrasting elements, a lack of unity is inevitable. Yet the trio's many poignant passages and moments of real beauty and its excellence of technical detail make it a worthy example of Smetana's pre-Nationalist style.

More than two decades later Smetana turned to chamber music again, to describe the course of his own life: both of his quartets bear the title *Aus meinem Leben* (From My Life). The first, in E minor, was written about 1876 and published in 1881 as Opus 115. Smetana supplied a complete program for the work.[6] The four movements depict the "romantic tendency and unsatisfied yearnings" of his early life, seen in a restless, but highly organized, first movement; the lighter side of his youthful existence, in a charming polka; "the bliss of my first love for . . . my wife," reflected in a moving and beautifully sustained slow movement; and, in the lively finale, "the discovery how to treat the National material in music." But also in the finale, "the beginning of my deafness, a glimpse into the melancholy future," mirrored in a sustained high E over a somber tremolo in the lower instruments.

The second quartet, considerably shorter than the first, and in a sense disorganized, is in D minor. Written about 1882–1883, it was published posthumously in 1889 without opus number. "The new quartet takes up—after the catastrophe" of Smetana's deafness, but goes no further in autobiographical detail. Composed during a time when Smetana was prey to intense morbidity and when his mental powers were fast waning, it is characterized by impulsive contrasts and lack of cohesion. Its four movements form a regrettably sad memorial to the unhappy fate suffered by the essentially cheerful Smetana. The first quartet, on the other hand, has by its effective writing, brilliance, and Nationalistic flavor won a commanding place in the literature. It stands as one of Smetana's characteristic works, one which combines program and Nationalistic traits in a predominantly musical framework.

Far more prolific in chamber music than Smetana, and perhaps of greater musical importance, was Antonín Dvořák. Born at Mülhausen, Bohemia, in 1841, his early life was not a happy one. His father's wish to have him trained as a butcher scarcely comported with his own desire to become a musician. In the end he broke away, self-taught to some extent, and became a member of a theater orchestra in Prague. He played viola and composed; but not until he was in his thirties did his compositions attract any favorable attention. From about 1875 he devoted himself exclusively to composition; friendship with Brahms and von Bülow helped him to gain

[6] Newmarch, in *Cobbett's Cyclopedic Survey of Chamber Music*, II, 427 ff.

favorable hearings for his works. During the course of a few years he gained considerable fame as a teacher of composition. Dvořák visited England several times between 1884 and 1891, conducting his own works at various festivals; his success and the quality of his works added to his personal renown. From 1892 to 1895 he served as director of the National Conservatory in New York and visited a Bohemian community in Spillville, Iowa. He returned to Prague in 1895, resumed his post at the Conservatory in that city, and in 1901 was made the director of the school. When he died, in 1904, he was secure in his position as Bohemia's greatest and best-loved composer.

Dvořák's chamber-music works include four piano trios, three piano quartets (one of them with two violins), a piano quintet, a trio for string instruments, eight string quartets, two string quintets, one sextet for strings, and almost a dozen (published and unpublished) early or smaller compositions—thirty works in all. In them one may see how Dvořák was influenced by one or another composer throughout his lifetime.

A series of early works written between 1861 and 1873 includes five string quartets, a string quintet, a piano quintet (not the more famous Opus 81), and *The Cypresses* (ten love songs arranged for string quartet as Opus 8). According to Sourek,[7] these unpublished works reflect at first Dvořák's adherence to Beethoven and Schubert; then, about 1870, a sudden infatuation with the methods and forms of Liszt and Wagner. That phase expired rather quickly; by 1874 Dvořák had returned to the path marked out by Classical models.

Between 1874 and 1877 lie three string quartets, Opera 16, 80, and 34, in A minor, E major, and D minor, respectively; a string quintet for two violins, viola, cello, and bass, in G major, originally planned as Opus 18, but eventually published as Opus 77; two piano trios in B flat and G minor, Opus 21 and Opus 26, respectively; and a piano quartet in D major, Opus 23. The B flat trio, lying about midway in the period, represents both the strengths and the weaknesses of Dvořák's style at this time. Its first movement is clear in form and straightforward in expression. But some of its rhythmic figures are

[7] In *Cobbett's Cyclopedic Survey of Chamber Music*, I, 355–370.

a bit obvious; phrase extensions and development episodes follow merely the usual course, and a general air of immaturity prevails. An otherwise beautiful slow movement is marred by the overuse of a few standard devices. Likewise in the finale: inane sequence passages destroy to some extent a forthright and vigorous movement. Only the third movement, a quasi-intermezzo, is free from such structural weaknesses.

The works which lie between 1878 and about 1890, on the other hand, show that Dvořák had freed himself from the somewhat rigid expression derived from his Classical models and had entered upon a period in which Slavonic elements predominated. Nine chamber-music works were written during those years: a string sextet in A major, Opus 48, in 1878; two string quartets, Opus 51 and Opus 61, in E flat and C major, respectively, 1878 and 1881; two piano trios, Opus 65, in F minor, in 1883, and Opus 90, in E minor, in 1890; a piano quintet in A major, Opus 81, in 1887; a piano quartet in E flat, Opus 87, in 1889; a terzetto for two violins and viola in C major, Opus 74, in 1887; a set of bagatelles for two violins, cello, and piano, in G major, Opus 47, written about 1878, but published in 1890. Of these works, the E flat quartet, the piano quintet, and the E minor piano trio may be singled out for closer attention.

The success of Dvořák's sextet, Opus 48, with its outspoken Slavonic elements, led to his being commissioned to write a string quartet embodying similar elements; [8] the E flat quartet, Opus 51, resulted. The Slavonic touches are seen in the first movement's themes, in the "Dumka" which constitutes the second movement, and in the brisk, dance-like finale. The *dumka* occurs so frequently in Dvořák's works that it may well be defined a bit more closely. A *dumka* is an elegy, hence may be expected to be melancholy in mood; but it also contains a middle section, usually in fast tempo and always contrasting sharply in mood with the elegiacal sections. Thus the *dumka* was a perfect vehicle for Dvořák, who was fond of abrupt emotional changes. *Dumky* is the plural form. But the E flat quartet as a whole is much more than an expression of Nationalistic elements. It is the

[8] *Ibid.*

reflection of a capable, sensitive, imaginative, and humorous composer; for Dvořák was all these things. The first movement breathes an air of good nature which is in no way incompatible with its contrapuntal excellence. The "Dumka" offers great contrasts between the sentimental and scherzo-like sections. The "Romanze" is a moving piece, and the finale delightfully boisterous.

The A major piano quintet again reveals a Dvořák who is essentially happy. Its first movement is melodious, brilliant, and altogether an excellent piece of music. Many of the rhythmic devices one associates with Brahms are here evident; what might be called rhythmic counterpoint becomes characteristic. This rhythmic vitality, which forms an important element of Dvořák's later style, appears in constructions like the following:

The second movement is again a *dumka;* its contrasting sections are poignant and lively in turn. The scherzo breathes the spirit of the *furiant,* an energetic triple-measure Slavonic dance. And the finale, a gay and boisterous dance-like movement, suggests a collection of national airs, without actually quoting such airs. One is continually struck by the variety of Dvořák's means of expression. Lyric tunes, melodies dripping with sentiment, brisk fugal passages, and sections containing elaborate contrapuntal devices—all are there. This variety is largely responsible for the charm and sterling qualities which his music possesses, and allows it always to be heard with pleasure.

The E minor piano trio, Opus 90, lies near the close of Dvořák's Slavonic period. Its content is unique: for virtually the only time in his chamber-music works he departed from the conventional four-movement form and wrote a collection of six *dumky* (hence the popular nickname of "Dumky Trio"). Alternations of slow and fast tempo, of somberness and abandon, are characteristic of the trio; inevitably so, the *dumka* form being what it is. But in Dvořák's hands that form did not always retain a simple ABA pattern. The return of the A (slow) section is seldom exact; rather is it a greatly modified recapitulation embodying changes of tone color, of instrumental figuration, even of harmony. As a result, the trio exhibits a certain lack of cohesion and gives the effect of being composed of many short fragments. Only the facts that the first three *dumky* are connected and harmonically related (E, C sharp minor, and A, respectively)— forming in effect one long movement—and that the fourth, fifth, and sixth are unrelated—thus completing the illusion of a four-movement form—save the trio from making a completely episodic effect. Inner threads of unity are provided by the contrasting moods which prevail: sentiment and pathos in the slow sections; abandon and forced gayety in the fast.

The years 1892 to 1895 mark the dates of Dvořák's stay in the "New World." Two chamber-music works were written during that visit: a string quartet in F major, Opus 96 (the "American Quartet") and a string quintet in E flat, Opus 97. These works are characterized by his "impressions" of American folk music (American taken in its widest sense to include many of the European and extra-Caucasian elements which find expression in that music), and not by direct quotation of American tunes. Thus, one finds in the quartet themes based on the Oriental pentatonic scale (F-G-A-C-D); in the quintet, rhythmic figures popularly associated with the American Indian; and in both works, a variety of mood which reflects the countless facets of life in the United States.

But apart from these local, quasi-descriptive elements, the works reveal Dvořák's depth of feeling, the resourcefulness of his technique, and his boundless imagination. Clear forms, subtle contrasts of texture and tone color, and great melodic charm combine to place these among his finest works. The "American Quartet" is deservedly one of the most popular of late nineteenth-century chamber-music compositions.

After his return to Bohemia, in 1895, Dvořák composed two more quartets: Opus 106 in G major and Opus 105 in A flat (obviously, the first written was the second to be published). With them his long activity as a chamber-music composer, extending across almost thirty-five years, came to an end. Filled with joy at returning to his native land, secure in the affections of his countrymen, and honored by all of Europe, Dvořák gave expression to his feelings of peace and contentment. No longer concerned with Nationalistic expression or exposed to an alien culture, he reverted to a Classical purity of form. The two quartets, despite several passages which are devoid of deep feeling, are among his most successful works.

Seen in retrospect, the chamber-music compositions of Dvořák reveal a composer second to none in technical ability, in melodic invention, and in formal perception. Contrasting moods are typical; passages in which one is suddenly transported from the depths of melancholy to the heights of wild abandon are found frequently in his pages. In only one respect does he fail to warrant a place among chamber music's immortals: in his almost total lack of profundity. All other types of expression are reflected in his music: passages of deepest morbidity and most intense joy, and all shades between. But the universally significant kind of music, the music which enthralls or inspires the listener, is missing. In that respect Dvořák is akin to Mendelssohn. Both composers succeeded in writing charming, dignified, and even moving music; but it is always a surface emotion that is touched. Many chamber-music composers in the late nineteenth century were technically superb and musically inspired; but only Brahms was able to write profoundly.

13

THE CONTEMPORARY WORLD

ONE WHO wishes to write convincingly about the direction of present-day music should be either a participant in that music's creation or a critic proficient in prophecy. Only then can he unerringly underline this or that trend, style, or composition and persuade his readers that it contains within itself the germ of the future; only then can he name "the" composer of the age in whose shadow later generations will stand. That contemporary music has a direction can hardly be denied. A backward glance over the music of the past few decades discloses a reaction to this, a counter-reaction to that, and a return to something else. In short, music is on the way to a new condition. Only the adherent of a particular style or the seer can venture to predict its path of development.

Being neither the one nor the other, this author can do no more than report events, describe new techniques, and summarize trends. Twentieth-century chamber music exists in large quantities; new composers emerge almost monthly. New compositions are hailed, performed once—and forgotten; new style tendencies are eagerly exploited, imitated—and heard of no more. This chapter attempts to survey that growing, changing field and to discuss its most significant aspects. Inevitably, it is an incomplete and, perhaps, superficial account of contemporary developments. But first a brief summary of the entire period under discussion, namely, the period from about 1890 to the present, may be of help in clarifying the complex situation in which modern music finds itself.

We had reached the last decade of the nineteenth century. The subjectivity, the outpouring of emotion, the extravagance which often led to bad taste, the attention to sentimental detail—in short, all the elements of post-Romanticism were in fullest bloom, were at the height of their influence. The grandiloquent, sometimes pretentious expression of Wagner was emerging, in the orchestral field, in the tone poems of Richard Strauss (1864–1949). Brahms was still contending against that type of expression, as he had struggled against it during his lifetime. But Brahms reacted, not by going forward to something new, but by endeavoring to restore the balance and the clarity of the past. Such a negative reaction was bound to fail; Brahms was himself too much a Romanticist at heart successfully to avoid becoming infected by the extravagant harmony and personalized expression which surrounded him.

A stronger, positive reaction was needed; inevitably, a forward-looking composer appeared, to give music a new direction. At the hands of Claude Debussy, in the 1890's, that new direction made itself apparent. Finding in Moussorgsky a freedom of melodic line and in Wagner a chromaticism which seemed to presage a new employment of tonal resources, Debussy seized upon those elements and created the musical style called Impressionism.

The new style was strong in its appeal from the first, influenced many later composers, and did much to clear the air of post-Romantic excesses. But neither during Debussy's lifetime nor up to the present moment has the subjective Romantic style died out completely. In the field of chamber music its rearguard included, through the early decades of the twentieth century, such composers as Fauré, d'Indy, and Dohnányi. These men modified their techniques, of course; but they remained tied, in some degree, to Romanticism's subjective point of view.

Impressionism in its early stages was also subjective in its point of view. The very term adopted to characterize the new style gives evidence of its personal nature. It remained for later Impressionists to become somewhat objective in their musical utterances, thus to employ the new style as a means of establishing a new aesthetic code. Influenced largely by Maurice Ravel, post-Impressionistic composers appeared in France, England, and the United States.

In the years before the first World War, about 1910 to 1913, Paris and the musical world were startled by the compositions, large ballet works for the most part, of a comparative newcomer: Igor Stravinsky. Characterized by a complete negation of accepted rhythmic, harmonic, and formal procedures, Stravinsky's works seemed unlike any music ever heard before. These negations were later seen to be logical extensions of customary procedures; the works were polyrhythmic, polytonal, and the like. In their use of a new, sentiment-free expression and in their air of stark primitivism, however, they pointed to a dissonant future.

About the same time Arnold Schönberg, a Viennese composer who had begun his work in the traditional, advanced Romantic style then current in Vienna, reached an expressive impasse. Convinced that significant musical creation did not lie merely in an extension of that style, Schönberg began his sensational development away from tradition. His experiments led to atonality, gave rise to spare, sparse tonal skeletons and culminated in the "twelve-tone technique." Simultaneously a Hungarian, Béla Bartók, working independently of Schönberg, was evolving in a related atonal direction, employing the additional element of Hungarian folk music.

The war years, to about 1920, put a temporary halt to international communication among musicians. When the smoke of battles had been dissipated, the musical scene revealed itself as one of frank experiment. Stravinsky, Schönberg, and Bartók went their several ways; Ravel and other post-Impressionists were strongly opposed by a group of French composers headed by Darius Milhaud. Experiments with extreme dissonance, with jazz elements, with oriental and primitive flavors led to a decade of wild extravagance and cacophony. Out of this period of experiment grew a desire to return—no one knew to what. The clarity of eighteenth-century music became one ideal, and a neo-Classicism arose. And out of Germany came Paul Hindemith, to bend the neo-Classicism to his own expressive purposes—one of which resulted in the style called "linear counterpoint."

In the years after 1930, with political upheavals in Europe and new war clouds looming over the horizon, many leading composers came to the United States. Here and elsewhere throughout the musical world, each had developed a following among native composers. In England, throughout Latin America, and in the United States the influence of Stravinsky, Schönberg, Bartók, Milhaud, and Hindemith has been felt. But native composers of the last two decades have also begun to write individually and to contribute to the formation of a definite, unique and indigenous American music. Among chamber-music composers Goossens, Bloch, Piston, Porter, and Harris have been most active.

The foregoing incomplete and generalized sketch of the years from about 1890 to the present will provide a basis for discussing the activities of chamber-music composers during the last half-century. It will enable us to group together those works which disclose similarities of structure and style and to relate the works of one style tendency to those of another. It will hope to show that contemporary composers differ in their expressive aims, in their technical means, and in their aesthetic results. They are not easily lumped together into one dissonant pot and disposed of with the term "modern."

Claude Debussy (1862–1918) made but one contribution to chamber-music literature: a string quartet in G minor, Opus 10, written about 1893. Outwardly, the quartet owes much to Franck: the cyclical-form principle is at work in three of its four movements. It owes as much to Russian contemporaries, of whose music Debussy had some knowledge: the whole-tone scale is an important element in the quartet's melodic line, as it is in certain Russian folk music. But its content, its sensitivity, and its general atmosphere are Debussy's own. In the 1890's, quantity of tone and instrumentation were closely related to musical quality—as they are in Richard Strauss's early symphonic poems—and richness of emotional expression was deemed an essential. The quartet's cool restraint and lack of blatancy immediately showed the way to a new kind of music. Suggesting rather than stating, concerned more with the color of the fleeting moment than with form and structure, and characterized by shimmering arpeggios and tremolos, the new music reflected the aims of the poets and the painters who were called Impressionists. Thus, the latter term stands in opposition to realism, the outstanding exponents of which were the post-Romanticists.

In later works Debussy's technique was expanded. Unprepared or unresolved dissonances made their appearance; a greater freedom of modulation based on enharmonic changes [1] became characteristic, and a texture became typical in which contrapuntal and outspokenly homophonic devices were freely alternated. The consistent use of the new technique created a style eminently suited to the aims of the Impressionists. Preoccupation with isolated sounds and with new color effects achieved through the increased use of dissonance, employment of a greater variety of chords, rapid changes of harmony, and a departure from the accepted methods of thematic development—all these became characteristics of the new music.

In the G minor quartet, however, not all the new techniques are yet apparent. Orthodox methods of theme development are still in evidence; a variety of simple repetitions, of sequence modulation, of rhythmic transformations, and even some contrapuntal imitation are present. The forms of the individual movements, too, correspond rather closely to the traditional patterns: sonata-allegro, scherzo with trio, and song form. With the retention of all these customary devices, it is inevitable that one feels the quartet's kinship with earlier works. But there is also a feeling of great originality in Debussy's employment of short melodic figures, of sustained trills, of colorful tremolos and repeated notes. The general atmosphere of the music is new; it is characterized by a refinement and elegance, by a delicacy of expression, and by a variety of veiled colors virtually unknown in earlier music. The originalities which Debussy introduced into this quartet became commonplaces in the works of later composers who were influenced by him. Thus, the quartet stands on the dividing line between the turgid, emotionally rich music of the late nineteenth century and the objective, somewhat intangible music of the early twentieth.

[1] The device whereby a note, E flat, let us say, is transformed (in notation) to D sharp, and whereby a whole new range of keys is made available.

Gabriel Fauré (1845–1924) composed his first chamber-music work in 1879: a piano quartet in C minor, Opus 15. Other works were written at long intervals across almost half a century. A second piano quartet, in G minor, Opus 45, appeared in 1886; two piano quintets in D minor and C minor, Opus 89 and Opus 115, were published in 1906 and 1921, respectively; a single piano trio in D minor, Opus 120, was written about 1923. Finally, a string quartet in E major, Opus 121, was written in Fauré's eightieth year, the year of his death.

Those six works are in a category separate from other chamber music of the time. Their general harmonic content, their melodic types, and even their forms are not essentially different from other post-Romantic works. A vigorous expression of honest sentiment, a mood that is forthright, delicate, or merry in turn, a fluency of utterance—all these are to be found in Fauré. And yet, such terms do not adequately describe this music, for over and above such characteristics is a poetic feeling, a combination of directness and reticence. What in Schumann was akin to moodiness must be called reflectiveness in Fauré; the dramatic passion of Brahms is transformed by Fauré into something disembodied, remote, and objective; the chromatic richness of Wagner becomes in Fauré a considered and controlled manipulation of the chromatic scale. Many other late Romantic devices are in evidence, yet all are refined and brought into balance. We are told that Fauré is so typically French that only a born Frenchman can enjoy his music. Surely, anyone with an ear for sensitive expression and subtle shading of tone quality can profit by the serene and dignified poetry which is reflected in Fauré.

With Vincent d'Indy (1851–1931) the case is somewhat similar. Two piano trios, Opus 29 and Opus 98; two piano quartets, Opus 7 and Opus 81; three string quartets, Opera 35, 45, and 96; a string sextet, Opus 92—these, with a few minor works, are d'Indy's contributions to the literature. The piano quartet Opus 7 was written in 1878; the piano trio Opus 98, about 1929. During those fifty-one years d'Indy remained faithful to a reserved and somewhat conservative style. As befitted a pupil of Franck, he made considerable use of cyclical-form principles; as a Frenchman, he strove for clarity of intention and refined expression.

But in that clarity itself lies a possible source of musical weakness. D'Indy's clear lines and forms appear as the result more of calculation than of expressive necessity. His cyclical themes are transformed under the influence of a dominating intellect, sometimes at the expense of warmth or even real musical interest. Reserve, austerity, and technical excellence characterize d'Indy's chamber music. Charming moments occur often; the presence of considerable rhythmic inventiveness contributes to that charm. Surrounded however, by a half-century of music which appeals either through its noble sentiment or technical innovation, the music of d'Indy appears dated and something less than eternal.

Ernst von Dohnányi, born in Hungary in 1877, must be placed in a separate category from the two preceding composers. In his early works the influence of Brahms was strongly felt; this was also the case with Fauré. But Dohnányi's original melodic turn and his contrapuntal skill came to minimize that external influence. The result, even in his Opus 1, the C minor piano quintet, published in 1902, is a quality of music that need yield to no other for freshness of thematic material, formal clarity, and rhythmic interest. Dohnányi's melodies often lean toward sentimentality, but invariably they are kept under control. In the quintet, as in many later works, Dohnányi wrote multivoiced passages which are unequaled for sheer melodiousness and unashamed emotional appeal.

The quintet of 1902 was followed by three string quartets: Opus 7, in A major, 1903; Opus 15, in D flat, 1907; Opus 33, in A minor, about 1926. A small but effective string trio in C major, Opus 10, was published about 1904; a second piano quintet, in E flat minor, Opus 26, in 1919. The quartets reveal in ever-increasing measure those of Dohnányi's style traits which were first seen in the C minor piano quintet. In addition come a complete mastery of form and a greater pungency and variety in the harmonic scheme. Not essentially influenced by contemporary developments, Dohnányi nevertheless progressed toward a more rugged melodic line and greater freedom in key relationships. The new developments are most strikingly revealed in the second piano quintet.

The outstanding features of the quintet are its contrapuntal texture and its angular melodic lines. The fugal last movement contains a plethora of augmentations, diminutions, inversions, and the like—to a degree virtually unknown in other works contemporary with it. True to his expressive code, Dohnányi does not allow his contrapuntal fluency to obscure the dramatic or colorful purposes to which it is applied. In form, also, the quintet is unique. Although not based on cyclical-form principles, first movement themes are quoted in the intermezzo and the finale and serve as unifying material. The intermezzo is a masterpiece of theme transformation and varied moods.

How shall one treat Max Reger (1873–1916)? No composer held in such esteem by so many sincere and intelligent musicians can be ignored. No composer who has written almost three dozen massive chamber-music works containing passages of real musical worth should be neglected. No composer whose technical attainments and contrapuntal skill are so self-evident dare remain unmentioned. Yet the forbidding quality of much of Reger's chamber music makes even adequate reporting of its content and direction more than difficult. In a book such as this, whose second part is devoted so largely to works in the present-day repertoire, one may be justified in attempting little more than a catalogue of Reger's chamber music; only a minute portion of its bulk has found a place in the permanent literature. For those readers who find his polyphonic massiveness appealing, the following list is appended: five string quartets; one clarinet quintet; two each of piano quintets, quartets, and trios; one string sextet; two string trios, and more than a dozen sonatas for various pairs of instruments. This author must honestly admit his own temperamental inability to look beyond its dryness, its thickness of texture, and its obscure forms to find the musical worth which its admirers claim for it.

The single string quartet of Maurice Ravel (1875–1937), like the quartet of Debussy, is an early work. Composed in 1902–1903 and dedicated to Fauré, it represents an early period in Ravel's development. The later typical preoccupation with isolated, glistening colors —to the virtual exclusion of thematic or formal interest—is not always present. Singularly melodious and regular in its sonata form, the first movement is precise and economical in its use of thematic material. The scherzo is agitated and broadly lyrical in turn. The final movement of the quartet, however, employs many of the devices which became typical in Ravel's later works. An expressive melody, for example, is suddenly interrupted by a vivid splash of colorful sound, introduced by means of rapid tremolos on a short melodic fragment. And again, sweeping arpeggio figures accompany a sustained phrase and serve to veil the underlying harmonies most effectively. The finale as a whole is a dramatic movement in which a variety of meters—5/4 and 5/8 among them—contribute to a restlessness of mood. It provides a striking preview of what the Impressionistic style will later contain.

The *Introduction and Allegro*, for harp solo with accompaniment furnished by flute, clarinet, and string quartet, was written about 1906. Although it is sometimes found on chamber-music programs, the work is essentially an orchestral piece, hence requires no further mention here.

In 1915 Ravel composed a piano trio in A minor. That work reveals the full development of his Impressionism. Extreme use of arpeggio figures, rapid repeated notes and tremolos through long passages, many harmonics (overtones) in the string parts, and increased range in the piano—all these contributed to the extension of Ravel's color palette. Harmonies based on parallel use of neighboring triads (akin to the old *faux bourdon*), added seconds and sixths in chords, unresolved dissonances—these gave the work its quality of freshness. Themes based on modal formulas and scales which create pentatonic patterns supplied an exotic tinge to the melodic line. Free phrase structures, an avoidance of symmetry and an absence of traditional development devices contributed to a breakdown of accepted forms. And above all, an avoidance of sentimental expression and emotional tumult gave rise to the cool, objective, colorful, and aloof utterance which is typical of Ravel's music.

Echoes of Impressionistic technique were not confined to the country of their origin. They appeared in the early chamber music of Eugene Goossens (b. 1893), born in France, but connected with English and American musical life since the early years of the century. In Italy, Ottorino Respighi (1879–1936) made use of them; in the United States certain works of Charles Martin Loeffler (1861–1935) are based on them. In France, Paul Dukas (1865–1935) and Florent Schmitt (b. 1870) continued the style established by Debussy and Ravel. Most of the composers mentioned here wrote chamber music; the works of Eugene Goossens have continued to the present (even though their style is not consistently Impressionistic) and may be examined in greater detail.

Of Goossens's several early works in the field, the piano trio *Five Impressions of a Holiday*, Opus 15, for flute or violin, cello, and piano, written in 1914, follows most directly the stylistic model provided by Ravel. Fragments of whole-tone scales, triads with added notes, a play with the sound of isolated chords, parallel harmonies, and the inevitable tremolos and arpeggios—all the elements of technical Impressionism are there. But with them is a ruggedness of expression and an energetic employment of the trio's full resources that remove the work from the category of objective, aloof music. Here are directness and vitality of a kind seldom found in related works of the time.

In half-a-dozen works written in the decade 1914–1924, including his first string quartet, Opus 14, Goossens grew away from Ravel's influences to some extent; became more dissonant and even more direct. Those tendencies culminated in the concertino for string octet, written in 1928 and published in 1930 without opus number. The concertino, which can also be played by a string orchestra according to the composer's preface, is in three connected movements. It is an example of that large body of works which came to be called "neo-Classical." Obviously, neo-Baroque would have been a better term for this piece, since elements of pre-1750 music reappear, Energetic themes based on diatonic scale lines, treated polyphonically and presented in square, solid rhythmic patterns are typical of the first movement. Considerable use is made of standard contrapuntal devices: close imitation, theme augmentation, and melodic counterpoint. The second movement is relaxed: "in the style of a folk song" is written at the head of the movement. In the third, the Baroque texture is again evident. But harmonically the concertino belongs to the twentieth century. Passages in parallel motion at dissonant intervals add a pungency to the tonal whole; free use of contrasting chords adds an element of polytonality.

The second quartet, Opus 59, was composed in 1940 and deserves the term neo-Classical. Its first three movements are written in strict forms, but with the freest of developments and great variety of rhythms. A few ever-recurring figures provide a feeling of unity and serve as points of reference as the extremely dissonant and contrapuntal fabric rolls by. The contrapuntal devices, extending as far as a fugato in the first movement, are skillfully employed. With all its neo-Classical elements, Impressionistic colors are still in evidence. The influence of Ravel, seen in Goossens's early works, is still alive in his latest.

The full import of Igor Stravinsky's (b. 1882) appearance on the musical scene in Paris about 1909 can be gathered only through a discussion of his music for the ballet. Since so full a treatment is not appropriate here, it must suffice to describe briefly the nature of Stravinsky's innovations. The works written between 1910 and 1914 (music to *L'Oiseau de feu* and *Le Sacre du printemps* are perhaps the best known) contained elements drawn from many sources. Impressionistic passages in *L'Oiseau* stood opposite sections based on almost primitive writing; extreme dissonance derived from new relations between individual tones, as in parts of *Le Sacre*, was contrasted with diatonic, clear consonance, notably in certain of *Petrouchka's* passages. Suggestions of polytonality appeared side by side with overt use of "old-fashioned" melodic devices. But several features dominated all these works: an avoidance of sentiment, a mechanized and impartial play with all the elements of the tonal system, and an experimentation with new concepts of instrumentation.

Out of such confusion of style tendencies came Stravinsky's early chamber-music works. Several sets of songs accompanied by small groups of instruments, three pieces for string quartet and a concertino for the same combination—these were written between 1914 and 1920. Another work, the *Histoire du soldat,* scored for clarinet, bassoon, trumpet, trombone, percussion, violin, and bass, and requiring the services of a narrator and conductor for its complete performance was written about 1918; a version for clarinet, violin, and piano was made subsequently. An octet for wind instruments (flute, clarinet, and pairs of bassoons, trumpets, and trombones) published in 1924 and a pastorale for violin and four woodwinds, about 1934, carried forward the search for complete objectivity, for new uses of dynamics and instrumental color. Stravinsky's later works, mostly orchestral compositions, disclose that he has synthesized many of the diverse elements which characterize one or another of his earlier compositions and has emerged with a restrained expression and a new regard for Classical form principles and for a certain integrity of tonality.

Had Arnold Schönberg (1874–1951) stopped writing in 1910, his place in the history of music would be easily defined. A string sextet, *Verklärte Nacht,* was written about 1899 and published as Opus 4, in 1905; two string quartets, Opus 7 and Opus 10, appeared in 1907 and 1910, respectively. In those works Schönberg disclosed himself as a fluent, impassioned Romanticist. The sextet employed the technique and the form of the tone poem and became a masterpiece of dramatic expression and emotional variety in a rich, eloquent, and subjective texture. The quartets, equally subjective in content, but characterized by four-movement patterns, represent other aspects of late Romanticism. The first quartet contains suggestions of cyclical form, in that many of its first-movement themes occur in later sections of the work; the second includes a part for soprano voice. All three works contain Wagnerian climaxes; chromatic harmonies and intense lyric melodies are found throughout. With these compositions the last step in the expansion of subjective emotional expression had been taken. Yet in some respects even these works contained within themselves tentative steps toward Schönberg's future style development.

The path that development was to take was revealed in the *Kammersymphonie*, Opus 9, written about 1906. There Schönberg abandoned the tonic triad to a large extent and based his themes on successions of fourths: the negation of tonality was made possible and the road to atonality was opened. In the quartets two further elements of his new style are to be seen: (*a*) a theme seldom appears in a concrete form, but is varied on each appearance, and (*b*) the melodic line becomes angular to an extreme degree, embraces leaps of major sevenths, minor ninths, and similar large intervals. Expansion of those elements, to the virtual exclusion of customary relationships between one tone and another, is seen in *Pierrot Lunaire*, Opus 21, written in 1912. In that work twenty-one short poems are set to music in a half-recited, half-sung style, to the accompaniment of piano, flute, clarinet, violin, and cello. Intricate contrapuntal passages, rhapsodic sections, and a wealth of new instrumental colors occur in the cycle.

Then followed a group of works in which Schönberg's probing among tonal resources became systematized. A serenade for mandolin, guitar, two clarinets, and string trio, with a part for male voice in one of its seven movements, was published as Opus 24 about 1923. A woodwind quintet, Opus 26, appeared in 1924. In 1926, as Opus 29, came a suite for piano, three string, and three woodwind instruments. A third string quartet was published, as Opus 30, in 1927. With this group of four works the principles of the "twelve-tone system" were clarified. Schönberg and his disciples became eloquent in their explanations of the system and have been of great influence on a whole generation of later composers.

The twelve tones refer to the complete chromatic scale. In the system, as finally laid down by several of Schönberg's pupils, the notes of that scale are arranged in an arbitrary manner; the resulting series of tones, called a tone-row, may be inverted, may be played backwards, and that retrograde version may be inverted. Those four chromatic lines then become the basis for the desired piece's construction. Melodies are drawn out of them, chords are constructed out of them (the first three tones of the row may form one "triad," the following three another, and so forth), and various other prescribed actions may be taken. Apparently, in some cases the entire series must be heard before any portion may be repeated.

The following examples, drawn from the suite, Opus 29, will illustrate the procedure. The basic form of the tone-row is as given below.[2] The examples disclose the manner in which the rules are ap-

By permission of the copyright owners, Universal Edition, Vienna.

[2] The author believes that he has abstracted the tone-row correctly. He regrets that the direction of his interests does not allow him to pursue his study of the twelve-tone system far enough to verify, in every measure of the suite, the truth of the series as he has given it.

plied in musical creation. And they disclose further the fascinating mathematical possibilities of this purely abstract, arbitrary system of composition.

It must be emphasized, however, that the twelve-tone system describes only the technical aspects of Schönberg's music. Every variety of music has its own principles and formulas; Schönberg has merely substituted his formulas for the diatonic, chords-built-on-thirds, tonic-dominant formulas which served music from the early seventeenth century to the late nineteenth. His compositions must be evaluated for their musical results, for the quality of the musical responses to which they give rise.

The experiments of Schönberg and his school, which in two large steps led from post-Romanticism to the tone-row technique, were soon seen as a reaction against the Impressionistic style. For Impressionism was concerned with color; the new atonal music was not interested in that element. Impressionism had its roots in the tonal system; the new music led away from that system in an attempt to develop its own. Impressionism often took the form of program music; the new music was abstract and severe. Early Impressionism provided an outlet for subjective sentiment; the new music, which soon came to be called "expressionistic," avoided emotional display and confined itself largely to bare, impersonal melodic lines. The term "expressionism" is obviously misleading, since it applies equally well to all music and is no longer in general use.

Schönberg's fourth quartet, Opus 37, was published in 1939. According to Ernst Křenek,[3] this quartet no longer exhibits the close imitations which were characteristic of the works of Schönberg's middle period (from Opus 26 to Opus 36). The tendency toward a dominant rhythmic flow is arrested here, nor is the clarity of form which was a feature of the third quartet attained in the fourth.

Of the number of composers who have to a large extent adopted the twelve-tone system, Anton von Webern (1883–1945), Alban Berg (1885–1935), and Křenek (b. 1900) may be singled out. A review of their works indicates that variety of expression is possible in

[3] Writing in *Modern Music*, XXI, No. 3 (March, 1944), 131-138.

that system, too. Von Webern remains largely within the style marked out by Schönberg, but attains a new degree of concentration, refinement, and brevity in its employment. A string quartet, Opus 28, written in 1938, and two earlier sets of pieces for quartet, 1909 and 1913, respectively, reflect those characteristics. The three movements of Opus 28 require barely six minutes for performance. The quartet's "thematic material" and its employment can best be described by appending a few measures of the first movement. A similar texture prevails throughout the entire work.

By permission of the copyright owners, Boosey & Hawkes, London and New York.

Alban Berg, one of Schönberg's earliest followers, was not primarily a chamber-music composer. Two early works, a quartet, Opus 3, from 1909, and a *Lyric Suite* for quartet, 1927, exhibit a tendency to introduce certain Wagnerian melodic devices into the system; [4] the evidence is strong that Berg attempted to combine the richness of late nineteenth-century Romantic expression and the twelve-tone technique. That he succeeded to some extent is revealed by the greater amount of emotional warmth in his music.

Ernst Křenek presents a more difficult case. His earliest works were founded on a solid contrapuntal style (Křenek was not at first a Schönberg disciple); a strong jazz influence is apparent in others, and an outspoken adherence to the twelve-tone system in the latest. Finally, a degree both of subjective feeling and experimental dissonance are typical of all his music. Thus his work is more than

[4] Evans, in *Cobbett's Cyclopedic Survey of Chamber Music*, I, 120.

eclectic; it summarizes many of the trends which prevailed from about 1920 to 1940. Among his published works are four string quartets; the first, Opus 6, 1922; the third, Opus 20, 1924; the fifth, Opus 65, 1930, and the sixth, Opus 78, 1937.

The six quartets of Béla Bartók (1881–1945) are among the most successful of twentieth-century chamber-music works. In a tonal language that is unique in its flexibility, Bartók created a series of works which are unsurpassed in the variety of their sonorous effects, in the power of their rhythmic appeal, but more especially in the rich expressiveness they achieve in their dissonant, atonal idiom. Beginning with the second string quartet (the first, written about 1908, belongs to a style category which Bartók did not pursue in later works), published in 1920, each succeeding one disclosed new musical possibilities. Thus, the second quartet contains moments of deepest gloom and frenzied energy in a sonorous and somewhat contrapuntal texture. Successions of fourths and fifths in the melodic line, considerable use of parallel seconds in the harmony, and complete modulatory freedom provide the work with a dissonant acridity which precludes any possibility of sentimental expression.

Contrapuntal writing is noticeably absent in the third quartet, published in 1927. In its place comes a preoccupation with brutal chords, with running scale passages, and with broken, hesitant rhythms. In spite of its apparent complexity of sound, much of the writing is two-part; octaves and unisons now became a characteristic of Bartók's quartet style. The fourth quartet was published in 1928. The great ability of Bartók to devise new instrumental effects, seen in the earlier works, here reaches new heights. Tight chordal formations, long glissandos, percussive bowing effects, concentrated tone clusters, new employment of pizzicato techniques—all are here in the fourth quartet, added to the emotional tension brought about by barbaric rhythms and unrelieved dissonance.

In the fifth and sixth quartets, written in 1934 and 1936, respectively, as in the *Contrasts* for piano, violin, and clarinet, of 1938, Bartók turned away from the relentless, acrid dissonance of earlier works. The fifth even bears some relationship to the key of B flat;

but it is a key in which major and minor are employed simultaneously, in which modal implications are present, and one which
Bartók does not hesitate to employ in its widest aspects. Certain
outspoken diatonic chords and even extended diatonic passages
occur. And in the sixth quartet the quantity of sheer dissonance is
lessened. In its place comes a melodically derived dissonance; the
progression of individual parts tends to absorb the tonal clashes, and
a degree of warm sentiment almost completely missing in earlier
works emerges.

From a late Romantic standpoint the quartets of Bartók seem cold,
forbidding, and devoid of expression. From any standpoint they are
reserved and impersonal. Yet their general quality, their indefinable
air of sincerity, plus the magnificence of their purely instrumental
effects and savage rhythms combine to give them a deservedly high
place in twentieth-century literature. One suspects that many of the
barbaric rhythmic effects and exotic turns of phrase in the quartets
are derived from eastern European folk music; Bartók's position as
one of the most eminent of folklorists makes the surmise likely. But
the variety of texture, the dignity of phrasing in the quieter moments,
and the subtle form extensions are purely his own. Of all the
many experiments which have led to a general widening of tonal
possibilities in the twentieth century, those of Bartók seem to hold
the greatest promise for the future.

In a history of harmonic processes since the sixteenth century, one
important topic concerns the enlarging of the basic harmonic unit:
the chord. In the time of Palestrina that chord was most often a triad
composed of thirds superimposed upon each other: C-E-G or G-B-
D. Each new development in harmonic complexity since that time
has been accompanied, among other things, by the addition of another third to the basic unit. For a considerable period the major
seventh chord, C-E-G-B, for example, represented the height of
harmonic daring. Later the ninth, and still later the eleventh and
thirteenth chords came into use. The latter, C-E-G-B-D-F-A in one
version, was with difficulty perceived as one chord; its extreme
spread and the fact that it contains within itself all the tones of the

diatonic scale, tend to divest it of any great chordal feeling. During the late nineteenth century the conviction arose that the thirteenth chord really contained the elements of several chords: the tonic triads of C major, G major, and D minor, respectively. Forward-looking composers made tentative use of such related chords, placing one harmony above another. Their use naturally suggested the employment of other unrelated chords. And so, in small steps and in full accord with historical precedent, the simultaneous use of two tonalities resulted. At the hands of Darius Milhaud (b. 1892) that expansion of harmonic resources received its most consistent employment; polytonality, for so the practice is called, became an important element in Milhaud's style about 1918.

The early quartets of Milhaud have all but disappeared from general circulation. According to Edwin Evans,[5] the first three (1912, 1915, 1916) are distinguished by excellent contrapuntal writing in a strictly diatonic setting and by great clarity of form. During the course of a diplomatic visit to Brazil (1917–1919) Milhaud composed his fourth quartet, in which polytonal devices received extended treatment. To make certain that the duality of keys was perceived, it became necessary to establish each tonality with the utmost clarity; diatonic writing in the several parts was essential. The latter, already a factor in Milhaud's earlier style, became even more pronounced in later works and led to the criticism that his melodic line was perfunctory and overly simple. No one denied its clarity and appeal nor Milhaud's technical competence.

Following his return to Paris and his association with the group of composers called "Les Six," about 1919,[6] Milhaud composed a fifth quartet, dedicated to Arnold Schönberg. Evans quotes passages from that work to illustrate the "uncompromising nature of the texture." The sixth quartet, 1922, and the seventh, 1925, mark a return to a relatively simple, unassuming, and melodious polytonality. In succeeding years Milhaud added to his series of chamber-

[5] In *Cobbett's Cyclopedic Survey of Chamber Music*, II, 140–145.
[6] Arthur Honegger, Louis Durey, Georges Auric, Francis Poulenc, and Germaine Tailleferre were others of "Les Six."

music works. His eighth and ninth quartets were published about 1936 and 1937; the eleventh was performed in New York during the winter of 1942.

There are few opportunities to hear Milhaud's late quartets outside metropolitan centers. One would like to gain more familiarity with his attractive idiom. The impassioned passages, the placid contrasts, and the musical worth one finds in his orchestral works are reputedly also present in the quartets. Those characteristics, added to the technical competence Milhaud has always shown, should give his chamber music a high place in the contemporary literature.

An eighteenth-century musician was expected to be a complete master of his craft. It was normal to find the activities of composer, performer on several instruments, teacher, and musical administrator combined in one person. In the twentieth century, with its high degree of specialization, such universality is a decided exception. Of all modern musicians, probably Paul Hindemith (b. 1895) meets eighteenth-century specifications most closely. Professionally active as a violinist and violist, he is reputed to be a pianist and a clarinetist as well; and he has privately admitted his prowess on the bassoon. As a conductor and a member of several university faculties, he has proved himself equally competent. Most importantly, his compositions give him a leading place in the musical world.

Hindemith's early works disclosed his great skill in contrapuntal writing and his daring in harmonic innovation, even though some passages reveal conventional ideas and a "post-romantic divagation." [7] Among these works is his first string quartet, Opus 10, in F minor. With the second quartet, Opus 16, performed at a Donaueschingen Festival in 1921, Hindemith's future path was revealed. Tendencies present in that work, notably the domination of melodic (horizontal) over harmonic (vertical) elements, led the way to the style of linear counterpoint with which Hindemith identified himself during the following decade. The third quartet, Opus 22, revealed the full development of that style.

That work, making great technical demands upon its performers,

[7] Evans, in *Cobbett's Cyclopedic Survey of Chamber Music*, I, 556–562.

contains a degree of free contrapuntal writing not found in the earlier quartets. Fugal passages and close imitations appear in large numbers. The counterpoints exhibit little of the old relationship between parts. Each part follows its own destiny, realizes its own melodic implications quite independently of the others. The resulting dissonances are thus of another type than the dissonances, say, of Schönberg, Bartók, or Milhaud. Hindemith's represent the logical completion of linear tendencies, while the others result from chordal complexes or melodic thickening. No concern with harmonious sound deflects the composer from his aim of making each voice really independent. In other sections of the quartet suggestions of poly-tonality, of thick chromaticism, or of merely expanded chordal writing provide the necessary contrasts of texture.

The fourth quartet, Opus 32, published in 1924, is the most con-sistent of Hindemith's chamber-music works in its employment of linear counterpoint. From beginning to end it embodies a polyphonic texture. The first movement contains a fugue (first theme) and a double fugue (second theme); one of that movement's episodes con-sists of a simultaneous development of all three themes. The second movement, whose inner voices are in canon with entrances an augmented octave (C flat-C) apart, contains a wealth of free con-trapuntal weaving in the outer parts also. The polyphonic complex is lightened to some extent in the third movement, a march; but even there a full-bodied texture is employed. The fourth is a passacaglia: twenty-seven variations of a seven-measure theme lead to a fugal coda in fast tempo. Throughout the entire quartet an intensity of purpose is felt: in the sustained rhythmic drive of the first movement, in the almost sixty-measure crescendo from *pp* to *fff* in the march, in the inexorable tonal growth of the passacaglia, and in the relentless hammering of the final coda. In all respects the quartet reaches new heights of concentration and sonority.

Hindemith's fifth quartet was written in 1943 and carries on its title-page an indication of tonality! Thus Hindemith, too, has made the return to a tonal framework—as did Bartók and Stravinsky, among others. But the tonality—E flat in this case—remains simply a point of departure. Modulations are abrupt, distant, and dissonant; major and minor modes occur simultaneously, and certain passages suggest polytonal writing. In earlier works dissonances were the inescapable results of the strict contrapuntal writing; here, in the E flat quartet, they serve as elements of harmonic color. Possibly as a consequence of the new treatment of dissonance, the texture is lightened considerably. Consistent use of polyphony is no longer characteristic; such contrapuntal passages as occur are incidental to Hindemith's processes of thematic development rather than essential elements of his style. With the return to tonality and the clarifying of texture come an increased directness and vitality in the music itself. Great energy has always been a characteristic of Hindemith's music; here the energy of earlier works has been transformed into vitality and driving power.

The second to fifth quartets, along with half-a-dozen works for various combinations,[8] give us a picture of a composer second to none in imagination, technical skill, and intensity. Hindemith's successive styles have been of incalculable influence on other composers; he is without doubt one of the most important of contemporary musicians. Having earlier shown the way to the logical expansion of polyphonic concepts which led to the dissonant style of linear counterpoint (i.e., counterpoint freed from all vertical, or harmonic, restrictions), he has now developed an equally vigorous but more restrained manner, which again allows subjective emotional expression to emerge.

Almost every musical work, to whatever style period it may belong, can roughly be classified according to the following categories: (a) it contains new elements which lead in the direction of a new style; (b) it is one of the masterworks which realizes the full implications of its particular style; (c) it discloses evidence of the style's decline; (d) it is directly influenced by works of a more powerful composer or is a pale imitation of those works; (e) it contains new

[8] One string trio, Opus 34, for violin, viola, and cello; one trio for two violins and viola, dated 1932; a trio for piano, viola, and Heckelphon or saxophone, Opus 47; a quartet for piano, violin, clarinet, and cello, from 1939; a quintet for clarinet and strings, Opus 30; a quintet for woodwind instruments, Opus 24, No. 2—these are the additional published and unpublished chamber-music works of Hindemith.

elements which, it can be seen in retrospect, lead nowhere; (*f*) it is purely of local or contemporary interest. Obviously, the categories are not mutually exclusive.

The chamber-music works discussed thus far in this book have in the main been representative of the first three categories. As such, their qualities are self-evident. But a sizable literature of contemporary works which must be placed in the minor categories (*d*, *e*, and *f*) exists also. There are literally hundreds of such works ranging from Bax to Zemlinsky. Space limitations, among other things, forbid the discussion of that literature. One group of them is seen to reflect the style characteristics of Ravel; another embodies the twelve-tone system of Schönberg or the linear counterpoint of Hindemith; still another employs sterile experiment. Nor are those works confined to individual countries: the new developments in twentieth-century music are worldwide in their effects.

A bare catalogue of names will illustrate the extent of this minor literature. Among the English, Arnold Bax (b. 1883), Frank Bridge (1879–1941), Waldo Warner (1874–1945), and Vaughan Williams (b. 1872) deserve mention. Italians include Alfredo Casella (1883–1947), Francesco Malipiero (b. 1882), and Ottorino Respighi (1879–1936). The Spanish Joaquin Turina (1882–1949), the Rumanian Georges Enesco (b. 1881), the French Jacques Ibert (b. 1890) and Arthur Honegger (b. 1892), and the Brazilian Heitor Villa-Lobos (b. 1890) have all written chamber music.[9] This incomplete list includes only the more prominent composers, and only those not primarily associated with the United States. With all due respect to the musical qualities of those composers' works—insofar as they are known to the present author—it seems advisable to let a later generation of musicians decide, on the basis of repeated performances, which of their works deserve to live and which had best be forgotten.

Three other composers, the Bohemian Bohuslav Martinu (b. 1890) and the Russians Serge Prokofieff (1891–1953) and Dmitri Shostakovich (b. 1906), are on a higher level. Martinu, after a hectic existence

[9] References to works of those composers written before 1929 may be found in the invaluable and unique *Cobbett's Cyclopedic Survey of Chamber Music*, on whose pages the present author has leaned repeatedly.

in war-torn Europe, has emerged in the last few years as one of the most imposing of Czech composers. His long residence in Paris, where he was influenced by the music of Stravinsky, perhaps accounts for the interest in rhythmic elements which his second quartet (1926) discloses. A play with cross accents and a variety of phrases written across measure lines are typical of those years. A piano trio (1930), on the other hand, is based on a solid polyphonic style. Other works have shown Martinu's tendency to employ first one, then the other of those styles. Thus, a string quintet and a string sextet, from 1929 and 1932, respectively, embody the rhythmic characteristics of the second quartet. A third quartet (1932) with overt jazz devices and a piano quintet from 1934, continue the rhythmic style. A later work, the piano quartet of 1942, discloses a return to the polyphonic style of 1930. Two other works, Martinu's fourth and fifth string quartets, from 1936 and 1938, are not available at present writing.

The major importance of Serge Prokofieff is in fields other than chamber music. As one of the leading figures in contemporary music, as one of the outstanding exponents of neo-Classical style tendencies, and in the forefront of contemporary developments, Prokofieff is one of the best known and most frequently performed of present-day composers. While his contributions to the chamber-music literature are few, they are significant in their stylistic aspects. Two string quartets (1930 and 1942) and a quintet for string and wind instruments (1924) are his principal works in the field. Prokofieff is seldom dull or heavy in his writing; a lightness of touch characterizes even the slow movements. Lyric melodies abound, suggesting at times a trace of Romantic sentiment. In spite of his free use of dissonance, Prokofieff does not often stray too far or too long from an established tonal center. Early works (we speak here of his compositions in other fields) were characterized by extreme instrumental range, by a fondness for the high registers, and by elements of grotesqueness and ironic humor. Later works disclose a renewed interest in lyric melody, a less abrupt rhythmic scheme and a partial abandonment of objective, remote expression.

Dmitri Shostakovich is in many respects similar to Prokofieff. Like the latter, Shostakovich's contributions to chamber-music literature are few: a string quartet written in 1938 and a piano quintet from 1940 are the principal works. A piano trio and a second string quartet are listed as having been written in 1944. Like Prokofieff again, the works disclose a Classical clarity of form, a mildly dissonant style, with strong elements of old-fashioned sentiment and a marked tendency to employ bizarre, humorous, or ironic musical devices. But in addition to these, there is in Shostakovich a blatant, pompous strain reminiscent of Tschaikowsky in his more inflated moments. One has the impression that Shostakovich writes with tongue in cheek, that many of his mawkish passages are burlesques, and that he does not mean them to be taken seriously.

In preparing for the writing of these final pages on chamber music of the United States, the author found it expedient to reread at one sitting, so to speak, all the issues of *Modern Music* [10] published between 1928 and the fall of 1946—book reviews, criticisms, advertisements, and all the pertinent articles. Two strong impressions remain from that intensive reading: that successive performances of certain contemporary works often reflected great changes of critical opinion—apparently one year's meat was another year's poison—and that American music is safe in the hands of a dozen composers. These composers are the most often performed, the most often published, and the most often written about—by each other. It is equally significant that the majority of them live within a few hundred miles of New York.

Other composers, geographically remote from that most important of American musical centers, receive little recognition, are critically disposed of with a few shakes of the pen, or are ignored. One may admire the energy, the versatility, and the verbal eloquence of the most prominent American composers; at the same time one may be led to suspect that others, less well known, may be of equal importance to the future of American music.

[10] *Modern Music* (New York, League of Composers, 1924–1946).

The majority of the better-known composers (details will appear below) have since the 1920's passed through an experimental period characterized by formal innovations and a wildly dissonant harmonic style—as did their European contemporaries. Many of them have since emerged on the fringe of a neo-Classicism in which restraint and a measure of stylistic refinement are respectable—again in the pattern of Hindemith, Stravinsky, and others. In so doing they have caught up with a number of lesser-known American composers who either did not experiment so intensively or kept their experimental work from a long-suffering public: the very composers whose works were held in scant esteem by the "progressives." Now, in the 1940's, a new generation is appearing which has profited by the innovations of the one group and the patience of the other. A quality of music with new expressive values is becoming characteristic.

Of earlier composers—the American Romanticists, post-Impressionists, or even atonalists—there is no need to speak here. Elements of their respective styles were derived largely from corresponding European models; [11] their works do not, in general, lead to the styles of contemporary American music. One exception to this statement is found in the works of Ernest Bloch (b. 1880). Born in Switzerland, he has lived in the United States intermittently since 1916. Much of Bloch's chamber music was written and published here; in certain respects he may be considered an American composer, if only for the influence he has had upon his American pupils.

A string quartet in B minor was completed in 1916, a piano quintet appeared in 1924, a set of three nocturnes for piano trio followed in 1925, and a second string quartet in 1947. These, along with several sets of pieces for string quartet, represent Bloch's contributions to the literature. They include elements of several styles, they contain personal mannerisms, in a form which is not far removed from the conventional. A richness of emotional expression which can be ascribed to Bloch's Jewish ancestry, a rhythmic vitality in the best

[11] The career of Charles Ives (born 1874) provides a notable exception to this general statement. Ives was experimenting and composing in a dissonant style years before his European contemporaries had gained wide recognition.

American tradition, a trace of Impressionistic concern with the sound of isolated harmonies, a few digressions into the world of quarter-tones—all are represented. Bloch seldom writes contrapuntally; many short thematic fragments, strongly supported by vital rhythmic figures or resonant chordal patterns are basic to the texture of his music. The occasional monotony which the consistent employment of this texture brings with it is in large part relieved by great emotional variety, ranging from intense lamentation to wild abandon.

Louis Gruenberg (b. 1884) is perhaps better known for his orchestral works and operas than for his chamber music. Several sets of pieces for string quartet (*Whimsicalities, Indiscretions,* and the like), written between 1920 and 1930, and a piano quintet from 1937 are his compositions in the latter field. An early interest in the formal possibilities of jazz led to the inclusion of that element in the shorter sets of pieces. In later works that interest has been abandoned to some extent.

Frederick Jacobi (1891–1952) was once attracted to the music of the American Indians. That interest was reflected in his first string quartet, from 1924; the themes of two of its movements are derived from Indian songs and dances. Jacobi's second quartet was published in 1935; a piano quintet, *Hagiographa: Three Biblical Narratives,* followed in 1942. In a harmonic idiom that is essentially conservative and tonal, and in a texture that is remarkable for its lack of counterpoint, Jacobi succeeds in writing dramatically and interestingly. The quintet in particular contains passages full of new instrumental effects and striking colors.

Walter Piston (b. 1894) is in a sense the most eclectic of American chamber-music composers. Dissonant counterpoint in the style of Hindemith, tight chordal formations similar to those of Stravinsky's early period, a melodic line whose leaps and angles sometimes reminds one of Schönberg, a rhythmic vitality akin to Bartók's—all these are found in his music. Yet these diverse elements are combined in a texture which is unique for its clarity and straightforwardness. Symmetrical forms and contrapuntal textures, along with excellent part writing, are most typical; probably to no other contemporary American composer does the term neo-Classical apply so aptly. Two string quartets, from 1933 and 1935, a piano trio written in 1935, but published in 1938, and a quintet for flute and strings dated 1942 are among his chamber-music works. One must admire the intellectual qualities which shine through Piston's music even while one may be repelled to some extent by its cool, detached tone. All the technical qualifications of an accomplished composer are everywhere apparent; one could wish for a greater degree of personal expression— even though it be couched in his contemporary, dissonant language.

That such a degree of personal expression is possible in the contemporary idiom is seen when the chamber music of Quincy Porter (b. 1897) is examined. More conservative in its harmonic style than Piston's, Porter's writing occasionally discloses a lyric quality which Piston's largely lacks. His four published quartets are as follows: No. 3, 1935; No. 4, 1936; No. 6, 1937; No. 7, 1943. In them is disclosed a style that has remained essentially unchanged for more than a dozen years (the third quartet was written in 1930). The quartets further reveal Porter's fondness for *ostinato* motives: a typical effect is created by the employment of two or three such motives to accompany a lyric melody. His thick part-writing produces a texture which sometimes lacks characteristic color, but it often develops large sonorous climaxes. A variety of moods emerge from the quartets; but, on the whole dramatic allegros, rather heavy slow movements, and agitated finales are typical. Other works of Porter's, most of which have remained unpublished, include a quintet for clarinet and strings, a piano quintet, and several smaller compositions.

A striking feature of the chamber music of Roy Harris (b. 1898) is its formal variety. In a style compounded largely of parallel writing, bitonality, sixteenth-century modes used in pairs, and manipulated rhythmic figures, Harris's outstanding works in the field present several formal innovations. Thus, his second quartet is entitled *Three Variations on a Theme* (1932); the third (1938) consists of four preludes and four fugues; a piano quintet from 1937 contains a passacaglia, a cadenza, and a fugue. His other works include a piano trio from 1934 and a string quintet from 1940; a string sextet written about 1932 and several smaller works complete the list.

The piano quintet discloses Harris's strengths and weaknesses of style, perhaps to a greater degree than do his other works in the field. Its massive, concentrated, polyphonic first movement, with its long melodic lines, builds up at great length to an imposing climax which seems foreshortened. The second, in which the instruments singly and together engage in free rhapsodic development of the first movement's passacaglia theme, is not well proportioned. The third, a masterful and compelling fugue on the same theme, suffers from overdevelopment; a mass of unessential figuration obscures the lines of the fugue and leads to a noisy climax.

The third quartet, as noted above, contains a prelude and a fugue in each of its four movements. In each case the prelude is cast in one of the old church modes, whereas the fugue employs two modes simultaneously. The resulting modal clashes create a new harmonic sound, redolent of the sixteenth and the twentieth centuries at once. The prevailing contrapuntal texture is logical and precise, but thick writing and a lack of real climaxes lead to a certain monotony of color. Again the abrupt endings are encountered, as in the piano quintet. But the work as a whole—and this is still more true of the quintet—testifies to the vigor of Harris's writing, to its freedom from contemporary transatlantic influences, and to its directness.

A number of American composers of the generation 1880–1900 have written isolated chamber-music works. In many cases such composers are primarily interested in orchestral or other fields; a discussion of their music based on one or two perhaps unrepresentative compositions would be erroneous. Among these composers, Eric DeLamarter (1880–1953), Howard Hanson (b. 1896), Roger Sessions (b. 1895), George Antheil (b. 1900), and Aaron Copland (b. 1900) may be mentioned as being the most prominent.

But an equal number of younger and less-prominent Americans have also written significant chamber music. Among those who have enjoyed less public recognition—in itself no measure of their music's worth—David Van Vactor (b. 1906), Robert Sanders (b. 1906), and

Anthony Donato (b. 1909) may be singled out for the excellence of their writing.

Van Vactor has written, among other chamber-music works, a quintet for flute and strings which reveals great competence in its handling of its diverse materials. In a texture which is melodious and rhythmic in turn, bustling or lyric themes develop along conservative lines. Sanders's music in general is characterized by vitality and rhythmic resourcefulness and by a naturalness in its tunes. His piano trio (1926) and string quartet (1929) reflect those elements. Donato is, perhaps, the most successful of the group in his writing for string instruments. Two string quartets disclose a power of invention, a richness of expression, and a variety of color seldom found in contemporary chamber music. Unpublished at the moment,[12] Donato's quartets are known only to a comparatively small audience.

Within recent years a new group of American chamber-music composers have gained recognition: William Schuman (b. 1910), David Diamond (b. 1915), and William Bergsma (b. 1921) among them. Schuman, with a piano trio and three string quartets to his credit, exhibits an emotional power which is not always held in control, and a quality of contrapuntal writing which tends to become conventional. Harmonically he leans toward polytonal devices. A quintet for piano, flute, and strings (1942) by Diamond reveals his attraction to the objective, detached style characteristic of the 1930's. Bergsma's lyric gifts and technical competence promise well for his future and for the future of American music.

One still hears on every hand severe criticisms of the expressive aims and dissonant styles of contemporary composers. One learns that beauty has gone out of music, that noise and confusion are modern musical ideals, that expression of feeling is not to be found. One may grant, grudgingly, that contemporary music is clever, that it is inventive, in short, that it is "different." So, in general, run the comments.

The makers of these and similar criticisms sometimes fail to realize

12 The first of Donato's quartets was published in 1947–1948 by the Society for the Publication of American Music (New York, G. Schirmer).

that in that very difference lies the hope for the well-being of music in the years ahead. Throughout the course of this book the author has attempted to show how music has always been on the march; how its forms, styles, and entire mode of expression have changed with each passing decade; how every new style has been derived from the old, has in a sense been an extension of the old. Chamber music was born amid diatribes and invectives; Artusi's pamphlet of 1600 was directed against the *nuove musiche* of his day. Out of that new music developed the forms and the styles of the late Baroque period. They in turn were outmoded while Bach was still alive, namely, before 1750, and another revolution in musical taste prepared the way for the style which culminated in the works of the late nineteenth century.

The conclusion is inescapable. Since the early 1900's still another musical revolution has been going on, one which in the last decade or two has shown signs of coming to a close. Out of that latest upheaval a new style emerged—is emerging—will emerge. It is the fate of progressive composers—and most great composers have been progressive—to stand some distance in advance of their audiences. It was true of Monteverdi, of Mozart, and of Beethoven; it is true of Stravinsky, of Bartók, and of Hindemith.

It would be trite to point out that as the world has become smaller it has also increased its rate of change. A musical development that might have taken half a century in the past is now consummated within a decade. From Frescobaldi to Bach was a hundred years; from Debussy to Stravinsky is barely twenty. In that speed of development, in the rapidity with which the new styles have encompassed the earth, lies the difficulty for many listeners to contemporary music.

The new styles are here to stay for several generations, even though they have probably not yet reached their definitive shapes. The gap which separates the most conservative listener from the most progressive composer has become noticeably smaller in recent decades. The expressive possibilities of the new music are vast, at least as great as they were in older music. Composers everywhere are tireless in their efforts to bring those possibilities to light. And in the future development of those possibilities the resources of chamber music will be called upon. Chamber music will play as vital and significant a role in music of the future as it has played in the music of the last three-and-one-half centuries.

DICTIONARIES, ENCYCLOPEDIAS, AND CATALOGUES

Altmann, Wilhelm. Kammermusik-Katalog. 6th ed. Leipzig, Hofmeister, 1945.

Apel, Willi. Harvard Dictionary of Music. Cambridge, Mass., Harvard University Press, 1944.

Baker, Theodore. Baker's Biographical Dictionary of Musicians. 4th ed. New York, G. Schirmer, 1940.

Cobbett, Walter W., ed. Cobbett's Cyclopedic Survey of Chamber Music. 2 vols. London, Oxford University Press, 1929–1930.

Eitner, Robert. Biographisch-bibliographisches Quellen-Lexikon der Musiker und Musikgelehrten. 10 vols. Leipzig, Breitkopf & Härtel, 1900–1904.

Ewen, David, ed. Composers of Today. 2d ed. New York, H. W. Wilson Co., 1936.

—— Composers of Yesterday. New York, H. W. Wilson Co., 1937.

Grove, Sir George. Grove's Dictionary of Music and Musicians. 5 vols. and supplement. 4th ed. by H. C. Colles. London, Macmillan Co., 1940.

Koechel, Ludwig Ritter von. Chronologisch-systematisches Verzeichniss sämtlicher Tonwerke Wolfgang Amade Mozarts. Rev. 3d ed. by Alfred Einstein. Leipzig, Breitkopf & Härtel, 1937. Reprinted by J. W. Edwards, Ann Arbor, Mich., 1947.

Kolodin, Irving. New Guide to Recorded Music. Rev. ed. New York, Doubleday & Co., 1947.

Leslie, George C., ed. The Gramophone Shop Encyclopedia of Recorded Music. Rev. ed. New York, Simon & Schuster, 1942.

Nottebohm, Gustav. Beethoven: thematisches Verzeichniss. Leipzig, Breitkopf & Härtel, 1913.

Riemann, Hugo. Musik-Lexikon. 2 vols. 11th ed., rev. by Alfred Einstein. Berlin, M. Hesse, 1929.

Thompson, Oscar. The International Cyclopedia of Music and Musicians. 4th ed. New York, Dodd, Mead & Co., 1946.

Walther, Johann Gottfried. Musikalisches Lexikon. Leipzig, W. Deer, 1732.

HISTORIES

Adler, Guido, ed. Handbuch der Musikgeschichte. 2 vols. 2d ed. Berlin-Wilmersdorf, H. Keller, 1930.

Bücken, Ernst, ed. Handbuch der Musikwissenschaft. 10 vols. Wildpark-Potsdam, Athenaion-verlag, 1928–1934.

Burney, Charles. A General History of Music. 2 vols. Rev. ed. New York, Harcourt, Brace & Co., 1935.

Dorian, Frederick. The History of Music in Performance. New York, W. W. Norton & Co., 1942.

Einstein, Alfred. A Short History of Music; tr. from the German by Eric Blom and others. 2d Amer. ed. New York, Alfred A. Knopf, 1938.

Grout, Donald J. A Short History of Opera. New York, Columbia University Press, 1947.

Haas, Robert. "Aufführungspraxis der Musik," in Ernst Bücken, Handbuch der Musikwissenschaft (Wildpark-Potsdam, Akademische Verlagsgesellschaft Athenaion, 1931), Vol. VIII.

—— "Die Musik des Barocks," in Ernst Bücken, Handbuch der Musikwissenschaft (Wildpark-Potsdam, Akademische-Verlagsgesellschaft, 1928), Vol. IV.

Howard, John Tasker. Our American Music. 3d rev. ed. New York, Thomas Y. Crowell Co., 1946.

Kretzschmar, Hermann. Führer durch den Concertsaal; I Abtheilung, Sinfonie und Suite. 3d ed. Leipzig, Breitkopf & Härtel, 1898.

Láng, Paul Henry. Music in Western Civilization. New York, W. W. Norton & Co., 1941.

Mersmann, Hans. Die Kammermusik. 4 vols. Leipzig, Breitkopf & Härtel, 1930–1933.

Moser, Hans Joachim. Geschichte der deutschen Musik. 2 vols., 3 pts. 3d ed. Stuttgart and Berlin, J. G. Cotta, 1923–1924.

Nef, Karl. Geschichte der Sinfonie und Suite. Leipzig, Breitkopf & Härtel, 1921.

—— An Outline of the History of Music; tr. from the German by Carl Pfatteicher. 3d printing. New York, Columbia University Press, 1939.

Oxford History of Music, The. 7 vols. 2d ed., with revisions. London, Oxford University Press, 1938.

Pruniéres, Henry. A New History of Music; tr. from the French by Edward Lockspeiser. New York, Macmillan Co., 1943.

Riemann, Hugo. Geschichte der Musik seit Beethoven. Berlin and Stuttgart, W. Spemann, 1901.

—— Handbuch der Musikgeschichte. 2 vols., 5 pts. 2d ed. Leipzig, Breitkopf & Härtel, 1920–1923.

Salazar, Adolfo. Music in Our Time; tr. from the Spanish by Isabel Pope. New York, W. W. Norton & Co., 1946.

Schering, Arnold. Tabellen zur Musikgeschichte. 4th rev. ed. Leipzig, Breitkopf & Härtel, 1934.

Slonimsky, Nicholas. Music since 1900. 2d ed. New York, W. W. Norton & Co., 1938.

Straeten, Edmund van der. The History of the Violin. 2 vols. London, Cassell & Co., 1933.

GENERAL

Abraham, Gerald, ed. The Music of Schubert. New York, W. W. Norton & Co., 1947.

Allen, Warren D. Philosophies of Music History. New York, American Book Co., 1939.

Arnold, Franck Thomas. The Art of Accompaniment from a Thorough-bass. London, Oxford University Press, 1931.

Artaria, Franz, and Hugo Botstiber. Joseph Haydn und das Verlagshaus Artaria. Vienna, Artaria & Co., 1909.

Artusi, Giovanni. Overo delle imperfettioni della moderna musica. Venice, Vincenti, 1600.

Bach, Karl Philipp Emanuel. Versuch über die wahre Art das Klavier zu spielen. Berlin, C. F. Henning, 1753.

Bauer, Marion E. Twentieth Century Music. New York, G. P. Putnam's Sons, 1933.

Beckmann, Gustav. Das Violinspiel in Deutschland vor 1700. Leipzig, N. Simrock, 1918.

Burney, Charles. The Present State of Music in France and Italy. London, T. Beckett & Co., 1771.

Castiglione, Baldassare. Libro del cortegiano. Florence, Giunta, 1531.

—— The Book of the Courtier; done into English by Sir Thomas Hoby, anno 1561. New York, E. P. Dutton & Co., 1928.

Crevel, Marcus van. Adrianus Petit Coclico. The Hague, M. Nijhoff, 1940.

Crocker, Eunice C. "An Introductory Study of the Italian Canzona for Instrumental Ensembles." 2 vols. Unpublished dissertation. Cambridge, Mass., Radcliffe College, 1943.

Drinker, Jr., Henry S. The Chamber Music of Brahms. Philadelphia, the author, 1932.

Duncan, Edmonstoune. Schubert. Rev. ed. New York, E. P. Dutton & Co., 1934.

Einstein, Alfred. Mozart, His Character, His Work; tr. from the German by Arthur Mendel and Nathan Broder. London, Oxford University Press, 1945.

Evans, Edwin. Handbook to the Chamber and Orchestral Music of Brahms. 2 vols. London, W. Reeves, 1933–1935.

Ewen, David, ed. From Bach to Stravinsky. New York, W. W. Norton & Co., 1933.

Gasparini, Francesco. L'armonico practico al cimbalo. New ed. Venice, A. Bortoli, 1708.

Geiringer, Karl. Brahms; Leben und Schaffen eines deutschen Meister. Vienna, R. M. Rohrer, 1935.

—— Haydn; a Creative Life in Music. New York, W. W. Norton & Co., 1946.

Heinichen, Johann David. Der General-Bass in der Composition. Dresden, the author, 1728.

Heuss, Alfred. Kammermusikabende. Leipzig, Breitkopf & Härtel, 1919.

Jahn, Otto. W. A. Mozart. 2 vols. 4th ed. Leipzig, Breitkopf & Härtel, 1905–1907.

Kilburn, Nicholas. Chamber Music and Its Masters. Rev. ed. by G. E. Abraham. London, Wm. Reeves, 1932.

Kinkeldey, Otto. Orgel und Klavier in der Musik des 16ten Jahrhunderts. Leipzig, Breitkopf & Härtel, 1910.

Leichtentritt, Hugo. Händel. Stuttgart, Deutsche Verlags-anstalt, 1924.

—— "Was lehren uns die Bildwerke des 14ten–17ten Jahrhunderts," in Sammelbände der Internationalen Musikgesellschaft (Leipzig, Breitkopf & Härtel, 1905–1906), Vol. VII, Pt. 3, pp. 315–364.

Lenz, Wilhelm von. Beethoven et ses trois styles. New ed. by M. D. Calvocoressi. Paris, Legouix, 1909.

Marliave, Joseph de. Beethoven's Quartets; tr. from the French by Hilda Andrews. London, Oxford University Press, 1928.

Mason, Daniel Gregory. The Chamber Music of Brahms. New York, Macmillan Co., 1933.

—— From Grieg to Brahms. New York, Macmillan Co., 1912.

Norlind, Tobias. "Zur Geschichte der Suite," in Sammelbände der Internationalen Musikgesellschaft (Leipzig, Breitkopf & Härtel, 1905–1906), Vol. VII, Pt. 2, pp. 172–203.

Ortiz, Diego. Trattado de glosas sopra clausulas y otro generos de puntos en la musica de violones [Treatise on ornaments over cadences and other kinds of notes in music for bass viols]. Rome, Dorico, 1553.

Pohl, Karl Ferdinand. Joseph Haydn. 3 vols. Vols. I–II, Berlin, A. Sasso Nachfolger, 1875, 1882; Vol. III (completed by Hugo Botstiber), Leipzig, Breitkopf & Härtel, n. d.

—— Mozart und Haydn in London. Vienna, C. Gerolds Sohn, 1867.

Riemann, Hugo. Beethovens Streichquartette. Berlin, Schlesinger'sche Buchhandlung, n. d.

Riezler, Walter. Beethoven; tr. from the German by G. D. Pidcock. New York, E. P. Dutton & Co., 1938.

Sandberger, Adolf. "Zur Entstehungsgeschichte von Haydns sieben Worte des Erlösers am Kreuze," in his Ausgewählte Aufsätze zur Musikgeschichte. Munich, Drei Masken Verlag, 1921.

—— "Zur Geschichte des Haydnschen Streichquartetts," in his Ausgewählte Aufsätze zur Musikgeschichte. Munich, Drei Masken Verlag, 1921.

Schauffler, Robert H. Florestan. New York, Henry Holt & Co., 1945.

Schnerich, Alfred. Joseph Haydn und seine Sendung. Zurich, Almatheaverlag, 1922.

Scott, Marion M. Beethoven. 2d ed. London, J. M. Dent, 1937.

Schwebsch, Erich. Johann Sebastian Bach und die Kunst der Fuge. Stuttgart, Orient-Occident-Verlag, 1931.

Shepherd, Arthur. The String Quartets of Ludwig van Beethoven. Cleveland, the author, 1935.

Steiner, Rudolf. Geheimwissenschaft in Umriss. 20th ed. Dornach, Switzerland, Philosophischer-Anthroposophischer Verlag, 1925.

—— Outline of Occult Science; tr. from the German by H. and M. Monges. New York, The Anthroposophic Press, 1939.

—— Die Philosophie der Freiheit. Rev. ed. Dornach, Switzerland, Philosophischer-Anthroposophischer Verlag, 1929.

—— The Philosophy of Spiritual Activity; tr. from the German by R. F. Hoernlé. New York, The Anthroposophic Press, 1932.

Strunk, Oliver. "Haydn's Divertimenti for Baryton, Viola, and Bass," in The Musical Quarterly (New York, G. Schirmer, April, 1932), Vol. XVIII.

Sullivan, John William N. Beethoven; His Spiritual Development. New York, Alfred A. Knopf, 1927.

Thayer, Alexander W. The Life of Ludwig van Beethoven; ed. by Henry A. Krehbiel. 3 vols. New York, The Beethoven Association, 1921.

Tovey, Donald Francis. Beethoven. London, Oxford University Press, 1945.

Tovey, Donald Francis. Essays in Musical Analysis; Chamber Music. London, Oxford University Press, 1944.

Turner, W. J. Mozart, the Man and His Works. New York, Alfred A. Knopf, 1938.

Wasielewski, Joseph W. von. Die Violine und ihre Meister. Rev. ed. Leipzig, Breitkopf & Härtel, 1927.

Werckmeister, Andreas. Harmonologia musica. Frankfurt and Leipzig, T. P. Calvisii, 1702.

Williams, C. F. Abdy. G. F. Handel. Rev. ed. New York, E. P. Dutton & Co., 1935

PERIODICALS

Jahrbücher für musikalische Wissenschaft; ed. by Friedrich Chrysander. 2 vols. Leipzig, Breitkopf & Härtel, 1863, 1867.

Modern Music. 23 vols. New York, League of Composers, 1924–1946.

Musical Quarterly, The; ed. by O. G. Sonneck, Carl Engel, Gustave Reese, Paul Henry Láng. New York, G. Schirmer, 1915–.

Sammelbände der Internationalen Musikgesellschaft. 15 vols. Leipzig, Breitkopf & Härtel, 1899–1914.

Studien zur Musikwissenschaft, Beihefte der Denkmäler der Tonkunst in Österreich. 21 vols. Vienna, Artaria & Co. and Universal Edition, 1913–1934.

Vierteljahrschrift für Musikwissenschaft. 10 vols. Leipzig, Breitkopf & Härtel, 1885–1894.

Zeitschrift für Musikwissenschaft. 17 vols. Leipzig, Breitkopf & Härtel, 1918–1935.

MUSIC, ANTHOLOGIES, COLLECTIONS, AND COMPLETE WORKS

*For additional music references see list of
chamber-music publications on p. 395.*

Attaingnant, Pierre. Quatorze gaillardes, neuf pavennes, sept branles, et deux basses danses (Paris, Attaingnant, c. 1530); facsimile ed. in Eduard Bernouilli, ed., Chansons und Tänze, Vol. IV. 5 vols. Munich, C. Kuhn, 1914.

Bach, Johann Sebastian. J. S. Bachs Werke. 47 vols. Leipzig, Bachgesellschaft, 1851–1894.

—— Joh. Seb. Bachs Werke. 38 vols. to 1937. Leipzig, Der neuen Bachgesellschaft, 1901–.

—— Das musikalische Opfer; modern ed. by Hans T. David. New York, G. Schirmer, 1944.

Beethoven, Ludwig van. Ludwig van Beethovens Werke. 25 vols. Leipzig, Breitkopf & Härtel, 1862–1888.

Brahms, Johannes. Johannes Brahms sämtliche Werke. 26 vols. Leipzig, Breitkopf & Härtel, 1926–1928.

Byrd, William. My Ladye Nevelles Booke (1591); modern ed. by Hilda Andrews. London, J. Curwen Sons, 1926.

—— Three Dances of William Byrd; ed. by Sir Granville Bantock. London, Novello & Co., n. d.

—— John Bull, and others. Fitzwilliam Virginal Book; new ed. by John A. Fuller-Maitland and Wm. B. Squire. 2 vols. London and Leipzig, Breitkopf & Härtel, 1899.

—— John Bull, and Orlando Gibbons. Parthenia (c. 1611); reprinted for The Musical Antiquarian Society, London, Chappel, 1847. New ed. by Margaret H. Glyn. London, Wm. Reeves, 1927.

Corelli, Arcangelo. Sämtliche Werke, Bd. I, in Denkmäler der Tonkunst, ed. by Friedrich Chrysander, Vol. III. Bergedorf, Weissenborn, 1871.

Davison, Archibald T., and Willi Apel. Historical Anthology of Music. Cambridge, Mass., Harvard University Press, 1946.

Denkmäler der Tonkunst, ed. by Friedrich Chrysander. 5 vols. Bergedorf, Weissenborn, 1869–1871.

Denkmäler der Tonkunst in Österreich. 83 vols. Vienna, Universal Edition, 1894–1938. Abbreviation: D.T.Ö.

Denkmäler deutscher Tonkunst; erste Folge. 65 vols. Leipzig, Breitkopf & Härtel, 1892–1931. Abbreviation: D.D.T.

Denkmäler deutscher Tonkunst; zweite Folge: Denkmäler der Tonkunst in Bayern. 36 vols. Leipzig, Breitkopf & Härtel, 1900–1931. Abbreviation: D.T.B.

Ecorcheville, Jules. Vingt suites d'orchestre du XVIIe siècle français. 2 vols. Paris, Fortin, 1906.

Erbe deutscher Musik, Das; erste Reihe. 13 vols. to date. Leipzig and Berlin, various publishers, 1935–.

Frescobaldi, Girolamo. Il libro primo della canzoni ad 1, 2, 3, 4 voci. 2d ed. Rome, Masotti, 1628.

Gabrieli, Andrea. Canzoni alla francesa—per sonar sopra istromenti da tasta; Lib. V e VI. Venice, Gardano, 1605.

Gabrieli, Giovanni. Canzoni et sonate—per sonar con ogni sorte di instrumenti. Venice, Magni, 1615.

Handel, George Frederick. Georg Friedrich Händels Werke. 96 vols., 6 supplements. Leipzig, Deutsche Händelgesellschaft, 1859–1901.

Haydn, Franz Joseph. Jos. Haydns sämtliche Werke. Incomplete. Leipzig, Breitkopf & Härtel, 1908–.

Klaviertänze des 16ten Jahrhunderts; ed. by H. Halbig. Stuttgart, Cotta, 1928.

Locheimer Liederbuch, Das [Lochamer], and Conrad Paumann, Fundamentum organisandi. Facsimile ed. by Konrad Ameln. Berlin, Wölbing Verlag, 1925.

Mendelssohn, Felix. Felix Mendelssohn-Bartholdys Werke. 36 vols. Leipzig, Breitkopf & Härtel, 1874–1877.

Mozart, Wolfgang Amadeus. Wolfgang Amadeus Mozarts sämtliche Werke. 24 series in 75 vols. Leipzig, Breitkopf & Härtel, 1877–1905.

Polyphonies du XIIIe siècle; modern ed. by Yvonne Rokseth. 4 vols. Paris, Editions de L'Oiseau-Lyre, 1935–1939.

Purcell, Henry. The Complete Works of Henry Purcell. 36 vols. London, Novello & Co., 1878–1928.

Riemann, Hugo, ed. Collegium musicum. 50 vols. Leipzig, Breitkopf & Härtel, n. d.

—— ed. Old Chamber Music. 4 vols. London, Augener & Co., n. d.

Schein, Johann Hermann. Johann Hermann Scheins Werke. 7 vols., 8 pts. Leipzig, Breitkopf & Härtel, 1901–1923.

Schering, Arnold. Geschichte der Musik in Beispielen. Leipzig, Breitkopf & Härtel, 1931.

Schubert, Franz Peter. Franz Schuberts Werke. 40 vols. Leipzig, Breitkopf & Härtel, 1888–1897.

Schumann, Robert. Robert Schumanns Werke. 34 vols. Leipzig, Breitkopf & Härtel, 1886–1893.

Tagliapetra, Gino, ed. Antologia di musica antica e moderna. 18 vols. Milan, G. Ricordi, 1931–1932.

Torchi, Luigi, ed. L'arte musicale in Italia. 7 vols. Milan, G. Ricordi, 1897–1903.

Vitali, Giovanni Battista. Sonate per 2, 3, 4, e 5 instrumenti; Opus 5. 2d ed. Bologna, Monti, 1677.

CHAMBER-MUSIC PUBLICATIONS
AND RECORDINGS

THE FOLLOWING list of chamber-music publications contains works of three classes: (*a*) those mentioned in the text, insofar as they are available in present-day editions; (*b*) a judicious selection of additional nineteenth- and twentieth-century European works, presented in the interest of rounding out the survey of the literature; (*c*) a representative collection of contemporary American chamber-music compositions, as reflected in the catalogues of the principal American publishers. Thus, it is by no means a complete list of all published chamber music. For such a catalogue the reader is referred to Wilhelm Altmann, *Kammermusik-Katalog*, 6th ed. (Leipzig, Hofmeister, 1945).

Instrumental combinations mentioned in the list are to be understood in their usual sense, as employed in the text. Thus, "trio sonata" includes two violins and cello, plus a keyboard instrument (although the cello part may be optional in many cases); "piano quintet" implies string quartet and piano. The exceptions and the unusual combinations are noted in each case.

The listed recordings are drawn from the latest catalogues of the principal American recording companies. European catalogues are sparsely represented, since European recordings are not generally available in this country. A few exceptions will be found, however, when the musical interest of the work in question warrants its inclusion.

NAMES AND ADDRESSES OF PUBLISHERS MENTIONED IN THIS LIST

A firm name in parentheses following that of a publisher indicates the American agent from whom works may be obtained.

American	American Music Center, 250 W. 57th St., New York 19, N.Y.
AMP	Associated Music Publishers, 25 W. 45th St., New York 19, N.Y.
Am-Rus	Am-Rus Edition, New York (Leeds).
Arrow	Arrow Press, New York (American).
Augener	Augener & Company, London (Broude).
B. & H.	Breitkopf und Härtel, Leipzig (AMP).
Bärenreiter	Bärenreiter Verlag, Cassel (Baron).
Baron	M. Baron Company, 8 W. 45th St., New York 19, N.Y.
Belaieff	M. Belaieff, Moscow and Leipzig (AMP).
Birchard	C. C. Birchard Music Co., 221 Columbus Ave., Boston 16, Mass.

Boosey & Hawkes	Boosey & Hawkes, Inc., 43 W. 23d St., New York 10, N.Y.
Broude	Broude Bros., 115 W. 57th St., New York 19, N.Y.
Chester	J. and W. Chester, London (Baron).
Columbia	Columbia Recording Corp., Bridgeport 8, Conn.
Compass	Compass Record Co., Inc., 1270 Avenue of the Americas, Radio City, New York 20, N.Y.
Composers Press	Composers Press, 853 Seventh Ave., New York 19, N.Y.
Concert Hall	Concert Hall Society, 250 W. 57th St., New York 19, N.Y.
Cos Cob	Cos Cob Press, New York (American).
Durand	A. Durand et Cie., Paris (Elkan).
Edwards	J. W. Edwards, Ann Arbor, Mich.
Elkan	Elkan-Vogel Co., 1716 Sansom St., Philadelphia 3, Penn.
Eng. Gram.	English Gramophone Co., London (Gramophone).
Enoch	Enoch et Cie., Paris (Baron).
C. Fischer	Carl Fischer, Inc., 56-62 Cooper Square, New York 3, N.Y.
J. Fischer	J. Fischer & Bro., 119 W. 40th St., New York 17, N.Y.
Gramophone	The Gramophone Shop, 18 E. 48th St., New York 17, N.Y.
Gray	H. W. Gray Co., 159 E. 48th St., New York 17, N.Y.
Hansen	Wilhelm Hansen, Copenhagen.
Heugel	Heugel et Cie., Paris.
International	International Music Co., 509 Fifth Ave., New York 17, N.Y.
Jurgenson	P. Jurgenson, Moscow and Leipzig.
Kalmus	Edwin F. Kalmus, P.O. Box 476, Scarsdale, N.Y.
Leduc	Alphonse Leduc, Paris (Baron).
Leeds	Leeds Music Corp., RKO Building, Radio City, New York 20, N.Y.
Litolff	Henri Litolff, Leipzig and Braunschweig.
L'Oiseau	L'Oiseau-Lyre Edition, Paris.
Marks	Edward B. Marks Music Corp., RCA Building, Radio City, New York 20, N.Y.
Music Press	Music Press, Inc., 130 W. 56th St., New York 19, N.Y.
Musicraft	Musicraft Corp., 245 E. 23d St., New York 10, N.Y.
Nagel	Nagel Musik-Archiv, Hannover (AMP).
New Music	New Music Press, New York (American).
Novello	Novello & Co., London (Gray).
Oxford	Oxford University Press (C. Fischer).
Peters	C. F. Peters, Leipzig (Summy).
Rahter	D. Rahter, Leipzig (AMP).
Ricordi	G. Ricordi & Co., 12 W. 45th St., New York 19, N.Y.
Roszavölgyi	Roszavölgyi & Co., Budapest (Elkan).
Rouart	Rouart, Lerolle et Cie., Paris (Elkan).
Russ	Russischer Musik-Verlag (Leeds).
Schirmer	G. Schirmer, Inc., 3 E. 43d St., New York 17, N.Y.
Schmidt	Arthur B. Schmidt Music Co., 120 Boylston St., Boston, Mass.
Schott	B. Schotts Söhne, Mainz (AMP).
Senart	Maurice Senart, Paris (Elkan).
Simrock	N. Simrock, Leipzig (AMP).
Skand.	Skandinavisk Grammophon Aktieselskab (Gramophone).
SPAM	Society for the Publication of American Music (Schirmer).
Summy	Clayton F. Summy Co., 321 S. Wabash Ave., Chicago 4, Ill.
Ultraphon	Ultraphon Records, Prague (Gramophone).
Universal	Universal Edition, Vienna (AMP).
Victor	Radio Corporation of America, RCA Victor Division, Camden, N.J.
Vox	Vox Records, 236 W. 55th St., New York 19, N.Y.

ABBREVIATIONS EMPLOYED IN THIS LIST

bsn.	bassoon	h.	horn	stq.	string quartet
cb.	contrabass	hps.	harpsichord	trp.	trumpet
cl.	clarinet	ob.	oboe	va.	viola
Eh.	English horn	org.	organ	vc.	cello
fl.	flute	p.	piano	vl.	violin

PUBLICATIONS AND RECORDINGS

Abaco, Evaristo Felice Dall'
> Sonata da camera, G minor, Augener.

Arensky, Anton Stepanovich
> String Quartet, G minor, Op. 11, Jurgenson.
> ✓ Piano Trio, D minor, Op. 32, Universal, International, Augener.

Arnell, Richard
> Prelude and Double Fugato, for fl., vl., va., and vc., Music Press.

Ayres, Frederic
> ✓ Piano Trio, D minor, SPAM.

Bach, Johann Christian
> Quartets, Op. 8, Nos. 1, 3, and 5, for fl. (or ob. or vl.), vl., va., and vc., Bärenreiter.

Bach, Johann Sebastian
> Fifteen Terzetti, for 2 vl. and va. (arr.), International.
> String Trio, A major, for 2 vl. and vc. (arr.), Augener.
> String Trio, D minor, for 2 vl. and vc. (arr.), Augener.
> String Trio, G minor, for vl., va., and vc. (arr.), Augener.
> *The Art of the Fugue*, arr. by Harris-Norton, Schirmer. Columbia M206.
> *The Musical Offering*, arr. by H. T. David, Schirmer. Victor DM709.
> Trio Sonata from the above, Schirmer.
> Sonata, C major, for 2 vl. and p., International.
> Sonata, G major, for fl., vl., and p., International.
> Complete Works (reprinted in 1947): Vol. IX, trio sonatas; Vol. XXV^1, *The Art of the Fugue;* Vol. XXXI^2, *The Musical Offering*, Edwards.

Bach, Karl Philipp Emanuel
> Trio Sonata, G major, Schirmer.
> Two Trio Sonatas, F major and D minor, Peters.

Barber, Samuel

    Serenade, Op. 1, for stq., Schirmer.

    String Quartet, Op. 11, Schirmer.

Bartók, Belá

    String Quartet, Op. 7, Universal. Victor DM286.

    String Quartet, Op. 17, Boosey & Hawkes. Victor DM320.

    String Quartet No. 3, Boosey & Hawkes.

    String Quartet No. 4, Boosey & Hawkes. Concert Hall A8.

    String Quartet No. 5, Boosey & Hawkes.

    String Quartet No. 6, Boosey & Hawkes.

    Contrasts, for vl., cl., and p., Boosey & Hawkes. Columbia X178.

Bax, Arnold Edward Trevor

    String Quartet No. 1, G major, Oxford.

    String Quartet No. 2, E minor, Schirmer.

    Quintet, G minor, for ob. and stq., Oxford.

    Piano Quintet, G minor, Oxford.

Beach, Mrs. H. H. A.

    Theme and Variations, Op. 80, for fl., and stq., Schirmer.

    Piano Trio, Op. 150, Composers Press.

Beethoven, Ludwig van

    String Trio, Op. 8, for vl., va., and vc., International. Columbia M217.

    String Trios, Op. 9, Nos. 1 and 3, for vl., va., and vc., International. No. 1, Columbia M384; No. 3, Columbia M397.

    String Trio, Op. 25, for fl., vl., and va., International.

    String Trios, Op. 3, Op. 8, Op. 9, Nos. 1–3, Op. 25, Universal.

    String Quartet, Op. 18, No. 1, Durand. Columbia M444.

    String Quartet, Op. 18, No. 2, Durand. Columbia M66, Victor DM601.

    String Quartet, Op. 18, No. 3, Durand.

    String Quartet, Op. 18, No. 4, Durand. Columbia M556.

    String Quartet, Op. 18, No. 5, Durand. Columbia M301.

    String Quartet, Op. 18, No. 6, Durand.

    String Quartets, Op. 18, Nos. 1–3, Augener.

    String Quartets, Op. 18, Nos. 4–6, Augener.

    String Quartets, Op. 18, Nos. 1–6, Kalmus.

    String Quartet, Op. 59, No. 1, Durand. Columbia M543, M256; Victor DM804.

    String Quartet, Op. 59, No. 2, Durand. Victor DM340.

    String Quartet, Op. 59, No. 3, Durand. Columbia M510.

String Quartets, Op. 59, Nos. 1–3, Universal.

String Quartets, Op. 59, Nos. 1–3, Op. 74, Op. 95, Kalmus.

String Quartet, Op. 74, Durand. Victor DM467.

String Quartet, Op. 95, Durand. Columbia M519.

String Quartet, Op. 127, Schirmer, Universal, Durand. Columbia M537.

String Quartet, Op. 130, Schirmer, Universal, Durand. Columbia M474, Victor DM157.

String Quartet, Op. 131, Schirmer, Universal, Durand. Columbia M429.

String Quartet, Op. 132, Schirmer, Universal, Durand. Columbia M545, Victor DM490.

String Quartet, Op. 133, Schirmer, Universal, Durand. Columbia X6, Musicraft M73.

String Quartet, Op. 135, Schirmer, Universal, Durand. Columbia M489.

String Quartets, Op. 127, 130–133, 135, Kalmus.

Seventeen String Quartets, in three volumes, Peters.

Seventeen String Quartet scores, in three volumes, Kalmus.

String Quintet, E flat, Op. 4, International.

String Quintet, C major, Op. 29, Universal, International. Columbia M294, M623.

Sextet, Op. 81b, for 2 h. and stq., International.

Septet, Op. 20, for vl., va., vc., cb., cl., bsn., and h., Peters.

Trio, Op. 87, for 2 ob. and Eh., Boosey & Hawkes.

Variations on a Theme by Mozart, for 2 ob. and Eh., B. & H. Musicraft Set 34.

✓ Piano Trios, Op. 1, Nos. 1–3, Schirmer. No. 3, Musicraft Set 2 (with Op. posth., 1812).

✓ Piano Trio, Op. 11, for cl. (or vl.), vc., and p., Schirmer.

✓ Piano Trios, Op. 70, Nos. 1 and 2, Schirmer. No. 1, Victor DM370.

✓ Piano Trio, Op. 97, Schirmer. Victor DM949.

✓ Piano Trios, Op. 44, Op. 121a, Op. posth. (E. flat), and Op. posth. (1812), Durand. Op. posth. (1812), Musicraft Set 2 (with Op. 1, No. 3).

✓ Eleven Piano Trios, complete, Universal, Augener.

✓ Piano Quartet, E flat (Bonn), Universal.

✓ Piano Quartet, D major (Bonn), Universal.

✓ Piano Quartet, C major (Bonn), Universal.

✓ Piano Quartet, E flat, Op. 16, Schirmer, Augener.

Berg, Alban
    String Quartet, Op. 3, Universal.
    Lyrische Suite, for stq., Universal. Vox 181.
Bergsma, William Laurence
    String Quartet No. 1, SPAM.
Bloch, Ernest
    String Quartet, Schirmer, Universal. Columbia M392.
    String Quartet No. 2, Boosey & Hawkes.
    Three Nocturnes for Piano Trio, C. Fischer.
    Paysages, for 2 vl., vc., and p., C. Fischer.
   √ Piano Quintet, Schirmer, Universal.
Boccherini, Luigi
    Three Trios, Op. 9, for 2 vl. and vc., International.
    Three Trios, Op. 38, for vl., va., and vc., International.
    Two Trios, for 2 vl. and vc., Music Press.
    Three String Quartets, Op. 32, No. 4, Op. 33, Nos. 5 and 6, International.
    Nine Selected String Quartets, Peters.
    Twelve Selected String Quartets, in four volumes, Ricordi.
    String Quintet, C major, for 2 vl., va., and 2 vc., International.
Borodin, Alexander
    String Trio, for 2 vl. and vc., Am-Rus.
    String Quartet, A major, Universal.
    String Quartet, D major, Universal, International.
Borodin-Glazounow
    Quartet on "b-la-f," International.
✸ Brahms, Johannes
    Three String Quartets, Op. 51, Nos. 1 and 2, and Op. 67, Kalmus.
        Op. 51, No. 1, Victor DM227; No. 2, Victor DM278. Op. 67, Vox 208.
    String Quartet, Op. 51, No. 1, Augener.
    String Quartet, Op. 51, No. 2, Augener.
    String Quintet, F major, Op. 88, International. Victor DM466.
    String Quintet, G major, Op. 111, International. Victor DM184.
    Quintet, B minor, Op. 115, for cl. and stq., Boosey & Hawkes. Victor DM491.
    String Sextet, B flat, Op. 18, International. Victor DM296.
    String Sextet, G major, Op. 36, International. Victor DM371.
   √ Piano Trio, B major, Op. 8, Schirmer, Augener. Victor DM883.
    Trio, E flat, Op. 40, for vl., h., and p., International. Victor DM199.

Piano Trio. C major, Op. 87, International, Augener. Columbia M266.

Piano Trio, C minor, Op. 101, Schirmer, Augener.

Trio, A minor, Op. 114, for cl., vc., and p., International. Musicraft Set 15.

Piano Quartet, G minor, Op. 25, Schirmer, Augener. Victor DM234.

Piano Quartet, A major, Op. 26, Schirmer, Augener. Victor DM346.

Piano Quartet, C minor, Op. 60, Schirmer, Augener.

Piano Quintet, F minor, Op. 34, Schirmer, Augener. Victor DM607.

Bridge, Frank

String Quartet No. 3, E minor, Augener.

String Quartet No. 4, G minor, Augener.

Three Idylls, for stq., Augener.

String Sextet, E flat, Augener.

Phantasy Piano Quartet, F sharp minor, Augener.

Piano Quintet, D minor, Augener.

Britten, Edward Benjamin

String Quartet No. 1, Boosey & Hawkes.

String Quartet No. 2, Boosey & Hawkes. Eng. Gram. C3536–3539.

Phantasy Quartet, Op. 2, for ob., vl. va., and vc., Boosey & Hawkes.

Bruckner, Anton

String Quintet, F major, International.

Intermezzo, for string quintet, Universal.

Buxtehude, Dietrich

Sonata, E major, Op. 2, No. 6, for vl., vc., and p., Nagel.

Trio Sonata No. 13, C major, Nagel. Skand. DB5249.

Carpenter, John Alden

String Quartet, Schirmer.

Piano Quintet, D major, Schirmer.

Casella, Alfredo

Five Pieces for String Quartet, Universal.

Concerto for String Quartet, Universal.

Serenata, for vl., vc., cl., bsn., and trp., Universal.

Siciliana e burlesca, for vl., vc., and p., Ricordi.

Chausson, Ernest

String Quartet, C minor, Op. 35, International.

Piano Quartet, A major, Op. 30, International.

Concerto, Op. 21, for vl., p., and stq., International. Victor DM877.

Cole, Ulric
    Piano Quintet, SPAM.
Coperario, Giovanni
    Four-part Fancy, for stq., Augener.
Copland, Aaron
    Vitebsk, for vl., vc., and p., Arrow.
Corelli, Arcangelo
    Trio Sonata, Op. 1, No. 1, Music Press.
    Trio Sonata, Op. 3, No. 1, Music Press.
    Trio Sonata, Op. 3, No. 2, Music Press.
    Six Chamber Sonatas, Op. 4, for 2 vl. and p., International.
    Trio Sonata scores, Opp. 1–4, two vols., Augener.
Couperin, François
    First Suite, for 2 vl., vc., and p., Durand.
    Second Suite, for 2 vl., vc., and p., Durand.
Debussy, Claude Achille
    String Quartet, G minor, Op. 10, Elkan, Kalmus. Columbia M467,
        Victor DM186 (*see* Glazounow).
    Sonata, for fl., va., and harp, Elkan. Victor DM873.
Delius, Frederick
    String Quartet, Augener.
Diamond, David Leo
    Quintet, for fl., vl., va., vc., and p., SPAM.
Dittersdorf, Karl Ditters von
    String Quartet, E flat, International.
    String Quartet, A major, B. & H. Musicraft Set 45.
Dohnányi, Ernst von
    Serenade, C major, Op. 10, for vl., va., and vc., International. **Victor**
        DM903.
    String Quartet, A major, Op. 7, Universal.
    String Quartet, D flat, Op. 15, AMP. Columbia M367.
    String Quartet, A minor, Op. 33, Roszavölgyi.
    Piano Quintet, C minor, Op. 1, International. Columbia M546.
    Piano Quintet, E flat minor, Op. 26, International.
Donato, Anthony
    String Quartet, E minor, SPAM.
Dowland, John
    Lachrymae, or Seven Teares, for 2 vl., va., 2 vc., and hps. ad libitum,
        C. Fischer.

Dumler, Martin George
    String Quartet, Op. 47, Composers Press.
☆Dvořák, Antonín
    Terzetto, C major, Op. 74, for 2 vl. and va., International.
    String Quartet, E flat, Op. 51, International. Columbia M480.
    String Quartet, C major, Op. 61, Simrock. Concert Hall B12.
    String Quartet, F major, Op. 96 ("American Quartet"), Kalmus.
      Columbia M328, Victor DM681.
    String Quartet, A flat, Op. 105, Simrock.
    String Quartet, G major, Op. 106, Simrock.
    String Quintet, G major, Op. 77, for stq. and cb., Universal.
    String Quintet, E flat, Op. 97, International.
    String Sextet, A major, Op. 48, International. Victor DM661.
  ✓ Piano Trio, B flat, Op. 21, Schirmer.
  ✓ Piano Trio, F minor, Op. 65, Universal.
  ✓ Piano Trio, E minor, Op. 90 ("Dumky Trio"), International.
    Bagatelles, Op. 47, for 2 vl., vc., and p., International.
  ✓ Piano Quartet, E flat, Op. 87, AMP.
  ✓ Piano Quintet, A major, Op. 81, Schirmer.
Elgar, Sir Edward
    String Quartet, E minor, Op. 83, Novello.
Enesco, Georges
    String Octet, C minor, Op. 7, Enoch.
☆Fauré, Gabriel Urbain
    String Quartet, E major, Op. 121, Durand.
  ✓ Piano Trio, D minor, Op. 120, Durand.
  ✓ Piano Quartet, C minor, Op. 15, International. Columbia M255.
  ✓ Piano Quintet, D minor, Op. 89, Schirmer.
  ✓ Piano Quintet, C minor, Op. 115, Durand.
Foote, Arthur William
  ✓ Piano Quartet, C major, Op. 23, Schmidt.
☆ Franck, César Auguste
    String Quartet, D major, Kalmus. Columbia M128.
  ✓ Piano Trio, F sharp minor, Op. 1, No. 1, International.
  ✓ Piano Quintet, F minor, Peters, Heugel. Columbia M334.
Freed, Isadore
  ✓ Triptych, for piano quartet, SPAM.
Frescobaldi, Girolamo
    Suite, D major, for 2 vl. and p., Elkan.

Gabrieli, Andrea
   Three Ricercari, arr. for stq., Music Press.
Gade, Niels Vilhelm
   Novelettes, Op. 29, for vl., vc., and p., Augener.
   √ Piano Trio, F major, Op. 42, Augener, C. Fischer. Skand. DB5244–
      5245.
Giannini, Vittorio
   √ Piano Quintet, SPAM.
Gibbons, Orlando
   Four Fantasies, arr. for vl., va., and vc., Marks.
Glazounow, Alexander
   Five Novelettes, Op. 15, for stq., International. Op. 15, No. 3, *In-
      terludium in modo antico*, Victor V7838 (part of Victor
      DM186).
   String Quartet, Op. 1, Belaieff.
   String Quartet, Op. 26, Belaieff.
   String Quartet, Op. 106, Belaieff.
   String Quartet, Op. 107, Belaieff.
Glazounow-Borodin
   Quartet on "b-la-f," International.
Glazounow-Liadow
   Festive Moods, for stq., International.
Glière, Reinhold
   String Quartet, A major, Op. 2, International.
Gluck, Christoph Willibald von
   Trio Sonata No. 2, G major, Music Press.
Goossens, Eugène
   Phantasy Quartet, Op. 12, for stq., Chester.
   String Quartet, Op. 14, Chester.
   String Quartet, Op. 59, Boosey & Hawkes.
   Five Impressions of a Holiday, for vl. or fl., vc., and p., Chester.
Grieg, Edvard
   String Quartet, G minor, Op. 27, International. Victor DM465.
Griffes, Charles Tomlinson
   Two Sketches based on Indian Themes, for stq., Schirmer.
Gruenberg, Louis
   Four Indiscretions, Op. 20, for stq., Universal.
   String Quartet, Schirmer.
Haba, Alois
   String Quartet, Op. 4, Universal.

String Quartet, Op. 7 (quarter-tone), Universal.
String Quartet, Op. 12 (quarter-tone), Universal.
Hadley, Henry
    String Quartet, Op. 132, Schirmer.
  ✓ Piano Quintet, Op. 50, Schirmer.
Handel, George Frederic
    Trio Sonata, Op. 2, No. 4, International.
    Trio Sonata, Op. 2, No. 6, International.
    Trio Sonata, Op. 2, No. 8, International.
    Trio Sonata, Op. 2, No. 9, International.
    Trio Sonata, Op. 5, No. 4, Music Press.
    Trio Sonata, E major, Music Press.
    Trio Sonata No. 3, E flat, Music Press.
Hanson, Howard
    String Quartet, Op. 23, Birchard.
Harris, Roy Ellsworth
    Three Variations on a Theme, for stq., Schirmer.
    Four Preludes and Fugues, for stq., unpublished. Columbia M540.
  ✓ Piano Trio, New Music.
  ✓ Piano Quintet, Schirmer. Victor DM752.
    Concerto, for p., cl., and stq., Arrow.
Haubiel, Charles
    Clasici, for stq., Composers Press.
Haydn, Franz Joseph
    Three Divertimenti, for vl., va., and vc., International.
    Two "London Trios," for 2 fl. and vc., Nagel. Musicraft Set 42.
    Eighty-three String Quartets, complete, Litolff (c. 1879), Peters
       (c. 1912). Op. 3, No. 5, Op. 33, No. 2, Op. 64, No. 6, and Op. 71,
       No. 1, Victor DM525. Op. 20, No. 5, Op. 50, No. 3, and Op. 76,
       No. 3, Victor DM526. Op. 20, No. 4, Op. 74, No. 2, and Op. 77,
       No. 2, Victor DM527. Op. 1, No. 1, Op. 20, No. 1, Op. 55, No. 3,
       and Op. 76, No. 4, Victor DM595. Op. 50, No. 6, Op. 74, No. 1,
       Op. 3, No. 4, and Op. 64, No. 3, Victor DM689. Op. 20, No. 5,
       Columbia M228. Op. 54, No. 1, Victor DM869. Op. 74, No. 3,
       Columbia X274. Op. 76, No. 3, Columbia M246. Op. 76, No. 5,
       Columbia M400.
    Thirty Celebrated Quartets, in two volumes, Kalmus.
    Six String Quartets, Op. 76, Nos. 1–6, Universal.
    Thirty-one Piano Trios, complete, Peters, Universal.
  ✓ Twelve Piano Trios, in three volumes, Peters, Durand.

Five Celebrated Piano Trios, International.
√   Piano Trio No. 30, B. & H. Musicraft Set 8.
Heilman, William Clifford
√   Piano Trio, C major, Op. 7, SPAM.
Heller, James Gutheim
Three Aquatints, Op. 1, for stq., SPAM.
Hill, Edward Burlingame
String Sextet, Op. 39, SPAM.
Hindemith, Paul
String Trio No. 2, for 2 vl. and va., Schott. Columbia M209.
String Quartet No. 1, Op. 10, Schott.
String Quartet No. 2, Op. 16, Schott.
String Quartet No. 3, Op. 22, Schott.
String Quartet No. 4, Op. 32, Schott. Concert Hall B2.
String Quartet No. 5, E flat, AMP.
Five Pieces, Op. 44, No. 4, for stq., AMP.
Holden, David
Music for Piano and String Quartet, SPAM.
Honegger, Arthur
String Quartet No. 2, Senart.
String Quartet No. 3, Senart.
Huss, Henry Holden
String Quartet, B minor, Op. 31, SPAM.
Ibert, Jacques
String Quartet, Leduc.
Indy, Paul Marie Théodore Vincent d'
String Quartet, E major, Op. 45, Durand.
String Sextet, B flat, Op. 92, Heugel.
√   Piano Trio, G major, Op. 98, Rouart.
√   Piano Quartet, A minor, Op. 7, Durand.
Ireland, John
√   Piano Trio No. 3, E major, Boosey & Hawkes.
Jacobi, Frederick
String Quartet on Indian Themes, SPAM.
String Quartet No. 2, G major, SPAM.
Hagiographa, Three Biblical Narratives, for piano quintet, Arrow.
Jarecki, Tadeus
String Quartet, Op. 21, SPAM.
Jenkins, John
Four-part Fancy, for stq., Augener.

Five-part Fantasy No. 1, for 2 vl., 2 va., and vc. (or 2 vl., va., and 2 vc.), Schirmer.

Kennan, Kent Wheeler

√ Piano Quintet, Schirmer.

Kodaly, Zoltán

String Trio, F major, Op. 12, for 2 vl. and va., Universal.
String Quartet, C minor, Op. 2, Universal.
String Quartet, Op. 10, Universal.

Koutzen, Boris

String Quartet No. 2, SPAM.

Křenek, Ernst

String Quartet No. 1, Op. 6, Universal.
String Quartet No. 3, Op. 20, Universal.
String Quartet No. 5, Op. 65, Universal.
String Quartet No. 6, Op. 78, Universal.

Kroll, William

Four Bagatelles, for stq., Schirmer.
Four Characteristic Pieces, for stq., Schirmer.

Lawes, William

Six-part Fantasy and Air, for 2 vl., 2 va., and 2 vc., Schirmer.

Leclair, Jean-Marie

Six Trio Sonatas, Music Press.
Trio Sonata, B flat, AMP.
Trio Sonata, D minor, AMP.

Lockwood, Normand

Six Serenades, for stq., Music Press.
String Quartet No. 2, SPAM.

Loeffler, Charles Martin

Music for Four Stringed Instruments, SPAM.
String Quintet in One Movement, for 3 vl., va., and vc., Schirmer.
Two Rhapsodies, for ob., va., and p., Schirmer.

Lœillet, Jean Baptiste

Two Trio Sonatas, A major and D major, International.
Six Trio Sonatas, Book I: Nos. 1–3, Marks.
Two Trio Sonatas, D minor and D major, Music Press.
Two Trio Sonatas, G major and B minor, Elkan.

Malipiero, G. Francesco

Rispetti e strambotti, for stq., Chester.
Ricercari, for 4 va., vc., cb., fl., ob., cl., bsn., and h., Universal.
Ritrovari, for above instrumentation, Universal.
Sonata a tre, for vl., vc., and p., Universal.

Markevitch, Igor
    Serenade, for vl., cl., and bsn., Schott.

Martinu, Bohuslav
    String Quartet No. 2, Universal. Ultraphon G14330–14332.
    String Quartet No. 3, Leduc.
  √ Piano Trio, Schott.

Mason, Daniel Gregory
    Quartet on Negro Themes, Op. 19, SPAM.
    Serenade, Op. 31, for stq., SPAM.
    Three Pieces, Op. 13, for harp, fl., and stq., SPAM.
  √ Piano Quartet, A major, Op. 7, Schirmer.

☆ Mendelssohn, Felix
    String Quartet, Op. 12, Universal, Ricordi, Augener.
    String Quartet, Op. 13, Ricordi, Augener.
    String Quartet, Op. 44, No. 1, Augener. Columbia M304.
    String Quartet, Op. 44, No. 2, Augener.
    String Quartet, Op. 44, No. 3, Augener.
    Four String Quartets, Op. 12, Op. 44, Nos. 1–3, International.
    Three String Quartets, Op. 44, Nos. 1–3, Universal.
    String Quartet, Op. 80, Universal, Augener.
    String Quartet, Op. 81, Augener.
    String Quintet, A major, Op. 18, Peters, Ricordi.
    String Quintet, B flat, Op. 87, Peters, Ricordi.
    String Octet, E flat, Op. 20, International, Ricordi.
  √ Piano Trio, D minor, Op. 49, Schirmer.
  √ Piano Trio, C minor, Op. 66, Schirmer.
  √ Three Piano Quartets, Opp. 1–3, Peters.

Milhaud, Darius
    Sonatine a trois, for vl., va., and vc., Music Press.
    String Quartet No. 1, Durand.
    String Quartet No. 2, Durand.
    String Quartet No. 6, Universal.
    String Quartet No. 7, Universal.
    String Quartet No. 8, Elkan.
    String Quartet No. 9, Elkan.

Moore, Douglas Stuart
    String Quartet, SPAM.

☆ Mozart, Wolfgang Amadeus
    Divertimento, E flat, K.563, for vl., va., and vc., International.
      Columbia M351, Victor DM959.

Sixteen Early Quartets, K.155–160, 168–173, 285, 298, 370, and 546, Kalmus. K.171, Vox 183. K.285 and 298, Musicraft Set 7. K.370, Columbia X21. K.546, Victor 12324.

Ten Famous Quartets, K.387, 421, 428, 458, 464, 465, 499, 575, 589, and 590, Schirmer, Universal, Augener. K.387, Columbia M374. K.421, Columbia M462, Musicraft Set 4. K.428, Columbia M529. K.458, Columbia M438, Victor DM763. K.464, Columbia M222. K.465, Columbia M439, Victor DM285. K.590, Victor DM348.

Eleven Famous Quartets, the above plus *Eine kleine Nachtmusik*, Kalmus.

Three Quartets, K.285, 285a, and 298, for fl., vl., va., and vc., International.

Quartet, K.370, for ob., vl., va., and vc., Boosey & Hawkes, AMP.

String Quintets, Vol. I, K.406, 515, 516, 593, and 614, Peters, Kalmus. K.515, Columbia M586. K.516, Columbia M526, Victor DM190. K.593, Victor DM350.

String Quintets, Vol. II, K.S.515, K.46, 174, 581, and 407, Peters.

Quintet, A major, K.581, for cl. and stq., Kalmus, Boosey & Hawkes, AMP. Columbia M293, Victor DM452.

Divertimento, K.334, for 2 h. and stq., B. & H. Columbia M379.

Sextet, *Ein musikalischer Spass*, K.522, for 2 h. and stq., International.

√ Piano Trio, B flat, K.254, Schirmer.
√ Piano Trio, D minor, K.442, Schirmer.
√ Piano Trio, G major, K.496, Schirmer.
√ Piano Trio, E flat, K.498, for cl., va., and p., Schirmer, Augener.
√ Piano Trio, B flat, K.502, Schirmer.
√ Piano Trio, E major, K.542, Schirmer. Musicraft Set 29 (with K.548).
√ Piano Trio, C major, K.548, Schirmer. Musicraft Set 29 (with K.542).
√ Piano Trio, G major, K.564, Schirmer.
√ Eight Piano Trios, complete, Universal.
√ Piano Quartet, G minor, K.478, Augener.
√ Piano Quartet, E flat, K.493, Augener. Columbia M669.
√ Two Piano Quartets, K.478 and 493, Marks, Universal.
√ Three Piano Quartets (arr.), E flat, K.452; A major, K.581; D major, K.593, Universal.

Seventeen Trio Sonatas, for 2 vl., vc., and org. or p. (Vols. IV and V with additional wind instruments): Vol. I, Nos. 1–6; Vol. II,

Nos. 7, 8, 10, and 11; Vol. III, Nos. 9, 13, and 15; Vol. IV, Nos. 12 and 14; Vol. V, Nos. 16 and 17, Music Press.

Adagio and Rondo, K.617, for harmonica (celeste), fl., ob., va., and vc., B. & H. Victor 11–9570.

Piano Quintet, K.452, for ob., cl., bsn., h., and p., International.

Nardini, Pietro
Six String Quartets, AMP.

Pergolesi, Giovanni Battista
Trio Sonata, G minor, Music Press.

Pierné, Henry Constant Gabriel
Trois pieces en trio, for vl., va., and vc., pub. unknown. Columbia X153.

Pisk, Paul Amadeus
String Quartet, Op. 8, Universal.

Piston, Walter
String Quartet No. 1, Cos Cob. Columbia M388.
String Quartet No. 2, Schirmer.
Quintet, for fl. and stq., Arrow.
√ Piano Trio, Arrow.

Porter, Quincy
String Quartet No. 3, SPAM.
String Quartet No. 4, Arrow.
String Quartet No. 6, SPAM.

Prokofieff, Serge
String Quartet, Op. 50, International. Columbia M448.
String Quartet, Op. 92, International, Am-Rus. Concert Hall A1.
Quintet, Op. 39, for vl., va., cb., ob., and cl., Russ.
Overture on Hebrew Themes, for stq., cl., and p., International.

Purcell, Henry
Trio Sonata, B minor, Augener.
Trio Sonata, A minor, Augener.
Trio Sonata, C major, Augener.
The Golden Sonata, Elkan, Augener.
Three Fantasies, for vl., va., and vc., Marks.
Twelve Trio Sonatas, first set, pub. separately, *L'Oiseau.*

Rachmaninoff, Sergei
Trio elegiaque, D minor, Op. 9, for vl., vc., and p., International.

√ Ravel, Maurice
String Quartet, F major, International. Columbia M425, Vox 180.

Introduction and Allegro, for harp, fl., cl., and stq., Durand. Columbia X167.

✓ Piano Trio, International.

Reger, Max

Two String Quartets, G minor and A major, Op. 54, Universal.

String Quartet, D minor, Op. 74, Universal.

String Quartet, E flat, Op. 109, Universal.

String Quartet, F sharp minor, Op. 121, Peters.

Quintet, A major, Op. 146, for cl. and stq., Peters.

✓ Piano Trio, E minor, Op. 102, Universal.

✓ Piano Quartet, A minor, Op. 133, Peters.

Reiser, Alois

String Quartet, Op. 16, SPAM.

Respighi, Ottorino

String Quartet, D major, Universal.

Quartetto dorico, Universal.

Riegger, Wallingford

String Quartet No. 1, Arrow.

✓ Piano Trio, SPAM.

Robertson, Leroy J.

✓ Piano Quintet, SPAM.

Roussel, Albert

Trio, Op. 4, for fl., va., and vc., Durand.

String Quartet, D major, Op. 45, Durand. Columbia M339.

Saint-Saëns, Charles Camille

String Quartet, E minor, Op. 112, Durand.

String Quartet, G major, Op. 153, Durand.

✓ Piano Trio, E minor, Op. 92, Durand.

✓ Piano Quartet, B flat, Op. 41, Durand.

Septet, E flat, Op. 65, for stq., cb., trp., and p., Durand.

Scarlatti, Alessandro

Sonata a quattro, for stq., Music Press.

Scarlatti, Domenico

Burlesca, for 2 vl., vc., and p., Elkan.

Scarmolin, A. Louis

String Quartet, Composers Press.

Schobert, Johann

Two Piano Trios, B flat, Op. 16, No. 1, and F minor, Op. 16, No. 4, Nagel.

Schönberg, Arnold
    String Quartet, Op. 7, Universal.
    String Quartet, Op. 10, Universal.
    String Quartet, Op. 30, Universal.
    String Quartet, Op. 37, Schirmer.
    Verklärte Nacht, for string sextet, International.
    Quintet, Op. 26, for fl., ob., cl., bsn., and h., Universal.
    Ode to Napoleon (text by Lord Byron), for stq., p., and narrator, Schirmer.
    Suite, Op. 29, for vl., va., vc., 3 cl., and p., Universal.

Schubert, Franz
    String Trio, B flat, for vl., va., and vc., International.
    String Quartets, Vol. I: Op. 29, Op. posth. (D minor), and Op. 125, Nos. 1 and 2, Kalmus, Peters, Augener. Op. 29, Victor DM225. Op. posth., Victor DM468. Op. 125, No. 1, Concert Hall.
    String Quartets, Vol. II: Op. 161, Op. 168, G minor, D major, and C minor, Kalmus, Peters.
    String Quartet, A minor, Op. 29, Universal.
    String Quartet, D minor, Op. posth., Universal.
    String Quintet, C major, Op. 163, for 2 vl., va., and 2 vc., International. Columbia M497, Victor DM299.
    Octet, F major, Op. 166, for stq., cb., cl., bsn., and h., Peters. Columbia M97.
    ⱽPiano Trio, B flat, Op. 99, Schirmer, Universal, Augener. Victor DM923.
    ⱽ Piano Trio, E flat, Op. 100, Schirmer, Universal, Augener.
    Nocturne, for vl., vc., and p., International.
    Sonata, for vl., vc., and p., Universal.
    Adagio and Rondo, for piano quartet, International.
    Quintet, A major, Op. 114 ("The Trout"), for vl., va., vc., cb., and p., International. Victor DM312.

Schuman, William Howard
    String Quartet No. 2, Arrow.
    String Quartet No. 3, Boosey & Hawkes. Concert Hall.

Schumann, Robert Alexander
    String Quartet, Op. 41, No. 1, Augener. Columbia M454.
    String Quartet, Op. 41, No. 2, Augener.
    String Quartet, Op. 41, No. 3, Augener. Columbia M319.
    Three String Quartets, Op. 41, Nos. 1–3, International.

Piano Trio, D minor, Op. 63, Schirmer, Universal, Augener.
Piano Trio, F major, Op. 80, Schirmer, Universal, Augener.
Phantasiestücke, Op. 88, for vl., vc., and p., Augener.
Piano Trio, G minor, Op. 110, Schirmer, Universal, Augener.
Märchenerzählungen, Op. 132, for cl. (or vl.), va., and p., Durand.
Piano Quartet, E flat, Op. 47, International, Universal, Ricordi.
Piano Quintet, E flat, Op. 44, Schirmer, Ricordi. Columbia M533,
    Victor DM736, Musicraft A29.

Search, Frederick Preston
    String Quartet, E minor, Composers Press.
    String Sextet, F minor, SPAM.

Sessions, Roger Huntington
    String Quartet, E minor, Arrow.

Shepherd, Arthur
    String Quartet, E minor, SPAM.
    Triptych, for soprano and stq., SPAM.

Shostakovitch, Dmitri
    String Quartet, Op. 49, International. Columbia X231.
    String Quartet, Op. 69, Am-Rus.
    Two Pieces for String Quartet, Op. 11, Am-Rus.
    Piano Trio, Op. 67, Am-Rus. Compass C102.
    Piano Quintet, Op. 57, Am-Rus. Columbia M483.

Sibelius, Jan
    Voces intimae, D minor, Op. 56, for stq., International. Victor
        DM344.

Sinding, Christian
    String Quartet, A minor, Op. 70, Peters.
    Piano Trio, C major, Op. 87, Peters.

Smetana, Bedřich
    String Quartet, E minor, Op. 115 ("Aus meinem Leben"), Univer-
        sal, International. Columbia M405, Victor DM675, Ultraphon
        G12610–12613.
    String Quartet No. 2, D minor, Universal.
    Piano Trio, G minor, Op. 15, International. Vox 628.

Smith, David Stanley
    String Quartet, C major, Op. 46, Schirmer.
    String Quartet, E flat, Op. 57, Schirmer.
    String Quartet, C major, Op. 71, SPAM.

Sowerby, Leo
    Serenade, G major, for stq., SPAM.

Spalding, Albert
 String Quartet, C minor, Op. 10, Schirmer.
Stravinsky, Igor
 Concertino for String Quartet, Hansen. Concert Hall B6.
 Three Pieces for String Quartet, Universal. Concert Hall B6.
 Octet for Wind Instruments, Russ. Columbia X25.
 L'Histoire du Soldat, for vl., cb., cl., bsn., trp., trombone, percussion, and narrator, Chester. Columbia M184.
 The above, arr. for vl., cl., and p., Chester.
Taneiev, Sergei
 Trio, Op. 21, for 2 vl. and va., International.
Tartini, Giuseppe
 Two Sonatas, G major and D major, for 2 vl. and vc., International.
 String Quartet No. 1, International.
 Sonata, D major, for 2 vl. (vc. ad libitum) and p., International.
Taylor, Deems
 Lucrece, suite for stq., Op. 21, J. Fischer.
Tschaikowsky, Peter Ilich
 String Quartet, D major, Op. 11, Kalmus, Universal, Augener. Columbia M407.
 String Quartet, F major, Op. 22, Universal.
 String Quartet, E flat minor, Op. 30, Universal, Augener.
 String Sextet, *Souvenir de Florence*, Op. 70, Rahter.
 Piano Trio, A minor, Op. 50, Rahter, Augener. Victor DM388.
Turina, Joaquin
 String Quartet, A minor, Op. 67, Rouart.
 Piano Trio, D major, Op. 35, Rouart.
 Piano Trio, B minor, Op. 76, Rouart.
Van Vactor, David
 Quintet, for fl. and stq., SPAM.
Veracini, Antonio
 Trio Sonata, C minor, Augener.
Villa-Lobos, Heitor
 String Quartet No. 2, Schott.
 String Quartet No. 3, Schott.
 Piano Trio No. 2, Schott.
 Piano Trio No. 3, Schott.
Wagenaar, Bernard
 String Quartet No. 2, Arrow.
 String Quartet No. 3, SPAM.

Warner, H. Waldo
>   Moods, theme and variations for stq., J. Fischer.
>   Suite in the Olden Style, Op. 34, for stq., J. Fischer.
>   Three Arias in the Olden Style, Op. 39, for stq., J. Fischer.
>   String Quartet, D major, Op. 49, J. Fischer.

Weber, Carl Maria von
>   Piano Trio, G minor, Op. 63, Peters.
>   Piano Quartet, B flat, Op. 8, Litolff.

Webern, Anton von
>   String Trio, Op. 20, for vl., va., and vc., Universal.
>   String Quartet, Op. 5, Universal.
>   Six Bagatelles, Op. 9, for stq., Universal.
>   String Quartet, Op. 28, Boosey & Hawkes.
>   Quartet, Op. 22, for vl., cl., tenor saxophone, and p., Universal.

Whithorne, Emerson
>   String Quartet, Arrow.
>   Piano Quintet, Op. 48, C. Fischer.

Wolf, Hugo
>   *Italian Serenade*, for stq., International.
>   String Quartet, D minor, Universal.

INDEX

Abendmusiken, instituted by Buxtehude, 121

A cappella, 12 f.

Accompanied recitative, 38 ff.

Adagio, 102

Adler, Guido, 159; editor of *Handbuch der Musikgeschichte,* 69; controversy with Riemann over the Mannheim composers, 167 f.

Affetti musicali (Marini), 63, 65, 66

Agrément, 88

Agricola, Martin, *Duo libri musices,* 15

Ahle, Johann Rudolf, 88 f.

"Airs," term used in 18th-century dance suites, 87

Airs, in eighteenth-century dance suites, 88

Albinoni, Tommaso, 145

Albrechtsberger, teacher of Beethoven, 242

Allemande, 77, 86; loss of dance-like character, 88

Amateur music, 18

American music, modern, 378 ff.

"American Quartet" (Dvořák), *see* Dvořák, string quartet in F major (Opus 96)

Ammerbach, Elias, 71

Ammerbach dance set, 72

"Andante Cantabile" (Tschaikowsky), 342

Antheil, George, 382

Antiphonal principle in music, 33 f.

Antiphonal style, 62

Antologia di musica antica e moderna (Tagliapetra), 78

"Archduke Trio" (Beethoven), 252 ff.

Arensky, Anton, 345

Artaria, August, 188

Art of the Fugue, The (Bach), 134, 138 ff.

Artusi, Giovanni, 25, 42; *L'Artusi overo della imperfettioni della moderna musica,* 20

Athalia (Handel), 132

Attaingnant, Pierre, *Quatuorze gaillardes, neuf pavanes, sept branles et deux basse danses,* 71

Attaingnant dance, 72

Aus meinem Leben (Smetana), 347

Bach, Johann Christian, 176; Mozart's knowledge of, 212; Mozart influenced by, 213

Bach, Johann Sebastian, 3, 12, 121, 133 f.; admiration for Purcell's music, 103; dance suites of, 109; *B minor Mass,* 133; *Passion According to St. Matthew,* 133, 169; *The Musical Offering,* 134, 135 ff.; Bach, *The Art of the Fugue,* 134, 138 ff.; lack of formal regularity in his fugues, 193; *B Minor Mass,* chromaticism in, 224; Mozart influenced by, 227; *St. Matthew Passion,* conducted by Mendelssohn, 300

Bach, Karl Philipp Emanual, 143, 152, 164, 176; works of, known by Haydn, 182

Bachgesellschaft, Schumann instrumental in founding of, 302

Bachgesellschaft edition of Bach's works, one of Purcell's *toccatas* in, 103

Bäurl, *see* Peuerl, Paul

Balbastre, organist, 115

Balletto (Monteverdi), 78

Ballo, 106

Banchetto musicale (Schein), 81, 83, 87, 157

Banchieri, Adriano, 36

Bardi, Count, 38

Baroque form, end of, 143

Baroque period, 20 ff.

Baroque style: persistence of, 145; review of, 147

Bartered Bride, The (Smetana), 347

Bartók, Béla, 356, 357, 370 f.; second string quartet, 370; third string quartet, 370; fifth and sixth string quartets, 370 f.

Basse danse, 70

Basso continuo, 40 ff.; invention of the term ascribed to Viadana, 46; of small importance in canzoni, 57; its use in

Basso continuo (*Continued*)
"Canzona francese a quattro, a riposta" (Viadana), 48; use in smaller canzoni, 58; in dance music, 84; decay of principle, 160 f.
Basso generale, 41
Basso ostinato, 88
Battista, Giovanni, 154
Bax, Arnold, 376
Becker, Diedrich, *Musikalische Frühlingsfrüchte*, 109
Beethoven, Ludwig van, 4, 10, 239 ff.; member of the Electoral orchestra in Bonn, 146; evidence of the Mannheimer style in works of, 171; assistant court organist at Bonn, 240; influenced by Neefe, 240; pupil of Mozart, 240; affected by his mother's death, 241; his father's death, 241; pupil of Haydn, 241 f.; pupil of Albrechtsberger, 242; pupil of Salieri, 242; deafness, 242, 251; love affairs, 243; guardianship of Karl van Beethoven, Jr., 243; death of, 244; interest in chamber music, 245; piano quartets, 246 f.; development of piano quartet simultaneously with Mozart, 247; trio in E flat for violin, cello, and piano, 247 f.; trio in G minor for flute, bassoon, and piano, 247 f.; *Rondino*, 248; piano trios, Opus 1, 248; variations in E flat (Opus 44), 248; use of modulations in piano trios, 249; trio for clarinet, cello, and piano (Opus 11) 250 f.; "Ghost Trio," 251; piano trios, 251 f.; "Archduke Trio," 252; trio in B flat, Opus 97, 252 ff.; piano trio in B flat, 254; *Adagio, Variations, and Rondo, Opus 121a*, 254 f.; octet in E flat, Opus 2, 255 f.; Opus 103, 255 f.; Opus 3, 256; Opus 25, 257 f.; Opus 9, 258 f.; Opus 71, 259; Opus 81b, 259; Opus 87, 259 f.; Opus 16, 260; septet for strings and winds (Opus 20), 260 ff.; string quintet in C major (Opus 29), 262 ff.; seventeen string quartets (Opera 18-135), 264 ff.; string quartet in F major (Opus 18) 265 f.; Opera 8 and 15, 265 f.; string quartet in D major (Opus 18), 267; string quartet in G major (Opus 18), 267; string quartet in F major (Opus 59), 268 f.; string quartet in E minor (Opus 59), 269 f.; string quartet in C major (Opus 59), 270 f.; string quartet

in E flat (Opus 74), 271; string quartet in F minor (Opus 95), 272; string quartet in A minor (Opus 132), 274; string quartet in E flat (Opus 127), 274; string quartet in B flat (Opus 130), 274 f.; string quartet in B flat (Opus 130), 275; string quartet in C sharp minor (Opus 131), 275; string quartet in F major (Opus 135), 275; string quartet in A minor (Opus 132), 275 f.; string quartet in B flat (Opus 130), 276 ff.; quartet in C sharp minor (Opus 131), 278 ff.; string quartet in F major (Opus 135), 279 f.
Beethoven, Karl van, 239; death of, 243
Beethoven, Karl van, Jr., Ludwig van Beethoven's guardianship of, 243
Beethoven, Maria van, 239
Bella (canzone da sonar), La (Vicentino), 31 ff.
Belli, Giulio, 57, 59
Berg, Alban, 368, 369
Bergsma, William, 383
Berliner Liederbuch, 15
Berlioz, Hector, 318
Bernardi, Stefano, 57
Birkenstock, Johann, 143
Bloch, Ernest, 357, 379 f.
B minor Mass (Bach), 133
Boccaccio, Giovanni, use of musical instruments recorded by, 13
Boccherini, Luigi, 229
Bocklet, Carl von, 295
Bonelli, Aurelio, *Il primo libro de ricercari et canzoni a quattro voci*, 36
Borodin, Alexander, *Sketch of the Steppes*, 344; string quartet in A major, 344 f.; string quartet in D major, 344 f.
Botstiber, Hugo, mention of "third and last" Haydn quartet, 209
Bourrée, 87
Brade, William, 76
Brahms, Johannes, 4, 10, 319 ff., 355; brilliant career for, prophesied by Schumann, 302; death and funeral of, 320 f.; trio in B major (Opus 8), 321 f.; sextet in B flat (Opus 18), 322 f.; piano quartet in A major (Opus 26), 323 f.; piano quartet in G minor (Opus 25), 323 f.; piano quintet in F minor (Opus 34), 324 f.; *Ein deutsches Requiem*, 325 f.; string sextet in G major (Opus 36), 325 f.; trio for piano, violin, and Waldhorn in E flat (Opus 40), 326 f.; string

quartets, in C minor and A minor (Opus 51), 327 f.; piano quartet in C minor (Opus 60), 328 f.; string quartet in B flat (Opus 67), 329; piano trio in C major (Opus 87), 329 f.; string quintet in F major (Opus 88), 330; piano trio in C minor (Opus 101), 330 f.; string quintet in G major (Opus 111), 331; quintet for clarinet and string quartet in B minor (Opus 115), 331 f.; trio for clarinet, cello, and piano in A minor (Opus 114), 331 f.; musical development of, 333 ff.; friendship with Dvořák, 348

Branle, 76 f.

Brentano, Maximiliane, Beethoven's piano trio in B flat dedicated to, 254

Bridge, Frank, 376

Brown, Count, Beethoven's Opus 9 dedicated to, 258

Brunelli, Antonio, 78, 97

Bülow, Hans von: friend of Brahms, 319; friendship with Dvořák, 348

Bull, John, 72, 73 f.; "Spanish Paven," 74; dances in the *Fitzwilliam Virginal Book*, 75

Buonamente, Giovanni Battista, 78, 97

Burney, Charles, 115, 158

Buxtehude, Dietrich, 121 ff., 142; *Suonate à doi, violino e viola da gamba, con cembalo*, 122

Byrd, William, 12, 13, 17, 72, 73; pavane by, 74 f.; dances in *Fitzwilliam Virginal Book*, 75; variations on a galliard, 75

Caccini, Giulio, 38; *Eurydice*, 41, 65; *Le nuove musiche*, 42, 45, 47, 65

Caldara, Antonio, 116, 117, 120 f.

Camerata, 37 ff.

Canale, Floriano, *Canzoni da sonare a quattro et otto voci, libro primo*, 36

Cannabich, Christian, 172

"Canzona francese a quattro, a riposta" (Viadana), 47 ff., 65

Canzone, 11, 17, 26, 30, 31 ff., 57, 66; indiscriminate use of term in first half of 17th century, 59; number of sections reduced to four, 68

Canzone a 2, 57 f.

Canzone a 3, 57 f.

Canzone a 8, 57

"Canzone auf den Schäfferstantz" (Widman), 82

Canzone da sonar, 32, 56 f.

Canzone style, 59 f.

Canzoni a due canti (Frescobaldi), 67

Canzoni a 4 et 8 voci (Rognioni), 36

Canzoni da sonar (Rossi), 58

Canzoni da sonare a quattro et otto voci, libro primo (Canale), 36

Canzoni, ovvero sonate concertate per chiesa e da camera (Merula), 96, 116

Capriccio a 4, canzona da sonar (Grillo), 52 f., 92

Cassation, *see* Divertimento

Cassel, *Landesbibliothek*, 77

Catholic Counter Reformation, *see* Roman Catholic Counter Reformation

Cavalieri, Emilio del, 38

Cavalli, Pietro Francesce, 108

Cavazzoni, Girolamo, *Intavolatura, cioè recercari, canzoni, himni, magnificat*, 29 f.

Cavazzoni, Marcantonio, *see* Marcantonio (Cavazzoni) de Bologna

Cazzati, Maurizio, 67

Cello; use in Haydn's quartets, 202; importance in Mozart's quartets dedicated to Frederick William II, 228 f.

Cento concerti ecclesiastici a 1, 2, 3, 4 voci (Viadana), 45 ff., 65

Chaconne, 88

Chamber music: advantages of, 4 f., 7 f.; early amateur status of, 5; development into a specialized field, 6; limitations of, 6 f.; number of players, 8 f.; definition of the term, 9 ff.; combinations in, 11

Chambonnières, Jacques de, 77, 86

Chanson, 16, 17, 18, 26, 28 ff.

Charles II, king of England, Purcell's patron, 104

Chaucer, Geoffrey, use of musical instruments recorded by, 13

Chausson, Ernest, a pupil of Franck, 336

Chopin of the North, The, *see* Gade, Niels

Chords, 371 f.

Chromaticism, in Mozart's quartets, 224

Chronologisch-systematisches Verzeichniss (Koechel), 216

Church music, 17 f.

Ciaconna, see Chaconne

Classical music, principal characteristics of, 314

Classical style, emergence of, 145 ff.

Classical symphony, French overture form influential in, 110
Clemenza di Tito, La (Mozart), 214
Collegium musicum, 18 f.
Combattimento di Tancredi e Clorinda, Il (Monteverdi), 65
Composers, conservative, see Conservative composers
Composers, progressive, see Progressive composers
Composition de musique selon la methode française (Kusser), 109 f.
"Concerto," indiscriminate use of term in first half of 17th century, 59
Conservative composers, in seventeenth century, 58
Consort Lessons (Morley), 75
Consorts, 75
Contemporary music, 354 ff., 378
Conti, Prince of, patron of Schobert, 175
Continuo: incorrect use of the term, 41; see also Basso continuo
Contrapuntal devices, in dance music, 84
Contrapuntal music, 17
Contrapuntal style, in Purcell's works, 103
Cooper, John, "Fancies for Viols," 76
Copland, Aaron, 382
Corelli, Arcangelo, 98 ff., 111 ff., 152; sonate da chiesa of, 115; sonata da camera of, 116; influence on Handel, 126
Cornett, 15, 48; see also Zinken
Costa, Gaspar, 36
Countermelody: its use by Marini, 66; improved by Merula, Cazzati, and Neri, 67 f.; used by Frescobaldi, 67
Counterpoint, its contrast to note-against-note style, 27
Counter Reformation, see Roman Catholic Counter Reformation
Couperin, François, 142
Couperin, Louis, 77, 86
Courante, 70, 77, 86
Court music, 18
Cramer, Wilhelm, 172
Creation, The (Haydn), 181, 183
Crequillon, 30
Crocker, Eunice C., 108
Cyclical principle, in Franck's chamber music, 337
Cypresses, The (Dvořák), 349

Dafne (Peri), 40 ff.

Dall'Abaco, Evaristo, 116 ff., 142, 152; similarity of Handel's sonatas to those of, 127
Dance movements in Corelli's sonatas, 112
Dance music, 69 ff.; development of, 16
Dance suite, 72 ff.; origin of, 69; summary of versions of about 1682, 110
Dance type of movement, 147 f.
Dantz und Nachdantz, 70
Danzi, Franz, wind quartet (Opus 56, No. 2), 173
"Death and the Maiden" (Schubert), 294
Debussy, Claude, 355; string quartet in G minor (Opus 10), 357 f.
DeLamarter, Eric, 382
Delle sonate over canzoni da farsi a violino solo e basso continuo (Uccellini), 94
Denkmäler der Tonkunst in Bayern, bibliography and thematic index of forty-seven Mannheim composers, 172
Detmold, court of, Brahms conductor at, 319
Deutsches Requiem, Ein (Brahms), 325 f.
Deutsche weltliche Gesang und Täntze, 79
Diamond, David, 383
Dido and Aeneas (Purcell), 101, 169
Dilettantism, in the Rococo period, 146
Distance between responsive entrances, see Responsive entrances, distance between
Divertimento, 158 ff.
Dohnányi, Ernst von, 355, 360 f.; second piano quintet, 361
Donato, Anthony, 383
Don Giovanni (Mozart), 214
Double, 88
Dowland, John, 76; Lachrymae, 75
Dramatic instrumental music, made possible by Camerata, 43
Dukas, Paul, 363
"Duke of Brunswick" (Bull), 75
"Dumka," 350 f.
"Dumky Trio," see Dvořák, piano trio in E minor (Opus 90)
Duo libri musices (Agricola), 15
Duple (imperfect) meter, origin of, in 14th century, 112
Dvořák, Antonin, 348 ff.; piano trio in B flat (Opus 21), 349 f.; Romanze, 351; piano trio in E minor (Opus

90), 351 f.; string quartet in A flat (Opus 105), 352; string quintet in E flat (Opus 97), 352; string quartet in F major (Opus 96), 352; string quartet in G major (Opus 106), 352; kinship to Mendelssohn, 353

Dynamics in instrumental music, innovations by Stamitz, 168 ff.

Echo effects, 59
Echo Song (Lasso), 169
Ecorcheville, Jules, *Vingt suites d'orchestre du XVII siècle française*, 77
Ehrenbreitstein, castle of, Beethoven's grandfather cook at, 240
Eichner, Ernst, 172
Einstein, Alfred: reviser of Koechel, *Chronologisch-systematisches Verzeichniss*, 216; comments on Haydn's influence on Mozart, 219; comments on Mozart's quintets, 233
Eisenstadt, 179
"Emperor, The" (Haydn), 206
Enesco, Georges, 376
Engelmann, George, *Fasciuculus quinque vocum concentum*, 81; *Paduana e galliarda a 5*, 81
England: dance music in, 72 ff.; 17th-century music in, 100 f.
Ensemble, conservative composers attracted by, 57
Estampie, 16
Eszterháza, 179 f.
Eszterházy, Prince Nicholas, patron of Haydn, 179
Eszterházy, Prince Paul Anton (d. 1762), patron of Haydn, 179
Eszterházy, Prince Paul Anton (the second), Haydn retired by, 180
Eszterházy family, Schubert teacher to a branch of the family in an estate on plains of Zelész, 290
Eurydice (Caccini), 41, 65
Eurydice (Peri), 41 f., 65

"Fancies for Viols" (Cooper), 76
Fancy, 72 f.
"Fantasia," indiscriminate use of term in first half of 17th century, 59
Fantasiestücke (Schumann), 312
Fantasy, *see* Fancy

Farina, Carlo, *Pavane, gagliarde, brandi, mascherata, arie francese, volti, balleti, sonate, canzone*, 84
Fasch, Johann, 155 f.
Fasciuculus quinque vocum concentum (Engelmann), 81
Faure, Gabriel, 355, 359; Ravel's string quartet dedicated to, 361
Fiddlers, guilds in 13th century, 13
Figured bass, 40 f.
Filtz, Anton, 172, 174
Finck, Heinrich, 15
Fischer, Wilhelm, 69, 87, 164
Fitzwilliam Virginal Book, 29, 73
"Five, The," 344
Five Impressions of a Holiday (Goossens), 363
Florence, the Camerata in, 37 ff.
Flute, 13
Folk songs (German), their transformation into instrumental music, 14 f.
Forelle, Die (Schubert), 290
Forellen Quintet (Schubert), 290
Form, The, 90
"Foscarina, La" (Marini), 65, 66 f.
France, the dance suite in, 76 ff.
Franck, César, 319, 335 ff.; fourth piano trio (Opus 2), 336; piano trio in F sharp minor (Opus 1), 336; quintet for piano and strings in F minor, 336 ff.; string quartet, 338 f.
Franck, Matthias, guardian of Haydn, 178
Franck, Melchior, 79 f.
Frederick the Great: theme given to Bach by, 135; patron of Karl Philipp Emanuel Bach, 164
Frederick William II, king of Prussia: Haydn's Opus 50 dedicated to, 201; Mozart's Frederick William quartets dedicated to, 201 f.; Mozart's visit to, 214, 227
Frederick William IV, Mendelssohn at the court of, 300
French overture form, 110
Frescobaldi, Girolamo, 52, 61, 96; *Canzoni a due canti*, 67; canzone of, 92 ff.; *Il libro primo della canzoni ad 1, 2, 3, 4*, 92
Friebert, Joseph, added vocal parts to Haydn's Opus 51, 204
Friends of Music concerts, Vienna, Brahms conductor of, 319

Fries, Count, Haydn quartet in B flat said to be dedicated to, 209
Froberger, Johann Jacob, 86
Fürnberg, von, employer of Haydn, 179
"Fugue form," inaccuracy of the term, 192 ff.
Fugues: composed by Mozart, 219; use of, by Haydn, 194
Fuller-Maitland, John Alexander, 101
Fux, Johann Joseph, *Gradus ad Parnassum*, studied by Mozart, 212

Gabrieli, Andrea, 30 f., 33, 59
Gabrieli, Giovanni, 33 ff., 52, 57, 59, 60, 61; *Sacrae symphoniae*, 34 f.; *Pian e forte*, 59, 169
Gade, Niels, 345
Galilei, Vincenzo, 38; *Lamentations*, 47
Galitzin, Nicolas Borissovich, Beethoven's Opus 127, Opus 130, and Opus 132 dedicated to, 273
Galliard, 70
Gantz neue Cantzon, Intraden, Balletten, und Couranten (Widman), 82 f.
"Gardana, La," (Marini), 63 ff.
Gardano, publisher of *Sacrae symphoniae*, 33
Gaultier, Denis, 77, 86
Gavotte, 87
Geiringer, Karl, 201
Geminiani, Francesco, 116, 143
Gerle, Hans, *Grosz- und Kleingeigen Quartet*, 15
German folk songs, *see* Folk songs (German)
Germany, the dance suite in, 76, 79; dominance in history of instrumental music from about 1750, 160; Italian influence on dance suites in, 82
Gesualdo, Carlo, 25
"Ghost Trio" (Beethoven), 251
Gibbons, Orlando, 17, 72, 73
"Gigg, A," (Byrd), 75
Gigue, 77, 86
Glazounow, Alexander, 345
Glinka, Michael, 341
Gluck, Christoph Willibald von, 143, 153 f.
Goossens, Eugene, 357, 363 f.; *Five Impressions of a Holiday* (piano trio, Opus 15), 363; influenced by Ravel, 364; second string quartet (Opus 50), 364

Gothic period, an uncomplimentary term, 20
"Gott erhalte Franz den Kaiser" (Haydn), 206
Gottlieb, Johann, 154
Gradus ad Parnassum (Fux), studied by Mozart, 212
Graun, Johann Gottlieb, 143
Grave, 102
"Great Consort" (Lawes), 76
"Great Fugue" (Beethoven), 276 f.
Gregorian plainsong, 18
Grieg, Edward, 345 f.; string quartet in G minor (Opus 27), 346
Grillo, Giovanni Battista, 52 f., 60, 66; *Capriccio a 4, Canzona da sonar*, 52 f., 92
Grosz- und Kleingeigen Quartet (Gerle), 15
Gruenberg, Louis, 380
Guilds, musical, 13
Guitar, 13

Haas, Robert, *Die Musik des Barock*, 62
Hagiographa: Three Biblical Narratives, (Jacobi), 380
Hammerschmidt, Andreas, 85, 87
Handbuch der Musikgeschichte (Adler), 69
Handel, George Frederick, 3, 117, 125 ff., 142, 152; French overture form in works of, 110; *Athalia*, 132; *Parnasso in festa*, 132; quartet in Opus 5, 162; string quartet, 163
Hanson, Howard, 382
Harp, 13
"Harp Quartet" (Beethoven), 271
Harpsichord: musical styles for, 17; discarded from trio sonata, 162; use in sonatas for keyboard instrument, 164
Harris, Roy, 357, 381 f.; piano quintet, 382; third quartet, 382
Hassler, Hans Leo, 17; *Sacri concentus*, 57; *Lustgarten*, 79
Hausmusik, 15
Haussmann, Valentin, 79 f.
Haydn, Franz Joseph, 3, 12, 18, 159, 178 ff.; influenced by Rosenmüller's technique, 108 f.; the controversy about the date of Opus 42, 201; string quartets mark beginning of classical style, 145; quartets, 166, 185 ff.; *The Creation*, 181, 183; *The Seasons*, 181; London symphonies, 183; trio sonatas,

184; string quartets, (Opera 1-2), 186; string quartets (Opus 3), 187; "Serenade," 188; string quartets (Opus 9), 188 f.; string quartets (Opus 17), 189 f.; string quartets (Opus 20), 190; string quartets (Opus 33), 194 ff.; string quartet in D minor (Opus 42) 201; string quartets (Opus 50), 201 f.; string quartets (Opus 51), 203 ff.; string quartets (Opera 54-55), 205; string quartets (Opus 64), 205 f.; "The Emperor," 206; string quartets (Opus 71), 206; "Gott erhalte Franz den Kaiser," 206; "The Lark," 206; "The Quinten," 206; "The Rider," 206; string quartets (Opus 74), 206; string quartets (Opus 76), 206; string quartet (Opus 77), 206 f.; "The Sunrise," 206; influenced by Mozart, 207 f.; numbering of quartets of, 208; "third and last quartet in B flat" mentioned by Botstiber, 209; influence on Mozart and influenced by Mozart, 222; style contrasted with that of Mozart, 225 f.; teacher of Beethoven, 241 f.
Haydn, Michael, 229
"He Who Wants the Little Daughter" (Ammerbach), 71
Hindemith, Paul, 356, 357, 373; third string quartet (Opus 22), 373; fourth string quartet (Opus 32), 374; fifth quartet, in E flat, 374 f.
Histoire du soldat (Stravinsky), 365
Hofdantz und Nachdantz, see Dantz und Nachdantz
Hoffmeister, Franz Anton, Mozart's quartet K.499 dedicated to, 226
"Holy Song of Thanksgiving to the Divinity by a Convalescent, in the Lydian Mode" (Beethoven), 275
Holzbauer, Ignaz, 172
Honegger, Arthur, 376
Hopper Tancz (Weck), 70 f.
Horn, 13, 15
Horn, Johann Kaspar, Parergon musicum, 109
Hornpipe, 87
Hummel, Johann, Opus 74, model for Schubert's Opus 114, 290
Humphrey, Pelham, 101

Ibert, Jacques, 376
Imitations, in dance music, 84
Impressionism in music, 355; Debussy, 358; Goossens, 363; Schönberg's "twelve-tone system" a reaction against, 368
Indiscretions (Gruenberg), 380
Indy, Vincent d', 355, 359 f.; pupil of Franck, 336
"In Our Deep Vaulted Cell" (Purcell), 169
Instrumental music: development of, 13 ff.; dramatic, see Dramatic instrumental music
Intavolatura, cioè recercari, canzoni, himni, magnificat (Cavazzoni), 29 f.
Intermezzo, in 18th-century dance suites, 87
Italy: the dance suite in, 78, 105 f.; sonata da chiesa and sonata da camera in, 90 ff.

Jacobi, Frederick, 380
Jannequin, Clement, 17
Jenkins, John, 73
Jesuits, 21
Jeune, Claude le, see Le Jeune, Claude
Joachim, Joseph, 319
Jongleur, 16

Kammersymphonie (Schönberg), 366
Kerll, Johann Kaspar, 86, 89
Keyboard instruments, before 1770, 234
Kleine Trauermusik, Eine (Schubert), 287
Koechel, Ludwig von, Chronologisch-systematisches Verzeichniss (K. or K.V.), 216
Kotter, Hans, 70
Křenek, Ernst, 369 f.
Kuhnau, Johann, 114
Kunst der Fuge, Die, see Art of the Fugue, The
Kusser, Johann Sigismund, Composition de musique selon la methode française, 109 f.

Lachrymae (Dowland), 75
Lamentations (Galilei), 47
Láng, Paul Henry, 137
Largo, 102
"Lark, The" (Haydn), 206
Lasso, Orlando di, 12, 13, 17, 18; Echo Song, 169
Lawes, Henry, 73
Lawes, William; "Great Consort," 76; "Royal Consort of Viols," 76

Leclair, Jean, 142
Legrenzi, Giovanni, 95 f.; "La Valvasona," 95 f.; "La Savorgnana," 96
Leipzig Conservatory, Mendelssohn's instrumentality in organizing, 300
Leipzig Gewandhaus Orchestra, Mendelssohn director of, 300
Leipzigischen Abendmusiken (Pezel), 109
Le Jeune, Claude, 17
Leopold II, Mozart's *La Clemenza di Tito* composed for, 214
Lessons for Consorts (Rosseter), 75
Libro primo della canzoni ad 1, 2, 3, 4, ll (Frescobaldi), 92
Lichnowsky, Prince, Beethoven's piano trios performed for, 248
"Linear counterpoint," 356; identified with Hindemith's compositions, 373 f.
Linke, Joseph, 295
Listener's attention, alteration of, 51
Liszt, Franz, 318
Little Consort of Three Parts (Locke), 76
Locatelli, Pietro, 117, 143
Lochamer Liederbuch, 15
Locke, Matthew, 86; *Little Consort of Three Parts*, 76
Loeffler, Charles Martin, 363
Löwe, Johann Jakob, 89
Lucino collection, 58
Lully, Jean Baptiste, 110
Lustgarten (Hassler), 79
Lute, 13; its use for transformed vocal music, 14; as substitute for voice parts, 29; early dance music arranged for, 70; its popularity in 16th-century Italy, 78

Machaut, Guillaume de, 14
Madrigal, 18
Magnificats, 17
"Maidens Are from Flanders, The" (Ammerbach), 71
Malipiero, Francesco, 376
Mannheim composers, 167; influence on Fasch, 155
Mannheim crescendo, 170
"Mannheimer sigh," 171
Marcantonio (Cavazzoni) de Bologna, 29
Marchenerzählungen (Schumann), 312
Marenzio, Luca, 22 f., 25
Marini, Biagio, 57, 58, 59, 61, 63 ff.; *Af-*

fetti musicali, 63, 65, 66; "La Gardana," 63 ff.; "La Orlandina," 63 ff., 92; "La Foscarina," 65, 66 f.; *Sonata da chiesa e da camera*, 96
Marriage of Figaro (Mozart), 214
Martinu, Bohuslav, 376 f.
Marxsen, Eduard, teacher of Brahms, 319
Maschera, Florentino, 52
Masses, 17, 18
Ma Vlast (Smetana), 347
Measures, 27
Meck, Nadejda von, 341
Melody, in Haydn's quartets, 194
Mendelssohn, Jacob Ludwig Felix, 299 ff., 303 ff.; *A Midsummer Night's Dream*, 299; death of, 300; friendship with Schumann, 302; sextet for piano, violin, two violas, cello, and bass (Opus 110), 304; string octet in E flat (Opus 20), 304 f.; string quartet in A major (Opus 13), 305; string quartet in E flat (Opus 12), 305; string quintet in A major (Opus 18), 305 f.; piano trio in C minor (Opus 66), 306 f.; piano trio in D minor (Opus 49), 306; string quartets in D major, E minor, and E flat (Opus 44), 306; string quintet in B flat (Opus 87), 307; string quartet in F minor (Opus 80), 307 f.; Opus 81, 308; adherence to Classical principles, 315
Merula, Tarquinio, 57, 67, 87; *Canzoni, overo sonate concertate per chiesa e camera*, 96, 116
Merulo, Claudio, 33, 52, 53 f.
Metastasio, Haydn's friend, 179
Midsummer Night's Dream, A (Mendelssohn), 299
Milhaud, Darius, 356, 357, 372 f.
Minuet, 87; use of, by Richter, 173; development of, 303
Minuet-scherzo type, position in Haydn's quartets, 197 ff.
Modal system, 23 ff.
Modern music, see Contemporary music
Modulations, Beethoven's use of, 249
"Moldau, The" (Smetana), 347
Monn, Georg Matthias, 167; quartets of, 163 f.
Monodic style, first application to a group of instruments, 52
Monody, 38 ff.; new principle of, 43 f.; broadened concept of, 47
Monteverdi, Claudio, 25, 33, 96; *Il com-*

battimento di Tancredi e Clorinda, 65; *Sonate, sinfonie, canzoni,* 65; *Balletto,* 78

Morley, Thomas, 17; *Consort Lessons,* 75

Morzin, Count Ferdinand Maximilian, employer of Haydn, 179

Motet, 17, 18; transformed into instrumental music by Machaut, 14

Motives in music, first use of, 55

Movements, first used by Uccellini, 94 f.

Mozart, Joannes Chrysostomus Wolfgangus Theophilus, 210 f.; *Versuch einer gründlicher Violinschule,* 210 f.

Mozart, Leopold, *Versuch einer gründliche Violinschule,* 210 f.

Mozart, Wolfgang Amadeus, 10, 210 ff.; evidence of Mannheimer style in works of, 171; works of, known by Haydn, 182, "Frederick William" quartets, 201 f.; influence on Haydn, 207 f.; concert tours of, 212; influenced by Schobert and Johann Christian Bach, 213; *La Clemenza di Tito,* 214; *Don Giovanni,* 214; *Marriage of Figaro,* 214; *Requiem,* 214; *Die Zauberflöte,* 214; numbering of his works, 216; string quartet K.80, 216 f.; divertimentos K.136-138, 217; quartet in B flat (K.137), 217; quartet K.138, 217; influenced by Haydn, 219; quartets K.168-173, 219; rapidity of his development, 219; as assimilator, 219 f.; fugues of, 219; quartets K.285, K.285a, K.Appendix 171, and K.298, 220; quartet for oboe and strings (K.370), 221; Haydn's influence on, 221 ff.; quartets K.387, K.421, K.428, K.458 ("The Hunt"), K.464, and K.465, 222 ff.; style contrasted with that of Haydn, 225 f.; quartet K.499, 226 f.; *Adagio and Fugue* (K.546), 227; chromaticism characteristic of, 224; Bach's influence on, 227; quartets K.575, K.589, and K.590, 228; virtuosity in quartets dedicated to Frederick William II, 228 f.; quintets, 229 ff.; quintet K.515, 231; quintet K.516, 231; quintet, K.581, 232; quintets K.593 and K.614, 232 f.; divertimento, K.361, 233 f.; quintet K.46, 233 f.; quintet K.407, 234; octet K.388, 233; piano trio K.254, 235; piano trios K.496, K.498, K.502, K.542, K.548, and K.564, 235 ff.; string sextet K.522, 237;

divertimento for strings K.563, 237 f.; piano quartets, 237; teacher of Beethoven, 240; development of piano quartet simultaneously with Beethoven, 247

Mozart, Maria Anna ("Nannerl"), 210; participation in Mozart's concerts, 212

Mühlfeld, Richard, 331

Münchener Liederbuch, 15

Musica ficta, 25; example of, 24

Musical Offering (Bach), 134, 135 ff.

Musical style, 56 ff.; changes after 1750, 11 f.; changes after 1600, 12

Musikalische Frühlingsfrüchte (Becker), 109

Musikalische Opfer, Das, see *Musical Offering, The*

Musikant, 16

Musik des Barock, Die (Haas), 62

Mussi, Giulio, 57, 58, 59

"Must I Die, Then" (Ammerbach), 71

My Country (Smetana), see *Ma Vlast*

My Ladye Nevelles Book, 73

National Conservatory in New York, Dvořák director of, 349

Nationalism in music, 318 f.; Bohemia, 346; Russia, 341

Neefe, Christian, influence on Beethoven, 240

Neo-Classicism in music, 356

Neri, Massimilliano, 67

Neubauer, Johann, "Neue Pavanen, Galliarden, Balleten, Couranten, Allemanden, und Sarabanden," 85, 87

Neue musikalische Intraden, 79

"Neue Pavanen, Galliarden, Balleten, Couranten, Allemanden, und Sarabanden" (Neubauer), 85, 87

Neue Zeitschrift für Musik, 301

Newe Paduan, Intrada, Däntz und Galliarda (Peuerl), 80 f.

Nicolas à Kempis, *Symphoniae 1, 2, 3, violinorum,* 93 f.

Nineteenth century, characteristic aspects of, 317 f.

Nocturne, *see* Divertimento

"Nocturne" (Borodin), 345

Note-against-note style, 27; characteristic of early dance music, 72

Nuove musiche, 20

Nuove musiche, Le (Caccini), 42, 45, 47, 65

Obbligato parts, 166
Oboe, 13
Oiseau de feu, L' (Stravinsky), 364
Operas, the direct result of Camerata's work, 43
Opus newer Paduanen (Simpson), 82
Orchestral music: limitations of, 6; emergence of, 109
Ordre, term used in 18th century for the dance suite, 87
Organ, 18; its use for transformed vocal music, 14; musical styles for, 17; transcriptions of chansons for, 29
"Orlandina, La" (Marini), 63 ff., 92
Ortiz, Diego, 40, 42
"Overture," term used in 18th century for the dance suite, 87

Padovana, *see* Pavane
"Paduan und Courante dolorosa" (Schein), 83
Paduana, *see* Pavane
Paduana e galliarda a 5 (Engelmann), 81
Palestrina, Giovanni Pierluigi da, 12, 13, 17
Parergon musicum (Horn), 109
Parnasso in festa (Handel), 132
Parthenia, 73
Partie, see Partita
Partita, 87
"Pasameza con variazioni" (Simpson), 82
Passacaglia, 88
Passacaile, see Passacaglia
Passage work, 59
Passamezzo, 70, 82
"Passamezzo d'Angleterre" (Ammerbach), 71
Passepied, 87
Passion According to St. Matthew (Bach), 133, 169
"Pastorum Dantz" (Ammerbach), 71
Paumann, Conrad, 15
"Pavana" (Bull), 75
Pavane, 69; loss of connection with dance music, 84 f.
Pavane, gagliarde, brandi, mascherata, arie francese, volti, balleti, sonate, canzone (Farina), 84
Paven, *see* Pavane
Pavin, *see* Pavane
Pergolesi, Giovanni, 143, 148 ff.; *Serva padrona,* 149; *Stabat Mater,* 149;

model for later composers, 154; his sonatas models for Karl Philipp Emanuel Bach, 164; innovations in the three-movement form, 187; musical form of, 202
Peri, Jacopo, 38; *Dafne,* 40 ff.; *Eurydice,* 41 f., 65
Petrouchka (Stravinsky), 364
Petrucci, Ottaviano dei, 70
Peuerl, Paul, 57; *Newe Paduan, Intrade, Däntz und Galliarda,* 80 f.
Pezel, Johann, *Leipzigischen Abendmusiken,* 109
Phonograph, role in development of chamber music, 6
Pian e forte (Gabrieli), 59, 169
Pianoforte music: development of, 164; Mannheim style transferred to, by Schobert, 175
Piano quartets, development by Mozart and Beethoven simultaneously, 247
Pièces de luth, 87
Pierné, Gabriel, pupil of Franck, 336
Pierrot Lunaire (Schönberg), 366
Pipers, guilds in 13th century, 13
Piston, Walter, 357, 380 f.
Piva, 70
Poco Largo, 102
Pohl, Karl Ferdinand: Haydn's biographer, 201; Mention of Haydn's divertimento, 208
Polonaise, 87
Polytonality, in Milhaud's music, 372
Porpora, Niccolò, 116; Haydn's friend, 179
Porter, Quincy, 357, 381
Prés, Josquin des, 22
Presto Largo, 102
Primo libro de ricercari et canzoni a quattro voci, Il (Bonelli), 36
Priuli, Giovanni, *Sacrorum concentum,* 57
Program music, development of, 318
Progressive composers, in seventeenth century, 58
Prokofieff, Serge, 376, 377
"Proportio, oder Galliard" (Ammerbach), 71, 72
Purcell, Henry, 26, 33, 73, 76, 100 f.; *Twelve Sonatas of Three Parts,* 100 ff.; *Dido and Aeneas,* 101, 169; *toccata* and fugue, copied by Bach, 103; "In Our Deep Vaulted Cell," 169; *Dido and Aeneas,* chromaticism in, 224

"Quartet serioso" (Beethoven), 272
Quartets, see String quartets
Quatuorze gaillardes, neuf pavanes, sept branles et deux basse danses (Attaingnant), 71
"Quinten, The" (Haydn), 206

Radio broadcasts, role in development of chamber music, 6
Rameau, Jean Philippe, codification of harmonic laws, 26
Rasoumowsky, Count, Beethoven's Opus 59 dedicated to, 267
Ravel, Maurice, 355; string quartet, 361 f.; piano trio in A minor, 362
Raverii collection, 52, 53, 54
Recitative, 38 ff.; see also Accompanied recitative
Recorder, 13
Reger, Max, 361
Reményi, Eduard, 319
Renaissance, 21, 37
"Reprise, La" (Ammerbach), 71
Requiem (Mozart), 214
Respighi, Ottorino, 363, 376
Responsive entrances, distance between, 51
Responsive style, see Antiphonal style
Reusner, Esajas, 89
Rhau, 15
Riccio, Giovanni Battista, 57, 58, 59
Ricercare, 17, 33, 55, 65 f.
Richter, Franz Xaver, 172 ff.
Richter, Jean Paul, influence on Schumann, 301
"Rider, The" (Haydn), 206
Riemann, Hugo, 52; controversy with Adler over the Mannheim composers, 167
Rigaudon, 87
Rinuccini, Ottavio, 38, 40
Rococo style, 145 f.
Rogers, Benjamin, 86
Rognioni, Giovanni, Canzoni a 4 et 8 voci, 36
Roman Catholic Counter Reformation, 21
Romanesca (Rossi), 62
Romanticism, 281 ff.
"Romanze" (Dvořák), 351
Rondeau, 53; in French dance suites, 88
Rondino (Beethoven), 248
Rore, Cypriano de, 33
Rosenmüller, Johann, 86, 89, 97; in-

troduction of German dance suite into Italy, 105 f.
Rosseter, Philip, Lessons for Consorts, 75
Rossi, Salomone, 57, 61 f., 65, 66; Canzone da sonar, 58; Varie sonate, 61, 62; Romanesca, 62; Ruggiero, 62; Sinfonie et gagliarde a 3, 4, et 5 uoci . . . per sonar 2 viole, ouero 2 cornetti, et un chittarone, 62; champion of instrumental monody, 63
"Rowland" (Byrd), 75
"Royal Consort of Viols" (Lawes), 76
Rubert, Johann Martin, 88 f.
Rubinstein, Nicholas, 341; Tschaikowsky's teacher, 343
Rudolph, Archduke of Austria, patron of Beethoven, 252
Ruggiero (Rossi), 62

Sacre symphoniae (Gabrieli), 33, 34 f.
Sacred music, limitations of, 6
Sacre du printemps, Le, 364
Sacri concentus (Hassler), 57
Sacrorum concentum (Priuli), 57
St. Matthew Passion, see Passion According to St. Matthew
Saint-Saëns, Camille, 339 f.
Salieri, teacher of Beethoven, 242
Salomon, Johann, manager for Haydn, 180 f.
Saltarello, 70
Salzburg, Archbishop of, Mozart concertmaster and organist to, 214
Salzburg, Court of, Mozart's birthplace, 210
Sammartini, Giuseppe, 154
Sanders, Robert, 382, 383
Sarabande, 77, 86
Satz-Quartett (Schubert), 291 f.
"Savorgnana, La" (Legrenzi), 96
Scarlatti, Domenico, 148, 162; deviates from Pergolesi's model, 154; string quartet, 163
Scheidt, Samuel, 57, 82, 83 f.
Schein, Johann Hermann, 57; Banchetto musicale, 81, 83, 87; "Paduan und Courante dolorosa," 83
Schering, Arnold, 77
Scherzi, 78
Scherzo: as used by Beethoven, 197; origin of the term, 197; development of, 303 f.

Schmitt, Florent, 363
Schobert, Johann, 174 ff.; Mozart's knowledge of, 212; Mozart influenced by, 213
Schönberg, Arnold, 356, 357, 365 ff; *Verklärte Nacht* (string sextet, Opus 4), 365; *Pierrot Lunaire* (Opus 21), 366; *Kammersymphonie* (Opus 9), 366; fourth quartet (Opus 37), 368; Milhaud's fifth quartet dedicated to, 372
Schubert, Franz Peter, 10, 282 f., 284 ff.; *Eine kleine Trauermusik*, 287; string quartet in B flat, 287; string quartet in C major, 287; string quartet in E flat, 287 f.; quartet for flute, guitar, viola, and cello, Kahl's account of, 288; string quartet in B flat (Opus 168), 288; string quartet in G minor, 288 f.; piano quartet, 289; string trio in B flat, 289; string quartet in E major (Opus 125, No. 2), 289 f.; *Forellen Quintet* (Opus 114), 290 f.; quartet in C minor (*Satz-Quartett*), 291 f.; string quartet in A minor (Opus 29), 292 f.; octet for wind and string instruments in F major (Opus 166), 293 f.; string quartet in D minor, 294 f.; quartet in G major (Opus 161), 295; trio for piano, violin, and cello in E flat (Opus 100), 295 ff.; trio for piano, violin, and cello in B flat (Opus 99), 295 f.; string quintet in C major (Opus 163), 297 f.; departures from Classical style, 314 f.
Schütz, Heinrich, 18, 26, 83, 121
Schuman, William, 383
Schumann, Clara (Wieck), 301; death of, contributed to Brahms's decline, 320; friendship for Brahms, 320; Brahms's friendship for, 328
Schumann, Robert, 301 f., 308 ff.; influenced by Richter, 301; marriage of, 301; friendship with Mendelssohn, 302; mental collapse and death of, 303; Eusebius and Florestan personalities, 309; piano quintet in E flat (Opus 44) 309 ff.; piano quartet in E flat (Opus 47), 311 f.; *Fantasiestücke* (Opus 88), 312; *Marchenerzählungen* (Opus 132), 312; piano trio in D minor (Opus 63), 313; piano trio in F major (Opus 80), 313; piano trio in G minor (Opus 110), 313 f.; conflict between

musical form and content, 315; admiration for Brahms, 319; friendship for Brahms, 320; death of, 328
Schuppanzigh, Ignaz, 295
Schwebsch, Erich, 141 f.
Seasons, The (Haydn), 181
Seconda aggiunta alli concerti raccolti dal . . . Francesco Lucino a 2, 3, e 4 voci, 57
Serenade, *see* Divertimento
"Serenade," misleading title for Mozart's K.388, 233
Serva padrona (Pergolesi), 149
Seventeenth century: turbulence of, 22; confused musical history of, 55 f.
Seventeenth-century music, neglect of, 3
Shostakovich, Dmitri, 376, 378
Siciliano, 87
Siebold, Agathe von, 325 f.
Simpson, Thomas, 76; *Opus newer Paduanen,* 82; "Pasameza con variazioni," 82
Sinfonia: indiscriminate use of term in first half of 17th century, 59; used by Rosenmüller in his dance suite, 106 ff.
Sinfonie et gagliarde a 3, 4, et 5 uoce . . . per sonar 2 viole, ouero 2 cornetti, et un chittarone (Rossi), 62
"Sir John Gray's Galliard" (Byrd), 75
"Six, Les," 372
Sketch of the Steppes (Borodin), 344
Smetana, Bedřich, 346, 347 ff.; *The Bartered Bride,* 347; *Ma Vlast,* 347; "The Moldau," 347; string quartet in E minor (Opus 115), 347 f.; string quartet in D minor, 348
Soderino, Agostino, 36
Sonata da camera, 10, 68, 87, 90 ff., 105 f.; characteristics at end of 17th century, 115
Sonata da chiesa, 10, 68, 90 ff.; term properly applies to Purcell's sonatas, 104; merger with *sonata da camera,* 105; for keyboard instruments, 114; characteristics at the end of the 17th century, 115 f.
Sonata da chiesa e da camera (Marini), 96
Sonata form, origin of, 55; changes in, 166 ff.
Sonata style, 59, 60 ff.
Sonatas: those by Purcell important in the development of the sonata type,

104; for piano solo accompanied by violin and cello, 164

Sonate a 2, 3, 4, e 5 stromenti (Vitali), 101

Sonate a 2 violini col suo basso continuo per l'organo, Opus 2 (Vitali), 97 f.

Sonate de camera (Corelli), 111 ff.

Sonate da camera cioè sinfonie, 106 ff.

Sonate, sinfonie, canzoni (Monteverdi), 65

Souvenir de Florence (Tschaikowsky), 344

"Spanish Paven" (Bull), 74

Spanyöler Tanez (Weck), 70 f.

Spillville, Iowa, visited by Dvořák, 349

Stabat Mater (Pergolesi), 149

Stadler, Mozart's quintet K.581 designed for, 232

Stamitz, Johann, 167 f.

Stamitz, Karl, 172; orchestral trio (Opus 1), 173

Starzer, Joseph, 155, 159 f., 162, 167

Steiner, Rudolf, 142

Strauss, Richard, 355

Stravinsky, Igor, 356, 357, 364 f.; *L'Oiseau de feu*, 364; *Petrouchka*, 364; *Le Sacre du printemps*, 364; *Histoire du soldat*, 365

"Stretto," 86

String instruments, early substitutes for organ, 31

String quartets, origin of, 162 f.; Haydn's importance in development of, 185 ff.

Style, *see* Musical style

Style galant, 161

"Suite," term adopted in France in 17th century, 87

"Sunrise, The" (Haydn), 206

Suonate à doi, violino e viola da gamba, con cembalo (Buxtehude), 122

Symphoniae 1. 2. 3. violinorum (Nicolas à Kempis), 93 f.

Tablature notation, 70

Tafelmusik (Telemann), 156 f.

Tagliapetra, Gino, ed., *Antologia di musica antica e moderna*, 78

Tartini, Giuseppe, 143

Tauler, Johannes, 142

Telemann, George Philipp, 117, 156 ff.; *Tafelmusik*, 156 f.

Tenors, 15

"Terrace dynamics," *see* Dynamics in instrumental music

Thematic dualism, 35

Theodore, Elector Karl, 167; patron of Stamitz, 168; quintets of Johann Christian Bach dedicated to, 176

Three Variations on a Theme (Harris), 381

Toëschi, Giuseppe, 172

Tomasini, Luigi, 189

Tonality, in Haydn's quartets, 198 ff.

Tonal system, 24 f.

Tone color, lacking before middle of 18th century, 19

Torelli, Giuseppe, 116, 121

Tourdion, 70

Tovey, Donald: opinion on date of Haydn's Opus 42, 201; comments on Haydn's style, 203

Tower music, 15 f.

Tremolo, 59; first use in violin music, 65

Trio, in dance suites, 88

Trio sonata, 10, 62, 90, 114, 115 ff.; established by Rossi, 63 ff.; origin of, 116; contrasted with style of divertimento period, 161

Trio sonatas, by Haydn, 184

Triple (perfect) meter, 12th and 13th centuries limited to, 111 f.

Trombones, 15

"Trout, The," *see Forelle, Die* (Schubert)

Trumpeters, guilds in 13th century, 13

Tschaikowsky, Peter Ilyitch, 341 ff.; string quartet in D major (Opus 11), 341 f.; string quartet in F major (Opus 22), 342; string quartet in E flat minor (Opus 30), 342 f.; piano trio in A minor (Opus 50), 343 f.; sextet for strings in D minor (Opus 70), 344

Tunder, Franz, predecessor of Buxtehude, 121

Turina, Joaquin, 376

Twelve Sonnatas of Three Parts (Purcell), 100 ff.

"Twelve-tone system," 366 ff.

Twelve-tone technique, developed by Arnold Schönberg, 356

Uccellini, Marco, *Delle sonate over canzoni da farsi a violino solo e basso continuo*, 94

"Valvasona, La" (Legrenzi), 95 f.
Van Vactor, David, 382, 383
Variations, in sonatas, 61
Varie sonate (Rossi), 61, 62
Venetian opera, overtures models for Rosenmüller's sinfonie, 108
Venetian school of composers, 33, 36
Venier, publisher of works of Haydn, Beck, Pfeiffer, and Schetky, 180
Veracini, Francesco, 142
Verklärte Nacht (Schönberg), 365
Versuch einer gründlichen Violinschule (Leopold Mozart), 210 f.
Viadana, Lodovico Grossi da: *Cento concerti ecclesiastici a 1, 2, 3, 4 voci*, 45 ff., 65; "Canzona francese a quattro, a riposta," 47 ff., 65
Vicentino, Nicolò, *La Bella* (*canzone da sonar*), 31 f.
Victoria, Tomás Luis de, 12
Vielle, 13
Viennese composers, first to discard *continuo*, 161
Villa-Lobos, Heitor, 376
Vingt suites d'orchestre du XVII siècle française (Ecorcheville), 77
Viola, appearance in chamber music, 162
Violin: musical styles for, 17; antiphonal style, 62; dominance of, in divertimento period, 161
Violin music, Marini's importance in development of technique of, 63
Viols: as substitutes for voice parts, 28; dance suites for, 75 f.
Virginal, 72
Virtuosity, in Mozart's quartets, 228
Vitali, Giovanni Battista, 96, 124; sonate, 97 f.; contrasted with Corelli, 99 f.; *Sonate a 2 violini col suo basso con-*

tinuo per l'organo, Opus 2, 97 f.; *Sonate a 2, 3, 4, e 5 stromenti*, 101
Vivaldi, Antonio, 142 f.
Vocal music, its transformation for lute and organ, 14
Voices, use of, by Giovanni Gabrieli, 34 f.

Wagenseil, 167
Wagner, Richard, 318
Walsh, publishers of Handel's works, 129
Warner, Waldo, 376
Weber, Constanza, Mozart married to, 214
Webern, Anton von, 368; string quartet (Opus 28), 369
Weck, Hans: *Hopper Tanez*, 70 f.; *Spanyöler Tanez*, 70 f.
Weelkes, Thomas, 72
Weltanschauung, 142
Wendling, Johann Baptist, 172
Werner, Joseph, 179
Whimsicalities (Gruenberg), 380
Widman, Erasmus, "Canzone auf den Schäfferstantz," 82; *Gantz neue Cantzon, Intraden, Balletten, und Couranten*, 82 f.
Wieck, Frederick, teacher of Schumann, 301
Willaert, Adrian, 33
Williams, Vaughn, 376
Wolf, Hugo, 4
"Wolsey's Wilde" (Byrd), 75
Woodwind instruments, early substitutes for organ, 31

Zauberflöte, Die (Mozart), 214
Zink, *see* Cornett
Zither, 13